National Cake Day in Ruritania

National Cake Day in Ruritania

Mark P. Henderson

First Published 2018 by Fantastic Books Publishing

Cover design by Gabi

ISBN (eBook): 9781-912053-83-4
ISBN (paperback): 9781-912053-82-7

Foreword

Anthony Hope's three novels gave rise to a minor literary industry. Since Hope set the precedent, several authors have chosen Ruritania as a fictional setting for adventure, science fiction and fantasy stories as well as tales in the 'Ruritanian romance' genre, the basis of certain feature films. Ruritania has also been a hypothetical milieu for academic arguments about politics and social organisation and for reflecting on European history. It's the archetypical 'micronation' on the entertaining website www.ruritania.net, and there are other online sources (e.g. McGill University's *Equatorial Cyberspace*). In the following pages I've borrowed from several of these creations (for instance, the design of the national heraldic crest, the 'Order of the Blue Primrose', the 1848 Peasants' Revolt, etc. are lifted – with consent – from www.ruritania.net), yet I claim originality in regard to plot and characters.

Every novelist adopts ideas from others, i.e. conducts research. The psychology paper discussed by Ariadne and Rory in chapter 47 is real (Robert Rosenthal, *Experimenter Effects in Behavior Research*, Appleton-Century-Crofts, New York, 1966), though – notwithstanding Ariadne's aspersions – the contrary results obtained by psychologists who repeated Rosenthal's experiment *were* published. 'Lekhissa's Riddle' and the puzzles constituting the logical maze through which Rory escapes in chapter 57 are adapted from Raymond Smullyan's brilliant *What is the Name of This Book?* (Prentice-Hall, Inc., Englewood Cliffs, New Jersey, 1978). I've also relied on William Poundstone's mind-bending

Labyrinths of Reason (Penguin, London, 1991), and, more obviously, on traditional 'fairy tales' and Classical myths.

Those who know my enjoyment of word-play (and are informed about British slugs) might spot the etymologies of some personal names. A reader who recalls Greek mythology will recognise the names of the gargoyle sisters (Othloc, Lekhissa and Sporota) as anagrams. The name of the horse 'borrowed' by Rory in chapter 63, 'Hobunay', is derived from the Estonian for 'horse'. Anyone familiar with popular English folklore will recognise 'Arraitch' and 'Eldzhay' as initials spelt out as names. But I don't expect my readers to know, or wish to know, any of the sources I've exploited or the way I've twisted them. A novel must stand alone and must entertain and engage, not instruct – though in the present case, some of the entertainment consists in blowing academic raspberries at instruction.

Just as authors depend on diverse sources for their research, so they depend on feedback to refine their manuscripts. No matter how careful a self-editor you are, you're too close to your own work to spot all the infelicities and inconsistencies in your 'final' draft. Skilled and disinterested eyes are needed to exorcise them. I had the good fortune to receive critiques on an early draft of this novel from my friend Valerie Hughes and from Lorena Goldsmith of Daniel Goldsmith Associates. Later, my submission to Fantastic Books Publishing benefited immeasurably from thorough, insightful and constructive criticisms and guidance by the firm's senior editor, Mae. Without that help, this book would never have been fit to unleash on the unsuspecting public.

Mark P. Henderson 2018

There is in human nature a servility which inclines us to adore our superiors, and an inhumanity that disposes us to contempt and trample underfoot our inferiors.

— *Adam Smith*

Man's capacity for justice makes democracy possible; man's inclination to injustice makes democracy necessary.

— *Reinhold Niebuhr*

Today we believe what we see ... but do not know whether further improvements in the means of observation will reveal what we assume is certain to be only illusion ... or, indeed, the contrary.

— *Wilhelm Kühne*

Because of Ruritania's interaction with the Faerie Realm, she is awash with spatiotemporal anomalies. This is why Ruritania is cartographically challenged, why she never appears on maps: she has no fixed size or location. She is supposed to be part of Europe but she never knows how, where or even whether to fit into the continent. Mostly she drifts between France and the Balkans, sometimes south to the Mediterranean coast, sometimes north to Estonia, and occasionally far to the west as though to escape from Europe altogether. She even makes tentative forays to the east, to the discomfiture of her people.

— *The Unideker Guide to Ruritania*

Chapter 1

Although there was no conclusive evidence, the Authorities felt the incident with the examination papers left them no alternative but to terminate Rory Redman's association with the College. Everyone was sorry to see him sent down, particularly the ladies, though many believed his departure made their possessions less likely to disappear. But it was never certain which allegations against him were true and which were fanciful. For instance, did he really steal the woollen socks that Professor Multiple had been wearing during dinner in the Great Hall? Mr Redman returned both socks to the barefoot professor that same evening while the port was being passed, by which time one of them was full of lumpy custard and the other of stewed prunes, but theft could not be proved. However, 'Nothing was ever proved' might stand some day as Rory Redman's epitaph. What is certain is that his expulsion deprived the University of one of its best-ever marathon runners and Morris dancers, and one of its most gifted young logicians.

— Cerberus D. Gardog: 'A College Porter's Recollections of Unconventional Undergraduates'

It was the wrong party.

The cascade of noise had lured him to the function room, past the big bright poster ('The Party's Here!'), past the coloured balloons and through the door before realisation dawned. Then the evidence was all around him: not a familiar face to be seen. Groups of guests chattered and laughed and clinked wine glasses

3

but none smiled at him, though his attire attracted attention: shorts and tee shirt and trainers, the outfit Paul had recommended because it lacked pockets capacious enough for valuables. However, Paul wouldn't have organised a DJ with drooping jowls to preside over a vacant dance area. No doubt about it: wrong party.

Nevertheless he lingered. Coincidences intrigued him. And he liked parties.

After he'd lingered for two minutes a lady in a long white evening gown approached and scrutinised his attire, her face a question mark. He said, 'Excuse me, Christine's husband invited me to her birthday party but I don't think … This *is* the Merlin Hotel, isn't it? And it *is* the tenth of May? And …' He glanced at his watch. Yes, seven minutes past eight. And he *was* carrying the card and the tastefully-wrapped gift.

Paul had phoned him six weeks earlier: 'Surprise party for Christine's thirtieth birthday, Merlin Hotel, tenth of May, eight o'clock. Please come.'

So Rory had come.

'Yes,' said the lady in the long white evening gown. 'This is the Merlin Hotel. And it's the tenth of May. And I'm Christine. And it *is* my birthday.'

But she wasn't the Christine he knew. Rory was too much the gentleman to guess her age, but water had passed under several bridges since she was thirty. Also, she was Afro-Caribbean and she didn't look interested in horticulture. Paul's wife was Caucasian and she looked after Rory's garden. And there was no sign of Paul.

'Many happy returns.'

'Thanks. Who are you?'

'Rory Redman. This isn't the right party. I mean, it isn't the party I was invited to. Wrong Christine. *Different* Christine. Sorry.'

He turned towards the exit, trying to calculate the probability of such multiple coincidences. The answer was close to zero.

'So you should be,' said the wrong Christine. 'Gatecrashers aren't welcome. But you mustn't leave.'

At this paradoxical injunction Rory muttered a half-apology, half-complaint and headed for the door with its poster and balloons. But a hand gripped his left shoulder and stayed him. It was a long, blue-veined hand with manicured nails. It was attached to an arm in a grey Armani sleeve. A Rolex glinted on the wrist. A voice spoke, grey as the sleeve: 'Ah, Rory Redman, the running man. I wish to speak with you. What I offer will redound to your advantage.'

Rory didn't recognise the voice and couldn't place the accent. He turned to confront the rest of the Armani suit. Under the jacket were a smooth white shirt and a tie indicating membership of something exclusive. Above this ensemble was a narrow lined face with prominent cheekbones and a white moustache and a crown of white hair combed back from a high forehead. The lips were thin and the eyes were blue and half-closed. The chin smelled of aftershave.

The man took his hand from Rory's shoulder and waved it backwards, once, without looking round; a casual flick of the Rolex-bearing wrist. The birthday girl retreated.

Rory said, 'I don't believe we've met'.

'We have met now, Rory. May I call you Rory?'

The hand returned to his shoulder and guided him to a corner of the room where four young party-goers sat. The quartet stood as one, bowed and headed for the dance area, leaving Rory and his companion alone. The DJ's jowls lifted.

Rory said, 'Who are you and what do you want? It seems I mistook the arrangements for the party I should have been attending.'

The Armani suit chuckled.

'You comprehend not the subtle dynamics of what common rabble dub *mistake* and *coincidence*. It is complex subject, which my people are elucidating. No matter. You are man of action, I believe, not man of science.'

'I still don't know who *you* are.'

'Few people in Britain do, Rory. Since you are man of action I come straight, as you say, to point.'

Rory learned he was being commissioned to run to a warehouse, collect a canvas sports bag, and deliver it to a particular person in a particular place at a particular time. He was told where the warehouse was, what number to phone to confirm his arrival and where to find the bag. Okay, he thought, it was a warm night and he was wearing running gear, but he'd expected to be drinking, not running. And what in the name of the wee man from Milton Keynes was this *about*?

The amalgam of mystery and challenge was irresistible.

'Door will be unlocked,' said the suit. 'Bag will be under desk in office at back of warehouse. You take it home for night. Hide it. In morning, seven o'clock, you take it to central library. Person carrying blue helium balloon bearing legend 'Happy Solstice!' will meet you outside main entrance. You give bag to this person and you receive envelope containing one thousand pound in used twenty pound note. You will tell no one of arrangement, you will ask no question, *and you will not look inside bag.*'

'I don't deal in hard drugs or firearms and I won't carry explosives.'

'I do not ask it. You will carry nothing immediately deadly. I choose you because you run fast. And have reputation.'

True, Rory was a runner. He ran operations and risks as well as marathons. And he did have a reputation: he'd never refuse a thousand pounds for carrying a canvas sports bag provided it didn't contain serious contraband. Also, the job sounded easy as well as intriguing. So he didn't shake his head, say thanks but no thanks, leave the Merlin Hotel and phone Paul to ask what the bloody hell had become of the party to which he *had* been invited.

'Why the cloak-and-dagger stuff?'

'No question, Rory. Now, I believe it is time you leave. You understand; this is private party.' There was a thin-lipped smile and the long left hand was extended. 'Before you go, you will return Rolex watch.'

As Rory set off in the specified direction he felt eyes following him. He couldn't see the watcher. He reached the warehouse about an hour later, paused under a sodium lamp, wiped his brow, put his mobile phone to his ear, talked briefly and entered the dark building. He was sure he'd attracted no attention yet he sensed scrutiny. More than ten minutes elapsed before he emerged, clinging to the shadows, carrying the bag. Under the monochrome streetlights it looked as black as his hair. He started to run again. When he reached his house he unlocked the front door and scuttled inside.

The sense of being watched had stalked him all the way. Perhaps the Armani suit had made him paranoid. And had given him too many instructions; Rory could be guaranteed to forget at least one of them. He showered, dressed and made a cup of coffee. And then he opened the bag.

The papers in it constituted an elaborate joke, he decided, though a joke by whom and at whose expense he couldn't guess. Was someone trying to embarrass the editors of a scientific journal? The covering letter said the papers were for publication in a special issue of the journal, but their provenance was fictitious and their titles fantastical.

With one exception. The document in the manila folder wasn't a scientific paper, and despite the mock geographical reference it seemed to have serious intent.

Serious enough for Rory to take a photocopy. Which he hid.

Chapter 2

The self-styled Socialist People's Army of Ruritania (SPAR) is an illegal underground organisation whose stated aims are to abolish the monarchy and aristocracy and establish a dictatorship of the peasantry with a healthy diet. Its leaders, notably the so-called Ulyanova, remain elusive. None of the SPAR activists so far apprehended by the police and the ekwyroj of the Order of the Blue Primrose have divulged information even when subjected to enhanced interrogation methods. Three of them were forced to listen to Spice Girls albums for three and a half hours, but they committed suicide rather than identify their leaders. This technique was a last resort: representatives of Her Majesty Queen Anastassia's government prefer to be humane. However, cruel and unusual punishments are not forbidden in Ruritania, and the need to eliminate SPAR's leaders, particularly the Ulyanova, has become urgent enough for heightened approaches to questioning to be deployed.

— Secret communiqué from the Strelsau High Bakery to MI7, London

Climbing towards the evening clouds above the darkening cityscape she watched him run through a maze of streets and alleys against a backcloth of neon signs, a man who preferred shade to light. His black attire concealed, or highlighted, muscle.

Even if he sensed her scrutiny he wouldn't see her. Klarissa was a climber. She could climb trees, walls, society; she had a head for heights. People who saw her found it hard to look away.

Beautiful, they said; maybe twenty-six, twenty-seven. Yes, said the few who knew her, she was beautiful, but she was older than twenty-seven, and much wiser.

As he cantered out of her field of view she scurried down roofs, scaffolding, ladders, drainpipes. A handbag swung from her shoulder. Padding barefoot over cobbles and pitted asphalt she tracked him; in the still air a whiff of sweat overlay the aromas of the city. She watched him pause under the sodium lamp beside the warehouse, wipe his brow with his forearm, put his mobile phone to his ear, talk for fifty-three seconds and enter the building, swift and surreptitious. The person he'd phoned would be hiding nearby, watching, ready to report; she made sure she remained invisible.

Twelve minutes and forty-three seconds elapsed before he emerged bearing a canvas sports bag. The bag looked black as his attire, black as his hair, but she knew it would be purple in daylight, with light brown handles. Her own sparse outfit also looked black under the yellow monochrome. Her teeth glinted.

He started to run again. Silent as ever she kept pace with him, still unseen. He reached a detached villa in West Didsbury, unlocked the front door and disappeared inside. She heard bolts close. She waited, recovering her breath, and took a navy blue track-suit from her handbag. As she put it on she scanned the area for watchers, spies, informers. There were none.

When dawn broke over Manchester's tower blocks and chimneys, throwing the Pennines into relief against the crimson east, she leapt atop his high garden wall and looked down upon trained fruit bushes, herbaceous borders, lawns and patio. There was an odour of moist earth, mown grass and night-scented stocks. But there was also *slug killer*. Her polished fingernails bit the heels of her hands. Conjuring comb and mirror from the handbag she straightened her hair and dabbed a Christian Dior perfume on to her ears and throat.

Three minutes after the sun rose he emerged from the conservatory and strode along the crazy-paved path. He wore a white shirt and a light camouflage jacket, jeans, white trainers and sunglasses. The canvas sports bag swung over his right shoulder. It was only half full but it wasn't light.

He was directly below her, still unaware of her, when she pounced.

As he lay face-down on the path she tore open the sports bag, scanned the papers inside, extracted a manila folder, exchanged it for a similar folder from her handbag, searched his pockets, and secured his wrists behind his back with Ann Summers handcuffs. She was over the garden wall and gone, handbag swinging around her, before he'd groaned back to consciousness. No one had seen her.

She headed for the central library: easy to climb, though the track-suit was inconvenient. Climbing would have been easier if she could have worn less but she didn't want to draw attention. From a pediment above the main door, she jumped. Twenty seconds later she'd merged with the rush-hour crowd in St Peter's Square.

A blue helium balloon bearing the legend 'Happy Solstice!' floated up into the Manchester sky. Its ascent was observed by two toddlers, a recumbent drunk and a dachshund. When it reached the stratosphere it burst. The drunk began to cry.

Chapter 3

Further to your recent communication, we will ensure that an agent will be outside the Manchester Central Library on the morning of 11th May (Gregorian calendar) to receive the package. We consider the scheme proposed to convey the manuscripts from your Academy of Science to the journal's London office to be overly complex, risking terrorist interference, particularly since an uninformed courier will be used for the penultimate stage. However, the President of the Academy has the right to insist on this scheme so we shall comply. Nevertheless we urge you not to include the plans for deployment of British military personnel in Strelsau on 4th-5th July (Ruritanian calendar) among the scientific manuscripts. Although terrorist agents might expose themselves to capture by attempting to ambush the consignment, the consequences should such an attempt succeed could be serious for both our countries.

— Secret communiqué from MI7, London, to the Strelsau High Bakery

'With these things. Took me half an hour to fiddle my way out of them.'

Rory tossed the Ann Summers handcuffs on to Christine's coffee table. Christine paused in the act of bathing Rory's head wound and almost suppressed a snigger. Paul didn't.

'No doubt they were fun, Rory. Sure you're okay?'

'Tip top. Broke my sunglasses on the path. Head aches where she thumped me.'

'*She?*'

'Smelled perfume when I was hit. And when I came round there were bare footprints beside the hydrangeas. *Small* bare footprints. No, Christine, the garden wasn't harmed, except all the slug killer had disappeared. So yes, Paul, apart from the headache and humiliation and broken sunglasses and being fifty quid lighter in the pocket and bloody cross about last night's party, I'm fine. Do me a favour and draw the curtains, will you?'

Christine went to brew coffee. Paul put on his spectacles and studied his guest. The venue for Christine's birthday party had been changed, he said, from the function room of the Merlin in Manchester to the upstairs room of the Whippet and Sausage in Stockport. Rory should have been advised of the change two weeks earlier.

'Why you *weren't* advised is a mystery. The krev promised to tell everyone who lived within a two mile radius while I alerted those travelling from further afield. It seems he told every invited guest in the neighbourhood except you.' Paul examined his watch. 'If you were assaulted just after sunrise, needed half an hour to – er – extricate yourself, and then took a taxi here, why did you only arrive in time for a late breakfast?'

'I went via the central library at seven o'clock to deliver this canvas bag to someone carrying a blue helium balloon. He or she was supposed to pay me, but he or she wasn't there. No blue balloon. So I came here to ask what the hell happened last night and what the hell I should do with the bag now. *Not* the obvious answer, please. Who's this krev? A creepy old git with a white moustache, an Armani suit and a penchant for being enigmatic? And what's a krev?'

'Ruritanian equivalent of 'Count' or 'Earl'. Cognate with Germanic 'Graf'. Similar titles in Finnish and Estonian. And your description does fit Krev Schammerbass: enigmatic, white moustache, expensive suit …'

Rory supposed the blow to his head had been worse than he'd presumed. There was no such country as Ruritania, he observed, except in stories and films, though the papers in the bag … He accepted a cup of coffee from Christine, who said, 'Thanks for the card and the tastefully-wrapped gift, Rory.' Rory said, 'Hope you'll like it, should match,' and drank the coffee.

'Contrary to rumour,' said Paul, 'Ruritania does exist. Krev Schammerbass is President of the Ruritanian Academy of Science. Two weeks ago, I learned he was hosting a birthday party at the Merlin for the wife of his disciple Jack Blackmeadow. Our arrangements clashed. We reached an agreement.'

'And he studied your guest list so he could contact *all but one* of those you'd invited who lived within a two mile radius. What did you tell him about me?'

Paul shook his head: nothing. But Krev Schammerbass, he observed, had the means to purchase information. Even by the standards of Ruritanian aristocracy he was wealthy. Apart from his castle and lands in Ruritania he owned large isolated houses throughout Europe: one overlooking Budapest, one just south of Lucerne, one in England.

Rory's mind tried to arrange his questions in logical order. First, he asked how Paul had come to know this Schammerbass fellow and why he supposed Ruritania to be real.

'Been there,' said Paul. 'Invited to the capital, Strelsau, to give an opinion about a land dispute. Ruritanian aristocrats respect British lawyers because we do everything slowly and in a convoluted manner and because we enjoy eating cake. My junior partner has studied Ruritanian law. She might emigrate there. You've met Ariadne, haven't you?

'Ariadne Sowerby? Yes.'

Rory retained a clear image of Ariadne: a woman about his own age, early thirties, with long auburn hair, intelligent eyes, ring-free fingers, a bust he estimated at 36DD and a dismissive response to his chat-up lines.

'She's Chair of the British Slug Defence League,' said Paul, 'so the Ruritanians are well-disposed towards her.'

Rory said Paul had now added two more questions to his list.

Paul said the contents of the bag might provide answers. Rory said the contents of the bag provoked even more questions.

'This krev character told me to collect the bag from the warehouse last night and run home with it and then deliver it to the balloon person this morning. He told me not to look inside it but he must have known I would.'

The bag contained papers, he said, plus a covering letter to the editorial board of the journal *Nurture*. All but one of the papers appeared to be spoof scientific manuscripts, allegedly by Ruritanian authors, which were being submitted for publication in a special issue of the journal. They included an article by Gottlieb Öst and Jamash Brün entitled *The Fractal Geometry of Faerie*, which was riddled with mathematical obscurantism. There were also three articles about the miasma theory of disease, a manuscript comparing methods for measuring the speed of dark, and a review of recent studies of the Philosopher's Stone.

'Those aren't spoofs, Rory,' said Paul, 'though some will be controversial. Take that Öst-Brün paper, for example. Öst and Brün claim their theory has solved a long-standing puzzle in the science of Faerie and they've won accolades for it. Many people regard it as taurocoprology, but Brün's got a huge grant to support his further studies. He's a friend of Krev Schammerbass.' Paul polished his spectacles, scrutinised them and put them back on. 'All but one of the papers, you said. What was the exception?'

'This.' Rory rifled through the contents of the canvas bag and pulled out a manila folder containing six pages of typescript. 'It isn't a scientific paper. And it almost – but not quite – resembles a manila folder I found in this bag last night. See what I mean about the contents provoking further questions?'

Paul glanced through the six pages of typescript and frowned.

'You mean your assailant substituted this folder for the one you took home in the bag? Slightly different document inside it?'

Rory nodded. He didn't mention the photocopy he'd made of the original typescript, the one that had been in the bag before the assault. The photocopy could be worth money.

Chapter 4

National Cake Day is the great midsummer solstice festival in Ruritania, the day before the annual general election. All the aristocracy, the krevoj and their families, have been master bakers for generations. Over the centuries, Ruritania's obsession with cakes has fattened and impoverished her people and made her bakers fabulously rich. As bankers are to the rest of the world, so bakers are to Ruritania – except that Ruritanian bakers hold explicit rather than covert power. All krevoj are bakers, and no one outside their families is permitted to bake except under their direction and supervision, on pain of removal of body parts. As National Cake Day approaches, the krevoj advertise cakes made to their own secret recipes and promise the electorate copious supplies of them throughout the year to come, if they'll vote for them.
   — The Unideker Guide to Ruritania

Klarissa inspected the mobile phone and punched in a number. A voice answered in a language known to few outside Ruritania.

'The oppressors' plan is in my hands,' said Klarissa. 'The papers had been sent to a warehouse in Manchester with a consignment of vermicelli machines, which is why we lost track of them. Schammerbass chose a courier who was ignorant of the material and would ask no questions. I followed the courier to the warehouse, then to his home. This morning I jumped him before he could deliver the bag to the MI7 agent … Yes, Arraitch, of course I left the papers! As far as the courier knows I didn't touch the bag. Even if he'd looked at the papers he won't have understood them so he can't have noticed the switch. I also eliminated the MI7 agent at the library; the courier will be blamed for that. And now I'll quit this benighted land of slug-slayers and return home before MI7 or the oppressors' agents notice me.'

The voice on the other end of the telephone asked questions.

'Yes,' said Klarissa. 'I put the fake plan into the canvas bag in place of the genuine one. The MI7 running-dogs will believe *it* to be genuine. The courier is reputedly a criminal, so he'll be suspected of stealing the bag of papers for sale to the highest bidder.'

She listened for a minute and smiled again. Her teeth were small and sharp and would have dazzled an onlooker.

'No, Schammerbass never saw me. He didn't recognise my assumed name so he–' She laughed. 'He's staying at the Midland, where all the ... Right now I'm going back to my room at the Merlin. Then I'll change my identity, eat lunch and catch a train to London. I'll stay in London until the next flight to Strelsau. I'll take a carriage from the airport to the usual address. Expect me in three days. I'll be in disguise.'

She listened again.

'Agreed. Blue Primrose will have sent agents but I haven't seen any.'

The voice in her ear grew urgent. For an instant, a slight frown blemished her perfect features.

'Grizelina Tupsroota?' Klarissa gave another small laugh. 'Her absence from Strelsau is Strelsau's gain. Yes, she *could* be. Thank you, Arraitch. I shall be vigilant. But Tupsroota and all her kind, and the royal family, and the aristocracy, will soon be history. The future is ours! We hold the original security plan and they have a useless fake. We need not hesitate to declare *Roll on the Solstice,* and *Viva la Revolucion*. Tell our comrades. Everyone and everything must be prepared for National Cake Day.'

Chapter 5

The Ruritanian calendar is more rational than its counterparts elsewhere. Each of the months January to December has twenty-eight days. There follows a thirteenth month, Extember, associated with the thirteenth sign of the Zodiac, Viverra (the Ferret). Extember has twenty-nine and a quarter days. At midnight on Extember 29th a six-hour period of celebration begins, inspired by the Scottish rite of Hogmanay, and at the end of those six hours the clocks revert to midnight and the new January 1st starts. This calendar was instituted in the hope of reconciling the solar and lunar cycles, but the objective was never attained because the sun declined to cooperate.
— *The Unideker Guide to Ruritania*

Paul and Christine perused the non-scientific document from the canvas bag. Rory peppered them with questions.

'What's this "Socialist People's Army of Ruritania (SPAR)"? Isn't it *passé* for a country to have an underground Communist movement? Very 1970s. And what's "National Cake Day"? And what are these "Blue Primroses" with upper-case initials?'

Paul took a deep breath.

'The ekwyroj of the Order of the Blue Primrose constitute a select security guard. Their official task is to protect the royal family and aristocracy. In practice they're part superior police force, part standing army. They're the only Ruritanians permitted to carry firearms. *Obliged*, rather. They find imaginative ways of interrogating suspects.'

'Ekwyroj?' Rory tilted his head.

'Plural of ekwyor,' said Christine. 'The most senior ekwyroj have a rank we'd label colonel or maybe general.'

'Okay,' said Rory, 'so Blue Primrose believes SPAR will start a revolution on National Cake Day this year and Britain will help to prevent it. And the plan in this folder indicates where and when British forces are to be deployed. So what's National Cake Day?'

And what, he wondered, was Britain's interest in Ruritania? Oil reserves?

Christine pulled a hardback copy of the *Unideker Guide to Ruritania* from her bookcase and handed it to him. The first page revealed why the country didn't appear on maps: unscripted shifts of size and location. Yeah, right, thought Rory, a country that travels the globe. Does she take her oil reserves with her? Christine drew his attention to the pages that explained National Cake Day and Ruritanian elections. Rory scanned them and grinned.

'So Ruritania's a feudal society with a monarch, and at the same time she's a democracy with a general election every June 22nd?'

'No, July 5th. Different calendar. National Cake Day is celebrated on the solstice, but in Ruritania that's July 4th not June 21st.'

Rory suspected his leg was being pulled but he smirked. He read more of the Unideker and shook his head. Ruritania's National Cake Day celebrations seemed extraordinary. The scenes in St Galen's Square in Strelsau must boggle the observer's mind: a simulated 'metacake', baked and decorated by the current head of government – the *krevjalem* – was ceremonially sliced by the Surgeon Archbishop of Strelsau amid magnificent pageantry.

A boggled mind, thought Rory, can't think. So maybe the purpose of pageantry in Ruritania, as in other countries, was to reduce the common mind to a condition of bogglement, thereby rendering it manipulable. And speaking of boggled minds, what in the name of the wee man from Milton Keynes was a *metacake*?

'I see. So all election candidates are krevs, and they seek to seduce the voters by offering cakes. What policies are debated?'

'Hardly any, Rory. The rival cakes are all-important. And the plural of krev is krevoj.'

Cake was the staple diet of Ruritanians, Paul told him. The only Ruritanians who didn't live on cake were the aristocrats, who made it, SPAR activists, who rejected it, and the Puritanical wing of the Asclepian Church, which was suspected of being pro-SPAR. Any non-aristocratic Ruritanian suspected of not eating cake was questioned. Painfully.

Rory was now sure at least one of his lower limbs was under traction.

'Okay. How many krevs – krevoj – stand for election, and who's allowed to vote?'

All of Her Majesty Queen Anastassia's subjects over the age of seventeen were entitled to vote, Rory learned. The majority determined which of the thirty-one hereditary krevoj would serve as head of government for the following year. The composition of parliament was otherwise unchanged.

There are thirty-one parliamentary seats, one for each krev, explained the Unideker. *Each seat acquires a new occupant only when the incumbent dies and the succession is resolved. This process usually involves legal wrangling, fratricide and sporadic fires.*

'So the country is always governed by the same élite oligarchy,' said Rory. 'But she's called a democracy because there are allegedly free and fair elections every year, following debates about cake policy.'

Paul shrugged.

'Every democracy and every tyranny evolves into an élite oligarchy. As Pareto said, élite oligarchy is the default form of government, though in all times and places it wears a mask.'

Paul was right, thought Rory. However, if SPAR was a political threat, as the manila folder suggested, why hadn't it been eliminated? Was Blue Primrose ineffective?

'How did you manage to visit Ruritania and return,' asked Rory, 'if the country has such an aptitude for accelerated tectonism?'

'You go by Ruritanian airways,' said Christine, 'which has Faerie powers. Not that I want to do it again. Paul found Ruritania quaint and congenial. I thought her backward and menacing.'

Rory asked about the Surgeon Archbishop, but Christine decided the time for late breakfast and explanations had passed and lunch must now take priority. The Unideker, she said, would tell Rory all he needed to know about the medical creed of the state religion and Ruritania's relationship to the Faerie Realm.

But it wouldn't tell him what to do with the canvas bag of papers now his rendezvous with the balloon carrier had failed. He scratched his chin and pondered. He could keep it, dump it in a skip, or perhaps find a way of collecting his thousand pounds.

Chapter 6

During the First World War, Military Intelligence Section Seven in Britain sprouted four sub-departments dealing with censorship and disinformation. After the War ended, MI7 was disbanded. As far as the British public is aware it was never re-instituted. However, there are many matters of which the British public is not aware. MI7 operates in the 21st century and is answerable to MIOCIA (the Ministry for Interfering in Other Countries' Internal Affairs).
— Anonymous letter to The Times; publication suppressed by the newspaper's owner

An elderly gentleman with grey eyes and matching beard and raincoat sat facing the screen. His right hand gripped the gnarled handle of an umbrella. As the CCTV images passed before his eyes he grunted, which might have signified annoyance, satisfaction, or a need to impress his authority on the minions juggling the tapes. Not that the minions needed impressing. They knew who was in charge: she was sitting beside the elderly gentleman. She radiated an aura of truculence and menace even when seated. When she stood up, anyone who met her eye tended to lose control of sphincters.

Neither she nor the elderly gentleman was disposed to sing a happy song. The agent hiding at the warehouse had watched Krev Schammerbass's bag of papers being collected, but he hadn't been able to keep pace with the courier so he'd lost track of him. *Ipso facto*, they'd lost track of the bag. And they didn't know who the courier was or where he lived.

'But although I couldn't keep up with the courier,' gasped the agent from the warehouse, still recovering from respiratory and cardiovascular distress, 'no one else followed him.'

The agent had an optometry appointment for the following week.

'There. See?' The elderly gentleman pointed his umbrella at the screen. He'd just watched the collapse of the balloon carrier outside the library. 'Play those last seven seconds again. Yes – there! By Jove, took him right out! Where the devil did she come from?'

'Above.' The voice was as feminine as a lioness's growl. 'Follow. Next camera. *No, fool*! There!'

If, thought the gentleman, 'above' is where she came from, then who is she? Young, agile, damned pretty; must be combat-trained to take out an experienced agent without being seen except by the cameras; brilliant climber – no scaffolding to help her …

It couldn't be coincidence. If she'd taken out the balloon agent she knew more about Waldemar Krev Schammerbass's too-clever-by-half bloody scheme than was healthy. Suppose, notwithstanding the warehouse agent's denial, she'd taken the krev's courier out as well. If so, either she'd known the bag of papers was in the warehouse or she'd followed the courier there, in which case she must have been at the Merlin. Or she and the courier were in cahoots. In any event, they must presume she now had the papers. What did she plan to do with them?

'SPAR?' he asked.

The female nodded and lit a cigar. The venom in her voice would have made a spitting cobra remember an urgent appointment elsewhere.

'It is *her*. Alterleta.'

'By Gad! Klarissa Alterleta? Here, in England? Thought she was older.'

'She is. She has live too long.' The tip of the cigar glowed with surrogate fury. 'They call her *Ulyanova*. Sometime she call herself *Klarissa Krefin Strlzhava*.'

The elderly gentleman drummed his umbrella on the floor and rubbed his beard. The legendary leader of SPAR had long evaded Ruritania's authorities. If she'd put herself at risk of arrest by travelling to Britain, at least three inferences followed.

First, SPAR had learned about Krev Schammerbass's convoluted scheme for getting the security plan to him without direct contact and without using diplomatic bags, which the krev deemed liable to interference. Like most Ruritanian aristocrats he was paranoid about SPAR; the krevoj saw Communist spies everywhere. How had news of the plan leaked?

Second, this Alterleta girl was smart and courageous, not to say foolhardy. The elderly gentleman acknowledged a surge of admiration, not untainted with lust.

Third, she was damned impertinent. No one except a spouse or immediate blood relative of a krev was permitted to use the honorific 'Krefin'; and to imply a relationship with the current krevjalem, Efeef Krev Strlzhav ...

'Follow those camera tapes and find out where she's staying: the Merlin or wherever.' He was accustomed to rapping out orders and seeing them obeyed. 'And we need to find the courier and trace those bloody papers before Schammerbass knows they're missing or we'll face the devil of a diplomatic row.'

'Krev Schammerbass choose courier. He choose criminal who run marathon, no close family, no work except crime. Nobody miss him.' The female grinned and the room temperature fell. 'We let krev deal with courier, make sure he stay silent. We find papers.'

The elderly gentleman demurred. His umbrella beckoned a minion, who marched forward, saluting like a soldier summoned by his commanding officer; which was exactly what he was.

'Find out *everything* about this courier: name, address, phone numbers, e-mail addresses, family, friends, life history, criminal convictions, girlfriends, boyfriends, hobbies, illnesses, known strengths and weaknesses, colour of underwear, what he eats for breakfast. I want a full report. *Now.*'

Chapter 7

Ruritania's state religion has a medical creed. The reigning monarch is the titular head of the Asclepian Church, but the Surgeon Archbishop of Strelsau is its spiritual, political and administrative leader. During its long history the Asclepian Church had undergone schisms. All branches are devoted to healing the sick and make token gestures towards feeding the poor, but conflicts among them have grown heated. The Puritan sect has become fractious during recent decades, accusing Asclepian traditionalists of covert pharmacolatry and other heresies. Its leaders are suspected of sympathising with SPAR. The more articulate Puritans have issued calls for National Cake Day to be abolished, murmuring about obesity, diabetes, heart disease, arthropathies, ingrowing toenails and terminal flatulence.
— The Unideker Guide to Ruritania

Smartly dressed, travelling first class, Rory studied the Unideker on the train journey to London. The Unideker confirmed what he'd learned from Paul and Christine and told him more. In particular, it answered the 'Surgeon Archbishop' question and gave an outline of academic life in Ruritania.

Sensible and economical, thought Rory, wondering whether his evaluation was ironic. Three cities in the country, one university in each. He read further. So Puritans are unpopular and the authorities are suspicious of them, he mused. I suppose the Surgeon Archbishop of Strelsau is *not* a Puritan.

The train reached Euston. Rory put the Unideker into his attaché case, slung the canvas bag over his shoulder, donned his new dark glasses and took a taxi to the *Nurture* offices. The two and a half mile journey took only fifty minutes; London traffic was light. He entered the building and navigated himself to the office of a thin bald man who was important enough to look harassed but not important enough for his underlings to look harassed. The thin bald man peered between his computer screen and the heap of files on his desk and scrutinised Rory through angry pince-nez.

'The balloon carrier was unavoidably detained,' said Rory, 'so I've brought the Ruritanian papers for your Special Issue.'

The thin bald man extended a thin bald hand and snatched the canvas bag. He opened it and flicked through the contents.

'And you are?'

Rory frowned.

'Was that a grammatically ill-formed indicative sentence or did the Australian-style rising intonation on the final syllable imply an interrogative?'

'*Who are you?*' The thin bald man barked like an enraged Chihuahua.

'Thank you. Much clearer. I'm Major Redman.'

'Are you indeed. And where did *you* spring from?'

'According to some authorities, the Garden of Eden.'

The thin bald man made a noise like a kettle on the verge of a nervous breakdown.

'*Who sent you?*'

'That information is classified. All the papers assembled by the Ruritanian Academy of Science are in the bag. End of message.'

Rory turned on his heel, marched out of the office and sniggered. He glanced at his watch. He could make it back to Euston in time for the next Manchester train if he avoided public transport. A two and a half mile run was no challenge. After all, his attaché case was empty except for the Unideker. And a manila folder.

All he had to do now was return to the Merlin Hotel, find Krev Schammerbass, and demand his thousand pounds. Plus travelling expenses.

But the krev wasn't at the Merlin. According to the reception desk he never had been. Rory scanned the guest list and noted the names 'Jack and Christine Blackmeadow': birthday party Christine and her husband. He went home, ate a salad in a plastic box he'd stolen *en route* from the café of a garden centre in Fallowfield, and changed into tee shirt and shorts and trainers.

To clear his mind, he needed a longer run than would have been possible in London.

Chapter 8

Just as Ruritania drifts among latitudes and longitudes, so her language has more roots than a banyan. Most of the roots are Indo-European. In Ruritanian you can identify fragments of Greek, Latin, Gothic, Polish, Hungarian, German, and – sometimes – mangled English, such as may be found in a British university student's essays. The language is so abstruse that the average Ruritanian often speaks English instead, with an accent like a second-rate British actor playing Johnny Foreigner in a black and white film. However, Ruritanian is invariably used during state occasions, and peasants in remote villages speak it while they chew straw.

— The Unideker Guide to Ruritania

Klarissa left the Merlin Hotel and caught the train to London. Three hours later, the elderly gentleman with the grey beard entered the hotel, displayed an identification card with attitude and demanded to see the guest list. Three recent departures: two men, one woman.

'Was this her?'

He showed the Reception clerk a photograph. It was a still from a CCTV tape but recognisable.

'Yes, sir,' said the clerk. 'Ms Sue de Nym. She took a taxi to Piccadilly station.'

The elderly gentleman snapped orders into his phone, then snatched a note from an attendant minion and read it. His face attained the hue of a beetroot receiving bad news. Beard bristling, he marched out of the hotel and snapped more orders.

Klarissa noted the time of the next flight to Strelsau; forty-three hours ahead. She booked a one-way ticket in the name 'Julneva Eidentyfeime', then took an executive suite at the Hilton using the same sobriquet. The receptionist's smile of greeting was high-grade plastic, camouflaging her envy of the guest's suit and jewellery.

'Welcome to the Hilton, Ms Eid … Eiden …'

'Thank you.' Klarissa signed the book and accepted her room key.

'Is this your first visit to London?'

'Ah … I know not how to say in English …' Klarissa continued in Ruritanian: 'No, but I hope it'll be my last because I hate the place and all of your benighted country. Look at *you*: all the advantages of living in a so-called advanced liberal democracy, yet the vacancy behind your eyes betrays the attitudes, values and sophistication of an illiterate peasant.'

The plastic smile intensified. The eyes above it strove for animation.

'Of course, ma'am. If you need any help in understanding our breakfast, lunch or dinner menus, room service arrangements or fire regulations, copies of all of which are available in your room, please telephone the desk at any time, day or night. Our experienced staff will be delighted to help you. Enjoy your stay at the London Hilton.'

'You have the voice of a robot and the worth of a department store mannequin,' replied Klarissa, not lapsing into English. She gave a sweet smile and glided towards the lift, designer handbag gracing her shoulder.

A uniformed youth trotted in her wake with her suitcase, his acne aglow, his eyes twin rabbits in the headlamps of her buttocks. The suitcase was empty. A notice beside the lift informed residents that the AGM of the Slug Defence League would begin at 7.30 the following evening in one of the smaller meeting rooms.

In the lift, Klarissa turned to examine the youth. She saw a small hopeful dog wagging its tail.

'You have British with interest in slug?' she said, making her English sound exotic.

The youth wagged a breathless response.

'Yeah, Lord Arion books a meeting room for the Slug Defence League AGM every year. Miss Sowerby will be chairing the meeting, 'cos she's, like, the chair of the Slug Defence League, and there'll be, like, Kelly Blackmantle, and …'

The lift stopped. Klarissa entered her room, gave the little dog a five pound note, sent him away and stared through the fog over Hyde Park. She went to check the adjoining rooms: empty. One couldn't be too careful. Then she returned to her suite and switched on her computer.

She smiled. The timing of the Slug Defence League meeting could prove convenient.

The youth stopped wagging and returned to duty, puffing his cheeks and wiping his brow. His acne fluoresced. His trousers felt tight.

Chapter 9

Since Mr Redman's departure from the College his friends have regaled me with tales of his antics, but it is hard to distinguish fact from fancy. I can believe the stories of cannabis deals and thefts from wealthy establishments, but not those involving violent offences. He might, for amusement, have committed acts of creative vandalism such as painting anarchist slogans on expensive cars, and he has probably defrauded banks, but I doubt the gossip about the security van in Glasgow. This much is certain: he has continued to enjoy an irregular relationship with the law, yet has largely avoided the customary fate of the criminal.
    — *Cerberus D. Gardog: 'A College Porter's*
      Recollections of Unconventional Undergraduates'

Clad in running gear, Rory dozed in his conservatory. The spirit of Professor Weisheitsliebhaber questioned him: 'Why did Krev Schammerbass make it so easy for a clever SPAR agent to rob you, Rory? Are you angrier with him or her?' Puzzlement often elicited half-dreaming encounters with Professor Weisheitsliebhaber, underlining his need for exercise.

He pulled himself awake, drank more coffee and left the house, switching into marathon mode. But as he turned to lock the front door, two men in black suits grasped his arms and propelled him towards a Rolls Royce with darkened windows parked beside his garden gate. They didn't speak. A shoulder holster bulged under each man's jacket. In the driving seat of the Rolls was a third black suit.

Rory struggled, then stopped; no point in provoking armed attackers. He muted his frustration with gritted teeth.

I should have known, yelled his mind. After the business with those papers, I should have known Schammerbass would … But it's stupid! *I* wanted to see *him*! Or – is someone else responsible for this?

Whoever was behind the abduction, he realised, was rich enough to own a Rolls Royce and employ at least three men who, to judge from their sizes and suits, were of the hench persuasion. He looked at the two who were holding him and asked questions. They didn't answer. They dragged him to the car and pushed him into the back seat. One sat on his left, one on his right. The third black suit drove, not exceeding the speed limit. All three remained silent.

Rory forced his body to relax but his mind spun. Who were these people? Where were they taking him? For what purpose? What could he do about it? Right now, the answer to the last question was 'Nothing'; he was outnumbered three to one and he was in a moving car. He stared through the darkened glass, trying to memorise the route they were taking. The roads soon became unfamiliar.

After forty minutes they had left the city and were driving along a country lane.

'Where are we?' he demanded. 'Where are we going?'

As if in answer, the car swung to the left, throwing Rory against the dark suit to his right. The suit pushed him upright again and then ignored him. Still none of the kidnappers spoke.

Rory wiped the perspiration from his hands on his running shorts and stared through the windscreen. The Rolls was now snaking along a gravel drive through an avenue of lime trees. After a quarter of a mile it glided to a halt outside a large white house with Georgian portico and bay windows and a weather-vane shaped like a slug.

The two black suits who'd seized Rory pulled him out of the car and propelled him into the building and up a curved staircase to a room with a high ornate ceiling and heavy furniture. One stood beside the door, the other beside the window. Both exuded menace. Rory wondered whether they were dumb.

But he was now certain that a Ruritanian had arranged the kidnapping. Emblazoned on the wall opposite the door was the heraldic crest of the Teesporn monarchs, who according to the Unideker Guide had ruled Ruritania for four centuries: cockerel rampant passant or, quartered with sword rampant and battle-axe couchant or, on field sable with bend sinister. The crest was surmounted by a portrayal of the Teesporn crown, a bejewelled gold replica of a three-tier wedding cake symbolising the marriage of the monarch to the country. But I suppose, he thought, SPAR sympathisers would see it as symbolising what the monarch and aristocracy do to the country on their metaphorical wedding nights.

On the wall adjoining the crest was a large painting of a cream cake with pink icing, couchant passant on cake stand argent. The play of light on the icing, the cream filling and the cake stand was depicted with delicacy. Rory guessed that cream cakes with pink icing were a speciality of the Schammerbass bakery.

No sooner had this conjecture formed when a bell rang, an electronic lock clicked, and he was ushered from the chamber into a larger apartment brimming with wealth and taste. The window, he noted, was bullet-proof. It afforded a prospect over lush parkland warmed by evening sunlight. Rory blinked and averted his eyes.

Seated in a black leather armchair beside the marble fireplace, clad again in Armani attire, was the man he'd wanted to see. His shoelaces were neatly ironed.

Krev Schammerbass uttered a command and the black suits effaced themselves. Then he narrowed his eyes and spoke.

'Rory. Forgive delay. Please be seated.'

His thin lips smiled. His eyes didn't.

Chapter 10

All three Ruritanian universities promote research into the physics of Faerie, and their philosophy and geography departments appoint chairs in Faerie Studies. The Faerie Realm is a major topic in Ruritanian philosophy, along with the Gödelpus Unsatisfiability Theorem and the logic puzzle dubbed 'Lekhissa's Riddle'. However, some Ruritanian philosophers devote themselves to the metaphysics of baking. There are debates about the ontological status of a metacake – or, according to classical Platonists, The Metacake. Materialists dispute claims for the fruit metacake and the cream metacake, idealists insist that The Metacake exists only as a mental entity, dualists declare you can have your metacake and eat it, and existentialists consider questions about the innate nature of the metacake empty since all that matters is the choice whether or not to metadevour it. These debates relate to the nature of the simulated metacake prepared each year in the krevjalem's bakery and taken by procession to St Galen's Square on National Cake Day.
— Dai O'Genies, A Primer of Ruritanian Philosophy

Paul answered the doorbell to an elderly gentleman with an umbrella in one hand and an identification card with attitude in the other. Looming over the gentleman's shoulder was what seemed on first glance to be a troll but on further inspection proved to be a female humanoid wearing a deep red uniform. Paul's heart sank. Rory was in trouble. Again.

'Paul Edict?' said the gentleman. 'Sorry to interrupt your evening but we need your help.'

Paul led his unwanted guests into the sitting room and introduced, 'My wife Christine and a partner in my firm, Ariadne Sowerby'. The elderly gentleman said, 'I'm Horatio Barrington; this is my colleague Grizelina Tupsroot.'

Paul nodded. 'Colonel. Ekwyor. Please sit down. How may we help you?'

The visitors sat in adjacent armchairs and exchanged glances: he'd used their titles, so he'd not only registered the details on Horatio Barrington's identification card but also recognised the female humanoid's uniform.

'I'm just leaving,' said Ariadne. 'Meeting in London.'

The colonel rose to his feet, the epitome of etiquette. He noted that Ms Sowerby was a damned fine-looking young woman with a straightforward gaze. He liked the cut of her jib, among other features.

'Before you leave, Ms Sowerby, may I ask whether you know a man called Rory Redman?'

'Met him.' Ariadne gave a tight smile. She considered Rory Redman an irresponsible kleptomaniac who needed to learn respect for the law. On a personal level he was attractive, athletic, clever and witty, but his advances were unsubtle. She wouldn't choose to encourage him until he showed less antipathy to commitment. 'Never felt inclined to further the acquaintance,' she prevaricated.

Paul saw her to the door while Christine brewed coffee. Colonel Barrington made a show of consulting his notes. When everyone was seated with coffee and biscuits, he spoke again.

'No doubt you've deduced why we're here. We know a lot about Rory Redman but certain details are missing. We understand you first met him at university thirteen years ago and you've remained in touch.'

Christine said Rory was interesting and entertaining, always in need of help with his garden and often in need of a lawyer.

'He visited you yesterday, the eleventh of May,' said the colonel. 'May I ask why?' Neither Paul nor Christine answered so the colonel prompted them: 'He accepted an assignment from Krev Schammerbass on the evening of the tenth and was supposed to complete it yesterday morning. He failed to do so. Since he visited you, perhaps you can explain.'

Christine said Rory had been assaulted and handcuffed and robbed of fifty pounds in his own garden. As per Krev Schammerbass's instructions he'd intended to deliver an item to someone outside the central library but the someone hadn't been there so he'd come to see them instead to ask what he should do with the item and to seek treatment for a minor head wound sustained during the assault. She went upstairs to the master bedroom and returned with the handcuffs. The colonel inspected them.

'Hmm. Mr Redman's assailant shops in Ann Summers, does he?'

'Rory said "she", not "he",' said Paul. 'Circumstantial evidence: an aroma of perfume and small bare footprints in a flower bed.'

The ekwyor said, 'Hah'. It sounded like an iron implement being driven into a sensitive part of a suspect.

'If Mr Redman sought your advice about the item he was supposed to deliver at the library, presumably his assailant didn't steal it. What was this item and what advice did you offer?'

Christine looked at her husband. Paul's face betrayed a rapid succession of thoughts.

'It was a canvas sports bag containing papers from the Ruritanian Academy of Science together with a covering letter to the editor of *Nurture*,' he said. 'Apparently Krev Schammerbass asked Rory to collect the bag but not to look inside it. But when he couldn't find the person outside the library he'd no alternative. He showed us the contents.'

The ekwyor leaned forward. Her snarl was an attempt to sound benevolent.

'Is anything in bag also than scientific paper and letter?'

Christine's mouth half-opened. Paul said, 'There were fifteen or sixteen manuscripts, mostly physics and medicine, plus the letter. Nothing else.'

The colonel met the ekwyor's eye.

'What did you suggest he do with this material?' he said.

'Return it to Krev Schammerbass,' said Paul.

'Sensible,' said the colonel. He rose; the ekwyor did likewise. 'That's all we need to ask. Thanks for your time, Mr Edict. And for the coffee and biscuits, Mrs Edict. I'm afraid we must relieve you of the handcuffs. Evidence.'

Paul and Christine showed the two visitors out. As they started down the garden path towards the colonel's Mercedes, the ekwyor turned and asked:

'Is Redman military person? Have officer status?'

'Rory?' Paul laughed. 'No! Never been in the armed forces and certainly not held a commission. Why do you ask?'

The ekwyor gave a chilling half-smile and marched to the car. The chauffeur held the passenger door open for her. She lit a cigar. The colonel sat behind her. The Mercedes purred away into the twilight.

Chapter 11

In Ruritania and Britain I'm known only as a lawyer with a passion for slugs. I never mention my physics degree. I avoid discussing most aspects of science, though I'm interested in how the teaching and practice of science differ between Ruritania and the rest of the world. It isn't a matter of who's right and who's wrong; it's about different accounts of reality suiting different cultures. Most people won't accept this because it undermines belief in certainties. They wouldn't believe in certainties if they understood the Gödelpus Unsatisfiability Theorem. Visiting Ruritania introduced me to the Theorem and left my mind awash with healthy confusion.
— *Ariadne Sowerby, 'First Impressions of Ruritania'*

'Mistakes were made.' Krev Schammerbass sighed. 'If I do not order you to look in bag you do not look. *Mea culpa.* But balloon carrier is assaulted and bag is not delivered. Your comment?'

'Do you imagine *I* attacked your balloon carrier, Krev Schammerbass? And why do you suppose I looked in the bag?'

The narrowed blue eyes pierced Rory. Did the krev need spectacles or was he wondering how Rory had learned his name?

'You deliver papers to *Nurture* office, therefore you read covering letter, therefore you look in bag. If you do not attack balloon carrier, who does? You know answers: you did not complete philosophy degree but you were expected to make first class.'

'Ditched the course so I wouldn't end up serving burgers and fries in Macdonald's.'

The response elicited no smile, not even a thin-lipped one.

'I was assaulted and robbed as I left my house this morning,' said Rory. 'When I recovered I took the bag to the library but there was no balloon seller. So I looked in the bag and took the papers to the address on the covering letter.'

Krev Schammerbass gave a half-smile, not too thin.

'So, *you* are assaulted and robbed. Who attack you? What is taken?'

'Fifty pounds went from my pocket. I didn't see the assailant. She knocked me unconscious and handcuffed me.'

The krev folded his arms and frowned. His voice seemed to drip incredulity.

'*She*? You say you are assaulted by *woman*? Not possible. You are strong healthy young man. If you do not see attacker, why say you it is woman?'

'I smelt perfume.'

There was a bark of laughter.

'I think you say such evidence would not stand up in court. What perfume?'

'God knows. It wasn't cheap scent, though.'

The krev shook his head.

'You were made unconscious, your senses deluded. A man with knowledge of philosophy should not draw inference from evidence so tenuous. What is "William Kemp Society"?'

Rory blinked.

'Why do you ask?'

'I am curious. You are Honorary Secretary of William Kemp Society. What is it?'

It was improbable that Schammerbass understood Morris-dancing. Few people did. If more communities engaged in it, thought Rory, there'd be less fighting in the world. Morris-dancing was guaranteed to ritualise and defuse aggression. Pacifists should encourage it.

'A group devoted to long-distance Morris-dancing,' he said. 'You know about Morris-dancing? It's an English tradition.

William Kemp was an actor in Shakespeare's theatre company. He had an argument with the Bard, walked out, and Morris-danced from London to Norwich in protest. We hold an annual London to Norwich Morris-dance in his memory.'

'You dance in protest also?'

'We honour a great Morris-dancer. Kemp made the journey in nine days spread over several months; crowds cheered him. We make it in nine *consecutive* days, thirteen or fourteen miles per day. Our cheering crowds number ten or a dozen.' Rory paused. His mouth was dry. 'I have a question for you, Your Excellency. Why did you select *me* as courier? Why would the President of the Ruritanian Academy of Science choose to convey a bag of scientific manuscripts to London via a marathon runner and a balloon carrier?'

Being scrutinised and appraised by Krev Schammerbass over a long silent minute and a short stretch of Axminster made Rory's palms sweat again. The scrutiny said 'I don't know how you've learned so much about me but it's *too* much.' Rory struggled to keep his face impassive. His heart thumped.

At length, the krev spoke.

'Special Issue of *Nurture* is devoted to paper by leading Ruritanian scientist. Dark forces plan to ambush consignment, prevent publication, set reputation of our science back. So bag is sent in secret to Manchester, hidden in warehouse, to be collected by courier not connected with Ruritania or science and handed to trusted agent … We learn you are intelligent, athletic, willing to take risk, criminal but dependable.' The krev shrugged. 'I am sorry birthday party venue change. You read papers in bag?'

Rory felt his fists begin to clench. The krev's side of the conversation comprised questions, diversions and insincere apologies. No mention of the manila folder.

'Flicked through them, saw the titles.'

'You take paper from bag before you hand to editorial office?'

'Of course not. What would I do with a scientific manuscript?' Rory examined his knuckles. 'I don't like being manipulated,

Your Excellency. And I don't like anyone manipulating my friends, as in making them change their birthday party arrangements. And I didn't like being attacked in my own garden and then abducted by your thugs and dragged here and interrogated when I planned to contact you anyway.'

The krev's face donned another smile.

'All is well, Rory. Paper are safe in London; I thank you. You are hurt; I am sorry. I suspect you of duplicity; for this also I am sorry. But all is well.'

He glided from his chair and his Gucci shoes creaked to the Louis Quinze cocktail cabinet opposite the window.

'I am poor host. What like you to drink?'

'Nothing, thanks.'

'You are sure? Your mouth is dry.'

'I'm sure.'

The krev inclined his head and poured a measure of virulent liqueur into a crystal glass.

'Now I keep my side of bargain.'

He raised his glass, drank the liqueur and rang a bell. One of the black suits re-entered. At a command from the krev his gun hand snaked to his shoulder holster.

He drew out an envelope bulging with twenty-pound notes and handed it to Rory.

'Task is complete, Rory,' said the krev. 'Now my men drive you home.'

Rory opened the envelope and counted the notes. Fifty-five of them.

'Travelling expenses added,' said the krev. 'It is what you wish, I think?'

Few things in life, thought Rory as the Rolls bore him homeward, are more annoying than feeling indebted to someone who's used you and then treated you like something he's trodden in. He concentrated on not shaking while the black suits were watching.

The Rolls let him out at the end of his street and slid away into the night. The black suits had spoken not a word. Perhaps they *were* dumb. But they were well trained and, Rory inferred, well paid, since they hadn't tried to steal his eleven hundred pounds.

But if Schammerbass had deduced I'd seen the manila folder before the SPAR activist stole it, he decided, I'd now be dead. And Prof Weisheitsliebhaber's question keeps nagging me: Why did the krev hatch a scheme that made it easy for a SPAR agent to rob me?

He went to bed, still musing, but the day's events had unsettled him sufficiently to induce bad dreams. They involved circus clowns, as his nightmares always did. He'd suffered from coulrophobia since childhood.

Chapter 12

Rory and I were friends at university and visited each other during vacations. My parents recognised his brilliance but deemed him unstable because he claimed to reject traditional values and beliefs. Nevertheless his behaviour was impeccable apart from the occasional theft and practical joke. Women found him attractive but he never formed a stable relationship, and he had few close friends except for me and Christine. His eccentricity is hard to explain. His parents were conventional people, much involved in local affairs. I suspect his father never took risks; his mother was cleverer than she believed; Ruby, Rory's sister, seemed ordinary. But despite his avowed contempt for convention, Rory once demonstrated an idiosyncratic brand of matchmaking that earned my gratitude.

— Paul Edict, 'Rory Redman as I Knew Him'

It was raining. After his morning run, Rory drank coffee, showered and donned smart-casual attire. Then he slipped his photocopy of the original security document under his hearthrug, together with the manila folder containing the fake, and stepped out again into the weather. The envelope full of twenty-pound notes nestled in his pocket.

As he headed towards the bank a gleaming black Mercedes whispered to a halt beside him and an elderly gentleman with grey eyes and matching beard and raincoat alighted from the rear seat, raising his umbrella.

'Mr Redman? Horatio Barrington. May I have a word?'

'What about?'

Rory stopped. Rain flattened his hair and trickled down his neck.

'The bag of documents you collected on the evening of May 10th,' said the gentleman.

Rory's fists clenched and his jaw tightened. He glared.

'No you bloody can't! I've had enough of this Ruritania tripe, people tossing me around like a cork on the tide, mugging me, tying me up, kidnapping me, interrogating me. Sod off! Get back into your poncy car and–'

'Why did you agree to run the errand for Krev Schammerbass?'

'It's none of your damned business!'

One of Krev Schammerbass's henchpersons, hunched against the rain, was talking to the occupant of the Mercedes's passenger seat and looking obsequious. Not dumb after all, thought Rory. Has he changed his suit since last night? There's a puzzle here …

'You're wrong, Mr Redman,' said the man in grey. 'Or should I say *Major* Redman? It's very much my business.'

He displayed the identification card with attitude. It revealed his name, rank and organisation. There was a crown on it.

'Yeah, right. *Colonel* Barrington. You think I'll fall for that? MI7 was disbanded before 1920. It's fictional.' Rage notwithstanding, Rory had to suppress a grin. Pretty much like Ruritania, he thought.

'That's what the public is meant to believe,' said the colonel. 'We know about your cannabis-dealing and petty thefts, Mr Redman. We know the circumstances under which you left university. And we know you only got away with those tricks with Barclays and NatWest, and the security van in Glasgow, because the police couldn't provide enough evidence to the CPS. *We* can supply the evidence.' He glanced back at Rory's villa and garden. 'Done well, haven't you?'

'I never touched the security van in–'

'Given the information we'd present, a jury would believe otherwise. Now put it all together, Mr Redman: bank frauds, security van, cannabis, thefts … Ten years inside? Twelve?'

Rory struggled not to grind his teeth. He might injure them. He hated dentists, drilling into carious premolars and precarious molars, filling one's head with fillings.

'What do you want, *Colonel*?'

'Answers to a few questions,' said the colonel. 'You have information we need. Cough it up and you've nothing to worry about. Play silly buggers and you're up to your neck in raw sewage. Now let's get into my car and out of this rain.'

Rory and the colonel dripped side by side in the back seat of the Mercedes. The driver wore a chauffeur's uniform. The passenger seat was crushed by a middle-aged woman built like a wrestler. It was easy to see why the henchperson had been obsequious. She too wore a uniform: it was dark red and embroidered with a fleur-de-lys, a blue flower and a crown.

'Cigar?' The colonel proffered a box of Havanas.

'Don't smoke tobacco,' said Rory.

Rory wanted to bank his eleven hundred pounds worth of twenty pound notes, not to sit around chatting to a supposed secret service officer.

'Sensible chap,' said the colonel. 'So Krev Schammerbass questioned you. What did you tell him?'

'I don't know why he sent his thugs to kidnap me. I'd already tried to see him again but he wasn't at the Merlin. I told him nothing he didn't already know except the person who attacked and robbed me was female. He pretended not to believe it. Changed the subject.'

The woman in the passenger seat turned and stared at Rory. Her eyes were hazel. They could have been used to hone the edge of a ceremonial sword. He stared back.

'Did you see this attacker?' said the colonel.

'No.' Rory sighed. 'And before you ask the obvious question, I smelt perfume in the split second before I was hit. Expensive perfume.'

The colonel grunted. The woman with carborundum eyes lit a Havana, muttered a few words and stared through the windscreen again. The chauffeur nodded and the car started to move.

'Where are we going?' asked Rory.

Carrying a wad of cash made him feel vulnerable.

'Somewhere we won't be disturbed. For a chat.' The colonel's face was unreadable. 'Why did you try to visit Krev Schammerbass before you were taken to him by force?'

'To explain why I hadn't completed his assignment.'

'But he already knew everything except the sex of your assailant? Tell me all about this assignment from beginning to … I almost said "end". I should say "this morning".'

Rory shook his head and sighed again. He summarised the story: the party at the Merlin, Krev Schammerbass, the run to the warehouse, the bag of papers, the assault, the recovery, the visit to Paul and Christine and the trip to London. He included everything except the manila folder. No one else spoke until he'd finished.

'Clear succinct report,' said the colonel. 'We could use a chap like you. You omitted only one piece of information.'

'What?'

'Something went missing from the bag somewhere between the warehouse and the *Nurture* offices.'

'Oh. Was it important?'

'Stop playing dumb, Redman. You're a bright chap with healthy curiosity, so after you took the bag home you examined its contents. One document caught your attention because it wasn't a scientific paper. How much of it did you read and what else do you know about it?'

Rory felt himself grow pale. Stereotypical persona notwithstanding, Horatio Barrington wasn't slow. He took a deep breath. He wasn't prepared to divulge the whereabouts of either the fake document or his copy of the original.

'I read enough to know it was a security plan relating to a country I didn't believe existed. I put it back in the bag. In the morning I set off early to the library. I was in a hurry to get rid of the bag, which is probably why I didn't notice the woman who attacked me. After I'd recovered and got out of the handcuffs I checked the bag: the folder containing the security plan was missing. I went to the library, found no balloon carrier, and went to ask Paul and Christine Edict for advice. They told me enough about Ruritania for me to decide to keep quiet about the missing document. I expected Schammerbass to question me about it last night. He didn't. I'm sure he knew it had gone, though. He paid me to keep my mouth shut.'

'Very well. You're certain your assailant was female?'

'Uncorroborated olfactory evidence can't establish certainty. But yes, she was.'

The colonel grunted, leaned forward and whispered to the woman in the passenger seat. She blew a cloud of cigar smoke and muttered to the driver in what Rory supposed was Ruritanian. The car turned off the road, bumped along a woodland track for three hundred yards and stopped. The colonel switched on his smart phone and showed a photograph to Rory. The woman in the photo had short raven hair, high cheek-bones, film-star pulchritude and startling green eyes. She looked fearless.

'Recognise her?'

'Never seen her. And it's not a face I'd forget.'

'Ever heard of Klarissa Alterleta? Or Ulyanova? Or Klarissa Krefin Strlzhava?'

'No. And it's not a name I'd try to pronounce.' Rory frowned. 'Is 'krefin' the feminine of 'krev'?'

'Diminutive, not feminine. Denotes a close relative of a krev. Which this woman isn't.' The colonel picked up his umbrella and opened the door. 'Let's go for a walk.'

Okay, thought Rory, now I know what she looks like I'm going to find her. She needs to be taught not to mug people and tie them up. I don't give a damn about the woman's politics but I do care about her manners.

His mind drew two other inferences. First, the colonel and the ekwyor wanted to talk to him out of earshot of the chauffeur.

Second, the puzzle he'd identified demanded a solution; or rather, three solutions. A rich Ruritanian aristocrat, a member of the government, had well-nigh engineered the theft of a sensitive security document by an alleged terrorist. Why? A Ruritanian security officer was hunting the terrorist, and a member of the British secret service was helping her. Why? And the servants of the seemingly duplicitous aristocrat had fawned on the security officer. Why?

Rory could never resist such challenges to his logical powers.

Chapter 13

Unlike most philosophy students, especially those with a passion for formal logic, Rory could put his academic skill to practical use. Christine had inherited a pair of pearl ear-rings from her grandmother and she loved them. She still does. One night I drank enough to tell Rory I was in love with Christine but she didn't seem to feel the same way. A few days later, her precious ear-rings disappeared. She was distraught. Rory gave me the name and address of a pawn shop I should visit. I followed his guidance. The pawnbroker asked me for proof of identity and then gave me the missing ear-rings. The person who'd pawned them had also paid the cost of redemption but had asked that the items be retained pending my arrival to collect them. As far as Christine knew, I'd traced her ear-rings and recovered them unaided. A few weeks later she and I were engaged.
— Paul Edict, 'Rory Redman as I Knew Him'

Rory walked between the colonel and the hazel-eyed wrestler. Water from the sky, the summer trees and the colonel's umbrella dripped on his head. The wrestler puffed her cigar, impervious to rain. The chauffeur stayed in the car, staring at the windscreen.

'Should have introduced you. Grizelina, this is Rory Redman. Mr Redman, this is my colleague Grizelina Ekwyor Tupsroot. Most Ruritanian ladies use a feminine surname inflection, but the ekwyor says 'Tupsroota' sounds like an online gambling game or an obscure Albanian delicacy.'

Rory proffered his hand. The ekwyor didn't shake it. Just as well, he thought; she'd have crushed it.

'Order of the Blue Phoenix?' he said.

She graced him with a beetle-browed glower. The glower persisted while her boot heel crushed the stub of her cigar into the mud. Seldom had Rory seen a boot heel crush with such relish.

'And you knew nothing about Ruritania three days ago?' Colonel Barrington almost smiled. 'By Jove, you *have* done your homework.'

Rory shook rainwater out of his eyes.

'Since an ekwyor of Blue Phoenix is here collaborating with a senior MI7 officer, and you're concerned about the missing manila folder, and you showed me a picture of an attractive young woman, asked whether I knew her and gave her what I suppose are Ruritanian names, should I infer that Klarissa What's-her-face is a SPAR agent, who concussed me and then nicked the folder along with fifty quid from my pocket, and that you're now keen to find her and recover the security plan before National Cake Day?'

The colonel's face grew bellicose.

'Try not to be so damned sharp, Redman. You'll cut yourself.'

'My mother told me that when I was three.'

'I think,' said the ekwyor, 'we keep Pan Redman under … what is word, Horatio?'

'Surveillance? Arrest? Protective custody? Wraps? Ground? Huh! When's the next flight from Heathrow to Strelsau, Grizelina?'

Ekwyor Tupsroot told him. He typed a message into his phone and sent it along with Klarissa's photo to seven colleagues. Rory considered handing over the fake manila folder to him, but decided not yet. And he wasn't prepared to relinquish his photocopy of the original document. Not without payment.

'She'll stay in London a couple of nights,' said Colonel Barrington, 'and she won't hole up anywhere cheap: she took a suite at the Merlin and we're told she wears gear from top fashion houses. So she'll use a good hotel. Typical Commie. She'll check in under another assumed name but the photo's unmistakable. We'll find her.' He turned to Rory. 'Come on, back to the car. You're soaked. Sorry to disrupt your life but you're coming to London with us. Too bloody risky to turn you loose considering all you've deduced, but criminal history notwithstanding we've no grounds for locking you up.'

'I trust you'll have the decency to take me home first so I can change and pack a suitcase.'

And, thought Rory, pick up my passport. And both versions of the security plan, the copy of the original *and* the fake.

He still hadn't made it to the bank to deposit his cash, but no matter: he was going to solve the puzzle.

Chapter 14

They say maths is the cheapest subject to teach because all you need is a pencil, a pile of paper and a waste bin for the wrong answers. But surely philosophy is cheaper because you don't need the waste bin. Rory is passionate about it, though. He told me he's a 'critical realist', meaning he believes in the world we all live and believe in but not in our everyday conception of it (or any conception, scientific or otherwise). He said Kant wrote something of the sort. And he agrees with an empiricist called Quine, who said things we perceive have objective existence but things we imagine, or mental entities, haven't; they're just words. I'd just returned from Ruritania when Rory told me all this. It struck me that a country so much influenced by the Faerie Realm would alienate him, so he'd better not go there. In any case, Ruritanian authorities don't take kindly to thieves.

— Paul Edict, 'Rory Redman as I Knew Him'

Klarissa's flight to Strelsau was scheduled to depart soon after sunrise. Her handbag contained both versions of the security plan: the original she'd stolen from Rory, and a copy of the fake she'd planted.

As she left the dining room she noticed a grey-suited man at Reception, holding his phone in front of the mannequin and questioning her. The mannequin's plastic smile had vanished. More men and women in grey suits populated the foyer, the two largest lurking beside the doors.

Klarissa side-stepped into a lift and directed it upwards. She glanced at her watch: seven o'clock. She made a short phone call. As the lift stopped and the doors slid open she leaned forward and scanned the corridor: nothing alarming. Yet. She ran to her executive room, made swift but drastic alterations to her appearance and her luggage labels, broke into the unoccupied adjoining suite, and then telephoned Heathrow and booked a first-class ticket to Vienna using the name on another of her passports, 'Gottlieba Weissfeld'. The Vienna flight would depart at five minutes to midnight, so she'd need to remain inconspicuous for two hours before she left for Heathrow. She knew there'd be a flight from Vienna to Strelsau the following morning; she'd buy a ticket at Schwechat.

*

As the black Mercedes purred into central London, Colonel Barrington's phone rang. The call lasted twenty seconds.

'Got her! She's at the Hilton, registered as Julneva Eidentyfeime, J-u-l – '

Rory groaned. 'Hell, is that the best she can do?'

'Booked on a flight to Strelsau tomorrow at sparrow-fart,' continued the colonel. 'Park Lane, driver – fast. Our people will hold the fort but Ekwyor Tupsroot must make the arrest.'

Ekwyor Tupsroot said something in Ruritanian and grinned. Her teeth were a peculiar colour.

'Tell me, one of you,' said Rory, 'how does air travel to Ruritania work if the country's of no fixed abode? I understand she gets around pretty freely.'

'The only flights in and out are by Ruritanian Airways. They can handle the geographical shifts. No one else … *God's molars, driver, get a bloody move on! To hell with traffic lights!*'

'Must be awkward, though, not knowing where you are from one day to the next,' said Rory.

'Do any of us? Damn this traffic! Look, Redman, I've no time for chatter. If you've anything relevant to say, spill it and be quick about it. Otherwise keep your trap shut. *Get a bloody move on, I said!*'

The Mercedes shot a red light on the wrong side of the road and induced a multi-vehicle pile-up, then took the corner into Mayfair at eighty miles per hour. Sirens began to approach from three directions.

This is fun, thought Rory. Aloud, he added: 'Someone above you in the chain of command has decided it's in Britain's interests to prevent SPAR's insurrection on National Cake Day, so you've been given the responsibility, Colonel. Any idea why intrusion into Ruritanian politics is in Britain's interests?'

'Some of us learn to obey orders, Redman, not question them. Useful ideas, I said, not guessing games!'

'Okay. Klarissa seems to combine expensive tastes with revolutionary proletarian zeal. How does she come by her wealth? The Hilton isn't cheap and neither's the Merlin.'

Ekwyor Tupsroot stared at him. Her expression softened to the abrasiveness of sandpaper.

'Wealth is easy: SPAR provide. Agree, Horatio? But we know not where SPAR get money.'

'Harder to account for her acrobatic agility,' said Colonel Barrington, 'and her intelligence and apparent fighting skill.'

'Influence of this so-called "Faerie Realm"?' asked Rory. 'Where once upon a time everyone lived happily ever after?'

'Don't mock, Redman. Someone once said to me, "There are more things in heaven and earth than are dreamed of ..." *Right. Stop here. Let's get inside!*'

The colonel's operatives were deployed within a minute. Every exit from the hotel was covered. Every lift was launched to Klarissa's floor with one man and one woman aboard, each of them armed. Pairs noted for fitness took the stairs.

'She left the dining room twenty minutes ago, Grizelina. She's not in the bar or anywhere else down here so she's most likely in her room. But just in case: you two – check the kitchens. You, the linen cupboards. You, the laundry.'

'Your people secure her, Horatio. We wait here.'

The colonel and the ekwyor formed an oasis of silence at the hub of the operation. Rory thought the silence would twang if you touched it.

On Klarissa's floor the operatives studied the photograph on their phones and scanned their surroundings. To the casual eye they didn't appear to be guarding the lifts or stairs. There was nothing obvious in their scrutiny of the elderly couple enjoying a quiet argument on their way down to the bar, the middle-aged man looking out for the escort he'd hired, the plump young businesswoman with the perfect suit and designer handbag, or the lame red-haired lady dragging her luggage to the lift. The operatives selected their targets.

'Excuse me, madam.'

'Yes?'

The businesswoman brushed a strand of brown hair from her face.

'Sorry to bother you; minor security matter,' smiled the operative. 'May I see your passport?'

'What? I leave it in my suite. I will not be travelling outside the country until next Wednesday. You wish me to return to my suite and bring the passport to you?'

The operative's mind logged the target as German or Austrian with blue eyes.

'Thanks, madam, that won't be necessary. Again, sorry to have troubled you.'

The businesswoman gave a tight smile and strode to the lift.

'Excuse me, madam,' said the second operative.

'Yes?' said the lame woman.

'Minor security matter. May I see your passport?'

'What? Ah, passport! But I do not go to airport until ten of clock, and now I have meeting down stair.'

The operative's mind logged the target as Unidentified Foreign with damaged face, red hair and brown eyes.

'You're travelling this evening? Where to?'

'Vienna. Why you ask?'

'Nothing you need worry about, madam, but may I see your passport?'

'Of course.'

Frowning, the woman ferreted in her handbag and produced the document. The operative studied the photograph and stared at the disfigured face.

'What's the meeting, Ms Marnikova?'

'It is at seven hours and the half.'

'No, I mean *what* meeting is it? What is it about?'

'Ah, I not understand. It is Annual General Meeting of Slug Defence League.'

'Have you been a member of the Slug Defence League for long?'

'No, I am not. It is for League in Slovenia. I go here for learning, yes?'

'Just a moment, please.'

The operative called Reception. She stared at the red-haired woman again. The woman returned the stare, anxious or impatient. Then the operative relaxed.

'Sorry to have troubled you, madam.'

She smiled and returned the passport. The red-haired woman limped to the lift, dragging her suitcases.

There were no more guests in the corridor. The silence jangled.

Weapons at the ready, the MI7 operatives burst into the executive suite registered to Julneva Eidentyfeime and conducted a rapid professional search. They'd learned how to do it by watching American cop films. The room was clear: no Julneva, no luggage, no sign of occupancy. They reconvened in the corridor. There was a short whispered argument and then their spokeswoman phoned Colonel Barrington.

'She's not up here, sir. No luggage. Shall we leave two in her room and two in the corridor while the rest are redeployed?'

Colonel Barrington's blood pressure climbed.

'Damn it, where's the infernal woman gone?'

The words were muttered; the voice seethed.

'She have not left hotel, Horatio,' said the ekwyor. 'We wait.'

'She *must* have left, Grizelina. We've checked everywhere, including store cupboards. Neither hide nor bloody hair of her.'

Colonel Barrington made more phone calls. Rory watched people trickling in ones and twos to the small meeting room. He saw Ariadne Sowerby march past them, making a point of not noticing him, and he felt his pupils dilate. He couldn't look away from her. His estimate had been right: 36DD.

'If Alterleta *have* left hotel, we secure her at airport, Horatio,' said Ekwyor Tupsroot.

Rory went to collect his suitcase from the Mercedes.

Chapter 15

Ghrunli is Ruritania's national sport. Much of the playing time is spent arguing about the rules, which vary. The rest is devoted to beating opposing players over the head with long sticks and trying to knock them into pits dug at each end of the playing field. There's a ball, but the players mostly ignore it. Crowd riots are de rigueur. When I attended my first ghrunli match I thought how our police and armed services personnel would relish the sport, but it's yet to catch on outside Ruritania. Negotiations with the International Olympic Committee continue.
    — Ariadne Sowerby, 'First Impressions of Ruritania'

The police were arresting the chauffeur on suspicion of reckless driving, criminal damage, criminal injury, seventeen moving-traffic offences and illegal parking. Rory strode from the Hilton into the evening drizzle, squared his shoulders and marched forward. The eyes of the older and larger constable probed him.

'Is this your car, sir?'

'Of course not. It's Colonel Barrington's car. What's going on?'

The constable jerked his thumb towards the chauffeur.

'This fucking idiot just drove it like he was in a Hollywood blockbuster car chase. We're throwing the book at him, the new leather-bound edition complete with appendices, glossary, bibliography and subject index. Who's Colonel Barrington when he's at home?'

Rory pointed towards the hotel and said, 'The colonel and his team are engaged in an operation it would be unwise to interrupt. He'll need his car soon. I'd advise you to back off.'

'Would you now? And who might you be?'

'I *might* be any youngish white male. Why not ask who I *am*?'

The constable evinced impatience. He thrust his jaw into Rory's personal space and opened his mouth to intimidate.

'If you'd asked the right question,' said Rory, 'I'd have answered "Major Redman, Military Intelligence". But you didn't. Now, I suggest you take my advice and release the colonel's chauffeur pronto.'

Indignation swelled the constable's chest and added roses to his cheeks. The roses were plum-coloured.

'Are you threatening an officer of the law, sir?'

'Yes. Get this straight, Constable: if you disrupt this operation and the target evades capture, the colonel will have your commander's guts for garters and the home secretary won't be amused. In which event I wouldn't care to be in your boots. Clear?'

The constable's cast-iron certainty began to fracture.

'I'll have a word with this Colonel Barrington of yours. Then we'll see what's what.'

'On your own helmet be it. He's not in the sunniest of tempers.'

The constable stalked into the Hilton, exuding dignity. His younger colleague eyed Rory with an amalgam of resentment and trepidation while keeping the chauffeur under restraint. It was the nearest he'd ever come to multi-tasking.

'Get my suitcase out of the boot,' said Rory, pointing at the Mercedes. When the young constable seemed disposed to argue, he bellowed, '*Now!*' and was obeyed. 'No, no, the red one! Right. About bloody time!'

A day in Horatio Barrington's company, he thought, seizing the case from the constable and glowering, and I've started to act like him. It's fun.

The cash from Krev Schammerbass was still in his pocket. He had his cards with him, too, and there was money in one of his accounts. Before he marched back into the hotel he glared at the chauffeur.

'The colonel will have words with you about this nonsense. Start thinking up excuses.'

A minute later he was seated at the bar ordering a pint of bitter. He wiped drizzle from his forehead. What a palaver to get my suitcase out of the car, he thought, and sank the pint in a single draught. Then he looked out of the window and grinned. The police car was departing with a rubbery squeal of chastisement and dudgeon. He wished he'd been a fly on the wall when the constable met the colonel.

Three yards away from him sat a well-dressed businesswoman with long brown hair, blue eyes and a designer handbag. She was too well-padded for the catwalk but merited a second glance. Her face, reflected in the mirror behind the bar, looked familiar. He dissected his memory but to no avail; his life had encompassed many encounters, mostly brief. She saw him staring and gave a non-committal smile. A few minutes later, as Rory was enjoying a second and more leisurely pint, she rose and walked towards the small meeting room. He watched, admiring her buttocks. Not bad beer, this, he decided.

A minute later a plump red-haired woman limped towards the small meeting room, carrying a handbag and two suitcases. Her left cheek appeared twisted and scarred. Rory frowned. Were the limp and the disfigurement real? Ariadne stepped out of the room, shot him a glacial stare, shook the newcomer's hand and took her to meet the rest of the Slug Defence League.

His mind began to work. He asked at Reception for directions to the Bessingham Art Gallery, which he knew was on the Norfolk coast, and while the mannequin was looking it up online he sneaked a look at the hotel register and located a certain guest's room number. Then he took the lift.

Had his skill with electronic locks grown rusty? Time would tell. But he'd need to be back in the bar before the Slug Defence League AGM ended.

Chapter 16

Slugs are magical creatures, which is why they can enter houses at night when all doors and windows are closed and are found the following morning scaling an inside wall or traversing the kitchen floor. Many portrayals of Faerie illustrate their magical qualities; for example, the clouds of silvery glitter surrounding Faerie folk and their wands in children's films and picture-books consist of slug-mucus. Slugs cross and re-cross the boundary between the mundane world and the Faerie Realm at will, opening or closing portals. In this article we discuss the mechanisms involved.

— *K. Blackmantle and A. Sowerby (2009) 'Slugs and Faerie Portals'. Ruritanian Journal of Faerie Studies* **73**, *117–134.*

The start of the AGM was delayed owing to the committee's reluctance to leave the bar. Ariadne Sowerby opened proceedings at 7.53 p.m.

'We have apologies from Sylvester Ash – woodworm in his leg again – and Cadwallader Radish, who has family problems; several of them have gone underground. Any others?'

There were no other apologies.

'We have two guests this evening. Sura Marnikova is founding a Slug Defence League in her native Slovenia and seeks our advice. We also welcome Gottlieba Weissfeld.'

The lame red-haired woman stood and gave a slight bow. Her lop-sided smile irradiated the room. Everyone thought she had lovely brown eyes. She resumed her seat and pondered the agenda. The brown-haired businesswoman raised a hand and smiled. Ariadne ignored her. Rory Redman's eyes had undressed that woman; she'd watched him do it. Goodness knows what he saw in her. Normally, he favoured women of less generous girth. She'd probably encouraged him. Not that he needed encouragement.

The minutes of the previous AGM were approved since no one had read them; *ipso facto* there were no matters arising. Ariadne read the chair's report. Lord Arion and Charisma Radula interrupted with points of order. Ariadne mused on an arithmetical symmetry: the amplitude of Charisma's voice in decibels equalled her body weight in kilograms, roughly one hundred. The acoustic assault startled old Ambrose Godsacre out of his slumber and his hearing aid emitted an electronic howl. Moving with unprecedented alacrity he tore it from his ear and threw it under the table, where it fell silent. He closed his eyes again.

Lord Arion delivered a rebuke to Charisma, his friend Jasper Milax winked and mouthed 'Nice one, Gavin,' and it took Ariadne two minutes to restore order. If she'd brought her legal skill to bear on the altercation it would have taken all night. Mr Godsacre snored. Sura Marnikova frowned. 'Gottlieba Weissfeld' was impassive.

Kelly Blackmantle delivered the secretary's report.

'Our correspondence with the RSPCA continues, but the outcome remains unsatisfactory. They still refuse to accord our twenty-four native slug species equal rights under the law with cats, dogs and horses, and they decline to lobby parliament for legislation to outlaw slug pellets or declare the application of salt and beer to our poor friends cruel. Moreover, they can't be persuaded to cull hedgehogs. The Royal Horticultural Society is equally intransigent. We've provided ample evidence that most non-carnivorous slugs eat leaf litter or fungi, not live vegetables, but they counter with defamation of the charming little round-backed slug and even the netted slug, which is such a delight to the eye. In one letter they accuse us of encouraging gardeners not to tidy their gardens so there will be enough leaf litter and fungi to keep our friends happy.'

'Damned good idea,' said Jasper Milax. 'I hate gardening.'

Mr Godsacre opened his left eye. 'I have a proposal, Ariadne,' he croaked.

'Yes, Ambrose?'

'Let's ask the RSPCA to lobby parliament to get slug pellets outlawed.'

Ariadne called for the treasurer's report. Jasper read it. No one listened and there were no comments. The meeting ended half an hour later and everyone adjourned to the bar. 'Gottlieba' looked at her watch and joined them. Sura did likewise.

Rory was back at the bar. 'Gottlieba' glanced once and ignored him. Ariadne glanced twice, seemed about to approach him and then thought better of it. He sighed.

The red-haired woman made friendly overtures to 'Gottlieba'. Soon they were chatting over a drink. Rory listened without seeming to notice them.

Chapter 17

That which opens the way may close the way, and that which closes the way may open it. The slug that throws wide the Faerie portal can seal it.

  — Old Ruritanian proverbs

When you hear our traditional proverbs, you understand why Ruritania was slow to adopt the corkscrew and the crowbar.

  — Dai O'Genies, A Primer of Ruritanian Philosophy

Rory listened for five minutes and then moved. The colonel and the ekwyor were nowhere to be seen and few MI7 operatives remained in the foyer. He made an inquiry at Reception and his mind drifted into a brief dialogue with the spirit of Professor Weisheitsliebhaber. Then he phoned Heathrow while he scanned the guest list again.

By the end of the call he'd established three facts: 'Julneva Eidentyfeime' and 'Gottlieba Weissfeld' occupied adjacent executive rooms; the latter was scheduled to fly to Vienna at 11.55 p.m., the former to Strelsau at 5.30 a.m.; and the red-haired Sura Marnikova, who pretended to be Slovenian, had booked on the same Vienna flight as 'Gottlieba'. If the colonel and the ekwyor had been present he might have shared thoughts with them.

*

The colonel would have liked to share thoughts with Rory, too. He took off his jacket and stared at his shirt cuffs. 'Where the hell are my silver cufflinks?' he demanded. The bedroom mirror vouchsafed no reply, but the colonel knew the answer. He fulminated.

*

Rory looked at his watch, returned to the bar and opened the Unideker Guide. Before he'd read two paragraphs, inspiration dawned. He went back to Reception and asked the mannequin to search the times of forthcoming Ruritanian Airways flights from Vienna. The search took ten minutes.

'There's one to Strelsau at 8.30 a.m. BST tomorrow, sir. That will be 9.30 in Vienna.'

'Yes. Thanks.'

Rory called Heathrow again and bought economy class tickets for both flights. He was sure 'Gottlieba', *alias* Klarissa, would fly first class, so perhaps she wouldn't notice him. But he'd need to avoid her at the airports; she'd recognised him in the bar. He watched Sura Marnikova ask something of 'Gottlieba', who nodded, approached one of the men from the Slug Defence League meeting and indicated Sura's luggage. He heard her say, 'You are very kind, Jasper. Thank you … Yes, please. I will share the taxi with Sura and ensure she is helped at the airport.' She made her accent exotic enough to sound sexy to the young male ear.

Then 'Gottlieba' and Jasper entered a lift. They reappeared five minutes later with her suitcase. The name on the luggage label read 'Trellarta Laskesia'.

Ah. 'Trellarta Laskesia', thought Rory. Anagram of 'Klarissa Alterleta'. I wonder whether that bastard Schammerbass would deem it a coincidence.

'Gottlieba', or 'Trellarta', or Klarissa, surrendered her room key. Sura did likewise. Then both women followed Jasper out of the hotel. He carried their luggage: Sura's cases looked heavy, Klarissa's very light. How gratifying, thought Rory, that chivalry isn't dead.

He looked for Ariadne but she'd disappeared. He waited five minutes and then collected his suitcase and attaché case. He took out the manila folder, begged an A4 envelope from Reception, put the fake security plan into it, addressed it to Colonel H. Barrington, and asked the mannequin to ensure the colonel received it. The photocopy of the original plan remained inside the lining of his suitcase.

He went to the taxi rank.

'Heathrow,' he said.

Chapter 18

According to the Öst-Brün theory of Faerie Realm physics, the mundane and Faerie worlds are connected via infinitely-dividing linear elements of local space-time. This is a difficult mathematical concept, but you can picture it as follows. Think of the mundane world as a tree of arteries branching ever more finely, and the Faerie Realm as a tree of veins branching ever more finely. The termini of the two trees are linked via a network of capillaries with zero diameter. (This network occupies a negative volume, but that can't be pictured.) Imagine you are a dimensionless blood cell: you pass down one set of branches and enter the other in less than zero time. This anatomical analogy breaks down because the transfer of the 'dimensionless cell' can be reversed, causing spatiotemporal distortion, but it will help you to visualise the Öst-Brün theory.
    — Jack Blackmeadow, 'In the Flutter of Gossamer: the Unity of Worlds'

Rory rubbed his eyes and altered his watch. He'd snatched two hours' sleep on the flight and was struggling to keep 'Gottlieba' in view. Notwithstanding the time, Flughaven Wien wasn't idle. Schwechat suffered worse aircraft noise than South Manchester. He changed his eleven hundred pounds for euros and bought a brightly-coloured baseball cap and a newspaper, a meagre disguise but better than none.

At a news stand he spotted a book in English: *In the Flutter of Gossamer: the Unity of Worlds* by Jack Blackmeadow, a popular-science eulogy on the Ruritanian physicists Gottlieb Öst and

Jamash Brün. He recalled a paper by those authors in the canvas sports bag: *The Fractal Geometry of Faerie.* The book's jacket blurb declared the Öst-Brün theory of Faerie Realm physics to be as epoch-making as Newton's theory of mechanics.

Jack Blackmeadow. Where had he heard the name? He bought a copy of the book and began to read, one eye still keeping watch. He saw the lame red-haired woman, 'Sura Marnikova', purchase a bus ticket and disappear into the lavatory.

Did Öst and Brün understand what they'd written, or did their abstruse mathematics only pretend to enlighten, leaving Blackmeadow to translate their smoke and mirrors into no less bewildering words?

Half an hour passed. 'Sura' reappeared. She'd lost her limp and her face was less scarred. Rory closed his book, followed her and watched her join a bus queue. Then he returned to his seat and went on reading.

A shadow fell over the page. Above him hovered a face gleaming with character, surmounted by auburn hair and underpinned with a Laura Ashley dress containing a 36DD bust. Ariadne wore discreet jewellery and carried an olive green suitcase.

'Well, well, how jolly. Here's Rory Redman, sitting in Schwechat Airport at blank o'clock on a May morning drinking second-rate coffee and reading third-rate popular science. From what fate is he fleeing this time? Or is he chasing a German businesswoman with a wobbly bum?'

'Ah, so you deigned to recognise me. You decided not to in the Hilton. Off on holiday?'

'In transit. So what about this German–'

'I never chase businesswomen, particularly German ones, and wobbly bums don't inspire me.'

'I'm *thoroughly* convinced.' Ariadne glared at the Blackmeadow book. '*Physics,* Rory? Has science seduced you from the arms of philosophy, the bums of businesswomen and the sirens of low-grade crime? What did you steal from the Hilton?'

'I'm contemplating such dreams as stuff is made of.'

Ariadne jabbed a finger at the book.

'Know why this thing was written? Jamash Brün pulled strings with the President of the Ruritanian Academy of Science, and over the next five years the most prestigious international journals published a succession of articles by Öst and Brün and their students, all saying the same thing. Readers who didn't or couldn't exercise thought believed the garbage they wrote. Jack Blackmeadow was commissioned to *exorcise* thought. He's the RAS President's lapdog.'

That's where I heard the name, thought Rory. Jack Blackmeadow is birthday-party Christine's husband. If I hadn't studied the Merlin's guest list when I was trying to find Schammerbass I'd never have known.

'And I was trying to educate myself.' He shook his head and flung the book on to an adjacent seat. A dachshund on a lead attached to an elderly woman in an incredible hat picked it up but deemed it indigestible and dropped it again. 'Let me buy you a second-rate coffee, Ariadne. You can tell me how a partner in a Manchester law firm came to know about "fairyland physics".' He recovered the book and waved it. There was a fine spray of dachshund drool. 'String pulling and corruption don't invalidate scientific theories, do they?'

He glanced around the terminal building. His target remained in view. Ariadne followed his gaze and her mouth tightened.

'No, Rory, but they persuade people to believe lies. Very few see through deceptions. In science, as in law courts and politics, "truth" is what manipulators establish by the continual and emphatic repetition of falsehoods. Blackmeadow is a paid manipulator. Brün is now a Fellow of the RAS and he's received a one-million raldol grant to continue his work. Öst presents seminars all over the world. There are television appearances and visiting professorships. Meanwhile, experts have proved their theory to be mathematically unsound, inconsistent with the data, founded on false assumptions and misleading in its applications. In other words, a total crock of–'

'Taurocoprology?'

'That's Paul Edict's word. Bastard etymology. Mixes Latin and Greek roots.'

'So? Haemoglobin does likewise. So do automobile, bigamy, electrocution … want me to go on?'

'Gottlieba' was buying a ticket for her next flight. 'Sura' was watching the transaction from her vantage point in the bus queue.

'If the theory's been so comprehensively falsified, Ariadne, Blackmeadow's book wouldn't be on sale.'

Ariadne's eyes blazed.

'All papers criticising the theory are rejected by the journals that published it because their editors won't retract what they'd backed. So the criticisms are published in less prominent journals, so they're ignored. Modern scientific publishing presents a crap theory as a work of genius, and the world believes it because dissenting voices are suppressed.'

Rory shook his head, revelling in Ariadne's indignation.

'A sad affair, Ariadne. What takes you to Ruritania via Vienna?'

She blinked.

'How about "I couldn't get a ticket for a direct flight to Strelsau"? Must I ask how you knew where I'm going? Did my passion about Öst and Brün make it ever-so-elementary-my-dear-Watson?'

'I read the label on your suitcase.'

Ariadne sighed.

'How long is it since a woman battered you?'

Rory smiled. His eyes continued to track Klarissa Alterleta, 'Julneva Eidentyfeime', 'Gottlieba Weissfeld', 'Trellarta Laskesia'.

'Four days.' Rory stood and stretched. 'Think I'll go to Ruritania, too. Never been, don't know anyone there, don't speak the language. Sounds like a plan.'

Ariadne sighed again.

'You don't change, do you? But if you go to Ruritania you will. Here.' She scribbled an address, tore the page from her notebook and handed it to him. 'When I'm in Strelsau I stay with these people. Great folk, hospitable, speak brilliant English. Thad is the Queen's personal press officer and closest adviser and he knows everyone in the High Bakery. Tomen's a socialite with a brilliant mind. They'll welcome you.' She glanced at her watch. 'Time to catch the flight. If you want a ticket for it you'd better hurry. There won't be another Ruritanian Airways departure for two days.'

'I'll get the flight but I'll travel pleb class.'

'So we'll be in different parts of the plane. I'm not going to impersonate a sardine. You'll need to move, though. Boarding shortly.'

'No sweat. See you at this address in Strelsau.'

Ariadne hurried away. Her suitcase was heavy enough to tilt her like the Leaning Tower of Pisa. Feminine physique notwithstanding, her retreating figure resembled a shore wader with a neurodegenerative disorder.

Rory's phone rang.

'Redman? Where the bloody hell are you and what are you doing? And where the bloody hell are my silver cufflinks?'

'Good morning, Colonel. Did you sleep well?'

Rory took the phone from his ear, waited ten seconds and then spoke again.

'I don't wear cufflinks. I'm at Vienna airport, reading a book. Let me guess: Julneva Eidentyfeime didn't appear at Heathrow for her 5.30 flight to Strelsau.'

'You know damned well–'

'But there's interesting news: the lame red-haired woman who occupied a suite on the same floor as Julneva's in the Hilton, registered as Sura Marnikova, is about to board a bus to Budapest. I believe I'll join her. I like Budapest.'

'Get back to London, Redman, *now*! Remember the evidence we can present to the CPS. Any further interference in this operation and you'll face ten years in jail!'

'Check at Reception for an envelope addressed to you, Colonel. I didn't waste my time at the Hilton. Goodbye.'

Rory switched off his phone.

He had to queue for his boarding pass, and the Ruritanian Airways flight was due to depart within minutes. He'd make it, though. He was the running man.

And now he was on the run.

Chapter 19

The basic units in Ruritania's system of weights and measures might seem half-familiar but they are distinctive. A 'fathom' (Rur. 'thlanmeng') is a unit of length, approximately six feet (or for readers who insist on metric units, a bit less than two metres). There are sixty smallbits (Rur. 'blamstiloj') in a fathom and two thousand five hundred fathoms in a league (Rur. 'eguale').

— The Unideker Guide to Ruritania

In a decrepit house in Vorgottenstrit, district 23K, one of Strelsau's notorious slums, Stanislas was keeping watch for signs of danger. He peered through the shutters at a carriage stopping ten fathoms along the narrow street. A plump young woman garbed in the crumpled elegance of a long first-class flight alighted carrying a suitcase and a designer handbag and handed the driver a ten raldol note. The carriage departed, leaving the gravel garnished with horse droppings.

Commercial carriages seldom stopped in area 23K, and for a rich-looking stranger to disembark in Vorgottenstrit was unprecedented. Stanislas strapped a knife to his waistband. Then the woman brought her handbag and suitcase to his door, glanced right and left and punched the gnome. Stanislas had flung the door open before the shriek subsided, one hand on his blade. The boy from the house opposite was shovelling up the horse droppings.

'Good afternoon, Stan,' said the woman. 'May I come in without being stabbed?'

Stanislas's suspicion metamorphosed to incredulity, then delight.

'*Ulyanova*! Mother of the Revolution! Is it really you? Thank Asclepius – you're safe, you're here!'

'Is the kettle on?'

Stanislas stood aside and Klarissa entered, removed her long brown wig and blue contact lenses, dropped them into her handbag and pointed at the suitcase. Stanislas scurried to her bedroom with it; it was still empty. Handbag over her shoulder, Klarissa strode to the kitchen. Cries of joy and hysterical yapping filled the house. The ancient woman seated beside the stove raised her withered arms and murmured, 'Dearest Great-Aunt. Asclepius be praised!' The tall powerful man in the hooded green jerkin and breeches bowed over his longbow and begged the Lady to recount her adventures. Vrero, a white long-haired Ruritanian Spitz – a flat-faced breed adapted to chasing parked vehicles – scrabbled at her legs and wagged at both ends. She patted his head. The children danced around chanting, 'Climb, Klarissa, climb, let's go climbing!' She knelt and put her arms around them.

'In a while, my bluebirds. First I need tea and I must change my clothes. I've had a long journey.'

Everyone rushed to brew tea.

'But Great-Aunt, you grow fat!' chided the old woman. 'Surely you're not infected with the malignancy of cake-eating?'

'Padding, Krohn,' said Klarissa. 'I needed the disguise to re-enter the country without being arrested. Even Stan didn't know me until he heard my voice.'

'True.' Stanislas sidled into the kitchen and grinned a yellow grin. 'Our Ulyanova spoke before I drew my knife, so my arms are not broken.'

There was laughter. Everyone gathered round. The best chair was pulled forward and embroidered cushions were plumped. Klarissa sat and drank tea.

'We have the oppressors' plan for the Solstice.' She drew two documents from her handbag. 'The original version sent from the High Bakery to Britain … and a copy of the fake version I left for the British running-dogs to find. Blue Primrose had anticipated risings in two quarters of Strelsau and wondered if we might also act in the north of the city. My alterations suggest further Revolutionary cells in southern and western districts. If our enemies believe those additions their forces will be divided. And those forces will be smaller than in the original plan.'

Her listeners applauded.

'*If* they act, Ulyanova? They won't dare ignore your additions!'

Klarissa continued: 'I planned to be out of Britain before MI7 traced me but Barrington was quick. He forced me to change my plans.'

'What you did, Lady, was brilliant and brave,' said the man with the green jerkin and longbow. 'But if this Barrington almost caught you, MI7 are cleverer than we supposed.'

Klarissa drank the rest of her tea. Stanislas refilled her cup.

'Barrington had help, Arraitch. First, Tupsroota was with him, as you guessed.'

There was an audible shudder.

'We shouldn't be surprised,' said Klarissa. 'MI7 have been ordered to support Blue Primrose so they must collaborate. But there was someone else: Waldemar Schammerbass's courier.'

Glances were exchanged.

'Surely the courier is of no account?' said Stanislas.

'He's a concern. Schammerbass chose well: the courier is criminal but clever, fit, single and solitary; his only living family is a sister he seldom sees. His name is Redman. I didn't expect him to realise the security plan had gone from the bag after I'd robbed him, but he did; Barrington and Tupsroota must have briefed him. He alone seems to have penetrated my disguise. He followed me to Vienna and then to Strelsau, trying to hide by flying economy class. Barrington and Tupsroota are still in London and can't reach Strelsau for at least forty-eight hours, so they'll rely on Redman for intelligence.'

The kitchen shimmered with tension. Vrero's tail sank.

'This is ill news,' said Arraitch. 'Would it have been better, Lady, if you'd taken the document from the warehouse, not from the courier Redman?'

'The warehouse was leased and guarded by agents of our London High Commission, Arraitch, and no one could have entered it without being recorded by security cameras. We had to be sure the cameras saw only the courier. And if Redman had reached MI7's agent at the city library our opportunity would have been lost. So to execute the task without being witnessed I had to rob him in his own garden, where there are no cameras. An MI7 agent from the warehouse tried to follow Redman but he was unfit.' Klarissa's emerald eyes scanned the kitchen. 'Nevertheless my face is now known to our enemies, so I can't stay in Strelsau even in disguise. Tomorrow I'll return to my village and remain in the countryside until Solstice Eve. Arraitch, you'll accompany me. When necessary, swift riders will bear messages between me and our comrades here and in Szipad and Hrincacz. The rest of you, note the photograph of Redman on my phone. Forward it to all SPAR cells. He must be inactivated, but without risking international protest, so don't terminate him; give him a debilitating illness.'

Rory's photograph was disseminated among SPAR's principal agents in Strelsau while Klarissa went to change her clothes and remove her padding. She returned to the kitchen slim, smiling and lightly garbed.

'Now,' she said, 'I've another commission. Children, you demanded I climb. Lead me to the trees and we'll see who can climb highest. Vrero, come with us!'

She took off her shoes and the children yelled with joy and clasped her hands and led her dancing barefoot from the back of the house, past the cesspit to their enchanted wood, the dog bounding around them.

The boy from across the street stopped shovelling the horse droppings and sidled away towards the centre of the city.

Chapter 20

There is much to disbelieve about Ruritania, such as the country's existence. Her geographical shifts are high on the list of incredibilia: impertinent parodies of tectonism, as though she were a speedboat dodging through a fleet of stately galleon-continents and thumbing her nose at them. Yet the learned of the eighteenth century were familiar with her habits. Her mobility inspired Jonathan Swift's fantasy of the flying island of Laputa, and the passion for cake among her inhabitants informed Marie Antoinette's solicitude towards the bread-starved citizens of Paris. It's been suggested that Ruritania also inspired William Blake's seldom-performed drama 'An Island in the Moon'. This conjecture has little support, but Blake's 'prophetic books' suggest he spent much of his mental life in Ruritania.
— *Ariadne Sowerby, 'First Impressions of Ruritania'*

Rory pondered his motives for travelling. Habitual impulsiveness, desire to thwart the colonel, longing for vengeance on Klarissa, plain curiosity, a holiday – all were plausible. Had introspection proposed lust for adventure (or for anything else) as a further ingredient he'd have repudiated it, but introspection grew weary of conjecture. Rory stared through the window and dozed.

Was the country to which he was travelling real? It appeared on no map.

Absence of evidence isn't evidence of absence, he mused. Ruritanian Airways will surely deposit me at Strelsau airport, which wouldn't be possible if the country didn't exist. But if

Ruritania is merely a mental entity then it *doesn't* exist. It's only a word.

The plane hiccupped through an air-pocket and began to descend. Rory dozed again.

'Can a country claiming a close relationship with the Faerie Realm be deemed "real" in *any* sense?' demanded the spirit of Professor Weisheitsliebhaber. 'And how might this relationship with the Faerie Realm relate to Britain's commitment to thwarting SPAR?'

'I intend to find out,' muttered Rory, alarming the occupant of the adjoining seat, whose husband was too discreet to talk in his sleep. He remained silent thereafter until the plane landed and they disembarked.

Blinking against the light, Rory scanned the view from the airport. The panorama fingered the misty border of recollection, taunting him with questions of where and when and how. But the meagre skylight of memory didn't clarify his ruminations. How could he remember a place he'd never visited? *Déjà vu* could never do more than tantalise.

This is absurd, he decided. Misty border of recollection, meagre skylight of memory? My metaphor mixer will fail its MOT. And my dark glasses are in my suitcase.

He spent two hours watching native Ruritanians flash their passports and leave the airport. 'Gottlieba' or 'Trellarta', *alias* Klarissa, was among them. At length he reached the front of the customs and immigration queue and presented his passport to an official dressed as a circus clown. His childhood coulrophobia reawakened, shuddering through his nervous system. His brow oozed perspiration.

'Do you visit Ruritania for business or recreation, Pan Redman?'

The clown's English was heavily accented.

'I've come to watch the National Cake Day ceremony,' said Rory.

The clown menaced him with jaundiced eye and greasepaint and then read from his script.

'Are you, or have you at any time been, a member of any non-human race?'

'No.'

'Are you aware of penalties for importing banned items into Ruritania?'

'All countries have penalties for importing banned items.'

'If you are caught carrying a banned item,' said the clown, 'the punishment may involve fines, imprisonment, questioning in a darkened room and confiscation of body parts.'

'Right.'

'So, does your luggage contain any of the following?' The clown read the list: 'Vermicelli machines, second-hand bee hives, iron walking sticks, uranium, adulterated leather, firearms, ammunition or explosives, sexy lingerie, slug pellets, any other substance that could put slugs at risk, unmounted artificial teeth, baking equipment including scale pans, mixing bowls, baking trays and wooden spoons, materials for baking including sugar, butter, flour and eggs, hamster cages, Communist propaganda, pharmaceuticals prescribed in your native country, or medical texts or other printed material promoting the Pasteurian Heresy.'

'I've never owned a vermicelli machine and I've given up sexy lingerie. But I've no objection to being searched.' Provided I'm not searched by a bloody clown.

The eye remained jaundiced. The menace of greasepaint intensified.

'What is your metaphysical stance?'

'I'm a critical realist.'

'And your epistemological position?'

'Quinean empiricist.'

The clown laughed, smiled a painted smile, drew a mouth squeaker and motor horn from his voluminous pocket, blasted them into Rory's face and opened the barrier.

'Welcome to Ruritania, Pan Redman,' he said, and bowed him through.

Rory changed his euros for raldols – 'raldoloj'– and entered one of those stores to be found at every airport in the galaxy, where he stole another pair of sunglasses. Outside the store, Ariadne greeted him. She looked unwell.

'How was customs and immigration?' she said.

'Why did the official have to dress as a damned clown?'

'Mine's always a piano teacher like the one who made my music lessons a torment when I was a child. Customs and immigration is the worst thing about Ruritania. Well, one of the worst.'

Beside them stood a trembling, white-faced man who looked as though he'd been interrogated by a giant frog.

Chapter 21

In accordance with the principles of Ruritanian geometry, St Galen's Square sometimes has five sides. One side is occupied by the late nineteenth century Dzhumpinpork Palace, residence of the Teesporn monarchs; its mediaeval forerunner was burned to the ground during the Peasants' Revolt of 1848. If you look towards the Palace from the centre of the square you see the parliament building (the High Bakery of Ruritania) on your left and the cathedral hospital of St Galen on your right. Behind the High Bakery are the civil service offices. Beside the cathedral hospital stands the Surgeon Archbishop's palace, surrounded by the mausoleums of great baker-aristocrats. If Ruritanian Gothic pains your sensibilities, you can feast your eyes on the delightful Gardens or look up at the brooding statue of St Galen, gleaming with pigeon poo. On the other side or two sides of the vast square, which you cannot see unless you turn your head and look askance, are the headquarters of the Order of the Blue Primrose. And the Labyrinth.

— The Unideker Guide to Ruritania

The boy who'd shovelled up the horse droppings in Vorgottenstrit sidled towards Blue Primrose HQ. He whispered to the guard at the Great Azure Door and waited, hands in pockets, glancing over first one shoulder then the other. Five minutes passed before a uniform containing a junior ekwyrin of the Order deigned to saunter out and sneer.

'Ekwyrin, I have news.' The boy's whisper was barely audible.

'Klarissa Alterleta has returned. I watched her enter a SPAR safe house in–'

'Who?'

'Klarissa Alterleta. Leader of the Socialist People's Army–'

'Wait here.'

The ekwyrin went indoors. Ten more uncomfortable minutes passed before the ekwyrin re-emerged with a more senior uniform, who brandished thirteen photographs of female faces.

'Are any of these women Klarissa Alterleta?'

The boy pointed with a ragged fingernail. The ekwyroj exchanged looks.

'Are you certain?'

'She arrived in disguise but she removed her false hair and contact lenses after she–'

'You have no doubt?'

'None, Ekwyor.'

'Are her name is "Alterleta"?'

'Some call her so, Ekwyor, some call her Ulyanova, and some … No, I won't say. But she isn't from Strelsau – they say she was born in a village near Hrincacz, beside Lake Brojginzha.'

'How and when did she arrive in Vorgottenstrit?'

'She came in an airport carriage, Ekwyor, number twenty-six. The shadows told me it was between eleven o'clock and noon.'

'She remains in the house?'

'Yes, Ekwyor.'

'You will watch her movements. You will report here every day. You will be paid.'

The ekwyor snapped her fingers and her junior colleague handed a hundred raldoloj to the boy. He stammered thanks. The ekwyroj went back into the building and the Great Azure Door slammed. The boy kissed the bank-notes, slid them into his pocket and began to retrace his steps to the south-eastern quarter.

As he traversed a refuse-dimmed alley between two thoroughfares a voice hailed him.

'Hey, Urtzhin! Out for a nice walk?'

The boy's complexion changed.

'Oh … Hello, Stanislas. I didn't expect … What brings you here?'

'Same as you, Urtzhin,' said Stanislas. 'Out for a nice walk. Got mates in Blue Primrose, have we?'

Urtzhin gulped.

'Er – yes, m-my sister …'

'Didn't know you had a sister. What's her name? How old is she? Been working for Blue Primrose long, has she?'

'Er …'

'Is she pretty? Maybe I'd like to meet her. You enjoy eating goose, Urtzhin?'

Urtzhin frowned. Did people eat *goose*? Was it like cake?

'Never tried it.'

'Oh, you must. In fact, you're going to try it right now. Goose with feathers on. I'll enjoy watching you swallow it.'

Stanislas put his fingers to his lips and whistled. Urtzhin turned and ran. He'd galloped almost eight fathoms before an arrow struck his throat and reappeared through the back of his neck. Stanislas grinned.

'Nice shot, Arraitch.'

He took the hundred raldoloj from the dead boy's pocket and his grin widened. Leaving the corpse in the alley he swaggered homewards, picking his teeth and singing a peasants' love song that made up in vigour what it lacked in subtlety.

Chapter 22

Hyperglykismaphagia is a medical condition caused by excessive consumption of cake. Ruritania has numerous sufferers. If the condition becomes chronic it can be fatal. The medipriests treat routine hyperglykismaphagia patients with emetics, enemas, purges and prayers. For recalcitrant cases they deploy a device resembling a hand-pumped vacuum cleaner with a sink plunger attachment. Most patients recover immediately when they see it.
— Ariadne Sowerby, 'First Impressions of Ruritania'

'What's with the sunglasses?' Ariadne's mouth sketched a sneer. 'Make you look *cool*?'

'Sensitive eyes. I have 20/20 vision but strong light gives me headaches. Prefer shade.' Rory curled his lips. 'So what brings *you* to Ruritania?'

'Take my final exam so I can practise law here. Visit my friend Kjym Krev Bauntzia and organise a slugfest for next year. And watch the National Cake Day festivities.' Ariadne frowned. 'Why've you *really* come, Rory?'

'Told you. Don't know the country or the language or the people.'

Ariadne marched out of the airport and summoned a carriage, which bore the number twenty-six. Rory helped her and her suitcase aboard and, to her manifest annoyance, followed. She sat in the corner and stared through the window, chin on fist. Rory was reminded of his sister, Ruby. His mouth twitched.

'Tell me, what's the fascination with slugs?'

She shrugged.

'They're gateways to the Faerie Realm,' she mumbled, 'which is why they're revered.' Then she stole a glance at Rory. 'This is my fourth visit to Ruritania but I'm still … confused. How does the country get around without crashing into other land-masses and causing earthquakes? The Faerie Realm must be involved, but how? And what about ecological consequences? Changing geography means changing climate, so sensitive species can't survive. And what about crops? Everyone dodges those questions.'

'They're good questions except for that "Faerie Realm" nonsense. Should we inquire at the Ruritanian Academy of Science or …? Hello, what's this?'

He snatched a luggage label from the carriage floor. The copperplate direction read: *Trellarta Laskesia, Vorgottenstrit 13, 23K Strelsau, Ruritania.*

'Interesting,' he muttered, pocketing the label. 'The President of the aforesaid Academy of Science told me his people were studying "coincidence". I wonder if they've made progress.'

Ariadne asked what Rory had found but he was either ruminating or dozing from exhaustion.

The carriage horse trotted slowly over pitted gravel roads and sporadic cobbles. And this, mused Rory, is the capital city. It's Third-World-ish. There was no motor traffic; pedestrians and a few riders passed; all transport was horse-drawn. There were horse droppings everywhere. The major streets were four carriages wide but the narrow lanes were dark and squalid. Strelsau stank. From behind the buildings came the grunting of pigs, the cackling of hens and the occasional virginal neigh of a unicorn. The houses, ramshackle confections of wood and masonry stuck together with no regard for architectural principles or gravity, were arranged higgledy-piggledy along the sides of the streets, their second or third storeys protruding vertiginously over the disagreeable pavements. Several ground floor frontages were shops.

'Mediaeval European towns must have looked like this,' said

Rory. 'Except there are tobacco shops and – are they *really* "suppliers of hamster food"? And cake shops outnumber all others.'

Ariadne said, 'It's a fair comparison. Mediaeval Europe was feudal, too, except for the sort-of-democracies of guilds.'

Strelsau's citizens wandered by under a pall of lethargy. To Rory's eyes their attire epitomised dinginess, their manner somnolence. They resembled characters in a Breughel painting but without the animation. Some were crippled. Some crawled. Most of them smoked. He considered the challenge of teaching Morris-dancing to them.

'Those people could never learn to dance,' he said.

'Many of them suffer from hyperglykismaphagia,' said Ariadne. 'Don't ask.'

'Colourful word,' said Rory. 'But the only colours I can see are on posters advertising cakes.'

'Exactly,' said Ariadne. 'The cakes *cause* hyperglykismaphagia. Public health's better in the countryside. Rural peasants work long hours. Some of them live well into their forties.'

After an hour the carriage halted in Klatzierstrit, north-west quarter. The driver unloaded their suitcases, proffered a callused left hand and departed with twenty raldoloj.

The houses in Klatzierstrit were more refined that those they'd passed *en route* but the quietness unsettled Rory: no motor vehicles, no muzak, no radios, no machinery. He lifted their suitcases and followed Ariadne to the address she'd given him at Schwechat airport: Klatzierstrit 27. He looked in vain for doorbell or knocker.

'Why's there a miserable-looking garden gnome stuck on the door?' he said.

Ariadne punched the gnome in the face. It shrieked. Half a minute later the door opened and they were admitted.

Chapter 23

The Gödelpus Unsatisfiability Theorem states: 'In any system of logically connected propositions containing at least one non-analytic premise there is at least one paradox'. In other words, as soon as you state something meaningful, something that is not merely true by definition such as '2 + 2 = 4' or 'all bachelors are unmarried men', you are bound to start contradicting yourself. Therefore, nothing can reliably be known; the clown feet of contradiction invariably trip the fall-guy of certainty. The Gödelpus Theorem is a logical proof of postmodernism.
— *Dai O'Genies, A Primer of Ruritanian Philosophy*

'She is found.' Ekwyor Tupsroot waved her phone and glared at Colonel Barrington, who had fallen asleep clutching the fake security document in the A4 envelope with Rory's writing on the front. 'Horatio! She is found!'

'Huh? Whassat, Mabel? Found what where?' The colonel blinked and shook himself. 'Sorry. What d'you say, Grizelina?'

'Alterleta is found. She is at terrorist safe house in south-eastern quarter of Strelsau. Report say she come from village near Hrincacz. If we find village, search and destroy.'

The colonel frowned and tugged his beard.

'Strelsau? How the devil did she get past airport security?'

'Disguise. False passport: "Trellarta Laskesia". But spy report to Great Azure Door and now watch safe house. Our people raid early morning tomorrow. Now they question others in street, airport carriage driver. We want whole terrorist cell.'

The ekwyor lit a cigar.

'Damned right.' The colonel stood, stretched and grunted. He shook the A4 envelope. 'What d'you think of this, Grizelina? Damned fishy, I say. Why do they want *eighty* men now instead of two-fifty? *Lightly* armed? And they want us to patrol more areas than we were first told.'

'I understand.' The ekwyor blew a perfect ring of cigar smoke and destroyed it with a kick of her left boot. 'We listen to spies. Spies believe we arrest SPAR leaders before National Cake Day. Raid on safe house will make it sure.' An anticipatory rictus bared her teeth. 'So High Bakery say only low-key British presence now needed for Solstice, but spread wide to crush disorder. Still have British presence because it is agreed.'

The colonel grunted again.

'Don't like it. Want to check this document with whichever pen-pusher produced it.' He yawned. 'Could use some shut-eye, but wish we could get an earlier flight and be in Strelsau for the safe house raid. Sooner we nab these jokers the better, and I'd like to be in on the interrogation. This plan might make more sense once we know the *enemy's* plans.'

The ekwyor stretched her lips. Once again her teeth tarnished the light.

'Question will be put. There will be full report. You talk to Budapest?'

'Five minutes.'

The colonel busied himself with communications, spoke, turned puce, spoke more loudly, swore, switched off the phone, stared at the ekwyor and shook his head.

'Redman is not on bus,' said the ekwyor, blowing more cigar smoke.

'Correct. Redman was not on the bus. Two more buses from Vienna Airport will be watched but I believe the scoundrel lied though his incisors. No intention of going to Budapest.'

'I am sure. He go Strelsau. We find out.'

'We *need to* find out. Bring him to heel before he upsets the whole damned applecart. In any case I want to wring the blighter's neck and make him cough up my cufflinks. Though I'd like to know how he came by this plan first.' The colonel punched buttons on his phone again. 'Something else, Grizelina–'

'Redman is nuisance but commit no crime. I say we arrest and lock away until task done but make no charge. What is something else, Horatio?'

'The woman called Sura Marnikova, the one Redman told us about; she *was* on the Budapest bus. Our people there have camera footage. She might be irrelevant but I'm taking no chances.'

Chapter 24

Concerning the origin and distinctiveness of western philosophy, there is a legend that encapsulates truth. What we call 'philosophy' began with Thales early in the sixth century BCE, but the Greeks dubbed Thales and his successors 'logographoi' not 'philosophers'. The term was pejorative. It meant 'those who understand the world through reason instead of looking to the gods'. (Nowadays we could call scientists 'logographoi'.) Three generations after Thales, Pythagoras founded his school in Kroton, where he faced the same suspicion as his predecessors in Asiatic Greece. One day, a citizen asked him, 'Hey, Pythagoras, you're another logographos, aren't you?' The old boy couldn't deny it, but being diplomatic he replied, 'I'm a lover of wisdom' – 'philos sophou' – and the label stuck.

— Dai O'Genies, 'A Primer of Ruritanian Philosophy'

'Ah, the Sleeping Ugliness has awakened! The fairytale prince has recapitulated his osculatory triumph!'

Ariadne was seated on a stuffed narwhal, the Ruritanian equivalent of a chaise longue. Her grin matched the narwhal's. Rory stepped into the room, stretched and rubbed his eyes. He was still tired.

'As I recall, Ms Sowerby, all fairytale princes were heterosexual.'

The room stank of cigarettes. After a day in Klatzierstrit 27, Rory was yet to grow accustomed to the company of smokers. Thad Masim wasn't at home; as Queen's adviser and press officer he was due to visit the Palace after his lunchtime lecture. In his place sat a thin elderly man with stooping shoulders, a sunken face and brilliant grey eyes.

'How long have I been asleep? My watch stopped again.'

'Another four and a half hours.' Tomen Comtra smiled. Her grey hair was neat, her eyes dark and warm and her waist enormous. 'We know now you like to drink coffee. I will prepare some.'

Once again Rory was overwhelmed by *déjà vu*. If the scene had been black and white and the actors less overweight he'd have imagined himself in an Ealing Comedy, his role ill-rehearsed. In fact the scene was coloured, though the colours were muted: décor, clothes and crockery were grey, sepia and olive green with the occasional touch of beige. The narwhal was mainly sepia.

'I'd be grateful, Tomen. But can't I do it?'

'You are our guest. And here is a visitor who wants to talk to you. May I introduce Dai O'Genies? Dai is a philosopher. Ariadne says you studied philosophy.'

Dai O'Genies tapped his cigarette on an olive green ashtray.

'I will stay my question, Rory Redman, until your mind is invigorated by caffeine.' Dai shook Rory's hand. There was mischief in his grey eyes. 'I am fascinated by history of thought. Amused by bad explanation. In sixth century BCE there is revolution in thought all over world: Confucius, Lao Tze, Gautama, Zoroaster, authors of Fourth Veda, great Jewish texts like First Isaiah, earliest Pre-Socratics … All within few years, no contact among them. Why? Climate change?'

Ariadne chuckled, wobbling the narwhal. The little man had *not* stayed his question.

'Perhaps there *was* climate change. So what?' Rory's voice was a caffeine-starved mutter. 'There's no plausible link between climate and an upsurge in attainment from Europe to China. No evidence for a global agricultural surplus. There was no efficient communication across cultural barriers or over great distances. I can't offer a credible answer.'

Dai gave a broad smile. Several of his teeth were missing.

'Ariadne, my friend, you are right. This man know history, and he prefer no explanation to bad explanation. Rory, you are man after my own cardiology. You will forgive me for hard question. But I want your opinion on Gödelpus Unsatisfiability Theorem.'

Despair shut Rory's eyes; moments later, rapture reopened them. A large olive green cup hovered before him. Its contents were beige.

'Thanks, Tomen, I might live. Bear with me, Dai.'

Rory focussed on his coffee for three minutes, then set down the cup and sighed.

'Dai wrote a primer of Ruritanian philosophy, Rory,' said Ariadne. 'His book includes a story about how the word "philosophy" was invented thanks to a piece of Pythagorean repartee. And after Pythagoras, all who'd been reviled as "logographoi" came to be venerated as "philosophers".'

'Not all,' said Dai. He drew a hundred cubic smallbits of cigarette smoke into his lungs and coughed. 'Plato have encourage flow and exchange of ideas and call it "dialektike" not "philosophy". So we speak of Plato "dialogues" and have word "dialectic".'

Rory took a deep breath and let caffeine weave its magic.

'I know the Pythagoras story,' he said. 'It's probably fiction, but so what? It's easier to grasp historical truth if you recreate it as fiction. Indeed, fiction's the best way to tell *any* truth. Or lie.' He stood and stretched. 'If you'll forgive me for changing the subject, can you tell me how to get to Vorgottenstrit in district 23K?'

Tomen's eyes widened.

'You wish to go to *south-eastern quarter, 23K*?'

'Bad place,' said Dai. 'Much crime.'

'Since you've never been to Ruritania before, Rory,' asked Ariadne, 'how come you …? Well, I suppose *you'd* gravitate to the slums anywhere. But why would you *wish* to?'

Rory clasped his hands on his knees and studied them.

'It's a long story, and I'm reluctant to tell it because it involves Ruritanian politics and I'm a guest in the house of the Queen's personal adviser.'

Tomen sat beside Dai, lit a cigarette and smiled.

'Please tell your story. You will not offend. About politics we are all cynical.' She turned to Ariadne. 'Everyone has been to Ruritania, Ariadne, though they might not know it.'

Thad Masim returned from the Palace and they dined. Rory recounted an edited version of his adventures, detailing his encounters with Klarissa, the colonel and the ekwyor but saying little about Krev Schammerbass save for his commission to deliver the bag of papers, 'Which,' he declared, 'still puzzles me'.

'Krev Schammerbass is an enigma,' said Tomen.

'A brilliant man,' said Ariadne, 'but too dedicated to the Academy of Science to seek political power.'

'Too often in Lucerne or Budapest or Manchester,' said Thad, 'dealing with scientific matters on the international stage, to have sufficient time for Ruritania's internal needs.'

Rory sensed that Thad was being diplomatic.

Daylight faded.

Chapter 25

Ruritania's largest river, the Vona, flows through the lower parts of the capital and empties into whatever sea or lake is available depending on the country's location. Experts have debated whether the River Vona was named after an ancient water goddess or a former krev who claimed ownership of the valley, but in fact 'vona' is Old High Ruritanian for 'river'.

— The Unideker Guide to Ruritania

Stanislas and Arraitch had reported the incident with the boy-spy Urtzhin, so Klarissa left Strelsau before dawn. Both men rode with her. Stanislas turned back as they crossed the city boundary, with orders to contact all SPAR cells.

'And Stan, move everyone out of Vorgottenstrit,' said Klarissa. 'If the spy told Blue Primrose the address they're in danger. And at all costs protect the security plan.'

Klarissa and Arraitch rode through woods and fields towards the breaking dawn, following the Vona upstream until the valley swung north towards the mountains. Then they climbed to the plateau and took country lanes eastward, avoiding the Szipad road. The sun rose, larks soared and woodlands sang. Their pace increased. After two hours they stopped at a village inn to rest their horses.

Inside the hostelry three male Blue Primrose ekwyrinoj smoked, drank, eyed the newcomers and muttered. Their guffaws oozed lechery. Arraitch and Klarissa sat well away from them and accepted obsequious mugs of ale from the innkeeper.

'Hey, peasant, give you ten raldoloj for your pretty girlfriend!' said the fattest ekwyrin.

Arraitch's hands itched for his bow. Klarissa shot him a warning glance and smiled.

'I'm not for hire, Guardian of the Queen's Peace. What brings you so far from the city?'

The hairiest ekwyrin said they'd heard about a terrorist leader travelling to somewhere near Lake Brojginzha. 'Some of our lads will scour the villages round there, but we reckoned we could catch the bastard on the way.'

'Get us promotions,' said the third. 'Then we can pay *more* than ten for you. Each.'

Klarissa laughed.

'If your terrorist comes this way, he'll visit the so-called SPAR enclave down the hill beside the stream. Don't you agree, Innkeeper?'

The innkeeper's hands waved denial. He was sure, quite sure, there were no terrorists anywhere near his hostelry. The enclave in the valley was news to the ekwyrinoj, too. If they could wipe it out and take one or two survivors back to Strelsau for questioning, promotions would be guaranteed.

'We don't know its exact whereabouts, Ekwyrin,' said Klarissa. 'Those terrorists stay hidden and move around for fear of Blue Primrose. We can lead you in the general direction, though. With your training and skill you're sure to find them. But please take care: they're rumoured to be armed with ceramic utensils.'

The Blue Primrose trio murmured disquiet. Huddling together, they followed Klarissa and Arraitch out of the inn, on to their horses, and down through the woodland. After two hundred fathoms, Klarissa and Arraitch accelerated from walk to canter and were soon out of sight. Angry shouts pursued them. They entered a clearing, leapt from their saddles and climbed the nearest trees. Just in time; Arraitch had scarcely nocked an arrow before the ekwyrinoj stumbled into the clearing, yelling and threatening. Two seconds later, the hairiest ekwyrin took

Arraitch's arrow in his chest and the fattest fell with Klarissa's throwing knife in his throat. The third turned to flee. Arraitch shot him in the back.

'Leave their weapons and uniforms,' said Klarissa, scrambling down her tree. She wiped her knife on the dead man's tunic and put it back into her handbag. 'Whoever finds the bodies will recognise Blue Primrose. They'll see their deaths as a foretaste of what's to come.'

'Indeed, Lady,' said Arraitch. 'But if Blue Primrose are scouring the villages near Hrincacz, you'll be in peril if you continue this journey.'

'The peril is to our people, Arraitch. They need our protection. I won't abandon them.'

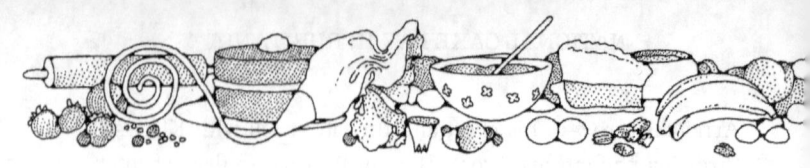

Chapter 26

Thanks to her biologists' expertise in genetic engineering, Ruritania produces the world's greenest electricity: giant hamster power. The generators are driven by huge treadmills on which hamsters the size of horses run. Animal welfare rules decree that the hamsters can only work two-hour shifts, so many are needed to keep the turbines turning. There is an intensive hamster breeding programme, and about twenty percent of Ruritania's agricultural land is devoted to producing hamster food: apples and blackberries, cranberries and grapes, strawberries and raspberries, bread soaked in whey, minced beef and chicken, soft cheese, grasshoppers and crickets, boiled eggs, nuts and seeds, broccoli and cabbage, carrots and celery, cauliflower and green beans, clover and dandelion leaves from the wayside; and sometimes lettuce, cooked peas, turnip, spinach and watercress. Thus, unlike the peasants who labour to feed them, the hamsters enjoy varied and balanced diets. Each generating station sells electricity to the city and pays the peasants and the carters. Giant hamster dung makes excellent fertiliser, a profitable by-product. The main technical problem is hamsters falling off their treadmills, causing power outages. A crane is required to lift the animal back into place and a vet must be present. The biggest danger for power station workers is hamster bites, which can sever an arm.
— The Unideker Guide to Ruritania

'Thank you for sharing your history, Rory. Few foreigners know about SPAR. Few of any nation have met the so-called Ulyanova. You must learn more of our country lest your perception become warped. Tomorrow we will take you on a tour of Strelsau. Later we shall visit 23K since that is your wish.'

Thad Masim lit a cigarette. He was a pear-shaped man with a head like a cannonball and a mind like a scimitar.

'Wouldn't it be better to go to 23K first, Thad?'

'No. Early in the morning, some residents will still be sneaking home from their night's activities. They will not wish outsiders to see them.'

The household watched a televised debate between the two main contenders for the forthcoming election. Rory wondered about the peculiarity of a nation in which transport required horses, yet some houses in the city had electric power and even television. Even mobile phones worked in Strelsau. But he was interested in the political posturings of the two principal krevoj, which seemed typical of politicians everywhere.

'What did you think of them, Rory?' said Ariadne when the debate ended.

Rory scratched his chin.

'As I understand it, Krev Hvimpy is promoting his new Caraway Angel Cake. He says if he wins the election there'll be a new public hovel-building programme to relieve homelessness. And his government will stimulate agriculture and raise tax revenues, though I couldn't grasp how, except he'll take bakeries opposed to his enterprise into public ownership. I gather that would be controversial.'

'Highly,' said Thad. 'His opponents will accuse him of SPAR sympathies. His gamble will cost votes in some areas but could win them in others.'

'I didn't understand the next part of his speech: increased investment in hamster-breeding to boost power provision and encourage technology. And what was that thing about a National Minimum Cake Provision to rise in line with economic performance? Will you vote for him?'

Ariadne grinned at Tomen. 'Told you,' said the grin. 'He can be quite quick.'

'About the hamster-breeding programme,' said Thad, 'look up "electricity generation" in your Unideker. As for Krev Hvimpy's policies, I doubt he would be willing to afford a National Minimum Cake Provision even if he could. And as for me: as adviser to Her Majesty I am politically neutral.'

Rory smiled. Thad seemed smarter than either of the leading krevoj.

'What's Queen Anastassia like?' he asked.

'She presides over parliamentary proceedings as your Commons Speaker does, though she exerts greater control,' said Thad. 'But she intervenes only to maintain order and decorum in the High Bakery. She entertains foreign dignitaries with regal magnificence. Loves her grandchildren, detests her son. She cast a spell on Crown Prince Elharic and transformed him into a frog, so he now lives near a stagnant pond deep in the enchanted forest. But she is shrewder and more intelligent than people realise. If she were a commoner I would hesitate to buy a used carriage from her.'

Rory smiled again.

'How does she rate Krev Schammerbass?'

'It is not for me to say, Rory. Perhaps there has been some tension … I know there was a disagreement between Krev Schammerbass and the Surgeon Archbishop, but there was no need for me to investigate the cause. How did you rate the other side of the political debate we've watched?'

'The skinny krev who sported the curly moustache was Strlzhav, I believe. Is he really the current krevjalem, seeking re-election?'

Tomen nodded.

'Yes, Rory. Did you understand *his* policies?'

Rory scratched his chin.

'Let's see. He promises continuing supplies of his low-cost Traditional Ginger Cake. He'll impose a one-year restriction on public cake benefits for everyone except the ten thousand poorest, though how will he decide who they are? He'll raise the threshold age for free cake donations from forty to forty-five–'

'The Queen won't consent,' said Thad. 'He'll have to compromise on forty-two.'

'– and he'll abolish cost reductions on all cakes for families with post-tax incomes over twenty-five thousand raldoloj,' Rory went on. 'I think he also said he'll curb the provision of richer cakes to the disabled, cut the cake allowance to senior civil servants by five percent, and offer short-term government loans to peasants who wish to purchase their own hovels.'

Thad and Tomen applauded the précis. Ariadne laughed, wobbling the narwhal again. Rory said it wasn't hard to grasp the essence of political promises because they were similar in all democracies.

'But why is there such emphasis on cake, Thad? You have a national obesity problem. It seems a "balanced diet" in Ruritania consists of holding one cake in each hand. The only non-fat Ruritanians I've seen are Krev Schammerbass and Dai, though the politicians on television were slim. And Klarissa Alterleta isn't what you'd call overweight except when she's disguised as someone else.'

'Cake is the foundation of our economy, Rory, and it's the main calorie source in the national diet. More than half our agricultural production goes into cake-making. Supply requires a corresponding demand, so everyone must buy cakes and eat them. The baker-aristocrats pay their peasants and millers and carters and retailers from their profits, but their income is vast. You see, freelance baking is illegal. Only the heads of aristocratic families and their employees are allowed to manufacture cakes. If you or I did it we would go to prison.' Thad lit another cigarette. 'The only non-obese Ruritanians are those who fail to contribute to society by eating cake four times a day: aristocrats, Puritans and SPAR supporters; and sick people, of course.'

'Dai didn't strike me as an aristocrat or a SPAR supporter.'

'He has bowel cancer. Ruritania's prosperity has its dark side.'

Rory went to bed and read more of his Unideker. It told him how the cities were provided with sufficient electricity to run televisions and other household appliances, but outside the cities there was no such luxury. Rural Ruritanians lived in a pre-television, indeed pre-electricity, era.

He put down the Unideker and flicked through the copy of Dai's *Primer of Ruritanian Philosophy* that Ariadne had lent him. After three quarters of an hour he set the book aside and lay awake pondering a cake-based economy, the nation's health problems, the alleged proximity of Faerie, the sad plight of Dai, and his persistent *déjà vu*. At last he fell asleep and dreamed a convoluted route through a smoky maze of fluctuating paths and shifting nodes. The spirit of Professor Weisheitsliebhaber told him it was a challenge: if SPAR ended the Ruritanian economy's reliance on cake, what would the Revolution put in its place?

Rory awoke at dawn still tired, unprepared for what was to come.

Chapter 27

The Réaumur temperature scale, named after René Antoine Ferchault de Réaumur (1683-1757), extends from zero (freezing point of water) to eighty (boiling point of water). Réaumur defined each degree on the scale by a 0.1% increase in the volume of the alcohol contained in the thermometer bulb at zero degrees. Sixteen Réaumur is sixty-eight Fahrenheit; or, for metricophiles, twenty centigrade. Official idiocy now insists on calling the zero-to-one-hundred scale 'Celsius' instead of 'centigrade', but the temperature scale invented by Celsius had zero as the boiling point and one hundred as the freezing point of water, so 'twenty degrees Celsius' is really eighty degrees centigrade, which is incompatible with most forms of terrestrial life. There's no such confusion or historical inaccuracy about the Réaumur scale. Ruritanian bureaucrats, unlike those in other nations, know something of the history of science. And the Academy of Science exerts influence.
— *The Unideker Guide to Ruritania*

Stanislas punched the gnome on a shabby door in the eastern quarter. Mouldering rubbish and untended cesspools cloyed the morning air. Unseen eyes dissected the visitor's intentions. Crows sang. The day would be warm; the temperature was already sixteen Réaumur.

The door creaked ajar and a curtained voice muttered, 'What tidings, Stanislas?'

Stanislas advanced into half-light. Six voices whispered welcome.

'Glorious news, Mangler. The Ulyanova's back. She's captured the oppressors' security plan and left their British running-dogs with a fake version.'

Muted satisfaction vibrated in the gloom.

'We're prepared, Stan. Will the Ulyanova amend the metacake?'

'No, I will. Do you know where it'll be housed?'

'In the upper chamber of the Strlzhav Bakery in Jubetitstrit. But it'll be guarded. The Ulyanova's climbing skill will be needed.'

'She's returned to her village, Mangler. Her image is known to Blue Primrose: British military intelligence obtained her photograph while she was in England. Their Ruritanian division is headed by Redman, who followed her to Strelsau – you've seen his photo. We must find him and put him out of action but his current location's unknown. She says he's not to be killed but must be given a debilitating disease. Do you have the means? We don't in 23K.'

'We put all we had into the single device, Stan. Our comrades in 14Q will help. Will debilitation suffice for this Redman?'

Stanislas shrugged.

'I'd rather eliminate him but the Ulyanova has given the order. He sent a spy to the Great Azure Door with news of her return. We killed the spy but the harm was done; she was no longer safe here. She rode out of town a few hours ago. Arraitch went with her.'

'Has Vorgottenstrit 13 been raided?'

'It hadn't when we left, Mangler. By now, who knows? But Blue Primrose will find nothing. Everyone's gone except the old woman and the children. Nothing remains to link the house to us. I won't return until tomorrow, but I'm not anxious.'

Mangler whispered to his five companions. Stanislas picked his teeth.

'We'll help to find Redman, Stan. Go to 14Q and obtain what's needed to dispose of him. How will you enter the Strlzhav Bakery to make the amendment?'

Stanislas grinned. He drew his knife and fingered the blade.

'One of their staff about my age and size will suffer stabbing pains. I'll borrow his uniform and hat and take his place. Alert me when the metacake arrives. I'll do the rest.' He surveyed the activists and nodded. 'Now I must visit all SPAR cells in Strelsau. Every comrade must be on the alert for Redman.'

Stanislas departed. Half an hour later he realised he'd lied. He'd said there was nothing left to link Vorgottenstrit 13 to SPAR, but there was: something incriminating. Something essential for the Revolution. Something he must recover without delay.

Chapter 28

All the bishops and priests who minister to patients in the cathedral hospitals and church surgeries are younger relatives of aristocratic families who have relinquished the bakery for medical school at the Universities of Strelsau, Szipad or Hrincacz. Hrincacz Medical School, on the shore of Lake Brojginzha, enjoys the highest reputation. State-of-the-art miasma research laboratories have been built there, and the School's success in alleviating or even curing miasma-related conditions is impressive. It may be coincidental that life expectancy in villages near Lake Brojginzha is higher than the national average, at least when the local krevoj and Blue Primrose see no need to cull the peasantry.
— *The Unideker Guide to Ruritania*

The western sky had crimsoned before Klarissa and Arraitch reached their destination, less than two leagues from Hrincacz. The house was bigger and sturdier than the village hovels.

'Beloved Klarissa, you should have warned us. But there's food in the larder, clean water in the well.'

'Snap decision, Bresina.' Klarissa hugged the corpulent woman and smiled. 'You and Egrienne still fulfil the role of parents, so I can impose without notice. I also impose on behalf of my companion.'

'Of course!' Egrienne Alterlet laughed. He was a four-square man with iron hair and velvet eyes. 'Arraitch, my friend, let's tend your horses and enjoy the new ale. Klarissa, we're hungry for news but you must rest first. Bresina, make up her bed, and one in the attic for Arraitch, then prepare food for our guests.'

In no other company would Klarissa have admitted to exhaustion. She bathed, then lay on the straw-stuffed palliasse and slept. Bresina busied herself in the kitchen. Egrienne and Arraitch drank ale and talked.

'Alone and unaided, facing hostile forces, she travelled to Britain, copied the government's security plan and brought it home.' Arraitch shook his head. 'More than once she evaded capture by the narrowest margin. It's scarcely thirty-six hours since she returned to Ruritania, and she's ridden beside me since before dawn. She's weary.'

Egrienne nodded and replenished their ale mugs.

'She never lacked courage or stamina and she's a born leader. For obvious reasons she was learned and skilled even before she went to university in England. They say she speaks the language like a native. She can defend herself. No one guesses her age unless they know the truth, so she uses her beauty as women do.'

'She also has a handbag.' Arraitch smiled. 'She says it can contain whatever she wishes because her stepfather made it and he understands Faerie physics.'

Egrienne chuckled.

'Ah, the handbag. It took me years …' He rose and went to the window. 'She'll be as safe here as I can make her, and you also. But you know my thoughts, Arraitch. Even if it succeeds, the revolution you plan will bring destruction and death, and the people don't want it. Most are content. And if it fails, the consequences will be tragic – for Bresina and me, and for your family.'

'Some are content because they don't perceive their oppression, Egrienne. Look at your village. Who owns it?'

'Some of us own our houses and hovels, others rent them.'

'You own them or rent them until the krev wants the land on which they stand. The fields belong to the krev. You grow wheat to send to the krev's mill to make flour for his baking, and beet to make sugar for him; you raise chickens to produce eggs for the krev; you breed cattle to yield milk to make cream for his cakes.'

'Yes, Arraitch, but we're paid for our labour, we meet our own needs, and the krev's bakery sells us cakes at special prices. The country moves among propitious climates so crops seldom fail and few go hungry. Not many are homeless, and the village cares for the old and crippled, though they're butts of jokes and cruelties. We've water to bathe and to brew ale and wine, the church surgery tends to our ills, there's schooling for those who want it, we entertain ourselves at the inn and the ghrunli field, so why would we want change? As a craftsman I'm respected. Would your revolution make people respect me more?'

'The Revolution will give you freedom, Egrienne; freedom to attain a university post, for example. You have education. You have great skill. Why should you live as a mere village craftsman just because you're not kin to an aristocrat?'

'Would a university post make me more respected? Would it make me happier? Would I achieve more than I do now? I admire your passion, Arraitch, I respect your beliefs and your courage, but you don't persuade me. Nor will you persuade others. If your revolution succeeded, what would you do with the unpersuaded? Force us to obey your dictates? Would this be the freedom you promise, or oppression such as you claim you'll overthrow?'

'Do you believe an accident of birth should determine your fate, Egrienne? Shouldn't merit and ability matter more? If compulsion is needed to promote merit, so be it; but I believe merit will find its own path when it's given the chance.'

'You'd replace a society in which the low-born serve the high-born with one in which the meritless serve the able. Would that make the world fairer?'

'You're caricaturing the Revolution. We'll replace an inflexible and immobile society with a flexible and mobile one, which *will* be fairer. And we'll end the national obsession with cake and introduce healthy eating. Cake is the staple diet only for the poor, and what's their life expectancy? Thirty-eight, forty? The aristocrats eat little cake and they live to seventy-five or eighty. Cake is an instrument of oppression. A killer.'

'Asclepius preserve us from Puritans!' Egrienne guffawed and grasped the ale jug. 'Drink again, Arraitch, and let's agree to differ. As Klarissa's loyal friend I drink to your health and happiness; as a revolutionary and a Puritan I reject all you stand for. But you're welcome to share my house as long as you will. Now, Bresina has food for us. Go and wake Klarissa and let our talk turn to lighter matters.'

The meal was merry with tales of village life, of everyday jealousies and feuds and maimings and rapes, but Klarissa's smile was knowing. As the platters were cleared and she declined her share of cake, she said:

'In my sleep, Egrienne, I heard your words to Arraitch. You're right: people resist change, even change for the better. But they can be persuaded without force. Britain is no model society – she pretends to democracy, but like Ruritania she's ruled by a political élite – yet she illustrates why the Revolution will prosper. Her government introduced a law prohibiting smoking in public places, including inns.'

'What?' Egrienne's jaw dropped. 'The British aren't allowed to smoke at an inn? And they call Britain the home of freedom?' He roared with laughter. 'Now *there's* a law the people would resist! Did they lynch the entire government or just the leaders?'

'No one was lynched. At first there were complaints, and some inns refused to comply until fines were imposed, but everyone soon accepted the new rule. British people now quit the inn to smoke in the open air.'

'Have they no backbone? They submit to smoking outdoors? In British weather?'

Klarissa joined in the laughter.

'They're decadent, Egrienne. There's much about them I could love and admire, but I can never decide whether to shed tears over them or bomb them. Yet there's a lesson for Ruritania. When we depose the Queen, turn the aristocrats out of parliament and install a government of the peasantry, there will be complaints and resistance; but soon the complaints will fall silent and resistance will fade. Our people will accept the new order, just as the British accepted the smoking ban. The British were persuaded by a promise of better health. Ruritanians will be persuaded by the promise of freedom as well as health.'

'You imagine a promise of freedom will move Ruritanian peasants?' Egrienne shook his head. 'No, Klarissa. I'll wager a hundred raldoloj the people of this village would respond to your cry of "freedom" with a tolerant smile and a return to their labour in the fields.'

'I accept your wager,' said Klarissa. 'Tomorrow, when the villagers take their midday meal, we'll summon them to the graveyard beside the church surgery. I'll tell them a story about freedom and we'll see how they respond. And you and I will each carry a hundred raldoloj and be ready to pay.'

Egrienne nodded.

'Agreed.'

Chapter 29

'NP-complete' is an abbreviation for 'Nondeterministic polynomial time complete'. It describes a problem that can – in principle – be solved by one or more (often simple) algorithms. In practice, however, the time required for solution grows exponentially with the size of the problem until it becomes effectively infinite, supercomputers notwithstanding – though it might be easy to check the solution if you can find it. Very large mazes and logic puzzles are NP-complete.

[...]

Turk Gödelpus (b. 1932) published an abstruse, contentious but uncontested proof of his Unsatisfiability Theorem while still a young man. Having thus demonstrated the impossibility of saying anything reliably meaningful he retired to a Trappist monastery. Little is known about his subsequent life, though he's rumoured to have remarked, on one of the few occasions when the monastic authorities permitted him to speak, 'The food here's bloody awful'. Opinion is divided as to whether that statement had meaning.

— *Dai O'Genies, A Primer of Ruritanian Philosophy*

At sunrise, after morning cakes, Thad and Tomen took Rory to show him the sights of Strelsau. Ariadne joined them. In the carriage, Tomen stubbed out her cigarette and smiled.

'Well, Logician, how do you interpret Ariadne's wish to accompany you to the slums?'

'She wants to know why Klarissa fascinates me and to witness my response when I meet her face to face.'

Tomen chuckled.

'But it is *Ariadne* who reads psychology papers. It is improper for men to understand female motives.'

'I often make forays into impropriety.'

'The person you're discussing in third-person terms is present in person, listening with mounting indignation and becoming personally affronted,' said Ariadne. 'And Impropriety should be your middle name, Redman Person.'

They entered the rich northern quarter with its hotels, library, opera house, concert hall and theatres. They drove past the Bank of Ruritania with its magnificent carvings of birthday cakes; the Strelsau Television Centre; the Academy of Science building with its committee-designed portico enshrouded in permanent scaffolding; the main University complex with its statues of aristocratic savants gazing at the heavens through closed eyes; and the National Ghrunli Stadium. No match was in progress; the ground staff were re-digging the pits and marking out the brutalisation squares.

Rory's *déjà vu* had become chronic. Everything hovered on the threshold of familiarity, as though scenes never before witnessed could evoke some half-forgotten dream.

'There's a paradox at the heart of the Gödelpus Unsatisfiability Theorem,' he said. 'I read about the Theorem in Dai's book, but Dai doesn't mention the paradox.'

'Dai studied with Gödelpus,' said Thad, 'so if he saw a fallacy in the Theorem he perhaps chose not to write about it. What is the paradox, Rory?'

Rory cleared his throat.

'Consider the statement "No knowledge of anything, no truth, can be objective". Consider "Nothing can be known for certain, bias-free". How can it be known for certain, without bias, that nothing can be known for certain, bias-free? How can we know, objectively, that no knowledge can be objective?'

Ariadne smirked.

'So the greatest contribution of Ruritania's greatest logician was taurocoprology.'

'Logically,' said Rory, 'the Theorem refutes itself. A proposition amounting to "All propositions are meaningless" is either meaningless, in which case it's consistent with the Theorem but invalidates it, or meaningful, in which case (no matter whether it's true or false) it's inconsistent with the Theorem and therefore disproves it. So why did a great logician make it his legacy? I think it's because the Theorem is *psychologically* valid. Each human individual believes a finite number of statements; but unless he or she is omniscient, some of those statements must be false. So everyone's beliefs are ultimately inconsistent. You can't believe all the things you believe without contradicting yourself somewhere along the line.'

Ariadne frowned; Tomen shook her head; Thad nodded. Rory went on thinking. He felt he'd discovered something at the core of Ruritania's idiosyncrasy but he couldn't put his finger on it.

Their route passed through a poorer part of the capital. Rory was still disconcerted by the lack of traffic noise and piped muzak. Piles of horse dung and the absence of tarmac evoked a bygone age. Odours redolent of decaying vegetables and blocked drains were omnipresent. He saw old men and women in their forties shuffling through the gravel, picking cigarette ends from the dirt and smoking them; skeletal dogs foraging in rubbish; bakers' shops at every corner selling carrot cakes, coffee cakes, chocolate cakes of numerous varieties, fruit cakes, cream cakes, sponge cakes. Election posters hung on walls, political leaders smiling beside their promised cakes. Beggars huddled in doorways. Victims of violence lay at the roadside or crawled moaning towards mirages of succour.

'Is the violence political?' asked Rory.

'Mostly street robberies and assaults,' said Tomen. 'The police are overstretched. Be warned: Area 23K is worse. But right now an emergency vehicle is about to pass us.'

Thad moved the carriage over to the pavement. Galloping hooves approached, accompanied by a glorious wordless song. The soprano voice raised hairs on the listeners' necks and bore them on waves of enchantment to the sides of the road, leaving a free path for the conveyance. It shot past at full speed, wheels spraying garbage, and Rory saw the singer. She sat on an inflatable rock atop the vehicle and was clad from neck to ankle in cerulean blue. Her hair was blue, her hands and feet and face were blue, and her song was magical. The carriage was out of view and earshot, leaving images of shipwreck in its wake, before anyone could draw breath.

'Whew … I suppose all emergency vehicles carry such singers,' said Rory. 'There must be a rigorous teaching and selection process.'

'Indeed,' said Tomen. 'It is a major commitment of police training schools.'

'Ah. The police, not Blue Primrose. Do the police and Blue Primrose cooperate?'

'They hate each other,' said Thad.

Clouds were gathering. Tomen said rain had been forecast. Rory took off his sunglasses.

They rode into St Galen's Square, parked the carriage and strolled through summer drizzle into the Gardens. Shabby old cripples adorned the wooden seats. Rory was tactful about the architecture of Dzhumpinpork Palace and the High Bakery and remarked on the relative austerity of the cathedral hospital and the Surgeon Archbishop's residence. Then he did a double-take.

'Hang on. There's the Palace on the far side, and the parliament building on the left, and the cathedral opposite, and – did you say Blue Primrose HQ behind us? And then there's … No, all four sides of the square are accounted for.'

Thad and Tomen exchanged grins with Ariadne.

'Can't you account for the unaccountable, Rory?'

'I need more sleep.' Rory stared at the Blue Primrose HQ. 'The square has a fifth side, but you can't see it if you look directly at it. What is it?'

'As a Brit, I'd have expected Blue Primrose HQ to interest you more. Two generations ago your upper classes used the expletive 'By Gad!' Most people suppose it to have been a corruption of 'By God!' but it was not; it was an acronym. British visitors to Ruritania had learned the importance to national security of the Great Azure Door of the Blue Primrose building.'

Rory shook his head.

'Would it be apposite to call that a "fairy story", Thad? Come on, what's on the fifth side of the square? You know what I've half-seen. Would you rather not talk about it? If so I'll stop asking.'

Tomen's voice was quiet.

'We do not talk about it much. It is the Labyrinth.'

'With a Minotaur?'

'There is no such thing as a Minotaur, Rory. But if you enter the Labyrinth there is no telling when or where or even if you will emerge. It is a refuge for those under imminent threat or in despair.'

Rory's interest was piqued. Somewhere at the back of his mind a bell rang. How could he have known about the Strelsau Labyrinth? He'd never heard of it, yet Tomen's words sounded familiar. *Déjà vu* again.

'If there's more than a single path through it then it's a maze, not a labyrinth,' he said. 'Mazes fascinate us, like logic puzzles. Challenges we're compelled to meet. Above a certain level of complexity they're insoluble in practice. Large-scale mazes and large-scale logic puzzles are NP-complete. Do you know how this so-called Labyrinth is structured? Total node number, mean path-to-node ratio, degree of connectedness?'

'No one is sure,' said Thad. 'People who have passed through it give conflicting accounts. It is a major intersection between the mundane world and the Faerie Realm. If you look at Blue Primrose HQ or the Surgeon Archbishop's palace, you will see through the corner of your eye innumerable slug trails; *nerjaportikhnoj*; evidence of Faerie involvement. The best description we have, Rory, is an ever-increasing path-to-node ratio, an ever-decreasing path width, and then a reversal of the trend, with time distortions.'

Rory frowned.

'It sounds like the Öst-Brün theory, the "fractal geometry of Faerie". Did the Labyrinth-maze inspire them?'

'Ah. You know their papers. Yes, a connection has been suggested. But the Öst-Brün work is controversial, just as the structure of the Labyrinth is controversial.' Thad studied his pocket watch. 'If you wish to visit 23K we must go. It will be best to return to a civilised part of the city before we want lunch, since food in the slums is to be avoided, and we would not wish to be anywhere near 23K when daylight starts to fade.'

Chapter 30

Much has been written about gargoyles, which spew rainwater from the eaves of religious buildings throughout Europe. Various authorities tell us they are caricatures of masons or prelates, or devices to ward off evil spirits, or fantasy decoration. In fact, they represent certain inhabitants of Faerie. Some are images of the female spirits Lekhissa and Sporota, who are sometimes only a smallbit (an inch and a half) tall so they might not be noticed. However, when they size-shift to a height of five fathoms (thirty feet) they cannot be overlooked. If you met either of them in her larger manifestation, you'd wee.

— *The Unideker Guide to Ruritania*

Clad in denim garb and wooden boots, cloth cap over her short black hair, Klarissa swung her scythe in harmony with the village. Bundles of winter feed for livestock tumbled at the peasants' feet and were lifted to haylofts. Voices sang and the chorus rose and fell with the reapers' blades. The meadows danced to the rhythm of the earth. The morning sparkled.

A youth leered.

'Hey, see the chick with the peachy bum? Five minutes behind the barn–'

The back of a hand struck his ear and sent him sprawling.

'Respect, boy! Don't you know who she is?'

The youth sprang up, fists bunched, but subsided before Arraitch.

'Oh. You mean she's –?'

'Yes.'

'Thought she was older. Thought she'd gone to foreign parts. Wouldn't come back to this dump.'

'The Lady will never forget her people.'

The youth bestowed another yearning look on Klarissa and resumed his labours. Arraitch watched him for half a minute and went on gathering hay.

As the sun approached its zenith Klarissa returned to the Alterlet house, laid down her scythe beside the well, washed, and dressed herself in a loose-fitting robe of brilliant white adorned with feathers. A gold circlet replaced her cap. She dabbed perfume on to her throat and ears.

Women and men, old and young, hale and lame, children clinging to parents or carried in their mothers' arms, gravitated from the fields to the church surgery and sat among the gravestones to eat their frugal meals of cake and ale. They watched as Klarissa glided barefoot through their midst, sprang from sundial to mullion to string course up the side of the building and stood high above them, each small foot planted upon the head of a gargoyle grimacing from the eaves, a vision in white with feathered wings and halo. She raised her hands and began:

'There was once an aristocrat, a skinny old baker who loved hunting. He looked like a weed fed on such rich manure it had grown a curly moustache. He couldn't shoot like Arraitch – after all he was only an aristocrat – but his aim was fair and his range was … moderate.'

Her audience chuckled. Already the story had a villain they could despise, and most of them recognised him.

'One sunny day he went into the enchanted forest, seeking to kill for pleasure. On a branch of a tree beside a clearing sat the most beautiful bird he'd ever seen. She had an orange beak and legs and crest, and golden feathers, and a great red curling tail, and when she stretched and opened her beak her glorious tail unfurled like a flag. The aristocrat stared at her and called, 'Beautiful bird, sing to me!' And the bird opened her beak and sang: *Nyaa nyaa ni nyaa nyaa, ni na ni na ni nyaa nyaa, nyaa nyaa ni nyaa nyaa, ni na ni na ni nyaa nyaa!'*

The villagers laughed. The children laughed loudest.

'The aristocrat said, "I've never heard such a disgusting song! If you sing it again I'll kill you." And the bird looked at him, raised her wings to the sides of her head and flapped them, and sang … Come on, everybody!'

Klarissa raised the feathery wings of her white robe and emulated the bird's gesture. Many of her audience joined in the song, laughing more loudly: *Nyaa nyaa ni nyaa nyaa, ni na ni na ni nyaa nyaa, nyaa nyaa ni nyaa nyaa, ni na ni na ni nyaa nyaa!*

'So the aristocrat took an arrow from his quiver and bent his bow, and – *Thwang.*'

Klarissa mimed the firing of the quarrel, then clutched her chest as though the point had pierced it. She toppled forward, leaning out over the gargoyles' faces until the crowd knew she would fall. They stopped laughing. But she righted herself and her story continued.

'The bird fell to the forest floor. The aristocrat picked up her body, stuffed it into his leather bag and turned to walk back to his castle. But as he walked, muffled singing came from the bag: *Nyuh nyuh ni nyuh nyuh, ni nuh ni nuh ni nyuh nyuh, nyuh nyuh ni nyuh nyuh, ni nuh ni nuh ni nyuh nyuh!'*

The audience laughed again, uncertainly.

'He was angry. The bird was supposed to be dead! As soon as he reached his castle he stormed into the kitchen, flung the bird on to the chopping board and tore off all her red and golden feathers. The bird lay naked on the board, her feathers scattered lifeless over the floor. The aristocrat grinned. And then the bird sang …'

Klarissa hunkered down on the gargoyles, wrapped her arms around her body for warmth, and shivered.

'*Nyaaaa nyaaaa ni brrrr nyaa, ni naa ni naa ni brrrr nyaa, nyaaaa nyaaaa ni brrrr nyaa, ni naa ni naa ni brrrrrrrr nyaa!'*

Young and old, the audience applauded with delight.

'He was beside himself. He seized his cleaver and chopped the bird into a hundred pieces, flung them into a cauldron of water and set it on the fire. But as the water boiled, a song arose from the cauldron: *Nyaa nyaa ni blubb blubb, ni na ni na ni nyaa blubb, nyaa nyaa ni blubb nyaa, ni na ni na ni nyaa blubb!* The aristocrat tore his hair. With ladle and fishing net he snatched all the pieces of bird from the cauldron and rammed them into a wooden box. Then he nailed the lid shut.'

She mimed the action of hammering. The audience was rapt.

'Out in the castle garden he dug a hole a fathom deep, threw the box into it, shovelled the earth on top and jumped up and down to flatten it.'

Again she mimed the action. Again the audience feared she'd lose her footing. She didn't.

'He went back into the castle and poured a mug of wine and drank it, for the bird was silenced at last. But as he drank he heard a sound from the garden, very faint but persistent.' Klarissa's voice fell to a whisper, but it carried across the graveyard to every ear: '*Nyaa nyaa ni nyaa nyaa, ni na ni na ni nyaa nyaa, nyaa nyaa ni nyaa nyaa, ni na ni na ni nyaa nyaa!*'

The audience's laughter returned.

'The aristocrat was at the end of his tether. He went back to the garden, dug up the box, dragged it to the river, tied heavy stones to it and flung it into the water. It sank to the bottom. Now, finally, he heard the song no longer.'

The audience fell silent. Klarissa let the silence hang. Then she resumed:

'Months passed. Fish nibbled the ropes until they broke, and the current washed the stones away from the box, and the box floated to the surface and was carried downstream. At a village not far away, children were playing at the riverside. They looked over the water and saw a wooden box floating towards them. A wooden box? Treasure! So what do you think they did?'

Klarissa smiled at a group of boys.

'They swam out and grabbed it!' cried the boys. 'And dragged it to the bank! And got a big stick and prised the lid off!'

'Yes, that's what they did,' said Klarissa. 'It took ages to force off the lid because the aristocrat has used so many nails. But finally, off it came … and the box was open … and … Out flew a hundred beautiful little birds with orange beaks and legs and crests and golden feathers and red curling tails, shining in the sunlight, and when those little birds stretched and opened their beaks their glorious red tails unfurled like flags. And as the children watched, the birds flew over their heads and away to the enchanted forest, and they found the tree beside the clearing and settled on its branches. Then who should appear but the aristocrat with his bow and arrows and his leather bag, and when the hundred little birds saw him they all opened their beaks and sang … Come on, everybody!'

The whole audience joined in: '*Nyaa nyaa ni nyaa nyaa, ni na ni na ni nyaa nyaa, nyaa nyaa ni nyaa nyaa, ni na ni na ni nyaa nyaa!*'

'The aristocrat couldn't believe it! Not one bird this time, but a hundred! He cried, "Who are you? What are you?" And the hundred little birds answered, "We are the freedom birds. You can shoot us with your arrows, you can put us into your leather bag, you can tear off our feathers, you can chop us into pieces, you can boil us in a cauldron, you can bury us in the ground, you can drown us in the river, but you can never kill the freedom birds! We are the birds of freedom, and freedom will never die! *We are the birds of* …" Come on, all together!'

'FREEDOM!' yelled the audience. 'FREEDOM!' And they laughed and danced, and the children sang the song of the freedom birds at the tops of their voices: '*Nyaa nyaa ni nyaa nyaa, ni na ni na ni nyaa nyaa, nyaa nyaa ni nyaa nyaa, ni na ni na ni nyaa nyaa!*'

Klarissa blew kisses to the crowd, leapt backwards from the gargoyles, and danced over the thatch and down the far side of the church surgery, a blaze of feathery white. Behind her, the villagers sang and danced and cried, 'Free-dom! Free-dom!'

'Well, Egrienne,' said Klarissa. 'Have they smiled a tolerant smile at the promise of freedom, or have they done as I foresaw?'

'No, Klarissa, they didn't smile. I owe you a hundred raldoloj.' Egrienne handed a bundle of banknotes to her. 'But let us join them again.'

Klarissa and Egrienne walked side by side around the church surgery to the graveyard, and there the villagers were growing quiet again. They no longer danced; they were tidying away the last crumbs of cake and finishing their ale. Then all of them, women and men, young and old, hale and lame, children clinging to parents or carried in their mothers' arms, went from the graveyard to the fields, took up their scythes and resumed their labour.

'We were both right,' said Klarissa, and returned the hundred raldoloj to Egrienne.

She went back to the house, shed the white robe and the golden circlet, put on her denim garb and cloth cap and wooden boots, picked up her scythe, strode to the fields, and worked beside the villagers until the day ended. Scythe and pitchfork, shoulder and thigh danced to the rhythm of the earth, the song of the harvest.

'Sheep,' she murmured. 'Contemptible sheep. I despise them. Filthy, ignorant peasants. They're my people. I love them. I'd die for them.'

Chapter 31

In principle, the greatest crime in philosophy, as in science, is to proceed without being sure that the stage your reasoning has reached is established beyond reasonable doubt. In principle, the same applies to the criminal law. All those disciplines exemplify the gulf between principle and practice.
— *Dai O'Genies, A Primer of Ruritanian Philosophy*

Colonel Barrington and Ekwyor Tupsroot settled into first-class seats and the flight departed. The ekwyor fulminated; the colonel was frustrated.

'I'm beginning to believe the damned woman is more Faerie than mortal.'

'Nonsense, Horatio. She is mere woman.'

'She's a bloody shape-shifter. Trying to catch her is like stapling jelly to the masonry. Do you have an update, Grizelina? Do your people know how she escaped the safe house raid?'

'Neighbours are questioned again. She leave Vorgottenstrit and ride from Strelsau before light.'

'Yes, yes, I'd gathered that. But where did she ride *to*?'

The ekwyor's face twisted, effecting no aesthetic improvement.

'It is not known.'

'God's armpit!' The colonel glared at a flight attendant, eliciting a tremulous smile. 'Didn't your HQ mention a village near Hrincacz?'

'There are many village around Lake Brojginzha. We have not time or people to search all. Also, peasant hide her.'

The colonel was silent for a minute.

'Of course, you've no register of births. Baptismal records might help if we knew the … Someone in Strelsau knows where she is. Did she ride alone?'

'Two went with her. Men. Names not known.'

The colonel snorted.

'The residents of Vorgottenstrit are covering for them. More questioning needed, Grizelina. If you get your hands on one or two SPAR activists, extract information. I know you have methods.'

The ekwyor glowered through the plane window. Rain started to fall on the land below.

'If,' she snarled.

The colonel refrained from shouting his opinion about the efficacy of Blue Primrose.

'Report from our Budapest people, Grizelina: the red-haired woman isn't called Sura Marnikova and she isn't Slovenian; her name is Sonja la Limace and she's Swiss. Seems she's on visiting terms with Waldemar Krev Schammerbass. But there's no intelligence about her. She's nothing to do with the terrorists. Redman sold us a red herring.'

'Sviss. Huh. Sviss Consortium blamed for Peasant Revolt of 1848. Nonsense. Sviss know nothing.'

'Never do,' said the colonel. 'Meanwhile, where the hell is Redman?'

'We have concern more pressing, Horatio.' The ekwyor's frown deepened. 'Unless he help escape of Alterleta from safe house.'

The colonel digested this hypothesis. Redman was a loose cannon if ever there were.

'You think he was one of the two who rode out of town with her? Bloody hell, you could be right, Grizelina. You could be right.' His eyebrows rose. 'Think he engineered her escape from the Hilton in exchange for the security plan? She'll have kept a copy, of course. If we're right, he's become a paid-up SPAR supporter. So he needs to be dealt with. Summarily.'

He tugged his beard and rapped out an order for whisky. The flight attendant bustled to oblige.

Chapter 32

Hi Paul, Christine. Mobile phones work in Strelsau, at least some of the time. You probably know that. This is just to say I'm in Strelsau (in case you hadn't guessed). Ariadne Sowerby is here too (you probably know that as well). So far, I've learned that Ruritania is the epitome of weirdness. Was it Haldane who said 'The universe is not just queerer than we suppose, it is queerer than we can suppose'? Well, for 'universe' read 'Ruritania'. I mean, why in the name of the wee man from Milton Keynes do customs and immigration arrange for every foreign visitor to be greeted by an official who scares the faeces out of them? As for the downside of feudalism, if it ever had an upside … Yeah, well, you'll have seen it. But thanks to Ariadne I'm staying in relative comfort (apart from the fag smoke) with her friends Thad Masim and Tomen Comtra, and I'm exploring the city. Dunno when I'll be back. If you wouldn't mind checking on my house and garden when you have chance I'll be grateful. Will try to call again soonish.

— Phone message sent by Rory Redman on 17th May (Gregorian), 25th May (Ruritanian)

'I'm leaving tomorrow, Thad, but I'll be back for the Solstice.'

Ariadne spoke from the back of the carriage. Tomen suppressed a smirk. She'd noticed Rory's transiently forlorn expression.

'Going to Castle Bauntzi?' asked Thad, urging the horses forward through the steady rain.

'Yes,' said Ariadne. 'Kjym and I are planning a slugfest for next year. She'll have to be here for National Cake Day, of course, so I'll travel back to Strelsau with her. And after the election I'll want to pick your brains, Thad. Final law exams are looming.'

'I hope the weather will improve for your journey,' said Tomen. 'We shall watch the weatherdancers this evening.'

Rory leaned towards Ariadne.

'Who *is* this "Kjym", and where's "Castle Bauntzi"? And did you say "weatherdancers", Tomen?'

'Kjym Krev Bauntzia is the cleverest of our krevoj, though she has never sought high office,' said Thad. 'She invested in vermicelli machine manufacture and her machines have become major exports. It is against the law to import such devices – or, indeed, vermicelli. She treats her peasants like family but she can be tough. Some say she would have the skill to broker a peace deal between the government and SPAR, given the chance. And I believe she and Ariadne are established friends.'

Rory asked how Ariadne intended to travel to Castle Bauntzi. Ariadne said she would *ride*, of course, along the Szipad road. How did Rory suppose one travelled around Ruritania except on horseback or on foot? Tomen asked Rory whether he too wished to see more of the country outside Strelsau. Her smile was merry.

'We could lend you a horse,' she said.

'I've never ridden one,' said Rory. 'I know nothing about horses. Well, I can tell the front from the rear, and I'd know if a horse was the wrong way up, but that's … Ah, is this Vorgottenstrit? You were right about 23K. It's a dump.' He took the luggage label from his pocket and re-read it. 'Vorgottenstrit 13. I'll punch the gnome. Anyone else coming?'

The south-eastern quarter stank. The sky was the colour of Krev Schammerbass's Armani suit. Drizzle fell. It was gloomy enough for Rory to keep his sunglasses in his pocket. He sensed impending catastrophe, though there was no obvious portent.

'Yes, you must not go alone, Rory,' murmured Tomen. 'We should all go.'

'No, Tomen,' said Thad. 'I am not disposed to leave a carriage and two horses unattended here. I will be with you if there is trouble. You three go. Stay together. I shall keep watch.'

All was not well at Vorgottenstrit 13. The door was broken. The entrance gaped. The gnome lay on the gravel a fathom away. Rory crept into the house, step by slow step, the hair on his forearms alert. Ariadne and Tomen followed, holding hands. A faint keening emanated from a back room. There was no other sign of life.

Rory sidled towards the source of the keening. It was a kitchen, or had been. He entered; the women tiptoed after him.

'Oh my God!' whispered Ariadne.

'Asclepius save us!' Tomen crossed herself.

Chairs and table were smashed. Shattered crockery, shredded cushions and ripped fabrics littered the floor. The stove was overturned. The back door swung crookedly on a single hinge. Outside was a cesspool; broken toys floated on it. Beside the stove lay the body of an old woman. A little boy was hunched near the ruined door, rocking to and fro, staring at nothing. He'd soiled himself. The keening came from his mouth. In the middle of the room sat a young girl cradling a dead dog, her face vacant. She looked up at Rory.

'*Spravaja, pan prejosz,*' she said, '*marak bressjiln Vreron.*' Her voice was a pallid monotone.

The dog's body bore signs of attention from iron-shod boots.

'What's she saying?' asked Rory.

'Please, dear sir, make Vrero better.' Tears trickled down Tomen's plump cheeks.

'Tell her we'll make sure Vrero is looked after. Ariadne, take your hands off your face and pull yourself together. Those kids need to be cared for. Tomen, we must organise a burial.'

No point seeking relatives, he thought, for people in this business. To those in authority, funerals are opportunities to make arrests.

Ariadne sat on the rubbish-strewn floor beside the girl, put her arms around her and whispered. The girl stared straight ahead, stroking the stiffening corpse of the dog. Tomen dialled numbers on an old mobile phone. It took time; her hands shook.

Rory went to search the rest of the house. He was back within minutes.

'Is there … Are there any more –?'

'No, Tomen. The whole place has been trashed but there's no one else, dead or alive. But the bastards who did it missed something.' He held up a document with a heraldic crest, then folded it and slipped it into his pocket.

'So Klarissa is … What? Dead? Captured?' Ariadne's voice was choked.

'I doubt it. More likely she flew the nest before this place was attacked.'

'How can you know that? God's sake, Rory, what kind of people did this?'

'Blue Primrose.'

'What? That's insane!'

'Think about it, Ariadne. This was a SPAR safe house, otherwise Klarissa wouldn't have come here after she escaped from London, and the luggage label says she did. No one except Blue Primrose would dare raid a SPAR safe house, or wish to. Tupsroot had told them Klarissa was back in Strelsau. Either she gave them this address or someone tipped them off. If they'd found Klarissa they'd have taken her away and interrogated her without wrecking the place or killing the old woman and the dog. They're the national security force, not vandals. And they'd have searched systematically and found the document I just pocketed. *Ergo*, they didn't find Klarissa, so they had to return to HQ empty-handed. They knew how the senior ekwyroj would react, so they went ape-shit. They probably questioned the old woman and she wouldn't–'

'Oh, right, clever dick, so where's Klarissa gone?'

'How the hell should I know? I'm not bloody clairvoyant!'

'You don't need to fucking shout at me! This isn't *my* fault, you jerk!'

126

'*Spravaja, pan prejosz,*' whispered the girl, '*marak bressjiln Vreron. Spravaja?*'

'Rory, Ariadne, please,' whispered Tomen. 'We are all angry, all distressed, but please, let us not–'

A new voice spoke from the kitchen entrance; a man's voice, trembling. A shaky arm seized Ariadne around the throat.

'What do you here? Who you are?'

Rory felt he'd half-anticipated the stranger in the dark red uniform, the automatic pistol in the unsteady hand.

'*Spravaja, pan prejosz,*' droned the girl, '*spravaja, spravaja, marak bressjiln Vreron.*'

Chapter 33

In Ruritanian, the formal appellation 'Voyalem Divlunir' or the less formal 'Voyalem' is applied to persons in charge. English equivalents of 'Voyalem' include 'chief', 'boss', 'chairperson', 'president' and 'big fish'. The noun is neuter, a fact of passing interest to sociolinguists. In this respect, 'Voyalem' is typical of a certain class of Ruritanian nouns; 'ekwyor' and 'krev' are also neuter. In all such cases the suffix '–in' betokens a subordinate status with no gender implication. 'Divlunir' is a term of respect, endearment or adoration. It is a unique adjective: it remains neuter whatever gender of noun it qualifies. The Ruritanian language may be a casserole of Indo-European leftovers, but dumplings of idiosyncrasy simmer in its depths.
— Teach Yourself Ruritanian

Eldzhay summoned the leaders of Strelsau's SPAR cells to a conclave at the Lenmir Hotel; the manager was a sympathiser. Six leaders presented themselves; each greeted Eldzhay with reverence. Stanislas wasn't among them. Eldzhay had just returned from an audience with the Ulyanova. He was weary and travel-stained.

'No, Comrades, only the Ulyanova should be addressed as "Voyalem Divlunir". I'm Eldzhay.'

The six leaders pointed out that Eldzhay had summoned the conclave and was chairing it so it was proper to address him as "Voyalem". As for "Divlunir", Eldzhay was respected because he'd once tossed a charging bull over a hedge. Also, he was Arraitch's biggest and most trusted lieutenant, and Arraitch was a SPAR legend. Eldzhay thumped the table, cracking its surface, and ordered the conclave to address him only by name.

The six brought him up to date with developments.

'The Ulyanova will not return before Solstice Eve.' Eldzhay stared around the conclave. 'She'll expect every part of the Revolutionary strategy to be in place. No detail can be overlooked. Where's the security plan detailing British military involvement?'

The leaders shifted in their seats.

'Er ... None of us has seen it, Eldzhay.'

'The Ulyanova brought two versions of the plan to Strelsau, thus laying a glorious foundation for the Revolution. The original version crystallises our operation: by knowing it, we can outmanoeuvre Blue Primrose. The fake version written by the Ulyanova will confuse the British running-dogs. Which version have you not seen?'

Brows sweated and chairs squeaked.

'N-neither, Eldzhay.'

'Where are they?'

The silence perspired. Then Mangler spoke:

'Before the Ulyanova returned to her village, Eldzhay, she stayed in Stanislas's cell at Vorgottenstrit 13 in 23K. She didn't take the plans east with her or she'd have given them to you, so either they're still in Vorgottenstrit or Stan has them.'

'Then where's Stan?'

Everyone agreed that Stanislas was hunting the British spy, Redman.

'And he's going to modify the metacake, Eldzhay.'

Eldzhay examined each leader like a vulture selecting a carcass.

'Each of you should have a copy of the original plan by now so you can rehearse your cell in its role. You must find the *original* immediately after this meeting, make six copies, and set to work. And bring the *fake* document to me.'

The vulture head retracted. The silence dabbed its forehead.

'All right,' said Eldzhay. 'Let's turn to other aspects of the Revolutionary strategy. Did you say Stan had undertaken to modify the metacake?'

'Yes, Eldzhay. But I'm not sure whether he's the right person to do so.'

'You're right, Mangler,' said Eldzhay. 'The Ulyanova would have been perfect for the task, though she's already done more than her share. Her absence is unfortunate but unavoidable. But Stan's never worked in a bakery. The metacake must seem undisturbed, its shape unchanged, its metaicing and metadecoration perfect. To effect the repair an experienced baker's labourer is needed. Who should it be?'

Another leader raised his hand.

'I'll volunteer, Eldzhay. Worked seven years for Hvimpy's lot. Bastards. I'll make the metacake good as new, scout's honour.'

Eldzhay gave guarded approval.

'Thank you, Sillias. But it's Strlzhav not Hvimpy who'll prepare the metacake. Yet again. For years now, our land has groaned under the yoke of a Strlzhav government. It must end ... Sillias, will you be able to make the repaired metacake look perfect? Won't the difference in practice between bakeries be a problem?'

'Nah,' said Sillias. 'All that "secret known only to my bakery" stuff's a load of unicorn shit. They're all the same. I've known labourers quit one bakery and start work in another the following day and there isn't none of them's never had no problem.'

Eldzhay wondered whether this was reassuring. At length he said: 'Okay, if you're sure. Now: preparations in Szipad and Hrincacz.'

Two leaders summarised the preparations in Szipad and Hrincacz. There was a risk of fatalities in Szipad, where the Surgeon Bishop was a habitual drunkard; he'd been a bosom friend of Crown Prince Elharic before the latter became a frog.

Eldzhay issued instructions.

'Next: the civil unrest campaign, to be initiated on June seventeenth. Strlzhav supporters will learn of a Hvimpy plan to take their bakery into public ownership. Of course there's no such plan, but a document with the Hvimpy crest outlining it will be leaked in all three cities simultaneously. On the following day a leaked document with the Strlzhav crest will appear, again in triplicate. It will call for Hvimpy to be arrested as a SPAR sympathiser and his bakery abolished. The police will be hard-pressed to control the ensuing riots.'

Six pairs of hands applauded, though with discretion. It ill became a secret conclave to generate noise.

'I've written both these documents. Tonight, those of you with the requisite equipment will prepare three printed versions of each, after you've corrected my spelling. Bring the results to me at dawn tomorrow. One copy of each document will be smuggled into each city. Will this be difficult?' (No one said 'Yes'.) 'There's also the matter of Strelsau's electricity generating station, but our tactic there hardly needs planning. Otherwise, I believe we've considered all strands of our strategy. There's much to do in a short time, but if we'd started earlier we'd have risked discovery. However, the most urgent tasks are to find, copy and share the original security plan, and deliver the fake one to me.'

Chapter 34

Got your message, Rory. You're crazy, but you know that already. I met Thad Masim in Strelsau and reckoned him as trustworthy as any royal adviser could be. If you stay with him and Ariadne and follow their guidance, even you should survive in Ruritania. I know you're as likely to accept advice as to take a holiday on Pluto, but as a friend I beg you not to steal anything in Ruritania, however trivial the item, to avoid Blue Primrose, and above all to have nothing to do with SPAR. I suspect you've gone there to catch up with the woman who mugged you. Please don't. Let the authorities deal with her. You have no idea how dangerous it is to embroil yourself in politics in Ruritania – wherever the country is right now. Oh, and if you're tempted to find an entry to the Faerie Realm and become the latest adventurer to imagine he can solve Lekhissa's Riddle, Don't. Everyone fails, and Lekhissa eats them with chestnut stuffing. She likes chestnut stuffing.

— Phone message to Rory Redman from Paul Edict on 18th May (Gregorian), 26th May (Ruritanian)

How, wondered Rory, do you say 'Oh, shit!' in Ruritanian? His attention jumped from the traumatised children to the women to the gun. His game-theory calculation excluded the heroic option. The gunman's hand shook, but not much.

'Let's deal with the priorities.' Rory's voice was steadier than the average jelly. 'Tomen has made funeral arrangements for the old woman.' He indicated Tomen. 'The first task is to take these children to a place where they'll be cared for.'

'No!' shouted the gunman. 'First thing, you tell what you do here. This terrorist house. You terrorist? *Then* care for children. Speak!'

'You and your kind caused this carnage. We've nothing to do with SPAR. I'll tell you why we're here but not until the children's needs are addressed. And *I* want answers from *you*.'

'Speak, I say! You think *you* dictate? I hold gun!'

'No you don't.' Thad appeared behind the ekwyrin and snatched his pistol. 'I watched you arrive. It seemed best to …' His eyes scanned the wreckage and his face whitened. 'Rory, you are right. The children come first.'

The gunman collapsed in the corner and burst into tears. The girl stared and raised the dead dog towards him. Her murmur rose to a shriek:

'*Spravaja, pan prejosz, spravaja marak bressjiln Vreron, marak bressjiln Vreron, spravaja,* spravaja!'

The child writhed screaming on the floor, her eyes white. Tomen seized her in a smothering hug. Ariadne massaged her throat and disengaged the dog's body from the little arms. Thad threw the pistol into the far corner and walked through the detritus to the boy. He put a hand on his shoulder and spoke. The boy went on rocking to and fro, staring straight ahead, keening. An urge to smash the ekwyrin's skull overwhelmed Rory. Instead, he punched the wall, tearing skin from his knuckles.

That was stupid, he thought, watching blood trickle from his fingers. I'd have better control if I understood the time-dislocation. A fraction of a second before I entered the kitchen I knew what I'd find. Then there were micro-anticipations of the gunman's appearance, what he said, Thad's intervention, and every little detail before and since. *Déjà vu* shouldn't last for minutes and hours and days. I've been like this ever since I reached the airport. It's bloody unsettling. I need a good long run. And weird though it seems I'm getting hungry.

Ariadne stood and said, 'Why don't Tomen and I take the kids to the nearest church surgery? You need to talk to our new companion, Rory. Thad, will you act as translator?'

'Gladly. Rory and I will take the ekwyrin to the carriage. The less time I spend in 23K the happier I shall be. There is a church surgery less than two hundred fathoms away, round the corner to the right. Can you ladies manage on foot with the children? The carriage cannot hold us all but we shall ride beside you.'

'Yes, Thad, we will manage,' said Tomen.

Tomen picked up the girl. Ariadne hefted the boy and wrinkled her nose.

'The sooner this little chap's decontaminated the better. We'll be back in Klatzierstrit in a jiffy, Thad.'

'We will wait in the carriage, Ariadne,' said Thad. 'I do not intend you to make your own way home from here. Rory, I presume your friend Klarissa is no longer in this house? Quite so.' He turned to the weeping ekwyrin. 'What is your name?'

'Huipi Krefin Hvimpy,' sniffed the disarmed gunman.

'Son of Krev Hvimpy?' said Rory. '*Were* you one of the gang of Blue Primrose thugs who trashed this place and murdered the old woman and killed the kids' dog? Yeah. Brave fellow. Your dad must be bloody proud of you.'

The miserable ekwyrin shook his head and wept anew. Thad picked up his pistol and examined it. It wasn't loaded.

'I need a long run, Thad,' said Rory. 'Right now. I'll find my way back to Klatzierstrit.'

Thad protested, but in vain. Rory had gone.

Chapter 35

When faced with something surprising, challenging or inexplicable, Rory often evoked 'the wee man from Milton Keynes', as in 'What in the name of the wee man from Milton Keynes ...?' On several occasions we asked him about this diminutive person, alleged to hail from the spiritual home of roundabouts, but he never explained. We once visited Milton Keynes and interviewed all the persons of restricted growth we could find, but we came no nearer to identifying the wee man whom Rory repeatedly evoked. It remains one of the unsolved mysteries about Milton Keynes.

— Paul Edict, 'Rory Redman as I Knew Him'

Colonel Barrington collected his suitcase at Strelsau airport and muttered into his beard. He looked ill.

'You are journey-indisposed, Horatio?' The ekwyor's face caricatured a smile. 'Soon you recover.'

'No, I'm not travel-sick, Grizelina, but that damned Edwardian nanny at customs and immigration upsets my stomach every visit. Don't they employ anyone else?'

'It depend who you are.'

The colonel deemed her reply too cryptic to be worth pursuing.

'First task,' he said, 'is to take a carriage to your HQ or the High Bakery offices and find who wrote this security plan. The infernal shape-shifter probably tinkered with it to put a mole-wrench in the works. And no doubt Redman had a hand in the tinkering.'

Ekwyor Tupsroot hid another smile. Much of colonel's animosity and suspicion arose from Redman's cleverness rather than the risk he posed. However, she said nothing; appearances notwithstanding, she understood diplomacy.

'Then we find where Alterleta go.'

'Right, Grizelina. Get her under lock and key and there'll be no revolution. The rest of the terrorist rabble will do nothing without her.'

The ekwyor thought the colonel's priorities were influenced by personal rancour. As with Redman, so with Alterleta or whatever she called herself: both had outsmarted the colonel. Nevertheless he was right: Alterleta was the 'Ulyanova', elusive and dangerous.

'We find if ekwyroj learn news of terrorist plans. Spies must report. We know SPAR try to disrupt National Cake Day. We know not how. This we must discover.'

'Once my team's here,' said the colonel, 'SPAR can try whatever they please. We'll be more than a match for them. But if we catch the woman first, my lads will have nothing to do. They can enjoy the National Cake Day shindig. There'll be no revolution. Knock down the flagpole and the red flag collapses.'

The ekwyor doubted whether the future would prove so simple.

Chapter 36

The English words 'curer' and 'curate' have the same etymological root (Latin cura = care); the Ruritanian 'yasimak' carries both meanings. The chief carer in a church surgery or cathedral hospital is addressed formally as 'voyalyasi' or 'voyalyasia', meaning 'cure-leader' or 'cure-director'.
— *Teach Yourself Ruritanian*

Stanislas was puzzled. Normally he'd have eliminated the cause of puzzlement without reflection, but circumstances weren't normal. He reported via a battered mobile phone.

He was the third visitor to Vorgottenstrit 13 within an hour. Sensing the house was occupied he watched from across the street, hand on knife. When the occupants emerged his puzzlement grew. Redman was among them but he ran off alone. Then the man who'd driven the carriage appeared, holding the ekwyrin's gun; he and the ekwyrin climbed into the carriage, arguing. Then the two women came out of the house carrying the children. For a moment Stanislas supposed the children were dead. Grief and fury clutched his gorge. Then he noticed movement. He spoke into his phone.

'The kids are alive! The two women are carrying ... church surgery, probably. Once I've searched the house I'll follow.'

The carriage moved forward at walking pace, staying alongside the women with the children. The man with the gun addressed the women as he drove. Stanislas watched for three minutes and then darted across the street and into the house.

Five minutes later he spoke again into his phone. His stomach heaved. He'd anticipated tragedy but the scene in the kitchen nauseated him. Failure to find what he sought worsened the nausea.

'They killed Krohn. They even killed the dog … I don't know yet … No, I don't think Redman *did* this, but he recruited the spy who …' (Could Redman have found what Stanislas had overlooked? As British military intelligence, he'd recognise it!) 'I'll find out. I'm going there as soon as I've finished here.' (But not until he'd conducted a further and more frantic search of the house.) 'Redman's set off running, alone. Seems to be heading towards the city centre. I can't understand why he came; he must have known Blue Primrose had raided the house.' (Unless Redman knew Blue Primrose had failed to find the security plan, so he'd come in person to steal it.)

Stanislas ended the call, stared across the kitchen, swallowed, swore, prayed, and went to search the rest of the ransacked house. Ten minutes later, relief weakened his legs: the manila folder was hidden between two drawers in a worm-eaten dressing table that lay on its back, legs and mirror broken. He kissed the folder and stuffed it under his jerkin.

'Mangler? Stan again. Found it … How would *I* know which? The Ulyanova will know … Oh, right, I never … Well, it's the only manila folder here. Maybe she *did* take the other. It would have been the fake version. This must be the original.'

As he spoke, Stanislas sidled out of the house and towards the church surgery. Two teenage muggers advanced to steal his phone, but they recognised him and decided they'd be safer several streets away. Besides, the phone was too old to be worth nicking.

Then Stanislas discovered the manila folder was empty. Fury pulsed in his muscles. He turned on his heel, leapt on to his horse and galloped after Rory.

Tomen and Ariadne entered the church surgery and the children were swept from them by the institution's *yasimakoj*, the efficient curer-curates. Reassurance was immediate: tattooed and shaven-headed door wardens with studded noses and black leather uniforms whispered kind platitudes to the women and proffered tea and cakes on pink china.

Chapter 37

If you have an enemy, kill him.
   — *Efeef Krev Strlzhav, quoting Niccolò Machiavelli:*
     'The Prince'

'Change will be gradual,' said Klarissa. 'We'll replace the structures of feudalism piece by piece with Revolutionary ones. We won't frighten the people by rushing. But krevs' courts will be the first institutions to go.'

'How then will village cases be tried and justice done?' said Bresina.

'You believe justice is done *now*? A krev's court decides in the krev's interests. If the krev's interests aren't involved the court cares nothing about its verdict.'

Bresina felt like an ageing mother unable to out-argue a mature but still-rebellious daughter.

'What will you put in their place?'

'Regional courts under trained lawyers for major cases, village assemblies for minor ones. Consensus will determine justice.'

At terrible cost, thought Bresina, to the unpopular, the eccentric, the solitary, all who are harmless but different. Even now they were targets for bullying; under Klarissa's plan they'd be expelled or driven to suicide.

'Village assemblies would tear themselves apart, Klarissa. Peasant hates peasant, family hates family; there are quarrels, fights, brutality. Could they administer justice by *consensus*?'

The wisdom of ages inclined Klarissa's head.

'Britain is no model nation but she's had remarkable leaders. Her greatest prime minister in a century imposed few decisions; he held

139

his cabinet on a light rein and let them form policies by majority vote. That cabinet included men who detested him, men who detested each other. Yet it was an effective government. It transformed British society within six years. The right leaders – men such as Egrienne – will run village assemblies with like success.'

Bresina shook her head.

'How many leaders are the equal of Egrienne? If the whole of Britain produced only one in a century, could every Ruritanian village produce its own? Local assemblies would be disastrous for their communities.'

'Some will fail, Bresina, so we'll have to intervene. The rest will work – some better than others, but experience will improve them. You're too much the pessimist.'

To answer 'I've lived too long to be anything but a pessimist' would be absurd, thought Bresina; she was talking to Klarissa.

'As for the anger coursing through rural communities, the feuds and jealousies, the brutality and acts of vengeance … the ghrunli field relieves tensions.' Klarissa smiled. 'And there's solidarity. Villagers support each other. Village societies are stable.'

Bresina sighed.

'What about contact with the Faerie Realm? Only in feudal societies can the portals open. If you modernise Ruritania, what price our relationship with Faerie?'

'The British have a saying, Bresina: you can't make an omelette without breaking eggs. Our relationship with Faerie has stultified Ruritanian society for centuries. For the communal good, some relationships have to be controlled, even terminated.'

Bresina was sure that Klarissa didn't mean what she said, but she made no comment. It was enervating to argue with a zealot, however deeply loved.

Chapter 38

I have no idea why Rory Redman asks questions in my name.
— *The wee man from Milton Keynes*

The sky sagged, though the drizzle had abated. Rory dashed from the beleaguered house to a bakery on the other side of Vorgottenstrit and bought a sandwich and a bottle of water.

'Rory,' said the spirit of Professor Weisheitsliebhaber, 'if Barrington is pursuing you and you're running from him, you've joined SPAR by default.'

Rory bit the unidentifiable sandwich and shook his head.

'A former American president once told his people "Either you're with us or you're with the terrorists". False dichotomy. Many people disapproved of America's actions but disliked the terrorists more.'

He studied the mysterious repast. Thad's voice called from along the road.

'Rory, come back to the carriage. There are better places to run. And you will not find your way. You are a stranger here.'

Rory swallowed water from the bottle. It had a curious flavour. He frowned.

'I'll retrace the route you took, Thad. I'll be fine. I *desperately* need to run.'

He looked around. Scruffy unsmiling children had encircled Thad's carriage. One's face was entirely free of dirt, suggesting uncaring parents. Eyes glowering from grimy windows exerted tangible pressure. The horses were restive in their shafts. In a couple of minutes the wheels could be off and the carriage

141

supported on bricks, and the horses' legs might be next. But Thad controlled the kids by force of personality.

Unsuitable attire notwithstanding, Rory set off like a regular marathon winner. The clouds began to lift and the afternoon brightened. He put on his sunglasses. The spirit of Professor Weisheitsliebhaber spoke again:

'Are you running from Barrington or towards Klarissa? You shouldn't run towards Klarissa. Men like you chase women they don't intend to treat honourably much as dogs chase cars they don't intend to drive. And she wouldn't be interested.'

Rory masticated the sandwich, a challenge for a human mandible. He didn't believe he was running towards Klarissa. Klarissa was interesting but Ariadne was fascinating, though he wished she'd show more interest.

'I want to meet Klarissa. I have questions for her.'

'You think she'd explain herself to *you*? What do you know about her?'

The professor's scorn was corrosive. Rory swallowed a mouthful of sandwich.

'I know she's an attractive intelligent woman with expensive tastes. She has amazing climbing skills; my garden wall is used to train fruit trees and exclude vandals. She's an ardent revolutionary, a mistress of disguise, and possibly the illegitimate daughter of a former or current Krev Strlzhav. Her name is Klarissa Alterleta but she uses umpteen pseudonyms, including Klarissa Krefin Strlzhava. People respect and obey her.'

'Oh, very good, Rory. You're *far* too clever to become an American president.'

'I'm not American.'

'But you still know little about Klarissa. She *won't* explain herself to you.'

Rory detached himself from his interlocutor and focussed on running. An angry horseman on a parallel road kept track of him.

'Sillias? Stan. Redman *is* running towards the city centre. Deflect him to St Galen's … I'll call the others … Of course there are places to hide … I'm on my way!'

Chapter 39

All members of the Government of Ruritania accept this prohibition of the use of miasma-based weapons and agree to be bound according to the terms of this declaration.

The present Protocol, of which the Ruritanian and English texts are both authentic, shall be ratified immediately. It shall bear today's date.

The instruments of ratification of and accession to the present Protocol shall remain deposited in the archives of the High Bakery of Ruritania.

The present Protocol shall come into force from the date of deposit of its ratification, and, from that moment, shall become law throughout Ruritania.

IN WITNESS WHEREOF Her Sublime Majesty Anastassia, by the Grace of Asclepius Queen of Ruritania, has signed the present Protocol.

DONE at Strelsau in a single copy, this seventeenth day of June, One Thousand Nine Hundred and Eighty-Five.

> *— Protocol for the Prohibition of Miasma-based*
> *Weapons in Ruritania*

Thad's carriage overtook Rory. Thad and Tomen exhorted him in vain to climb aboard.

'Typical philosopher. Logographos,' said Ariadne. 'You'll never persuade him. Concrete mind: all mixed up and firmly set. He'll attract trouble as he always does, but he'll survive.'

'I wish you may be right.'

Thad drove on. Rory waved adieu. One or two other carriages

passed him as he ran. Riders trudged by on worn-out nags. Quiet for a capital city, thought Rory, but this was an area to avoid. The brightening sky did little to improve it.

'What's that rhyme about British weather?' he asked a dazed-looking tramp. *'We muse, while winters freeze our blood, Or we're welly-deep in summer, That though the British climate's good, The weather is a bummer.'*

But this is Ruritania, he reflected, where the weather seems better controlled. Recalls Ariadne's question about geography and climate and ecology and crop growth. Does the country's adjustable location ensure agricultural production is maximised? How else could the bakeries thrive and the hamsters be fed?

The professor's spirit intruded again on his thoughts.

'Random musings achieve nothing, Rory. You must make decisions. Who was it who asked, 'What has it got in its pocketses?' What has Rory Redman got in his pocketses?'

'I know what I've got in my pocketses. Someone was damned careless to leave it unattended. But I suppose they had to run when Blue Primrose arrived.'

'The SPAR leaders will need copies of both versions. And Barrington is smart enough to recognise the version you left at the Hilton as a fake.'

'It might take him long enough for the insight to be useless.'

Whew, thought Rory. Stomach not brilliant. Wanted food but ate too soon before running. Not sure about the bottled water. Don't like the look of the gang at the end of the street. Take detour. Rely on sense of direction. If they chase I'll outrun them despite stomach. Hand's sore, too. Hurts when you punch a wall.

'You now have two copies of the original document: one in your pocket, one in the lining of your suitcase,' said the professor. 'In your pocket is the one Klarissa stole from the canvas bag in Manchester. So neither SPAR nor Blue Primrose has the original. If you give it to SPAR, the Revolution will proceed and SPAR could win. If you give it to Blue Primrose, the Revolution will be crushed and many will die. But in the process you'll deliver yourself to Barrington and Tupsroot, who'll imprison you. Therefore, what you have in your pocketses can determine Ruritania's future, and yours.'

'Yeah. Well, I don't like Barrington and Tupsroot.'

'Careful, Rory. Emotional reaction against Blue Primrose and Colonel Barrington isn't conducive to rational decision-making. Basic dilemma: you keep the document, in which case Klarissa and friends could bite the dust; or you return it to SPAR, so you conspire with others to overthrow a nation's elected government, making you a foreign terrorist.'

Must everything have a meaning? thought Rory. *Beware the paradox, my son* … I really don't feel well. Light's out of focus. Alley's blurred. Is that another gang? If I turn here, then left at the next junction … *And while in uffish thought he ran, the paradox with eyes of flame* … Now I'm mumbling nonsense. Unoriginal nonsense. Keep running. Not well. Hand hurts. Can't decide. Where am I? Deploying logic to decide a nation's fate and can't find my way home. Wait. Big building yonder … I think … Could pick up a public carriage from there. Yes! How did I get *here*?

Head spinning, stomach churning, Rory staggered into St Galen's Square. Gasping and clutching his sides, he tottered through the Gardens. A voice spoke from a wooden seat beside the statue.

'Rory Redman! Well met once more!'

It was Dai O'Genies, author of the *Primer*, whom he'd met at Tomen's house.

'Huh? Dai! What are you doing here?'

'I belong on wooden seat. I am shabby old cripple. Did you not say it?'

Rory didn't recall saying it yet the phrase seemed familiar. *Déjà vu* again. Perhaps he understood why this chronic micro-anticipation was unsettling: the time interval between foreknowledge and event, if it existed, was too brief for action or speech to be amended. It seemed to shackle free will to the cold dungeon wall of determinism.

'Don't think so. Can't be sure. Mind on logic puzzle.'

'Ah. Paper that amuse Ariadne? She tell you statistic joke?'

'What paper? What joke? I don't know–'

Suddenly, people around them were running and shouting. As Rory wondered what had amused Ariadne, as he wrestled with his dilemma about the security plan, something rolled to a halt at his feet with a noise like an underwater firework. A rising spiral of green fumes embraced him. There was a yell of warning. Rory frowned.

'There could be a … what's the word? Problem. That's it – problem. Contradiction. Fallacy. Dizzying prospect. Vertiginous.' Something caught his eye. 'Oh, look! Isn't it glorious?'

Through thickening haze he saw Colonel Barrington and Ekwyor Tupsroot step through the Great Azure Door, point, and rush towards him. He smiled, enraptured. The Labyrinth shone with a thousand effulgent colours in multidimensional splendour, iridescent beauty beckoning the world. A skein of a hundred slug trails scintillated through a network of paths, lost in the vastness of light. Behind the sunglasses, Rory's eyes dilated with ecstasy.

From another world came cries and screams of fear and fury, shouts of command, gunfire, the whistle of flying arrows.

He took three wobbling steps towards the Labyrinth and fell over.

Chapter 40

The High Bakery goes into recess three weeks before the Solstice and the krevoj retire to their castles to prepare for the election. Their televised debates are pre-recorded. Hundreds of political minions distribute leaflets and posters in the cities, even in villages, and every back street bakery girds its loins for the imminent inundation of cakes for free distribution to the electorate. Ruritanian politicians are adept at cajoling voters.
— The Unideker Guide to Ruritania

In cellars below guarded hovels in three of Strelsau's less salubrious districts, forgers wrought by the light of tallow candles. Presses turned. The papers hand-written by Eldzhay were transmuted into parchment proclamations under the seeming authorisations of Hvimpy and Strlzhav. If Eldzhay approved, couriers would bear these masterpieces around the three cities, where they'd unlock the gates of havoc. If Eldzhay didn't approve, strips of them would grace the Lenmir Hotel's lavatory cubicles and the labours in cellars would resume.

*

In Castle Strlzhav, the krevjalem was modelling his new ceremonial robes: white cotton uniform, white apron and hat, embellished with family crest and Ruritanian fleur-de-lys. All Members of the High Bakery would attend the ceremonial cutting of the metacake in St Galen's Square on National Cake Day, together with the Queen and the rest of the royal family (except the Crown Prince, who would be croaking beside a swamp in the enchanted forest). All would be garbed in ceremonial robes. The moment when the Surgeon Archbishop wielded his sacred scalpel above the metacake would shimmer with national pride; packed crowds of hoi polloi would cheer and a thousand Ruritanian flags would wave. Once again, Krev Strlzhav would head the procession into the Gardens and assume the principal place. New robes were obligatory for the leader of the outgoing government. Impressive apparel could tilt the balance in the election.

No news of SPAR's activities had reached the krevjalem or his parliamentary colleagues or rivals; Blue Primrose had limited intelligence. So Krev Strlzhav was unaware of the forgeries in the guarded cellars, ignorant of the Ulyanova's arrival in far-off Strelsau. Aside from the fitting of the ceremonial robes, his mind was focussed on his castle bakery. He was determined to produce the most memorable metacake of the century. (SPAR shared his determination, albeit in a different sense of 'memorable'.) He was also intent on undermining Krev Hvimpy's electoral position.

Robe fitting completed, the krevjalem dismissed the tailors and summoned his family, chief retainers, secretaries, church clinicians, musicians and principal minions to the banqueting hall. Three ekwyroj of the Blue Primrose Order attended. He took his gilded seat on the dais, accepted the proffered goblet of Szipad Riesling and lit a specially-imported cigarette.

'Let us be clear about our mission,' he began. 'Government must ensure economic stability. It must seem to protect the poor and vulnerable, though at no cost to itself. It must keep a tight rein on the nation's purse strings. Government promises must appear to be delivered. Do any of us doubt we can appear to deliver them?'

There was a chorus of non-doubt.

'The electorate must be persuaded of the vacuity of Hvimpy's pledges. Of course they're seductive; they're meant to be seductive. *Ad hominem* attacks in political debate are distasteful, but Hvimpy is as treacherous as a baby's arse. He's the only krev who can hide behind a spiral staircase. He couldn't cross an empty room in a straight line. And his son is a disaster. To consign Ruritania's future to Hvimpy would be to descend into nightmare. If he were elected he'd either renege on his promises or ruin the country. He bleats about stimulating agriculture. How? He won't say. He wants to raise tax revenues. How? Only by imposing a greater tax burden on those who have no wish to afford it! He claims this crippling burden will finance his national hovel-building programme. Taurocoprology! Hovel-building is the business of private owners, the krevoj and their families, who will attend to it in their own time and their own interests. Relief for the homeless must be left in the hands of the wealthy, not trampled under the clod-hopping boots of government. As for Hvimpy's much-vaunted National Minimum Cake Provision, he says it will rise in line with economic performance. But his policies will *depress* economic performance, so what price his National Minimum Cake Provision? Anyway, his Caraway Angel Cake is crap.'

There was a standing ovation. The hall echoed. Krev Strlzhav stubbed out his cigarette in an onyx ashtray. A minion scuttled forward and replaced the ashtray with a silver one.

'This,' continued the krevjalem, 'is our message to the voters. They know we never vacillate, never diverge from our course. But we *must* make them realise disaster would ensue were they to elect our main rival. Can we, during the short time left before election day, hammer this message through enough of their thick ignorant skulls to ensure that responsible government is maintained?'

The audience was unanimous. Krev Strlzhav's followers were ready to go forth and hammer.

'Do we,' wondered His Excellency, 'have any questions or concerns?'

'There's a message from Krev Schammerbass, sir, asking whether the science budget will be increased next year – assuming, that is … well, you understand.'

149

The krev smiled and lit another specially-imported cigarette.

'Is Krev Schammerbass still in England or Hungary or Switzerland, or has he returned? No matter: he'll be here for the Solstice. Tell him adjustments to the science budget may be discussed after the ceremony, if I have time. Anything else?'

'Update on the terrorist threat, Your Excellency.' An ekwyrin displayed a self-important clipboard.

'Yes, Ekwyrin? I understand the British military personnel will arrive tomorrow. The rumours of insurrection planned for National Cake Day may be unfounded, in which case their presence will be unnecessary; we have faith in the Order of the Blue Primrose; but the first duty of the nation's government is to ensure the security of her people, which is to say her aristocracy. What is your update?'

'Britain's Colonel Barrington has arrived in Strelsau, Your Excellency, along with Ekwyor Tupsroota. His soldiers will follow shortly. We believe many peripheral members of SPAR have been scared into sanity by the prospect of action in place of rhetoric and rumour, so any attempted insurrection could be stillborn. Nevertheless ...'

'Yes?'

'Your Excellency, this is delicate information. You might prefer to hear it in private.'

'No, Ekwyrin. Discretion is necessary for security matters; otherwise we have no secrets in this hall, private affairs excepted.' The krev smiled around the room. 'I'm sure no one will be indiscreet. I dislike having to rip out tongues. So *messy*. Speak on, Ekwyrin.'

The ekwyrin licked his lips and evinced an urge to urinate.

'Er ... An alleged leader of SPAR, perhaps *the* leader, has entered Ruritania. We received intelligence of her whereabouts in Strelsau–'

'*Her*? You mean the so-called Ulyanova? A real person, not just a tale to frighten children? Is she in custody? Has she been interrogated?'

'Unfortunately not, sir. We sent a force to arrest her but she'd gone. We … Well, we're sure she's left the city. It's … er … it's suspected she could be somewhere around here.'

'Around here? You believe she could be *somewhere in my own krefmark*? Where? Don't you *know*?'

'Not exactly, sir. Of course, we're searching–'

'I should hope so, Ekwyrin! What *is* known about this female?'

'We have her photograph, Your Excellency, and her real name is believed to be Klarissa Alterleta. But she uses assumed names. Er …'

'Well?'

'I beg Your Excellency's pardon, but it seems she's been calling herself … er … Klarissa Krefin Strlzhava.'

A murmur rose and swelled until the hall boiled with vocal rage. Krev Strlzhav opened and closed his eyes several times. Then he smiled and raised a manicured hand. His gold signet ring shone. Silence fell like a guillotine blade.

'Impertinence of such magnitude almost merits respect,' he said. 'An example will be made of this female; after the trial, needless to say. I look forward to it. We've not had a public execution in Strelsau for several years.' His face grew reflective. 'What's the expression? *Pour décourager les autres*?' He nodded to the ekwyrin and rose from his gilded seat. Everyone stood. 'That will be all. Attend to your duties. Hammer the skulls of the unwashed. Ensure Hvimpy is not elected. Capture the impertinent female and make her talk, in between screams. I shall now return to the bakery.'

The metacake was almost ready for dispatch to Strelsau. It would be dispatched under heavy guard, he decided. SPAR was unlikely to be well enough organised to interfere with it, but he wouldn't trust Hvimpy a smallbit.

The castle musicians accompanied his stroll to the bakery.

Chapter 41

Television weather forecasts in Ruritania are conveyed through the medium of dance. Most people find the routines easy to interpret once they grow accustomed to them. Some extreme weather events cannot be danced before the nine o'clock watershed, but these are rare. There is a cause-effect debate among experts: does the dance foretell the weather or does it cause it? This long-running controversy dominates many issues of the Journal of Terpsichorean Meteorology. Laypeople care little about the answer; they wish only for assurance that the prediction, or magical intervention, is approximately accurate.
— The Unideker Guide to Ruritania

The evening meal in Klatzierstrit 27 was tense. Where was Rory?

'I suppose the silly chump's got into another scrape and will have to be rescued,' said Ariadne. 'I'd like to know where he is, though.'

While she phoned around hire stables for a horse to take her to Castle Bauntzi, Thad switched on the television. Two people were dancing, without music, in front of a weather map. Ariadne recalled that the forecast always preceded the news. According to the weatherdancers it would continue fine and warm in the east of the country, with light rain during the nights, but there would be cloud and occasional showers around Strelsau with a maximum temperature of seventeen Réaumur. The dancers finished their routine, bowed to the camera and departed. The weather map faded.

Advertisements appeared. An enthusiastic man in a track-suit extolled a new dried cream-cake formulation, or perhaps the packet containing it. There was a furniture sale, eulogised in a gabble verging on hysteria. Then the news began. The lead item pulled all three viewers in Klatzierstrit 27 to their feet.

The cameras focussed on St Galen's Square. Police and Blue Primrose officials guarded a crime scene, ignoring each other. The reporter's tone was grave.

A miasma grenade had been thrown in the Gardens that afternoon. The perpetrator was believed to have been a SPAR activist. He and two of his accomplices had been shot dead by Blue Primrose ekwyroj. Several bystanders and two officials had been injured, one seriously. Other terrorists were believed to have been wounded in the fire-fight following the incident but had escaped. An inquiry had been launched. The miasma victims had been rushed by Faerie Flight to intensive care in St Avicenna's cathedral hospital in Hrincacz. One victim, described as a British tourist, was in a critical condition. According to a statement from the Great Azure Door he'd been arrested. Blue Primrose ekwyroj were guarding him at St Avicenna's. If he recovered he would be questioned after his discharge from medico-ecclesiastical care.

Two bakers' assistants were interviewed. They feared the incident could herald a spate of similar attacks in public places.

An expert in the studio pontificated about the history of SPAR and the implications of such an atrocity in the centre of the capital city when National Cake Day and the election were imminent.

Klatzierstrit 27 echoed with the muffled drum-beat of heavy hearts. No one heard the rest of the news. What had Rory done? Was he still alive?

'We have to go to Hrincacz,' said Tomen.

Chapter 42

Mr Redman's success in avoiding the forces of law, notwithstanding his imaginative enterprises, testifies to his cleverness and good fortune. But cleverness has its limits and good fortune runs a finite course. Sooner or later, therefore, Mr Redman's luck will run out and he will fall into the hands either of law enforcement agencies or of criminals more ruthless than himself.

— Cerberus D. Gardog: 'A College Porter's
Recollections of Unconventional Undergraduates'

An activist stumbled faint from blood loss into the Lenmir Hotel. Her darkening mind knew she must tender a report. The manager guided her to a sofa in a private room and summoned Mangler. Mangler assembled fragments of news from her and felt his face whiten. He must tell the other leaders and they must send information to the Ulyanova.

'We'll get you to a church surgery run by Puritans,' he said. 'You're going to be okay.'

It was the conventional lie to the fatally wounded. He prised the blood-stained manila folder from the activist's hand as consciousness bade her farewell.

Eldzhay's rage when he heard the news was disquieting. Neither his voice nor his face betrayed emotion, but the furniture seemed to hide in the room's dark corners.

'Mangler, your cell must recover the bodies of Stanislas and our other comrades. You, together with Sillias, must then prepare to amend the metacake.'

Mangler nodded.

'The messenger from St Galen's Square brought this, Eldzhay.' He handed over the folder. 'She took it from Stan's pocket.'

Eldzhay opened it and scowled.

'Empty. Where did Stan put the document? Why carry just the folder? And why did he throw a miasma grenade in the middle of the afternoon in full view of the Great Azure Door?'

Mangler said he believed Stanislas had been following Klarissa's order to dispose of Rory Redman. He had no idea where the security plan was.

'Eldzhay, Blue Primrose raided Vorgottenstrit 13, and Stan reported that Redman followed them there. If the document was in the house, not just the folder, it follows that Redman took it and left the folder behind.'

Eldzhay rose and went to the window. The view over the city was bleak.

'Where is Redman?'

'Taken to Hrincacz, Eldzhay. He might be dead; he might recover. At least he's out of action. But he's under arrest. Blue Primrose are guarding him in St Avicenna's.'

There was a short burst of inarticulate fury, but Eldzhay recovered his self-control in the clenching of a loaf-sized fist.

'Redman doesn't command the British force. The British will be led by Colonel Barrington. The Ulyanova told me and Arraitch. She couldn't have declared Redman… Who's responsible for the misunderstanding?'

'We only received her order via Stan, Eldzhay. When the Ulyanova returned from Britain she stayed with him in Vorgottenstrit 13. She must have had reason for issuing the order.' Mangler gulped. 'Perhaps Stan … misinterpreted.'

Eldzhay nodded.

'Stan can no longer answer questions.'

'I wish the Ulyanova were here,' said Mangler. 'Sillias and I will deal with the metacake as best we can but she'd do it better.'

'You'll do it equally well because you've no choice. However, there's an even more urgent task. I'll summon another conclave in two hours.' Eldzhay turned from the window and stared at Mangler. 'If Redman stole the security plan from Vorgottenstrit and is now in St Avicenna's, we must get to him there despite the Blue Primrose guard so we can recover the plan. And since he's now had time to read it, we must ensure he remains inactive until the Revolutionary government is in place. Or permanently. Understood, Mangler?'

Chapter 43

Feverfew (Tanacetum parthenium L.) (Asteraceae) is deployed to treat fevers, migraine headaches, rheumatoid arthritis, stomach aches, toothaches, insect bites, infertility, labour pains, psoriasis, allergies, asthma, tinnitus, dizziness, nausea and vomiting. It is used to combat cancers, inflammation, cardiac insufficiency and spasms, and to prepare an excellent enema for worms. The herb has a long history of medical use, especially among Greek, Persian and early European herbalists. It is cultivated widely, particularly in Ruritania, where there are increasing reports of its therapeutic efficacy against several categories of miasmata.
  — *The Hrincacz Herbal*

Rory thought it an adumbration of the afterlife, albeit blurred: a high stone-vaulted roof, gentle stained-glass light, impressions of passing angels, the soft chanting of a choir. His bed was comfortable and his mind floated. But there was contrary evidence: a headache, a sore back, a bandaged hand, and aromas of sickness and disinfectant mingled with incense. There was also a recent and unsettling dream, which for once didn't involve clowns; a fairytale prince's kiss had forced his eyes half-open. He lacked the will and the energy to wipe his mouth or spit.

'Ah. Methinks the sleeper awaketh.'

The words were half-recognisable. The voice seemed familiar but its levity cloaked the imminence of tears. If he could turn his head and keep his eyes from closing he might identify the speaker. He – no, she – might want to discuss the paradox in the Gödelpus Theorem. Or had that discovery been another dream, a chimera, doomed to fade in the light of day or Paradise? He contrived to look to his right without head movement. The figure beside him was out of focus but it had a 36DD bust.

'Ariadne?'

The figure gasped and leapt to her feet.

'He's awake, he recognised me!'

Two angels zoomed towards them. Ariadne put her hands over her face and sobbed.

'Explains dream,' whispered Rory.

One of the angels addressed him in English. Its voice was deep, calm and accented.

'Can you tell us dream, Pan Redman? Is Pana Sowerby in dream?'

'No. Prince. Fairy.'

Ariadne and the angels exchanged questioning looks.

'Dream tell us treatment, Pan Redman. For cure, it is needed you recall dream soon you wake … as soon as you waken. Try to tell us dream.'

Rory let his eyes close.

'Many dreams,' he muttered.

'Talking is hard. This we know. But try, please, tell all you can.'

Rory breathed without speaking. A minute passed. Ariadne and the angels waited. Through a haze of semi-consciousness he sensed their expectation.

'Colours,' he murmured. 'Shapes. Labyrinth. Flying … No, boat; rough river. Contradiction in Theorem. Face down in desert. Back burned. Old professor, talked about Mill. Greatest happiness. Green snake climbed me. Asky touched my head. Asky said …'

'Yes, Pan Redman? What said Asky?'

'*Tanacetum parthenium*. Then prince. Kiss. Ugh!'

Ariadne stopped crying.

'Oh, bugger,' she said, 'he's going to puke again!'

'No, dear madam. Stomach is voided. Allow him now to rest. Asclepius has spoken.'

Rory went to sleep. The two Blue Primrose guards beside the door remained awake. Ariadne picked up her bag and walked down the south aisle of the cathedral hospital. The medipriest followed her.

'Those two have one mediocre brain between them,' said Ariadne, pointing at the guards, 'and I don't appreciate the way they search me when I enter or leave the building. Tomen will come and sit with Rory soon, or maybe Thad … Look, Cure-director, I don't mean to seem rude, but treating a patient as sick as Rory with antiquated herbal remedies seems to me like treating a car crash victim with reflexology.'

The medipriest smiled.

'You are brought up in Pasteurian-Kochian heresy, Pana Sowerby. True medical religion is unknown for you. Your doctors are not trained in miasmology. Is this not so?'

'You're right. We believe infections are caused by microorganisms, not miasmata. We'd call the thing that nearly killed Rory a germ warfare weapon, and they're banned by international treaty. *Our* doctors would have him wired up to a dozen monitors and they'd be treating him with glucose-saline drips and massive doses of broad-spectrum antibiotics, not with dream-derived herbal cures and venesection and cupping glasses and purges and incense–'

'And your doctors make him live, Pana Sowerby, or does he in your country die?' For a moment the medipriest looked ferocious, then he smiled again. 'Forgive, please. I ask not fair question. This I tell you: miasma grenade is illegal also in Ruritania, and maker must go into prison.' The medipriest looked around the chapel-cubicles, each with its bed, and his voice softened. 'Your presence beside patient does much for cure. I thank you. Before you leave, I ask help. Much of Pan Redman's dreaming I understand. Visit of Asclepius – "Asky" in dream – is most important. Green snake is fume from grenade *and* sign of

Asclepius. Bright colour: he see light when he wake, maybe
Strelsau Labyrinth when attack made. Rough river, Faerie Flight
journey. Much about philosophy; he is philosopher. But at end,
he say "prince" and "kiss", and somehow it is about you. Can you
explain this?'

Ariadne managed a weary grin.

'I can guess. When he arrived in Strelsau he was exhausted
and slept for ages. When he came downstairs I said something
potty about the fairytale prince kissing him awake. I think he
sensed I was beside him here when he started to recover
consciousness, so he recalled my daft remark and it turned into
a half-waking dream.'

The medipriest bowed. There was no mockery in the gesture.

'You come work with us, dear madam, as dream interpreter.
Again I thank you.'

Chapter 44

To the foreign visitor, the Ruritanian general election may seem a charade. If the composition of the High Bakery remains unchanged after the election and only the title 'krevjalem' is at stake, why do political debates become heated, even vitriolic? Why should there be an electoral contest at all? The answer is that the krevjalem's bakery will profit during the year that follows, and all his or her supporters in the High Bakery will prosper. The loser of the election, and those who backed him or her, will profit less. Therefore, money not policy lies at the core of political debate in Ruritania. In this regard, Ruritania no doubt differs from other nations.

— The Unideker Guide to Ruritania

Krev Hvimpy cackled. His castle artist had designed a new election poster. It portrayed the visage of Krev Strlzhav flanked by the faces of Groucho Marx on one side and Joseph Stalin on the other. The juxtaposition revealed Strlzhav as a moustachioed amalgam of comedian and tyrant, an amalgam compounded by a mad alchemist in a lightning-bedevilled garret. Still cackling, the krev flung a thousand raldoloj on to the cold stone floor, patting the artist's head as he scrambled after the reward. The omnipresent draughts of Castle Hvimpy amused themselves with the scattered bank notes.

The krev's buoyant mood persisted: the opinion poll he chose to believe put him slightly ahead of Strlzhav. He cackled again, placed a cigarette in a gilded holder and lit it from a bejewelled methane lamp.

Krev Hvimpy wasn't handsome, even in his own estimation. He was small and slight, his hair was thin, and a fall from a horse in early life had twisted his spine and afflicted him with what the medipriests called 'extorsion of the eye and vertical diplopia caused by trauma to the trochlear nerve'. There was no effective treatment, they said. He'd tried falling off the other side of his horse but that hadn't helped. So he tilted his head whenever he read documents or talked to people. The tilt compensated for the extorsion of the eye and it conveyed an impression of cunning, wisdom and deceitfulness, invaluable in a politician. To suppress his back pain, he drank. To suppress his disappointment about his son, whom he'd compelled to join Blue Primrose to make a man of him, he drank more.

He retired to his private chamber to slurp a goblet of mead and contemplate his post-election glory: the joy of watching Strlzhav make his defeated way to Dzhumpinpork Palace and tender his resignation to the Queen; Her Majesty's summons; her command to form the new government; his humble acquiescence. He'd hold a banquet the same evening and he'd invite Strlzhav. Always, he sniggered, one must be generous in victory. He grinned at his reflection in the gilded mirror and raised his goblet in salute.

A minion scratched at the door and entered, head bowed.

'Your Excellency, an ekwyor of Blue Primrose craves an audience.'

'Does he?' The krev gulped the rest of the mead. He loved mead. He paid to maintain the hives; his peasants collected the honey and fermented it; he pocketed the proceeds. It was a perfect economic cycle. The peasants were content because they received supplies of Caraway Angel Cake. 'Right, send him in.'

The krev lounged in his ornate chair. The ekwyor marched into the room on authoritative boots, big and grim and pulsating with urgency. He greeted the krev with brusque deference and held out a crumpled, mud-smeared sheet of paper.

'Szipad's crawling with copies of this. There's a riot. The police are as effective against angry mobs as a stream of cat wee against a forest fire, and the Surgeon Bishop's pissed out of his head as usual. I respectfully ask Your Excellency to read the paper.'

His Excellency read it and his buoyant mood evaporated. His face couldn't decide whether to turn puce or pale. He leapt to his feet, screwed up the paper and threw it across the room.

'It's a damned lie, Ekwyor! It's as near as dammit a statistic! My government will make changes, but – nationalise Strlzhav's bakery? Can't everyone see the notion's absurd? The nation's purse couldn't afford it!'

'Yes, sir. But Krevjalem Strlzhav's supporters in Szipad don't think it's absurd. Bakeries on both sides have been attacked: there are fires, lootings, armed gangs roaming the streets … I understand the same thing's happening in other cities. I'm bound to ask, sir, whether you knew anything about this document before it became public.'

'Of course I didn't! Do you imagine I'd countenance something so fantastical and inflammatory? Do you?'

'No, sir, but some of your less intelligent supporters might. There are people who're always eager to cause trouble, and saving Your Excellency's presence, election times give them opportunities.'

'I won't tolerate such people among my supporters, Ekwyor! Have you spoken to Krev Strlzhav? He needs to know. He's still krevjalem, still head of government, so it's his job to suppress civil unrest.'

The ekwyor swallowed.

'It's being done, sir. If I may suggest it, Your Excellency might wish to issue an unequivocal denial of involvement in this matter and appeal to your supporters for calm.'

The krev glared.

'Fancy yourself as a politician, do you? Got your own bakery? Family connections? Maybe you're right, though.' He pulled a rope beside the mirror. A bell tolled in the bowels of the castle. 'My secretary will compose the denial. I thank Blue Primrose for drawing the matter to my attention.'

163

He nodded, but the ekwyor didn't bow himself out. He remained, upright and forbidding.

'Is there something else?'

'With respect, Your Excellency: if your supporters weren't responsible for this fake proclamation, who was?'

The krev began to ask how the devil he should know when the answer sprang up and smacked him between the eyes.

'Are you suggesting this is the work of terrorists?'

The ekwyor's head gave a single nod.

'Seems likely, sir.'

'What motive …? Oh, of course. They want to provoke civil unrest. They want to keep Blue Primrose and the police at full stretch while they throw their tedious little tantrums about usurping the democratically elected government and imposing healthy diets and all the rest of their infantile nonsense. Do you know what they're planning?'

'We're not clear about it, sir. It's not for me to judge, but if this *is* the work of SPAR, it could mean the rumours of a major insurrection on National Cake Day are true. Our British advisers take it seriously.'

The krev held up his hand for silence. He paced the room and tried to look as if he was thinking. The secretary arrived, glanced at the scene and remained outside. The krev beckoned her in.

'We've a denial to issue, Trescreya. The phrasing must be precise. Thirty copies to be ready for distribution around all three cities by midnight.' The krev turned again to the ekwyor. 'SPAR involvement may seem plausible, but is there evidence?'

'No direct evidence, Your Excellency, but terrorist activity has increased. A couple of days ago there was a miasma grenade attack in the middle of Strelsau. Three terrorists were shot dead and there were other fatalities including an ekwyrin. We'd received intelligence two days earlier of a SPAR leader returning to the country, perhaps the so-called Ulyanova. She's now believed to be hiding in a village near Lake Brojginzha. A detachment of five ekwyrinoj under the command of an experienced ekwyor was sent to arrest her. News reached us two hours ago: three of the ekwyrinoj have been found with arrows through their hearts. The others in the detachment are missing.'

The secretary gasped. The krev felt faint.

'This happened in Strlzhav's krefmark? Great Asclepius, how does the fool think he can govern the country when he can't control his own peasants? Take reprisals, Ekwyor. Krev Strlzhav should select a village for extermination. If this terrorist leader doesn't give herself up, wipe out another, then another. News will spread. If the female still doesn't hand herself in, the riff-raff will drag her to you before more than a handful of villages have been destroyed. And there'll be no significant loss of productivity. Peasants breed fast. They'll replace the labour force in two wags of a Spitz's tail.'

Chapter 45

While Asclepius was a baby, his mortal mother Koronis having died in childbirth, his father – the god Apollo – carried him to the centaur Chiron, who raised him and taught him the art of medicine. As a child, Asclepius exhibited kindness to all creatures, especially slugs; and in return, a giant slug licked his ears clean and taught him secret knowledge of healing. According to some traditions, a green snake rather than a slug licked out the child's ears, which explains why the sign of Asclepius is often a rod wreathed with a snake rather than a slug. As he grew older, Asclepius surpassed both Chiron and Apollo in his proficiency as a healer.

— The Hrincacz Herbal

Rory contemplated the vaulted ceiling: half-recalled dream or forgotten episode of consciousness? No choir sang now but soft footfalls echoed. The stained glass light had gone; candles flickered in sconces and lanterns hurried to and fro. Tentative experiments proved he could move his limbs. His head ached less but his back was sore.

He looked to the right. On the pew beside his bed sat Thad Masim.

'Thad!'

A shout from the rooftop would have elicited no greater response than his hoarse whisper.

'Rory! Awake! Ariadne has been beside your bed since you were admitted. Now she has gone to the hotel to sleep. I shall call the duty medipriest.'

Rory wanted to ask 'The what?' but Thad had disappeared. He returned a few moments later accompanied by a middle-aged woman wearing white clerical garb and plastic gloves. A green snake coiled around a large cross was embroidered on the front of her gown. She carried a stethoscope.

'Pan Redman. How feel you?'

'Full of clichés.'

The woman's face demanded enlightenment. Thad shook his head.

'We do not comprehend.'

Rory paused.

'Cliché the first: where am I?'

'You are in cathedral hospital of St Avicenna, Hrincacz.'

Rory digested this.

'Cliché the second: what happened? I remember talking to Dai ... then just dreams, I think.'

Thad recounted the St Galen's Square drama and explained the Faerie Flight emergency transport system.

'It is the only means of rapid travel to Hrincacz. It required authorisation, but His Eminence the Surgeon Archbishop responds quickly in a crisis. It was just as well he does, Rory. Miasma grenades are nasty. Blue Primrose will seek the perpetrators.'

Rory frowned. What in the name of the wee man from Milton Keynes was a miasma grenade?

'Cliché the third: how long have I been here?'

'Three days.'

Rory's frown deepened. He was about to speak again when the woman rapped:

'No more talk, Pan Redman, until I examine. Category 3B miasma should not be fatal, but you have also evil stomach content. You almost die.'

The examination was not unlike its British counterpart. The woman grunted and wrote on a slate. Rory lay passive until the lantern was brought near his face, whereupon his eyes watered and he flinched. When the ritual ended the medipriest stood.

'You are lucky.'

'First time for everything,' said Rory.

'Others not lucky.'

'Meaning?'

'Dead.'

'Dai?'

'Dead on arrival.'

Rory felt sorrow clench him. Dai had had bowel cancer, but death by terrorist atrocity was even more unfair than death by natural causes.

'What's the prognosis, Cure-director?' asked Thad.

The woman's smile warmed her face by two point five degrees.

'Pan Redman make full recovery. He have luck because young, fit, healthy, and good friend, and best care we can make. Stimulate mind, make him to walk. Now I go treat new hyperglykismaphagia case.'

She strode towards another chapel-cubicle, carrying a device resembling a hand-pumped vacuum cleaner with a sink plunger attachment. Rory started to climb out of bed.

'What are you doing?' said Thad.

'Making me to walk. You heard the lady. Tread beside me, Thad. As we walk, stimulate mind. Don't let me fall but please don't touch my back; feels scalded.'

The ten-minute journey took them to the far wall of the cathedral hospital and back. The two Blue Primrose guards left their post beside the door and followed them; Rory ignored them. Candlelight shone on faces surrounding a bed, transmuting the tableau to a Joseph Wright painting. Those fixed stares belied the false levity, uncomfortable solemnity and compulsive loquaciousness of hospital visitors everywhere. Rory sensed guarded references, taboos upon everyday words.

'Were Dai's family with him?' asked Rory.

'He had no family except an estranged son. Tomen and I made funeral arrangements.'

'You are kind people.'

'We brought your suitcase.'

'Ah. There's something in it … Thad, how *do* people rate Krev Schammerbass?'

Thad smiled.

'What do you mean by "people"? Those who know him and his work respect his intellect and diligence. Some do not trust him. He lives abroad much of the time, but he keeps his finger on the pulse of Ruritanian science. And on politics, though from a distance.'

'I know he has houses abroad. Thad … could he be a SPAR supporter?'

Thad was silent.

'He believes SPAR's revolution will succeed,' said Rory, 'and he's afraid someone is trying to kill him. His house in England is isolated. It has bullet-proof windows and armed guards. And when I took that batch of papers from the warehouse, he made it easy for a well-briefed agent to mug me and steal what SPAR wanted.'

'Klarissa, you mean. The Ulyanova.'

'Yes. So if and when the revolution succeeds, he'll be able to claim–'

'It is fine to say this to me, Rory, but please do not let others overhear. Krev Schammerbass has influence. He is powerful and rich; a natural enemy of SPAR, not a friend. And he is not a man to cross.'

'You don't say. I could add more suspicions … However, if you look inside the lining of the lid of my suitcase, you'll find a photocopy of what our MI7 people were supposed to receive from him: the document Klarissa stole from the consignment. Use it as you think best. MI7 and Blue Primrose have a useless fake version, which I believe Klarissa wrote.'

Thad took the photocopy and said farewell. No one with lesser authority could have smuggled it past the Blue Primrose guards, who were now back in post beside the door. And while the guards were arguing with Thad, Rory took the original document he'd recovered from Vorgottenstrit from his jacket pocket and hid it in the niche behind the statue of St William Harvey in his chapel-cubicle.

Chapter 46

The role of contiguity and territorial issues in conditioning rival forces toward increasingly intense conflict has been a persistent theme in the literature concerning civil unrest. In this article we investigate one particular aspect of the escalation puzzle in regard to these two dimensions, namely, their influence on the probability that militarised disputes will escalate in hostility and severity once the initial threshold of conflict has been passed. Ordinal level analyses reveal an interesting pattern: neither geographical proximity nor the type of issue underlying the conflict produce the expected positive effect in terms of hostility escalation. However, both these factors significantly increase the likelihood that conflict episodes will be marred by increasing numbers of lives lost, once force has first been used.

— *W. Sniper and B. Crater (2012), 'How to escalate civil disturbance', Journal for Stating the Bleeding Obvious in a Needlessly Obscure Way 14, 17-35.*

The ekwyor watched Krev Strlzhav's moustache gyrate. He imagined it was on the verge of parting company with His Excellency's upper lip and flying who knew whither.

'No doubt Hvimpy deserves this absurd threat.' The krevjalem's voice was silky with wrath. 'However, the meanest intelligence could see it's forged. Of course, our unwashed hoi polloi lack the meanest intelligence. You suggest the forgery was produced by terrorists. I suggest it's Hvimpy's pathetic attempt to discredit me. All he's accomplished is to set fire to Hrincacz.'

'Well, not *all* of Hrincacz, sir, but there's been burning and looting right enough. Same in other cities: gangs of rival supporters wandering the streets, drinking looted wine, singing out of key, beating each other's heads with big sticks and ceramic utensils ... Noisy, it is. Gangs throw bits of cake, too. Police run away.'

His Excellency made a rude noise and lit a specially imported cigarette.

'Yesterday, sir,' said the Ekwyor, 'another document appeared, supposed to have been written by Krev Hvimpy, and it–'

'I know. I thought it was genuine, but after today's outrage I suppose it too could have been forged. Both documents have caused riots. No one benefits from riots except rioters.'

And terrorists, thought the ekwyor.

'Thing is, Your Excellency, with all this happening, HQ haven't been able to send any reinforcements from Strelsau, so we don't have the numbers to hunt the female terrorist leader; you know, the one who's supposed to be hiding around here. This trouble in the cities will drag more of us away. And we've lost five ekwyrinoj and an ekwyor in the hunt, sir.'

'What do you mean, "lost five ekwyrinoj and an ekwyor"? Losing six colleagues is rank carelessness, Ekwyor. Where are they?'

'Dunno about three of them, sir, they've just disappeared, but the other three are underground. I don't mean sneaking around in plain clothes. I mean we've had to bury them on account of them being dead.'

The krev crushed out his cigarette and lit another. He ruminated.

'How did they die?'

'Shot through the heart. No idea who done it, but they knew the area and they knew how to use bows and arrows.' The ekwyor cleared his throat. He didn't mention that three other ekwyrinoj had been found slaughtered not far from the Szipad road. 'Could suggest bad apples in Your Excellency's peasant barrel.'

'Undoubtedly.' The krev's moustache stopped writhing and metamorphosed into a pediment over a noble smile. 'You won't catch the murderers unless other peasants name them, Ekwyor. There's little room in my heart for Krev Hvimpy – there's barely room in my dungeon – but he's suggested how the terrorist female can be nailed. I heard about it earlier. I'm sure you're prepared to implement his proposal.'

'With pleasure, sir, but we'll need your permission because this is–'

'My krefmark. Of course. You have my consent; indeed, you have my order. My secretary will give it to you in writing.'

Chapter 47

Experimental results in psychology usually require statistical analysis. The statistics tell you how credible your conclusion is. It works like this. Suppose the conclusion's wrong, i.e. your experimental findings are misleading. In that case, if you repeated the same experiment a hundred times, only a very few of the repetitions would, by chance, give the same misleading results. However, if out of the one hundred replicates you got the same results ninety-five or more times, you'd have good grounds for believing your conclusion. We describe such results as 'significant at the five percent level', i.e. there's no more than a one-in-twenty chance they're misleading you. In practice, life's too short to repeat an experiment a hundred times, so you do the statistics instead.

— I.M. Conningyu, 'Statistics for Psychology,'
Ruritanian Academy of Science Press

'You sure about this?'

Ariadne watched Rory walk across the cathedral hospital in a straight line, unsupported, under the eyes of the Blue Primrose guards. The effort was palpable.

'Yep. Want to know more about Faerie physics, since a so-called Faerie Flight got me here.'

'Will the medipriests let you travel to Hrincacz University for a public lecture?'

'Ask them, Ariadne. We can go in the carriage you took from the hotel, so what's the problem? Apart from making me pay my half of the fare. Of course, those Blue Primrose guards will have to accompany us to make sure I don't run away. Do them good to have an outing and a bit of education. They're getting bored. I've cajoled the medipriests into convincing them that a visit to the physics department is part of my treatment.'

Ariadne aimed a punch at Rory's ear and half-suppressed a grin.

'You're impossible.'

'I can't be impossible; I exist. I'm just improbable. *En route*, you can explain the psychology paper with "amusing statistics" Dai was trying to tell me about when the miasma grenade went off. "Stimulate mind", as one medipriest put it.'

They left the cathedral hospital and Rory mounted the carriage unaided, albeit slowly. He and Ariadne sat side by side, facing two Blue Primrose guards who epitomised sulk. A medipriest with a mischievous grin placed himself between them.

'Yes, that paper,' said Ariadne. 'It was about experimenter bias in psychology experiments. The authors studied a class of students. Each student picked twelve naïve subjects, mainly friends and family. Each subject was shown photos of different people and was asked the same question about every photo: "Is this person experiencing success or failure?" Half the students had been told to expect mostly "success" responses, the other half mostly "failure" responses. Most subjects said "success" if the student had been told expect "success" answers, and "failure" otherwise. The experimental design was rigorous; valid, no question. The results were significant at the five percent level. Conclusion: there's experimenter bias in psychology experiments.'

Rory frowned.

'No. The conclusion should be "There has been experimenter bias in one psychology experiment". But if the design was valid beyond reasonable doubt, there's a paradox.'

The medipriest's eyebrows rose. The Blue Primrose guards looked vacant. Ariadne grinned.

'Oh, you and your paradoxes! What struck *me* were the follow-up studies. There were nineteen separate attempts to repeat the experiment. They all gave negative results, showing there's *no* significant experimenter bias. *None of them got published.*'

Rory shrugged.

'Remember what you told me about Öst and Brün? Negative findings are hard to publish unless the principal author is pals with an editor. As for the paradox arising from the paper, let's play Socratic dialogues for the rest of this journey.'

'Not sure I know how.'

'Of course you do. I'll play Socrates to begin with, then we'll swap. Ignore the statistics for now, Ariadne. The conclusion of the paper is either true or false. Do you agree?'

'Yes, Rory. It must be true or false.'

'Therefore, it is either the case that psychology studies are prone to experimenter bias, or – if the conclusion is false – at least one psychology study is *not* prone to experimenter bias. Is this not so?'

'I see no alternative, Rory.'

'Let's suppose it's true. In other words, psychology studies are prone to experimenter bias. But wasn't the experiment itself a psychology study?'

'Undoubtedly so, Rory.'

'So assuming the conclusion to be true, the study demonstrating its truth was subject to experimenter bias.'

The medipriest scratched his head. The Blue Primrose guards were almost asleep. Ariadne pondered Rory's reasoning.

'The inference is inescapable, Rory,' she said at last.

'But if a study is susceptible to experimenter bias,' said Rory, 'it can't be valid. Do you not agree?'

'Certainly. A valid experiment must be bias-free by definition.'

'So the experiment could not have been valid.'

'No, Rory, it couldn't.'

'Yet the experimental design was valid. Therefore, because its design was valid, the experiment proved itself to be invalid.'

'Indeed, assuming the conclusion to be true has led to a paradox!'

'Does this not compel us, then, to deem the conclusion false?'

'Of course, Rory. *Reductio ad absurdum*.'

'In other words, *not* all psychology studies are prone to experimenter bias. But any experiment yielding a false conclusion is necessarily invalid, is it not?'

'Yes, indeed, Rory. No valid study can give a false conclusion, by definition of "valid".'

'But the conclusion of the experiment was that psychology studies *are* prone to experimenter bias. So again, because the design was valid, the conclusion was invalid.'

'So no matter whether the conclusion of this study was false or true, the study was invalid because of its demonstrable validity. Therefore, *no* study of experimenter bias can ever be valid. Hurrah!'

Ariadne applauded and the medipriest chuckled. Rory nodded and winked at him. The Blue Primrose guards looked as though they wanted to arrest someone but they weren't sure who.

'There we have it,' said Rory. 'There might or might not be experimenter bias in psychology studies, but whether there is or isn't can never be known.'

'It's the paradox of the liar rewritten as valid/invalid!' Ariadne grinned. 'By extension, *every* test of *every* belief must be biased. Science tries to eliminate bias, seek absolute objectivity, but … Look at the history of science. Francis Bacon spoke of "idols": preconceptions, cherished hypotheses, common knowledge, authorities, profitable beliefs, seductive beliefs. Idols we can't eliminate. No knowledge of anything, no truth, can be objective. *Nothing* can be known for certain, bias-free.'

'I suppose you're right, Ariadne.'

'So the invalid-because-valid psychology paper is a model for all failed attempts to remove bias from systems of thought.'

'This seems hard to accept, but I see no way of denying it, Ariadne.'

'No belief can ever be proved valid.'

'It seems inescapable, Ariadne.'

'This is what postmodernists say, is it not?'

'It's impossible to make sense of anything postmodernists say. But it's probably what they *imagine* they say.'

'So – are we now back to the Gödelpus Unsatisfiability Theorem?'

Rory and Ariadne caught each other's eye and burst out laughing. The Blue Primrose guards shook their heads and looked glum. The medipriest smiled again and wrote notes.

'Ah, I needed a bit of intellectual wotsit,' said Rory. 'My mind's regaining its vigour. I'm looking forward to the physics lecture now.'

'Me too,' said Ariadne.

She'd have held his hand if he hadn't insisted on managing without support.

Chapter 48

I've never witnessed the National Cake Day celebrations because I've always had to return home from Ruritania before midsummer, but I've seen the build-up in Strelsau. It's frenetic. The visitor (and the less agile resident) is advised to stay clear of major bakeries. Until I saw the bakers' assistants galloping in and out of the buildings and along every street and alley during the fortnight before the Solstice, yelling slogans, brawling, handing out cakes to all and sundry, I'd supposed Ruritania's pace of life to be slow.
— *Ariadne Sowerby, 'First Impressions of Ruritania'*

'Who's the fastest rider in your cell, Sillias? While we're busy, he'll need to go and book fresh horses for me at three villages on the Hrincacz road.'

'Who d'you think you are, Mangler? Find your own rider!'

'None quick enough in my cell. Sorry, pal: Eldzhay's orders. As soon as we've finished the metacake job I'm to ride east and recover the security plan. Redman stole it, so it's in St Avicenna's. Have to travel fast.'

'If you were really ill you could use the Faerie Flight system.' Thinking made Sillias look like a bulldog chewing a caramel. 'But if you were really ill they'd keep you in St Avicenna's. How did Redman get to nick this security thingummy?'

'Found it in Vorgottenstrit, they say. Zip your lips, Sillias; nobody else needs to know. Find a rider to help me and let's get down to Jubetitstrit.'

They had no need to pinch Strlzhav uniforms; hasty copies of

178

the insignia on their white hats and aprons escaped scrutiny because every pair of hands was needed. A Hieronymus Bosch painting of the Stock Exchange could have portrayed the Jubetitstrit bakery. Thousands of Traditional Ginger Cakes were being baked to the krevjalem's new recipe and assistants were racing all around Strelsau with them, distributing them as free gifts. They were armed in order to ward off robbers and dogs and urchins and to engage in combat with assistants from the Hvimpy bakery, who were dispensing Caraway Angel Cakes. The election campaign was gathering pace. There were riots in parts of the city but the assistants didn't care.

An overseer noticed Sillias's efforts.

'Good work! Excellent! You, you, get those cakes out of here – I want another ten dozen in 3H and the same in 19E within the next hour! Drop any and I'll cut unnecessary bits off you with my bread knife. Yes there are, I can think of a couple. You and you, get those ovens emptied, this batch is ready. Sillias, check them and sort out the mis-shapes, you seem a good quality-control man. Where's the next consignment? What the hell do *you* lot think you're doing? This isn't a rest home for retired layabouts! You, where are you going? You can have a cigarette break in mid-shift, not before. Back to work! You – what in the name of Asclepius do you call *those* things?'

Mangler had mastered the art of looking busy while he did what he wanted. Within minutes he'd located the upstairs room housing the metacake. He exchanged jokes with the two guards, returned to the maelstrom of the ground floor and carried a few Traditional Ginger Cakes to and fro.

'Sillias!'

'What? Sod off, Mangler, I've got to get these into shape before–'

'I've found it!'

'Found what?'

'The target!'

'Eh? What target?'

'Asclepius preserve us. The m-e-t-a-c-a-k-e.'

179

Sillias shook his head. Spelling wasn't his forte. Mangler bent his face to his partner's ear.

'The metacake is upstairs in a locked room with two armed guards outside.'

'We're buggered, then. Let's shift these ginger cakes. Tell you what, it's a brill recipe, wouldn't mind a full-time–'

Mangler picked Sillias up and shook him. There was a cloud of flour dust.

'Listen carefully, Sillias. We need the keys. K-e-y-s. Who carries keys? The overseers. So *you*, Sillias, will detach the keys from an overseer's belt without being caught. To achieve this, we'll arrange a collision between the loudest overseer and two or three assistants with laden trays. You will go to rescue the fallen cakes and in the process you'll take the keys and put them into your pocket. Meanwhile, I will cause a further diversion by kicking the assistants. Do you need me to repeat any of this?'

'Uh … Two things at once? Rescue cakes and pinch keys?'

'Yes. You'll then follow me upstairs. We'll relieve the guards – they're dying for a smoke. Once they're gone we'll unlock the door, alter the metacake, ensure it looks as good as new, leave the room and re-lock the door before the guards return. Later, we'll ask which of the overseers has dropped his or her keys, return them, and be rewarded with sobs of relief and a basket of cakes that have only recently gone stale.'

'Er … right. Yeah. Er … Mangler, why not wait a bit?'

'No time to lose. Got to ride east.'

Sillias sighed and returned to his quality-control work.

'Okay, Mangler, I'll do it, scout's honour. When?'

'Five minutes. I'll tell the guards we'll relieve them for a fifteen minute fag break as soon as my mate's finished checking the new batch.'

'Have you got the thing? You know, for stuffing into –?'

'Keep your voice down! Yes. Four minutes thirty seconds.'

The collision was easily arranged; one tripped assistant, one domino effect. The overseer shouted bad words. Sillias was so concerned about the fallen cakes that Mangler had to kick him to refocus his attention. While the cakes were being righted and the overseer was beating the assistants, Mangler and Sillias sneaked upstairs. The filched keys rattled in Sillias's pocket.

'Cheers, mates, we owe you,' said the guards. 'Remember, no one goes in there except the krev or his deputy. If an overseer tries to open the door, tell him to sod off.'

'Hope we get the chance.' Mangler grinned. 'How about that, pal? Krev's permission to tell nosy overseers to sod off!'

'Yeah.' Sillias nodded. He looked through the barred window into the locked room and was mesmerised by the metacake.

A minute later they were trying keys. One after another.

'Come on, come on …'

Two minutes passed. Then the lock clicked and the door opened.

'Keep the key in the lock, Sillias. We don't want the same trial-and-error when we leave.'

'Oh, Mangler, look! Most beautiful cake in the world! Did you ever see anything so exqui – esc – so nice? Mangler, we can't spoil it. It's a work of art.'

'We won't spoil it. You'll make it perfect again.'

Mangler was swift with knife and scoop. Within three minutes he was repairing the metacake. Sillias wept at his comrade's handiwork.

'Here, Mangler, let me. Please, let me …'

Mangler let him. Sillias's adoring hands caressed the metacake's delicate surface with the silver utensils provided for last-minute adjustments. Mangler glanced at his watch. Eleven minutes. Sillias was indifferent to time, aware of nothing but the masterpiece it was his privilege to restore. Even now Mangler could see no imperfection, but Sillias detected a miniscule unevenness here, a fractionally misplaced metadecoration there, a tiny imbalance, a barely-perceptible departure from the horizontal or vertical.

Thirteen minutes. Mangler grew conscious of his bladder.

'Sillias, we have to go!'

'Just one minute …'

'*Now*, Sillias! The guards will be here!'

'Okay, Mangler, just one moment …'

Mangler seized his colleague by the collar, dragged him out of the room and turned the key in the lock as the nicotine-refuelled guards stumped upstairs. A glance through the barred window reassured him: the metacake looked untouched.

'Cheers again, mates,' said the guards. 'Anybody try to get in there while we were out?'

'Nah,' said Sillias. 'We'd have sorted them out. Beautiful, that metacake. Wouldn't never let nobody near it. Might breathe on it.'

Chapter 49

The science of kriadalethargics developed in 19th century Ruritania. The word 'kriadalethargics' is derived from the Greek κρύο (cold) + λεθη (forgetfulness) + αργος (idle). Kriadalethargics concerns the interconversion of different forms of anergy. Its main principles are encapsulated in three laws. Students of kriadalethargics must learn how those laws are derived mathematically, but they can be expressed qualitatively in the following words:

1. Cold and idleness are interconvertible forms of anergy.

2. Any attempt to recover idleness from cold in an isolated kriadalethargic system increases the anergy in that system.

3. When the cold of any isolated kriadalethargic system is increased without limit, the total anergy of that system becomes infinite.

— Waldemar Krev Schammerbass, 'A Textbook of Intermediate Physics'

Rory and Ariadne entered the physics department of Hrincacz University in time to see Professor Reciprocus meandering along the hall past the stuffed and mounted forms of his predecessors, each in his dusty glass case with identifying label. Only the glass cases and the identifying labels distinguished the former occupants of the physics chair from the current one. The latter was more mobile, but the faces of those who had gone before shared his expression of benign bewilderment.

'Even at first glance,' said Rory, 'you can identify his calling.

Although he could be a professor of metaphysics rather than physics.'

They took their places in the lecture hall. The Blue Primrose duo dogged Rory's steps and noticed nothing remarkable; or indeed, anything at all. The medipriest kept writing notes.

'I know what "physics" means,' said Ariadne, 'but I've never been sure what "metaphysics" means.'

'Metaphysics bears the same relationship to physics as metempsychosis bears to psychosis.'

'Cheers, Rory, that's *really* helpful. But the Academy of Science publications I've read reveal how different Ruritanian physics is from ours, so I'm not sure what relationship it might have to either metaphysics *or* psychosis.'

Professor Reciprocus drifted to the podium surrounded by a cloud of lucubration and chalk dust. He cleared his throat, scrutinised the glass beside the lectern, sipped from it and peered at his audience. Were these people (his face seemed to inquire) first-year undergraduates, or final year undergraduates, or postgraduates, or conference delegates, or interested members of the public who neither possessed nor sought academic qualifications?

A white-haired man in the front row leaned forward and whispered: 'We're interested members of the public who neither possess nor seek academic qualifications.' The professor blinked and said, 'Oh. Yes, I see. Thank you.' He sipped from the glass again and addressed his audience. His English was almost devoid of accent.

'Er ... Ladies and gentlemen, I wonder, if I may – er – whether each of you will be kind enough to inform me, by the simple expedient of raising either your left or your right arm, if you are a visitor from another country.'

Three quarters of the audience raised an arm. Three quarters of the three quarters raised their right arms. Rory inferred that the number of people in the audience was divisible by sixteen.

'Ah. Then only twenty-five percent of you are native

Ruritanians.' Professor Reciprocus nodded as though he'd confirmed a theoretical prediction. Perhaps he had. 'If I may crave the indulgence of that twenty-five percent, I shall begin by explaining something of the distinctive character of Ruritanian physics. The visitors among you might believe that when I counted the number of raised arms a moment ago, light – *photons* – from these objects above our heads' (he indicated the onyx chandeliers) 'were reflected from those arms into my eyes, exciting receptors in my retinas and informing my brain of the – er – er – the information it sought. But we offer a different account, which is more consistent with reality because of that final fact: *it is the brain that seeks information.* The brain is the prime mover in acts of perception. Yet, ladies and gentlemen, if each of you could look inside your brain at this moment, without opening your cranium, what would you see?'

He raised his hands in expectation or supplication and the audience shifted and murmured. Then Rory called out, 'Nothing.'

'Precisely, sir!' The professor's hands rose higher, in triumph or applause. 'You would see *nothing.* Why? Obviously you would see nothing because the brain is flooded with dark! You see, these objects' (again he pointed to the onyx chandeliers) 'are *skotophages*, entities that devour the particles of dark we term *skotons.* Skotophages are skoton sinks. Of course, "particle" should be understood in its quantum mechanical sense, something that exists as a potentiality, a probability wave; but I digress. Skotons are omnipresent; the tenebriferous aether, which permeates space and matter at every level, teems with them.'

'So,' said a woman on the back row, 'the sun is the ultimate … skotophage?'

'In our part of the universe, madam, it is. It sucks skotons from all parts of space, lowering the tenebrous anergy level everywhere according to a precise mathematical relationship.'

Professor Reciprocus scribbled a formula on the board. Ariadne recognised it: the inverse square law with the signs changed.

'Did he say "anergy"?' said Rory. 'Opposite of "energy"?'

'Yes,' said Ariadne.

'There was something in that bag of Academy of Science papers I took to the *Nurture* office about the interconvertibility of different forms of anergy and the three laws of kriadalethargics.'

'Kriadalethargics is the Ruritanian equivalent of thermodynamics.'

Rory shrugged. Professor Reciprocus was explaining how skotons could – in a relativistic sense – be motionless but would travel towards any available skotophage faster than everything else in the material universe.

'This is why,' he said, 'many of our best minds have dedicated themselves to measuring the speed of dark. That the task has been accomplished must stand as a triumph of Ruritanian science. We now have an accurate value for the speed of dark.'

The screaming of a fire alarm interrupted him. There was a moment of collective thought before panic erupted, then everyone except Professor Reciprocus rushed to the nearest exit. Soon he was lecturing to an empty auditorium, miffed at the persistent clamouring of the alarm.

Outside the department, everyone saw that the fire wasn't local. Buildings burned throughout the city. The entire population seemed to be in the streets, screaming and running, brawling and looting. Rory thought it resembled Liverpool on a Saturday night when supporters returned from an away match, except for the emergency vehicles bearing blue-clad singers with magical voices, which are seen and heard in Liverpool only by persons in illegal states of mind. Of course, he thought, you never see Morris-dancing in Liverpool. Or, I suppose, Hrincacz. Hence the civil disorder. The billowing smoke caught his eyes and throat and he coughed.

'Back to St Avicenna's!' shouted the medipriest, covering his face with a cloth.

Thanks to the company of two Blue Primrose guards, the medipriest contrived to heave his patient on to a carriage and direct it through the churning chaotic crowd, back to the cathedral hospital.

Rory looked round, desperate to pull Ariadne into the carriage, but she'd vanished among the mob. He tried to leap out to find her but it would have been a hopeless endeavour even if the ekwyroj hadn't restrained him.

Chapter 50

All members of the Government of Ruritania accept this prohibition of the use of ceramic utensils as weapons and agree to be bound according to the terms of this declaration.

The present Protocol, of which the Ruritanian and English texts are both authentic, shall be ratified immediately. It shall bear today's date.

The instruments of ratification of and accession to the present Protocol shall remain deposited in the archives of the High Bakery of Ruritania.

The present Protocol shall come into force from the date of deposit of its ratification, and, from that moment, shall become law throughout Ruritania.

IN WITNESS WHEREOF Her Sublime Majesty Anastassia, by the Grace of Asclepius Queen of Ruritania, has signed the present Protocol.

DONE at Strelsau in a single copy, this fifth day of Extember, Two Thousand and Four.

> *— Protocol for the Prohibition of Ceramic Utensils as Weapons in Ruritania*

Bagpipes played; residents listened and went to check their livestock. Eighty British squaddies, primed and alert, marched from the airport into Strelsau.

'Looks foreign.'

'Like the pictures in a fairytale book I had when I was a nipper. Everything's falling down.'

'Your fairytales smell like this dump, then? Stone the bleeding crows, it's howling!'

'Yeah. Blighty stinks, but not this bad.'

'Looks foreign, smells foreign.'

'Dunno. Okay, it's full of foreigners. Well, so's London full of foreigners, right? So what's the bleeding difference?'

'There are architectural distinctions. The predominant style is an idiosyncratic Gothic with influences from–'

'Oh, shut your intebloodylectual arsehole.'

'You think England never stinks this bad? Ever marched behind Mikey after he's eaten a vindaloo? The atmosphere's incompatible with most forms of terrestrial life.'

Mikey cast aspersions on the speaker's parentage and expressed pessimism as to his future wellbeing.

'Tell you what, lads, thought I was back in barracks when we come through immigration. Fucking nightmare.'

'Customs and immigration aren't that scary in England, mate!'

'Yeah, that's what I meant. How come Ruritania customs recruited a load of British Army sergeant majors? Getting through immigration felt like coming back to camp when you're pissed out of your head and carrying contraband and can't remember the password.'

Masculine accord grunted along the marching lines.

Half a league further into the city, the squaddies' honed senses picked up disturbing signals.

'Something's burning.'

'My missus is cooking again. Didn't know *she'd* be here.'

'Crowd noise, too. Football match?'

'Dunno if they play footie here. It's foreign.'

'Yeah, but foreigners play footie, too.'

'Nah, it's not a football crowd, not unless Millwall are playing. Too violent.'

A few fathoms later the captain ordered his troops to take up defensive positions.

'There's a riot ahead. Local police can't control it so we'll need to disperse the crowd. Don't shoot until I give the command, then fire over their heads. Rubber bullets.'

The troops took up defensive positions, looking questions at each other.

'Thought the balloon wasn't supposed to be going up 'til the twenty-first. Or the fourth on *their* daft calendar.'

'Some silly bugger's inflated it early, then.'

'Yeah, well, we're not … *Fuck me, lads, get down!*'

Everyone fell flat on their faces as missiles flew past them and exploded.

'Great Scot!' hissed the captain. 'What the devil were those?'

'Ceramic utensils I think, sir.'

'Gad! The fiends!'

Chapter 51

Cupping therapy entails the application of heated glass bulbs (cups) to target areas on the patient's skin. As the bulbs cool, a partial vacuum within them draws the skin upwards. The cups stay in place for fifteen minutes. The increased blood flow in the treated areas has many therapeutic benefits if the cupping is combined with appropriate herbal treatments.

— The Hrincacz Herbal

'The speed and extent of your recovery are remarkable, Rory.' Thad shook his head. Rory was washed, shaved and dressed and had eaten a light breakfast, and his handshake was firm, though he hadn't slept well.

'Is Ariadne okay? Is she safe?'

'She is safe for now, in the hotel with us. But everyone who can is leaving Hrincacz.'

A wave of relief flopped Rory on to the bed. The Blue Primrose guards watched him flop. They'd been much more alert since they'd been caught up in the rioting.

'Thank goodness.' Rory released a long-held breath. 'I was … Well. Weight off my mind. This music, this glorious chanting – do you know what it is, Thad?'

'It is a mediaeval polyphonic setting of the Hippocratic Oath in Old High Ruritanian. It is chanted every morning before ecclesiastical ward-rounds. No one understands the words. Rory, less than a week ago you were unconscious and we feared you would die.'

'The medipriest said I was lucky. Few have the good fortune to be attacked with a miasma grenade while suffering food poisoning. My treatment looked crazy to non-Ruritanian eyes but I suppose it's worked. Or else my recovery was pure coincidence, which would interest the President of your Academy of Science. I asked a medipriest why my back was sore and she explained about cupping glasses. I thought it was stark raving eccentric, but she said the method was also used in other countries until the twentieth century. Apparently the heating and skin-pulling make local immune cells fight infections – sorry, miasmata.'

They sat on the pew beside Rory's bed. The guards' attention on Rory didn't waver despite the presence of the Queen's closest adviser. Thad eyed the statues of medical saints in sterile niches along the wall. Rory studied his face.

'What's wrong, Thad?'

Thad told him about the seeming proclamations from Krevoj Hvimpy and Strlzhav, which had caused the riots. Claims by both sides that the proclamations were forgeries had fallen on ears deafened by crowd fever and minds intoxicated with looting and arson. The riots were spreading to villages and Hrincacz was now dangerous.

'Yeah,' said Rory. 'I was forced into a carriage after the alarm went off in the physics lecture. Ariadne was left stranded.'

'I know. She realised it was not your fault she was left behind. Nevertheless she blamed you.'

'If my heart had cockles,' said Rory, 'that news would warm them. Proves she's female.'

Thad said the hotel had become a refuge for frightened citizens. He'd ordered Tomen and Ariadne to stay in the building. Ariadne was waiting for a horse she could ride to Castle Bauntzi, as she'd planned to do before Rory was rushed to hospital.

'Once she has left, Rory, I must take Tomen back to Strelsau. There is trouble there, too, but we shall be close to security headquarters and the north-west quarter should be safe. I wish we could take you but you are better here; no Ruritanian would attack a cathedral hospital.'

Rory didn't mention the tendency of fires to spread among buildings with thatched roofs.

'In any case I'm under arrest and can't go anywhere until Barrington sends guards to escort me back to Strelsau and either to prison or out of the country. So from my point of view the riots are a blessing. At least they delay the inevitable.' He gestured at the Blue Primrose pair beside the door. 'Bet those two can't wait, though.'

Thad's eyes twinkled.

'I think you have a saying, "Every cloud has a slug-trail lining".'

'The usual wording's a little different. Tell me what was in those inflammatory proclamations.'

Thad summarised the contents.

'Either both krevoj had gone insane,' said Rory, 'or the papers *were* forged. Who'd have the skill or the equipment to produce convincing counterfeits? Will this affect National Cake Day? If I've got my sums right it's only a week or so ahead.'

Thad's face remained sombre.

'The Solstice will be celebrated as always, Rory. Everyone will crowd into St Galen's Square. All citizens will relinquish rioting for National Cake Day.'

'I'd love to see it but I'm unlikely to have the chance.'

Thad painted a word portrait of Ruritania's great annual ceremony: the procession of aristocrats from the High Bakery; the arrival of Her Majesty and the royal family; the ceremonial presentation of the metacake by the outgoing krevjalem; the solemnity of the Surgeon Archbishop and his senior medipriests; the raising and plying of the sacred scalpel beneath the statue of St Galen; the cheering and flag-waving; the Queen's address to the people; the fireworks. Rory looked thoughtful.

'So the head of government designs the metacake, bakes it to the highest specifications and stores it in a safe place until the great day. Then it becomes the centre of the national ceremony in St Galen's Square, surrounded by Ruritania's royalty and aristocracy. The incision with the sacred scalpel must be … I suppose the common folk have to keep their distance. And the police and Blue Primrose presence will be stronger than ever this year since an insurrection is feared.'

Thad shrugged.

'Perhaps, Rory. Yes, it is hard to imagine a more apt celebration of our national identity: the epitome of cakehood at the centre of power, the focus of communal attention.'

Rory closed his eyes. Thad feared the patient was tiring.

'I should leave, dear friend. In any case I must take care of Tomen, and Ariadne too.'

'Yes, Thad, you must. I might not see you again before I'm imprisoned or deported, but I'll remain in your debt. You and Tomen have been generous beyond the call of duty.'

'Rory, there is no debt. Ariadne is right: aside from your intelligence, you are stimulating company because trouble follows you like a pet Spitz. You have made our lives more exciting. We hope you will soon return.'

'I can't compete with your graciousness,' Rory smiled; his eyes remained shut. 'Before you go … about Dai. I was sad to learn he'd passed away. Did you know he was talking philosophy again when the grenade struck? Had he been a university lecturer?'

'I think I told you he was once a student of Turk Gödelpus. When Gödelpus published the Unsatisfiability Theorem and quit the university, Dai gave up as well; he relinquished study, teaching and respectability. He went to live in a barrel, ate nothing but cake and drank nothing but rough home-brewed wine, seldom washed, and told all passers-by they should never believe anything to be valid.'

There was a disturbance at the west door. Rory opened his eyes. Three Blue Primrose officers had arrived. Their leader wore a senior ekwyor's uniform. She issued orders to the duty guards. They saluted. She reciprocated the gesture and marched forward. Her two subordinates followed.

'Well,' said Rory, 'it was bound to happen sooner or later, though there are surprising details. Thad, a safe journey home, may everything be well in Klatzierstrit 27, give my good wishes to Tomen and my love to Ariadne, and accept my thanks again for your many kindnesses. While you remain in here, please don't keep looking at the statues.'

Aware that his face had whitened, he smiled, stood, and walked towards the Blue Primrose trio, determined not to stumble or shake.

'Bring your suitcase and jacket, Pan Redman,' ordered their leader. Her English was accented but clear. She didn't echo his smile. 'You will not return here.'

The sun had risen. Rory put on his dark glasses. His mouth was dry.

Chapter 52

After successful treatment at a church surgery or cathedral hospital, the recovering patient is expected to sacrifice a pig, goat or cow, depending on the duration and intensity of therapy. The sacrifice is a token of gratitude. It also provides food for subsequent patients, not to mention the medipriests. For cures of minor ailments, the sacrifice of a rabbit can suffice.
— The Unideker Guide to Ruritania

'I haven't paid for medical care.' Rory cleared his throat. 'I don't suppose Ruritania has anything like Britain's National Health Service.'

They were approaching a copse. Two hundred fathoms behind them, the cathedral hospital was silhouetted against the fire and smoke of Hrincacz. Ahead, to the north, lay meadows and pastures, fields of wheat and barley, trees and clear sky.

'Then you *will* return. You must sacrifice a cow.'

Rory blinked.

'Right. Cow. I should have guessed. Am I being rescued or abducted, Pana Alterleta?'

Klarissa hitched her handbag over her shoulder. She didn't deign to look at him.

'I am Ekwyor Laskesia.'

'Yeah, I'm Abraham Lincoln. May I call you Trellarta? Or *Klarissa*?'

This time she faced him. Despite his anxiety, the green fire of her eyes made his viscera tingle.

'No. And I will not call you Rory.'

Her two male companions mounted horses. Klarissa sprang into the saddle of a third, which submitted to her touch. She pointed her riding crop at the remaining animal. Rory shook his head.

'I've never ridden a horse. How do you get on the thing?'

The Ruritanians held a short conference. The two men glowered at Rory. Klarissa pointed at the larger of them.

'You will ride behind Comrade Arraitch, Pan Redman.'

'I'll go on foot. I can run.'

'You are not recovered. You will do as I say.'

Rory was helped on to the back of Arraitch's horse. He gripped the saddle and his palms perspired. His suitcase was strapped to the fourth horse. They rode a meandering track through the copse to the open land. Klarissa smirked.

'I trust you are as comfortable as a British spy deserves. A spy who unleashed bloodshed in our safe house in Vorgottenstrit.'

'You know I'm not a spy and I didn't unleash any bloodshed. Blue Primrose trashed Vorgottenstrit 13. You didn't answer my question. Is this a rescue or an abduction?'

Klarissa glanced around the fields: no witnesses. She held out her left hand. Her right rested on the rein. Her handbag swayed as the bay horse walked on.

'Give me what you took from Vorgottenstrit 13.'

'I haven't got it,' said Rory.

'Stop,' ordered Klarissa. Everyone stopped. 'Search him.'

She sat in the saddle, arms folded, while Rory and his suitcase were searched. The men found no security plan.

'Where is it?'

'It was in my pocket when the miasma grenade exploded. It isn't there now. I was arrested by Barrington and Blue Primrose.'

'If they did not know you had it they did not take it. Did you give it to them? If not, where is it?'

'I haven't seen it since I put it into my pocket in your safe house, pana prejosza.'

Klarissa edged her horse up to Arraitch's so Rory's right leg was squeezed between the equine flanks. Her handbag nudged his abdomen. Her voice was as soft as a wolverine's fur.

'Comrade Mangler' (she nodded at the third rider) 'is adept at encouraging people to reveal information. Immediate recovery of the security plan is essential. Your survival and wellbeing are not. Do you understand?'

Mangler drew from his saddle bag a selection of corroded metallic implements of uncertain but imaginable function. He leered.

'I'm not impressed. He looks tired.' Rory's mouth was drier than ever.

'Tired men are impatient, Pan Redman, and Comrade Mangler is assiduous. Where is the plan? Once you've handed it over we will have no further use for you.'

Mangler reached again into his saddle bag and brandished Ann Summers handcuffs, a battery-powered CD player, a set of headphones and a *Spiceworld* CD. His leer widened.

'Okay,' said Rory, 'it's behind a statue in the chapel cubicle I occupied. But I'm afraid, pana prejosza, that you'd struggle to find an excuse to enter the Cathedral Hospital again. Incidentally, thanks for answering *my* question. This is abduction.'

Klarissa moved her horse aside and spoke to her companions. Mangler put the CD and implements back into his saddle bag and rode away. Rory wondered why SPAR was desperate to recover the plan since they knew Barrington and Tupsroot had a fake version; then light dawned. My wits are still slow, he thought. Well, they don't know I gave a copy of the original to Thad.

'We shall stay near here,' said Klarissa. 'Soon, one of us will accompany you back to St Avicenna's, where you will sacrifice the cow and then hand over the plan.' She looked Rory full in the face. 'You are quite intelligent. You even try to learn Ruritanian. But to address a woman as "pana prejosza" with ironic intent is insulting.'

'Since our encounter on the eleventh or nineteenth of May, depending on calendar, you've mugged me, kicked me unconscious and handcuffed me, had a miasma grenade thrown at me, abducted me from hospital and threatened me with torture. A quite intelligent woman would *expect* insults. A more intelligent woman would expect worse.'

'You are nevertheless a fool, Pan Redman. Why did you follow me to Strelsau? Barrington's orders?'

'I don't take orders from Barrington or anyone. And what makes you suppose I followed *you*? I followed someone more interesting. Your stunts are designed to draw attention but they're not clever. If the Blue Primrose guards at St Avicenna's had been smart enough to notice the obvious, your latest one would have backfired.'

She studied his face and urged her mount into a trot, leading the horse that carried the suitcase. Arraitch rode beside her, Rory clinging to the saddle.

'What should the guards have noticed?'

Rory felt unwell. Aside from the after-effects of the grenade, his situation was perilous and the undulating movement of the horse made him sea-sick.

'Even if they ignored the colour of your eyes, they should have spotted the repaired holes and bloodstains on your uniforms. I don't know whether bullets or arrows made those holes, but the uniforms' original owners are dead. Ruthless lot, aren't you?'

Arraitch spoke to Klarissa, his tone respectful. Klarissa laughed.

'You call *us* ruthless? Six Blue Primrose officers were hunting us. Do you know what they would have done had they captured us? We left three of their bodies where they would be found and took the uniforms of the three we buried. For your information, the holes were made by arrows. Only Blue Primrose use firearms.' She looked at Rory again and shook her head. 'Your powers of observation and deduction could be useful, Pan Redman, and your history suggests scant respect for authority. It is sad you make no commitment. Now, Arraitch urges us to rest because you are too sick to travel further. There is a village less than a league ahead. We will rest at the inn until noon.'

Rory wondered whether Mangler would find them at the village inn but he lacked the energy (or had too much anergy) to ask. Despite his sunglasses the light made his head ache, even when they entered another wood. He closed his eyes, clutched Arraitch's saddle and waited for the horses to stop.

They stopped at the edge of the wood within sight of the village. What remained of it.

Chapter 53

Strelsau's a waste of space. Food lousy, women fat, no decent telly. Not even much square bashing – sergeant's always pissed. At least there's no vindaloo, so Mikey's guts haven't turned into a weapon of mass destruction that threatens the ozone layer and makes the solar system a confined space. He's eating tons of cake, though. Mikey's alimentary canal has a towpath beside it.
— From the Diary of a Squaddy

Colonel Barrington's squaddies had dispersed the rioters and confiscated several ceramic utensils and were now enjoying cake and recreation. Eight prisoners were crammed into a subterranean portion of Blue Primrose HQ. The colonel loomed beside the dungeon door while his Ruritanian colleagues interrogated them. They weren't cooperative.

After an impatient hour and a half Ekwyor Tupsroot shouted a command, whereat a junior ekwyrin scurried forward bearing a CD and headphones. The interviewee's eyes dilated and he waxed loquacious, his voice a blend of pleading wheedle and hysterical squeak.

'He know not true name of Alterleta,' snapped the ekwyor. 'Only "Worshipped Leader" and "Ulyanova". He speak true, Horatio; he have seen CD.'

The colonel agreed. The squeak and wheedle betokened veracity.

'When he's back from that comfort break, ask him why they were rioting.'

'Already it is asked. He say it is Hvimpy threat for State to steal Strlzhav bakery.'

The colonel frowned.

'Thought these dregs would favour Hvimpy over Strlzhav. Damned if I understand Ruritanian politics, Grizelina.'

'They call Krevjalem Strlzhav oppressor. His government make anger among poor, so terrorist more loved. Krev Hvimpy kinder to poor, so not such love for terrorist.'

'Ha! Scum can be subtle. But where *is* this so-called Ulyanova?'

The ekwyor grated out more questions. The interviewee shook his head. His voice grovelled. The ekwyor shrugged.

'He say she is far from here. He know no more.'

The colonel snorted.

'One of these jokers knows, Grizelina.'

But none of the prisoners knew Klarissa's whereabouts. None could reveal the addresses of SPAR's new safe houses, either; all the known ones had been empty when raided.

'Why,' said the ekwyor, 'do you align yourselves with SPAR? It's illegal, dangerous, not to be trusted.'

'They're our only friends,' explained the most forthcoming prisoner. 'We're sediment in the ditch of life. We beat and kick our dogs to make them obey; the rich beat and kick us. I couldn't provide a goat for my wife's medical treatment, but SPAR paid the church surgery and now she's well. They give hope to the hopeless, belief to the disenchanted, purpose to the disaffected, money to the destitute.'

'Where does SPAR get its money?'

None of the prisoners knew.

The day lengthened. No further information was elicited. But as the interrogations ended a message arrived for the ekwyor. Her rage startled even the colonel.

'Krevjalem Strlzhav send six Blue Primrose officer to capture Alterleta. Three are murdered, maybe all six.'

'God's toenails,' muttered the colonel.

'Now I leave you to command here, Horatio. English interpreter help. I go myself, take new force to Lake Brojginzha and Castle Strlzhav. I find her. I make end of her.'

202

Chapter 54

The words 'dakh' and 'khad' puzzle historical linguists. In Old High Ruritanian, 'dakh' meant 'yes' and 'khad' meant 'no'. Then their meanings were switched: 'dakh' became 'no' and 'khad' became 'yes'. Not everyone kept pace with the change, causing misunderstandings in parliamentary debates, law courts, navigation, family life, and seduction. In modern Ruritanian it is therefore customary, and sensible, to establish what 'dakh' and 'khad' mean at the outset of any conversation, for example by asking, 'Does two plus two equal four?'

— Teach Yourself Ruritanian

Rory had grown accustomed to the absence of motor traffic, aircraft, power tools, muzak, alarms, loudspeakers, bustling crowds, drunken parties and all the manifold dins of civilisation. He imagined Ruritania could be a haven of tranquillity. But the silence of those sunlit fields was the silence of death. No birds sang. No livestock gave voice. The reek of bloodshed and burning cloyed the breath. Smoke rose from the remains of two dozen hovels. The air tasted of atrocity.

Klarissa and Arraitch looked down from the edge of the wood upon what had been a village. Arraitch mumbled and crossed himself. Rory opened his groggy eyes and assimilated the scene.

'Blue Primrose?' he croaked. 'Orders from Strelsau? Done to prevent the riots spreading?'

Klarissa shook her head, said 'Khad', and spoke to Arraitch. They descended the grassy slope at walking pace. The horses fretted, testing their riders. The stench grew noisome. Bodies lay scattered among the ruins, men, women and children slaughtered as they fled. Rory let his eyes close again but his mind saw everything in colour.

'No, Pan Redman. Orders from Strlzhav.'

Strelsau, Strlzhav … was 'Strlzhav' the older name of the capital, mutated to 'Strelsau' at a time in history when Ruritania had been too tightly attached to Germany, a circumstance common among European nations? Rory commanded his eyes to reopen. His companions' faces were set.

'Orders from the *krevjalem*?'

'Dakh. This is Strlzhav's krefmark. Blue Primrose could not massacre any of his villages without his command.'

'Why would a krev order his own peasants to be slaughtered?'

Klarissa answered first in Ruritanian, then in English:

'He is searching for us. He will destroy village after village until we give ourselves up. Unless we stop him.'

Arraitch nodded, lifted his bow and snarled. Rory's headache worsened. Klarissa pointed her horse towards the church surgery, which had escaped the flames. Of course, thought Rory, any survivors will have taken refuge there.

'You call *us* "terrorists".' Klarissa's voice was velvet.

'I've never used the word about SPAR,' said Rory.

Arraitch spoke again and Klarissa nodded, sprang from the saddle, tore off her Blue Primrose uniform and conjured denim clothes from her handbag. She applied perfume to her throat and ears. Rory blinked and saw Arraitch was now standing beside his horse dressed in green hooded jerkin and breeches and calfskin boots. He realised he was the only one still on horseback. The animal sensed his panic and bucked. Arraitch brought it under control but Rory fell off. Winded, he lay dizzy and nauseous, unable to stand. He saw Klarissa framed against summer sky and trees, clad in denim, and her beauty gave him a physical shock. For a moment he feared Arraitch's bark of laughter was occasioned by his sudden arousal rather than the inadvertent dismounting.

The village yasimak met them at the church surgery door. She recognised her two visitors and the fear left her face. She confirmed that the krev had ordered the massacre. One by one, the few surviving villagers crept from the shadows of the building and peered around her. Their eyes, shocked and vacant, passed over Rory with offhand curiosity. Klarissa spoke; her voice remained gentle but she was issuing orders. 'She has the gift of inspiring and uplifting people,' said Rory to the tainted air. Arraitch stood powerful and aloof, arms folded, bow over his shoulder, watching Klarissa with something like adoration.

Four villagers squeezed through the doorway and headed towards the four points of the compass. One rode a donkey and the others went on foot. All four were grubby and ragged and two were children. They scurried across the fields and into the woods. The remaining survivors including the yasimak tottered into the midday light and sought spades and mattocks.

'I guess those four travellers have gone to warn other villages,' said Rory, 'and the rest are preparing to bury their dead. What now? The inn's burned to the ground.'

'Khad,' said Arraitch.

'One has gone to my own village with a message for Comrade Mangler,' said Klarissa. 'Other villages will send help for the burial and rebuilding.'

So calm was her voice that Rory was slow to register the depth of her rage and compassion.

'Strlzhav will pay for this,' she whispered. Then she spoke to Rory again. 'Mangler will return from my village and take you back to St Avicenna's to pay your cow and collect the plan. We shall wait here.'

Chapter 55

The little time I've spent in Ruritanian villages has proved memorable. The villagers are hospitable to strangers, though it's unwise for a visitor to appear wealthy. There's solidarity and compassion among them, and the sick are well treated, yet the old, the crippled and the eccentric are targets of physical and verbal brutality, and women are continually at risk unless their families protect them.
— Ariadne Sowerby, 'First Impressions of Ruritania'

Egrienne Alterlet opened his arms to the little messenger but the message enraged him. He set his house about the ears.

'Bresina! This child must be washed, clothed and fed. His village is destroyed and his parents are dead. The survivors need our help. Mangler, the boy brings a message for you, too.'

Mangler was desperate to recover the security plan, but Bresina's priority was to see her little guest washed, fed, comforted and respectably clothed; so time passed before the child could tell his story. Then Mangler rose to his feet.

'I'll take the boy back with me, but if his home's been destroyed–'

'Leave him, Mangler,' said Egrienne. 'We've cared for many orphans. I'll take him back as soon as I've raised ten men to help rebuild his village.'

He shook his head. He'd always been sceptical about Klarissa's plan for a revolution. Was she right after all? What sort of government leader slaughters defenceless villagers at a whim without imagining reprisals?

Mangler hugged the child, bade farewell to Egrienne and Bresina and leapt into his saddle. He could assure the Ulyanova that her own adopted village and family were unharmed. As he urged his horse into a gallop he heard merry laughter behind him, mingled with agonised squeals. The village children were torturing a baby squirrel to death.

Evening was deepening by the time he reached the burnt-out village. Klarissa and Arraitch exchanged words with him and then rode away on a new mission. He watched them depart, then carried Redman back to St Avicenna's. He was exhausted; Redman, clinging to his saddle, was barely awake. Fumes from the newly-quenched fires of Hrincacz assailed his senses. He dressed again in his stolen Blue Primrose uniform and dragged his captive through the west door of the cathedral hospital.

'This prisoner,' he said, 'has returned so a cow may be sacrificed for his treatment. He offers to pay a yasimak to perform the sacrifice.'

The medipriest insisted on re-admitting the patient, who was clearly ill, but Mangler was adamant: Rory was a terrorist suspect who must be taken to Strelsau for questioning. While the two argued, Rory staggered to the statue of St William Harvey, unearthed the security plan and hid it under his jacket. Then he stumbled back to the west door.

'I'm fine. Just tired.'

He contrived a smile at the medipriest, handed over a fistful of raldoloj and left the cow sacrifice to an appointed yasimak. 'Perhaps the Surgeon Bishop in person,' he was assured as the money was counted.

'Not the Surgeon Bishop of Szipad, I hope!' Mangler laughed. 'He'd be too pissed to know one end of the cow from the other.'

At least, thought Rory as Mangler pushed him out of the building into the twilight, I don't have to turn butcher. But I'm short of cash now. And I need food and drink. I'm starving.

Mangler seized the security plan from him and grinned.

'Now we finish with you, Redman.' He drew a knife. 'You are British spy and will not live.'

207

Rory saw the blade flash in the fading light and adrenalin reignited his muscles. As Mangler lunged he fled towards the east end of the cathedral hospital, dodging the flying buttresses. He had no idea where he was going. He heard Mangler's feet hammering the ground behind him. He sensed hot breath on his neck.

Before him was a maze of yew hedges. He plunged into it and went on running.

Chapter 56

A krev's castle is his home. Woe betide those that enter uninvited.
  — Old Ruritanian Proverb

Klarissa and Arraitch tied their horses to trees at the forest's edge. The air was damp. Two hundred fathoms ahead, the silhouette of a castle loomed vast and bleak against the clouded night. To Arraitch's eyes it was a fissure through which the blackness of eternity beckoned.

'Lady, I beg you … Even under the noon sun this place is grim. At night, beneath cloud, it speaks of death.'

'It must be done, Arraitch, or the slaughter won't stop.'

'Let me go in your stead.'

Klarissa pointed to the top of the central tower. A bat skimmed her hand.

'The krev's private chamber is behind that window. Could you climb there?'

She flung off her outer clothes and shoes and applied perfume to her throat and ears. Two minutes later her bare hands and feet were groping up the castle's carapace. Her teeth gripped the haft of her throwing-knife; its blade whispered through the lightless air. Her handbag swung from her shoulder. Arraitch sighed, stowed her attire in her saddle-bag and ate an apple. As foretold by the weatherdancers, light rain fell.

Krevjalem Strlzhav, tired and truculent as any politician when an election is imminent, retired to his chamber to review his woes. The rioting in Hrincacz and (he was assured) Szipad had been suppressed, but the unrest had spread. Blue Primrose detachments were patrolling pockets of discontent. The metacake was secure in the Jubetitstrit bakery and free cakes were being distributed, but the expense was damnable. Two villages in his krefmark had been destroyed but the terrorist leader still eluded capture. Now, however, Ekwyor Tupsroota had brought a strong detachment to his castle, so he expected soon to meet the so-called Ulyanova face to face. He rubbed his hands, snatched the gold candlestick from the minion who bore it and kicked him downstairs. His wife had sought her private quarters two hours earlier, enervated by his pre-election tantrums.

Warm in the candlelight, the red velvet hangings of his canopy bed promised repose. But someone was sitting in his high-backed chair! He started and held the candle aloft. The intruder was a beautiful young woman, sparsely clad and smiling; the room was graced with perfume. His surprise yielded to expectation, but when the woman spoke his delight was stillborn.

'I hear you've been looking for me, Efeef.'

His moustache writhed. No one but his wife and his mother dared use his forename. Who was this woman? What did she mean?

'Who are you? How did you get in here?'

She pointed to the open casement; drizzle was staining the floor. Had she flown? Was she a denizen of Faerie? He felt his face whiten. His hand reached for the bell rope.

'Bad idea, Efeef. It would take forty-five seconds for your guards to reach this chamber. By then they'd be breathless and you'd be dead.'

He froze.

'How dare you trespass here and threaten me? How dare you use my personal name? Don't you know who I am?'

'Of course I do. And if you thought for a moment, you'd know who *I* am – and why I'm here.'

He blinked seven times. By Asclepius! *Her*? Alone, unarmed? She'd given herself up! Just two villages wiped out and he had her! Ekwyor Tupsroota's detachment wouldn't be needed after all! He gave a triumphant laugh and his hand reached again for the bell rope.

He never saw Klarissa move, but the air between them hissed and a howl was wrenched from his throat. His hand was pinned to the wall; the knife's ebony handle quivered. Blood ran down the panelling. His eyes dilated and his knees buckled. The rope remained unpulled.

'Be quiet or I'll kill you.'

He believed her. His cries of agony were muted to sobs. He concentrated on not fainting; if he fell, his hand would be torn in half. Then his outrage was reignited.

'You're the one who'll die, bitch!'

She rose from the chair, glided across the room and put her face ten smallbits from his. Her perfume made his eyes water. Her voice was gentle.

'It would be a pity if you were unable to preside in St Galen's Square on the Solstice, Efeef, but if one more village is attacked, if your hired scum hurt a single hair on the head of one more peasant, you won't live long enough. Don't imagine this threat is empty. See how easily I entered your chamber.' She stepped back. 'You ordered atrocities against the very peasants you should protect. Aristocratic trash!'

She sprang upwards and kicked him under the ribs. Air gushed from his lungs. He vomited and collapsed, opening the wound in his hand.

The disturbance had been heard. Boots pounded up the stairs. Voices shouted.

Klarissa snatched her knife from the panelling and leapt to the window. As the guards burst into the chamber she wriggled through the casement and began to scramble down the rain-soaked wall, hand over hand. Her left toes found a string course and she transferred her weight to it.

It crumbled beneath her and she fell.

Chapter 57

The greatest challenge in Ruritanian logic is attributed to the gargoyle Lekhissa. Lekhissa's riddle may be phrased as follows. Choose any statement; you wish to know whether it is true or false. To find out you may ask Lekhissa exactly one question, to which her answer must be 'dakh' or 'khad'. But will 'dakh' mean 'yes' or will 'khad' mean 'yes'? You do not know. And will she answer truthfully or will she lie? You do not know. Remember: you have only one question, and the dakh/khad answer must tell you whether your statement is true or false. Many have tried to solve this riddle in order to satisfy their need for vital information, but all have failed, so they have satisfied nothing save Lekhissa's craving for mortal flesh with chestnut stuffing.
   — Dai O'Genies, A Primer of Ruritanian Philosophy

Rory kept running. Slug trails, *nerjaportikhnoj*, led through the darkening maze. He followed the brightest. Then the path narrowed and divided into three branches. He heard Mangler thrashing among the hedges behind him.

At the openings of the three paths lay stones, each bearing an inscription. *This way is good*, said the first. *This way is not good*, said the second. *The first way is not good*, said the third. A banner hung over the three-way junction: 'At most one of the three inscriptions is true'.

Rory's mind whirled. The first and third contradict each other, so if the banner's correct, one of them must be true. So the second is … false! He dived into the second path and ran

212

onwards, hoping the puzzle would delay Mangler, hoping there was an exit from the maze.

The inscriptions were easy to read, he realised. So it was daylight again, the sun high in the sky. Had he slept? Had time gone out of joint?

Within a few fathoms the path bifurcated. At each opening was a stone bearing an inscription. *This is not the right way*, said the first. *Exactly one of these two inscriptions is true*, said the second.

'Wish I weren't exhausted.' Rory spoke aloud. Seconds passed as his mind assessed the options. Behind him, Mangler shouted Ruritanian obscenities.

'Got it!' Rory ran down the first path. He could no longer feel his legs. His knees were buckling. 'Come on, Redman,' he muttered, 'you can ... Oh, in the name of the wee man from Milton Keynes, not more!'

It was another trifurcation. Once again there was an inscribed stone at the entrance to each path. *This is the way*, said the first. *This is the way*, said the second. *At least two of these inscriptions are false*, said the third.

'Okay, if the third one is false, then the other two are true, which is impossible because they contradict each other. Therefore the third one is true. So the other two are false.'

Rory plunged into the third path and the maze vanished. He found himself in a world glowing with flowers and birds and butterflies. Figures flew around him, changing shape and species at every breath: now humanoid, now monstrous; now tiny, now gigantic. There was a diminutive Dai, a Disney fairy furnished with wand and suburban hairstyle flitting among flowers ... and then a gargoyle's head on a chitinous body supported by too many legs. Her mandible was impressive. Rory scuttled behind a tree.

'Greetings, Rory Redman,' said the gargoyle. 'I am Lekhissa. Come forward when your bladder is empty. Be glad you've met me and not my sister Sporota. So, you who disproved the

Gödelpus Theorem, you've solved your way through my maze! But now you must solve my riddle.' Her growl grew hungry. 'You have thirty minutes. If you succeed I will grant you one wish. If it is a good wish each of my sisters will also grant a wish. If you fail I shall eat you with chestnut stuffing. And all mortals fail.'

The gargoyle expanded to immense size and placed a bucket of chestnut stuffing in front of Rory. She licked her lips, a miracle of lingual agility considering the size of her mandible and her multiplicity of fangs. She emitted an aroma redolent of drains and charnel houses.

'Half an hour, Rory Redman. Enough time to whet my appetite.'

She recited her riddle: 'Choose any statement; you wish to know whether it is true or false. To find out you may ask me exactly one question, to which my answer must be "dakh" or "khad". But will "dakh" mean "yes" or will "khad" mean "yes"? You do not know. And will I answer truthfully or will I lie? You do not know. Remember: you have only one question, and the dakh/khad answer must tell you whether your statement is true or false.'

She grinned a gluttonous grin and salivated.

Chapter 58

Most krevoj guard their castles with mediaeval vigour. Along with moats, battlements, barred gates and armed guards, the castles are protected by ferocious hounds known as agriotytes. In this regard, as in others, Castle Bauntzi is distinctive: Krev Bauntzia keeps two or three pet Ruritanian Spitzes, which befriend everyone and everything except parked carriages, which they chase.
— Ariadne Sowerby, 'First Impressions of Ruritania'

Klarissa spread her arms and legs and pushed her face close to the rugged wall, fingers and toes scrabbling for crevice or ledge. Angry stones scraped skin from her knees and thighs and forearms and slashed the front of her sparse attire. She felt a toenail go. Ten fathoms of blackness gaped beneath her, a famished beak opening to a gizzard of sharp rubble. Pain and desperation gasped from her mouth. She almost dropped her handbag.

Her right hand sensed a window and a millisecond later it clutched the narrow sill. The sinews of her shoulder strained. She swung her body. Her left hand grasped the same wet ledge of flint and mortar. Her feet kicked for tenuous holds. Relentless drizzle sluiced perspiration from her brow. Blood seeped from her skin. Her throat was parched. For five seconds she hung motionless, the commotion from the krev's chamber drowned by the thundering of her heart, and then a gunshot split the night in two. The bullet struck the wall half a fathom from her head and whined into the darkness, ripping away a lump of stone like flesh from a rotting corpse.

215

'Stop shooting!' yelled a voice. 'I want her alive! Get out there!'

The unheeding gun crashed out another bullet, gouging away more stone. Fragments fell on Klarissa's head and dust stung her eyes. She scrambled downwards again. From above came a cacophony of imprecations, struggling bodies and a fist striking a chin. Down she went, hand over hand; another window space; another mossy sill; more rough stones. She listened for an arrow hissing towards the chamber window. Instead, a deep voice called from below:

'Jump, Lady! I'll catch you!'

How far was it?

She shut her stinging eyes, let go and plummeted. Time stopped. Then she felt her body strike hard muscle under a coarse jerkin. There was a breathless grunt, a buckling of knees, and she and Arraitch and the handbag were tangled amid soaking weeds and rubbish. She gasped, sprang to her feet and winced.

'Horses, fast! Where are my clothes?'

'In your saddlebag. Lady, you're hurt!'

'Strlzhav is worse hurt but alive. Go, Arraitch!'

Horses neighed in the castle courtyard, hooves stamped, hounds bayed; there were shouts of rage, commands, the clang and creak of an opening gate.

'Lady, you're not fit to ride, you must–'

'*Go*, Arraitch. Ride east. Gather as many comrades as you can, rouse the peasants in every krefmark. We'll meet in Strelsau at the Lenmir.'

She staggered towards their horses. Arraitch outpaced her, untied their mounts, flung her into her saddle, mounted his dun gelding and kicked him into a gallop. He heard Klarissa's bay mare crash through the undergrowth, heading north-west. His great heart sank. She couldn't escape unless the pursuers chased him instead of her, but they were too many and too skilled to be misled. She was lost, the Revolution was lost, because of her oath to wreak vengeance on Strlzhav. He could do nothing now but obey her final order.

There was an interlude of confusion among the hunters. They heard two riders gallop in opposite directions: which was their quarry? Then three agriotytes dashed baying and salivating towards the trees where the horses had been tethered. Their fangs, and the hog-like bristles on their backs and muzzles, suggesting kinship with Lekhissa. The kennel guard halted them with a command. Ekwyor Tupsroot rode up and dismounted. Her detachment and the castle retainers followed with Krev Strlzhav carried on a litter, hand bandaged, his wife and two medipriests fussing in attendance.

The ekwyor ran her hand through the grass and held it beside her lantern. Her subordinates wished she wouldn't grin.

'Blood.' Her gravel voice relished the word. 'She could mount and ride but one of those bullets must have struck her so she won't get far. Which doesn't let you off the hook, Lascar; you disobeyed an order. Krevjalem, your hounds will follow the trail of blood, but will they kill the female?'

'They're trained not to kill, Ekwyor,' replied the kennel guard, 'just to immobilise intruders and inflict non-fatal injuries.'

'Good. Let them go; we'll follow.' She turned to the krevjalem. 'With your consent, Your Excellency, we'll take the female to Strelsau for questioning, confession and trial.'

'Hold her until after the election, Ekwyor.' Klarissa's kick had reduced the krev's voice to a croak; the medipriests feared injury to the organ that rendered their master splenetic. 'I wish to witness the questioning, but I'll have no time before then.'

He'd announce the arrest of the Ulyanova at the start of the National Cake Day ceremony. He'd display his injured hand to prove his part in her capture. He'd be a hero; election victory was assured. He lit a damp cigarette and started to feel better.

The ekwyor saluted him and led her twenty-strong force in the hounds' wake. Her agate eyes gleamed. Never had a hunt excited her more.

An hour later, after the wounded krev had been lulled to sleep, his wife inspected his wardrobe. A legend had been written in black marker ink on his new white ceremonial robes: *Zitagu Epanastijan*. She shook her head.

'Long live the Revolution', indeed,' she said. 'How childish.'

She ordered a minion to bleach out the offending words.

Chapter 59

The tales of Faerie are Grimm but the reality is Grimmer.
— Old Ruritanian Proverb

Bread, meat and wine were laid out on a beautiful woven carpet so Rory could eat and drink while he wrestled with the riddle. Lekhissa liked her dinners well-fed. Two tiny men served him, smoking pipes, flitting above the greensward on iridescent wings.

If (thought Rory) I asked Ruritanian A 'If I asked Ruritanian B, who comes from a time or place where 'dakh' and 'khad' have meanings opposite to those in your time and place, whether two plus two equals four, what would she reply?' – then I'd hear the word for 'No' in Ruritanian A's time and place. Which wouldn't help.

'So faerie folk *are* tiny,' he observed.

'Taurocoprology,' snapped one of the little men, reverting to human size. 'Perspective, mortal. Things and people look smaller when they're further away.'

'In this realm,' said the other, 'space and time shift. The near becomes far, the brief grows long; the far shrinks to near, the long dwindles to brief.'

I could ask 'Is 'Dakh' the correct answer to the question, 'Are you from the same time and place as Ruritanian B?' but then I'd be relying on the willingness of my Ruritanian to tell the truth. If she was truthful I'd hear the word for 'No'. It still wouldn't help. Whether 'dakh' means 'yes' or 'no' is irrelevant.

Rory felt hyperaware, perhaps because of the exquisite location and the imminence of being eaten with chestnut stuffing. Or was it an effect of recent traumas, or the much-needed food and wine?

He supposed the condition resembled mescaline intoxication or religious ecstasy, though he'd experienced neither. The soil exhaled the scents of time and custom. Every sense was a vibrating reed blown by a nature spirit, transmuting the Arcadian scene to a simulacrum of Otherworld. His mind glowed with the emanations of the fecund landscape, the fractal geometries of cumulus clouds and the rotation of the earth; or did he sense the geographical drifting of Ruritania? Trees danced sarabandes in the verdant breeze; their myriad leaves were limpid and munificent, ineffable in their loveliness. Birds with white and gold and orange plumage sang for the joy of singing. Effulgent flowers dazzled the eye and enriched the air with their presence, countering the noisome odour of Lekhissa. Multihued butterflies abounded. Rory was glad of his sunglasses. A city-dweller for whom the countryside was a novelty, he was enchanted; and he felt he'd started to understand his chronic *déjà vu*.

I could ask Lekhissa, 'Is it true that if "Dakh" means "Yes" then you're a gargoyle?' She'd have to answer with whichever word means 'Yes'. But that wouldn't help, either. Enchantment notwithstanding, I'm going to be eaten. And I won't enjoy it.

The setting was idyllic, the scents (Lekhissa excluded) intoxicating, the meat and wine delicious. But how, in this place where beauty and horror cohabited, could he crack an intractable logic puzzle within half an hour?

He wished he could discuss it with Ariadne. She wouldn't be able to solve it but she'd inspire him! Where was she? Was she safe? Had she reached Castle Bauntzi, wherever that was?

He fell into a half-doze and explained Lekhissa's riddle to the spirit of Professor Weisheitsliebhaber.

Chapter 60

Mortals who enter the Faerie Realm and return from it are 'transformed'. Their minds and bodies may acquire new powers but they experience a sense of loss. This can cause them to use their powers for personal gain rather than the common good. A central theme in Ruritanian moral philosophy concerns the rightness or wrongness of entering the Faerie Realm and choosing whether to return, and the ethics of the returnee's subsequent behaviour.
— Dai O'Genies, 'A Primer of Ruritanian Philosophy'

Klarissa heard the hounds behind her. She was dazed and bruised and sore. Drizzle soaked her hair and her ruined garb. She shivered in the saddle and clutched her handbag. The agriotytes were gaining. Horses were following – many horses. She wrestled her mind into focus, slowed to a walk and turned off the track into the dense forest. Low cloud hid the stars and the crescent moon.

She alighted and led her mare through the undergrowth. In a clearing stood the remains of a deserted shack that had once sheltered a charcoal-burner or an outlaw or hermit. She tethered the horse to a tree at the edge of the clearing and crawled into the squalid hut, not touching its walls for fear they'd collapse. There was barely enough roof to cover her but there was a small patch of dry ground in one corner. She hunkered down on it.

The agriotytes arrived a minute later, a trio of deep-throated growls with dripping jaws. Klarissa uttered a low crooning chant and remained still. The growls diminished, then ceased. She continued to chant. The hounds' lips relaxed, their jaws stopped dripping and their mouths closed. Three muzzles sniffed inquiry. Within four minutes the animals were lying on the ground, one on his back. Still chanting, Klarissa reached out and stroked his tummy. He wagged and whimpered. His companions demanded like attention. She stroked them and they fell into stupefied slumber.

She stopped chanting, opened her handbag and applied salves and plasters to her injuries. The nail-less toe gave most pain. She dressed it with herbal ointment and wrapped a small bandage around it. Then, taking exaggerated care, she stripped off the remains of her attire. Tiptoeing past the sleeping hounds she went to the horse, patted her and recovered her clothes from the saddlebag. Dressed in dryish denim she felt warmer, though the rough garments chafed her torn skin and the wooden shoes hurt her battered feet. She rubbed her hair with a cloth, returned to the hovel, curled up on the dry portion of floor and sank into fitful sleep.

Ekwyor Tupsroot and her fellow-hunters rode onwards. Within a quarter of an hour they knew they'd lost the trail.

'The quarry's gone to earth,' snarled the ekwyor, 'but where are the agriotytes? They must have found her. Why haven't they spoken? Kennel-man, summon them!'

The kennel guard called and whistled: no response.

'Was the female armed?' asked an ekwyrin. 'Could she have killed the dogs?'

'Three fierce hounds?' said another. 'Unlikely. In any case we'd have heard the noise.'

The wet darkness hid the ekwyor's frown.

'A charm could account for their silence. The female's climbing skills suggest Faerie Realm connections. She must be hiding in the wood so we won't find her in the dark. We'll divide into five groups of four, take up positions three hundred fathoms apart starting half a league from Castle Strlzhav, and wait for daylight. There are no other horse-ways nearby so she must return to this track. Her injuries will force her to seek help, so even if she escapes us here we'll find her in the nearest church surgery. She can't elude us for long.'

Chapter 61

The characters in fairytales change yet the tales remain the same.
  — *Old Ruritanian Proverb*

'Consider the question you wish to answer, Rory,' said Professor Weisheitsliebhaber. 'Ask Lekhissa if she'll answer it. Link this by double implication to a question with a *known* 'Yes' answer.'

Ah, thought Rory, a glimmer of light.

Lekhissa's snarl roused him.

'Time's up. And as a mere mortal you can't have solved my riddle.'

Her salivating grin did nothing for Rory's *sang froid*. He cleared his throat and his voice was almost steady.

'There's a question I want to be answered so I've incorporated it into my solution. Here goes: *Will you tell me why Britain has become involved in the government's attempts to eliminate SPAR, if and only if you would answer "dakh" to the question "does two plus two equal four"?*'

Lekhissa made a noise like an organ pipe with a sixty-four-foot appetite and big teeth. Few entities in either the mundane or the Faerie Realm are less alluring than an unhappy gargoyle.

'Dakh.'

'Thanks.' Rory wiped his brow. 'I really want to know.'

'The answer will be shown to you.' The gargoyle growled. 'Congratulations. No one has ever solved my riddle until now.'

'First time for everything.'

'I was looking forward to a delicious morsel of mortal. Now I'll have to eat the chestnut stuffing on its own. Want some?'

223

'No thanks, the meat and wine are enough. Great riddle, Lekhissa! Would you mind metamorphosing to something less terrifying before you grant my wish?'

'Least I can do.'

Lekhissa shrank to little more than twice human size, shed her scales, retracted her muzzle, shrank her fangs, reduced her number of legs to two, developed a blonde suburban hairdo, attired herself in a white sequinned dress and grew two gossamer wings. She smelt better, too.

'I don't understand how the Faerie Realm operates,' said Rory. 'I know Ruritanian academics have published various conjectures.'

'They haven't a clue,' said Lekhissa. 'The question embedded in your solution pleased me, Rory Redman. You've become concerned about Ruritania's needs and future. After I've shown you the answer my two sisters will each grant you a wish. Close your eyes.'

Rory closed his eyes and felt himself flying through time and space, beyond when and where, from here and now to there and henceforth, until he squelched to a halt beside a stagnant pond. Insects buzzed. Of Lekhissa there was no sign.

'Who're you?' asked the handsome prince idling miserably by the water's edge. A fat blonde woman fawned on him, stuffing her face with cake.

'Rory Redman. I'm … visiting. May I ask who *you* are?'

'The Frog Prince.' The man shot out a tongue half a fathom long, captured a fat mosquito and swallowed it. '*Alias* Crown Prince Elharic.' He pointed his thumb at the fat blonde. 'People like her go around kissing frogs. Ugh!' He screwed up his face, wiped his mouth, then shot out his tongue and swallowed another insect. 'See what she's done to me? The food's good here, but I want be in frog shape, not getting kissed humanoid by millers' daughters and lost princesses and other stupid bimbos.'

His tongue captured a dragonfly.

'Wasn't it your mother the Queen who –?'

224

'Yeah, yeah, everybody knows that.' The prince munched the dragonfly and swallowed. 'Want to be taken before the King?'

Rory frowned.

'I thought Ruritania was ruled by the aforementioned Queen.'

'You're in the *Faerie Realm*.'

'Things are different here, mortal,' said a passing witch. She was bent and warty, her nose almost touching her hairy chin, and the black conical hat on her greasy hair bore occult symbols. She wore a shabby black cloak and carried a knobbly stick. She had just one large tooth. 'Nevertheless, *your* lands would have no stable culture without us. Deep down you believe in us because you're brought up on our stories. We're the spiritual glue that binds your collective past to your present and future. You'd have no civilisation without tales of kings and princes, spells and curses, hapless maidens and brave heroes. Always a king rules in the Faerie world. The king has a beautiful daughter with many suitors, and then an unlikely hero arrives ...'

Yes, thought Rory, it all begins from the mind. The Faerie Realm *exists in the mind*, Popper's World Three emanating from World Two. Without it, our everyday World One would collapse about our ears. So much for critical realism and Quinean empiricism. No wonder the clown at the airport laughed when I told him. Professor Reciprocus told us how Ruritanian physics begins from the mind. And even *I* could see that the Gödelpus Unsatisfiability Theorem is psychologically though not logically true.

'So if SPAR's revolution succeeds and eradicates feudalism in Ruritania–'

'Her people could be severed from us,' said the prince. 'Slugs guarding the portals could prevent any mortal from entering our Realm again. Why do you think *your* tales of Faerie are set in what to you is a feudal past?'

'Gizza 'nother cake,' said the fat blonde.

'Come, mortal,' said the witch, 'dine at my gingerbread café and bistro deep in this enchanted forest. My Hansel and Gretel pie is second to none.'

'Will Rapunzel be there?' The prince sounded both hopeful and hopeless.

'Probably,' said the witch, 'but she's had a new haircut. Looks good on her. Far more practical and less likely to dislocate her neck than those six-fathom-long tresses she wore. Took a dozen maidservants to brush it every morning and Asclepius knows how many parasitic invertebrates dwelt in it.'

'Those parasitic invertebrates,' mourned the prince, 'were all I admired about her.'

In a trice, Rory found himself at the gingerbread café and bistro. The Hansel and Gretel pie smelled delicious. He opted for a green salad. The prince sat outside devouring flies, dreamily eyeing the middle distance where a youth clad in Elizabethan garb played the lute and sang a haunting roundelay. Rapunzel, dressed in jeans and trainers and a loose-fitting sweater, hair boyishly short, neck muscles bulging, ignored everyone and tucked into a platter of pie. Gravy trickled down her pretty chin.

Then Rory was airborne again. He closed his eyes and landed on a mossy bank at the forest's edge, many leagues from the maze beside St Avicenna's, Lekhissa stood nearby, grinning. Even in humanoid guise the grin was unsettling.

'Is your question answered, Rory Redman?'

'I believe so.'

'Now I'll answer a question you haven't yet asked. SPAR will provoke the peasants into attacking the castles in every krefmark. They'll burn them and murder the krevoj and their families. Do you, with your new-found concern for Ruritania, want this to happen?'

'How could I prevent it?' said Rory.

'By deciding what wishes you'll ask my sisters to grant.'

Chapter 62

Much of Ruritania is covered with forest, some of it enchanted. Almost all the rest, apart from the mountains in the north where the Vona rises, is agricultural land. Few tracks lead through the forest so highwaypersons make good incomes. Some highwaypersons have become folk heroes; their deeds are said to contribute to SPAR's income. Blue Primrose seem powerless to stop them; the police seldom try.

— Ariadne Sowerby, 'First Impressions of Ruritania'

Klarissa awoke at sunrise sore and stiff. She licked rainwater from the leaves but there was nothing to appease her hunger except a few fat green caterpillars. The agriotytes still slept. She murmured and they rose, stretched, wagged and lapped water from a puddle. She led her horse towards the track but halted; ahead of her were four ekwyroj, two asleep, two smoking, guns at the ready. She bit her lip and retraced her steps, hushing the horse. The ekwyroj heard something, but they'd been hearing noises from the forest all night. One cracked a joke.

Klarissa returned to the hovel and lay down. Her stomach complained about the caterpillars. She was hungry and nauseous but she managed to doze, and it was past noon when she moved again. The four ekwyroj were still in place.

She stole westward through the trees, parallel to the track, leading the mare. The hounds followed. Another Blue Primrose quartet waited in ambush. She moved on again. Notwithstanding her resilience, she was exhausted by the cocktail of fright, injuries,

227

hunger, the night's exertions and discomforts and the fear of capture. She saw a third Blue Primrose group, then a fourth.

She stopped and hid again. Each group was organised: two rested and slept while the other two kept watch, then they changed places. They had rations for another twenty-four hours. She hadn't.

The sun sank towards the horizon beyond Strelsau. The prospect of another night alone in the forest held no appeal. Klarissa's entire body hurt; her needs for food, shelter and medicine were pressing. If she rode hard, she thought, she might outmanoeuvre her enemies. They'd divided into at least four groups so they'd need time to reassemble. She took a deep breath, prayed, led her horse on to the track and mounted. Her handbag snuggled against her ribs. She urged the bay mare into a trot, a canter, a gallop.

The agriotytes gave her away. They caught the scent of their master on the evening breeze and charged towards him, barking. The kennel guard heard, rushed to meet them, spotted the target and blew his hunting horn. The fifth and final Blue Primrose group were relaxing after afternoon rations, but the blast of the horn thrust them into their saddles, guns drawn. Given another half minute, Klarissa would have found them unprepared and could have galloped past them. In the event she had no chance.

Four ekwyroj blocked her way; sixteen were closing in behind her. She considered options. If she bolted into the wood her horse would be shot, and she was too weak to outrun twenty of the government's élite forces on foot. She looked upwards; there were branches on which she could swing and climb if her captors were distracted for a few seconds, but there was nothing to distract them. She had all their attention. She reined to a halt.

Four fathoms from her captive, Ekwyor Tupsroot snapped orders. Then she lit a cigar and walked her horse forward, grinning. Surrounded, weary, hurt, famished, sick, wrists now roped together behind her back, Klarissa sat upright in the saddle and spoke not a word.

'I've looked forward meeting you, Pana Alterleta,' said the ekwyor. 'I relish the prospect of questioning you in Blue Primrose HQ. You caused the deaths of six ekwyroj and we'll make you pay for them. You assaulted and injured the krevjalem of Ruritania in his own castle and you'll pay for that too. Your full confession, including the names of other SPAR leaders, will be recorded. It will take time, but you'll tell us everything.'

There was contempt, even amusement, in Klarissa's eyes. The ekwyor raised her right gauntlet and smashed it across her face. The prisoner swayed but in a moment she was upright again, staring at her enemy. The rope around her wrists was tight; she made surreptitious experiments but couldn't free her hands.

To the twenty ekwyroj her calmness seemed eerie. Ekwyor Tupsroot blew cigar smoke into her face.

'Our noble krevjalem wishes to participate in your interrogation. He'll enjoy watching our men operate in shifts.' She paused, seeming to ruminate. Around her, nineteen uneasy chuckles sounded. 'One detail we'll need to consider is when to relieve you of your pretty eyes. Once you're blind, what's coming next will be a surprise, and we all love surprises. On the other hand it could be more amusing if you *can* see what's in store, so perhaps we'll leave one eye until later.'

Klarissa smiled. The ekwyor raised her hand to strike her again but changed her mind.

'We'll leave now,' she said, blowing a smoke-ring. 'As we ride, you may ponder what awaits you.'

Then, as she turned her horse westwards, someone crashed towards her through the undergrowth at the forest's edge and called her name. She halted and stared.

Chapter 63

Morris-dancing has so many variants among English villages that its origin was surely polygenic. But since it could have sprung from 'Moorish' dancing, or from fourteenth century Spain, or elsewhere, why has it become exclusively English? Should we not seek to export at least some variants to other countries?

— Honorary Secretary's report, AGM of the William Kemp Society, 2012

Lekhissa was right: her big sister was scarier than her. Rory didn't like Sporota's shears.

'I wish,' he said, 'for a horse with all necessary tack, and the skill to ride it; including the ability to mount and dismount without disgracing myself.'

Sporota grinned. Rory preferred the shears.

'Easy,' she said. 'But to satisfy your *unspoken* wish I'll abduct a shining white charger from the stables of Castle Bauntzi. He'll know his way home.'

'How did you know I want to go to Castle Bauntzi?'

Lekhissa laughed.

'We divine your wish to re-unite … No, *unite* yourself with the mortal female Ariadne. We'll ensure you can ride the horse.'

Rory tilted his head. Lekhissa was quite pretty in her fairy guise, though she was still taller than him, but Sporota had the aesthetic appeal of a traffic accident.

'Thanks. Lekhissa, if you can read my mind, why didn't you know I'd solved your riddle?'

'Mind reading has limits.'

Really? thought Rory. Even in the Faerie Realm, even for gargoyles, mind reading has limits? Aloud, he asked: 'Do you know if Ariadne is at Castle Bauntzi?'

'Yes. Thad Masim took her there. It was a diversion from his route to Strelsau but it ensured she wasn't robbed, raped and murdered *en route.*'

Relief flooded him. So it isn't smart for a woman to travel unaccompanied through Ruritania, he thought. Mind you, some women I know wouldn't be at risk, unlike such fools as chose to attack them. However, if these three sisters have told the truth–

'Dakh,' chorused the gargoyles.

'What wish,' said Othloc, toying with spindle and distaff, 'do you want *me* to grant, Rory Redman?'

Since he'd met Lekhissa, Rory had seen Ruritania in a new light: the people moved with the rhythms of the land because they were part of it. Therefore, only if the rhythms were disordered would castles burn and blood be spilled. If they were brought into harmony there could be peace, perhaps even happiness.

'I doubt whether this wish is feasible, Othloc, but here goes.' He smiled at the least menacing sister. 'If the peasants could learn Morris-dancing it might divert them from their rampage of arson and murder. But there isn't nearly enough time to teach them before National Cake Day. Even with Faerie Flight it would take weeks to get around ... And they'd need the right equipment and the right personnel.'

'Tell us what you'll require,' said Sporota, clicking her shears. 'We can accomplish the impossible, up to a point.'

'Green.' Rory was thinking aloud. 'SPAR supporters favour green, with white ... We'll need bellpads, baldrics, rosettes, waistcoats, knee-length breeches, wooden clogs, straw hats, neckerchiefs and armbands, small silvery bells. If we could establish a team in every village we reach ... But can I even *start* to teach the peasants and still reach Castle Bauntzi before everyone leaves for Strelsau?'

'Leave the time dilation to us,' said Lekhissa. 'It's delightfully simple and completely inexplicable.'

'Like a woman?'

'If Ariadne heard that remark she'd beat you over the head with a ceramic utensil. Klarissa would ignore it. Kjym Krev Bauntzia would laugh. Tomen Comtra would sigh.'

'How well you understand mortal women. Can we really achieve what I wish?'

'We can reach thirty or thirty-five villages without straining the temporal bubble,' said Lekhissa. 'The clothing will be easy; I'm nifty with a measuring rod, and as you see my little sister has her distaff and spindle. What else will be needed?'

'We'll adapt local dance forms and go for sets of six or eight depending on the size of village. Music … pipe and tabor if possible, but we can use any instruments – fiddle, flute, shawm, crumhorn, slide trumpet, ram's horn, dustbin lid, barleycorns in dried pig's bladder … I'll act as foreman while we're teaching, then each village can appoint its own foreman and squire and bagman-come-ragman. I'll encourage each team to elect a fool for better communication, maybe a beast …'

Sporota ran eighteen of her fingers over her scales, yawned and crunched her mandible. The click of her shears echoed.

'You'll need to explain what sets are, and what the foreman and squire and the rest are supposed to do.'

'I know, enthusiasm's a bore. It's been a while since I danced. Er … am I *right* to believe that widespread adoption of the Morris would reduce the risk of mayhem?'

Lekhissa's smile sweetened. She'd enjoyed the chestnut stuffing, even without mortal.

'The peasants *might* be persuaded to express their anger and frustration through dance rather than burning and slaughtering; but if you want to be sure, you must ask the Oracle in the Coracle.'

Yeah, I suppose that figures, thought Rory. Aloud, he added: 'I wonder whether we should persuade the people to dance before or after the local ghrunli match … Details, details. Come, dear gargoyles, let's visit the Oracle in the Coracle and then get – dare I say "weaving"?'

232

Chapter 64

Ruritania, like Britain, has a constitutional monarchy, an institution most of the world has set aside. British anti-monarchists see it as a relic of feudalism, Ruritanian anti-monarchists as feudalism's principal bastion. They ask how any country can preach democracy when she has an unelected head of state, and consider all rulers whose status is granted automatically by right of birth to be descendants of robber barons and warlords. Monarchy, they say, entrenches hereditary privilege at the core of public life: it embodies social inequality and fosters a conservatism that only pretends to be apolitical. Moreover, these supposedly 'neutral' monarchies are not mere constitutional decoration: if they choose, monarchs can exert unaccountable influence because the judiciary, the police and the military pledge allegiance to the Crown, not Parliament. Monarchists counter by claiming that royal families boost the economy by attracting overseas visitors. Also, royal births, marriages and funerals unite the country in celebration or sorrow. But, say their opponents, that's because the media and the political class form a sycophantic phalanx around the institution, reporting royal events in tones befitting a one-party state while bleating about stability and continuity. The media create rather than voice majority opinion, making dissent seem petty and ill-natured. However, would a presidential system be better? To see the resurgence of the hereditary principle in countries that have rejected monarchy, consider North Korea.

— Ariadne Sowerby, 'First Impressions of Ruritania'

Kjym Krev Bauntzia closed Ariadne's book and smiled. She and her guest, both casually attired in tracksuits and trainers, had been discussing the slugfest for days. Politics made a refreshing change.

'You understand Ruritania.' Kjym's English betrayed her Oxford education; her poise revealed her hereditary privilege. 'But in your book, shades of opinion dance over the polished floor of objectivity. You overlooked one compelling argument for monarchy: a president is the country's chief executive but must also discharge ceremonial duties such as entertaining visiting heads of state. For one individual to fill both roles is exhausting and therefore counterproductive. Constitutional monarchy allocates the two functions to different people.'

Kartor stirred in his cradle and gurgled. The baby's father, Nadhan, had not yet returned from refereeing a ghrunli match between two of Kjym's villages.

'I wouldn't dare voice anti-monarchist opinions in Ruritania.' Ariadne sighed. '*First Impressions* hasn't sold well. Most people don't believe your country exists.'

She poured tea from a gilded china pot shaped like a rabbit with bright blue ears. Her eyes had accommodated to Kjym's décor, but Rory would need his dark glasses. Where *was* Rory? Still in St Avicenna's? Or had Blue Primrose dragged him back to Strelsau? She wished he were with her. Then she could at least try to keep him out of further trouble.

'You are thinking of Rory Redman again,' said Kjym.

If people read my mind so easily, thought Ariadne, I'll fail as a lawyer. Of course she'd confided in Kjym, so Kjym knew about Rory's dealings with Krev Schammerbass, his attempts to find the Ulyanova, the miasma grenade and the arrest at St Avicenna's. Kjym had drawn inferences.

'Why would I be thinking about *him*?' said Ariadne. 'I know, he's brilliant, athletic, gorgeous … but he's impulsive, totally irresponsible, never makes a commitment. Continually takes risks and gets into trouble and has to consult our firm in Manchester. That's how I met him.'

Kjym drank tea. Her eyes twinkled like sapphires.

'Of course. No sensible woman would fall in love with such a man. He must be sad that you are sensible. Has he involved himself with SPAR?'

Ariadne snorted.

'Wouldn't put it past him. He'd see it as an *adventure*. A wizard wheeze. And they say this Klarissa looks stunning.'

The three Ruritanian Spitzes made frenzied leaps at the castle door as minions rushed to unbar it and admit Nadhan.

'*Jappi, Hvaggi, Phlebag, hiri-jats!*' shouted Kjym. '*Hiri-jats, jetz!*'

The dogs duly came here and came here now. Like the humans in Kjym's krefmark they obeyed her without hesitation. Nadhan limped in their wake and greeted Ariadne with a grin and Kjym with a kiss. He was a healthy young man, handsome except for the bruised face and injured right arm.

'How was the match?' said Kjym.

'Second Village knock most of First Village into pits before I blow final whistle. Medipriest deal with worst injury.' He winked at Ariadne. 'Unlike most ghrunli referees I lose not teeth. Yet.'

He patted the dogs, then went to the cradle and woke Kartor by singing a nursery song. The baby began to cry. Kjym rolled her eyes at Ariadne.

'More serious,' Nadhan added. He sat the baby on his lap and poured a drink from the blue-eared rabbit pot. 'Ah. This is need … When Second Village players go home I follow with trophy. You cannot guess what rest of villagers do.'

'Anything I need to deal with?' said Kjym.

'No, but strange. Eight wear crazy dress and dance with stick and bell and white rag, rest play motley instrument or watch and cheer. Ghrunli player join them. I see nothing like it.'

Oh, but I have, thought Ariadne. Her heart quickened. I know only one person who would have taught a group of peasants such a dance. But how? And where is he?

'Strange, Nadhan, but not serious,' said Kjym. 'Is there something else?'

Nadhan's discomfort was palpable. He hugged the baby.

'When I took horse back to stable, one animal is missing. It is Hobunay. None of minion say where he go even when I crack whip.'

Kjym's face paled and darkened at the same time.

'Hobunay?' she whispered. 'No! How?'

Chapter 65

One of the legends of Lake Brojginzha, near Hrincacz, concerns the 'Oracle in the Coracle'. According to this tale, a traveller in the Faerie Realm may seek the Oracle's guidance. She is said to emerge from the mists of the lake on a frail round unicorn-skin boat, and if the supplicant crosses her palm with silver she inhales the toxic fumes from the water and answers his or her questions about the future. Her answers are alleged to be less cryptic than those of most oracles.

— The Unideker Guide to Ruritania

Lake Brojginzha was smelly. Rory wrinkled his nose and stood beside an ancient palm tree. The three gargoyles had retreated to the forest edge. Forest edges seemed to play significant albeit passive roles in Faerie Realm events.

The frail craft coalesced from the mist. At first Rory thought it was empty, but a figure in a long grey gown slowly took shape in it. The scene belonged in a spooky black and white film, though there was no creepy music. The figure stood tall and placid, propelling the coracle with a single oar. Her voice seemed to travel from afar and yet to whisper in Rory's ear.

'Cross my palm with silver.'

I can't reach your hand from here, thought Rory, so how …? Oh, right.

He took one of Colonel Barrington's cufflinks from his pocket, scratched the shape of a cross on the palm tree's trunk, and stuck the cufflink into the middle of it. The Oracle nodded.

'Yes, I can,' she said.

'Can you really foretell the future?' said Rory.

'They will,' said the Oracle.

'Will the peasants in all the villages the gargoyle sisters and I have managed to reach continue to practise Morris-dancing?'

'Yes,' said the Oracle. 'Morris-dancing peasants won't distress any poor helpless effigies by burning the aristocrats they're of.'

'Will Morris-dancing distract the peasants from burning and looting the krevoj's castles and destroying the Queen's peace?'

'SPAR will not love you for it.'

'What opposition will there be to my scheme?'

Okay, thought Rory, I can live with that. Now he truly understood the meaning of *déjà vu*.

'Any more questions and you must cross my palm with silver again,' said the Oracle. After a pause she added, 'Don't mention it.'

'I've asked enough questions,' said Rory. 'Thanks for your guidance.'

The oar stirred the oily water. The coracle and its occupant faded into the mist, which swirled and closed like a vaporous curtain. Rory watched, then turned away.

The scene before him was transformed. He was still in a black and white film but the forest edge had vanished. Now he stood in a ruined town – ancient, mediaeval, perhaps eighteenth century. Houses gaped as though battered by cannonballs or bombs. Broken walls rose from a riot of rubble and furniture. Here was half a mill, there a church with smashed windows and half its roof missing, rafters like bones in a decomposing body. Closest to Rory tottered a mansion or palace, its ballroom open to the winds yet replete with wealth: ornate furnishings, mirrors, candelabra, servants dispensing wine and dainties to the dancers and assembled gentry. A small ensemble played: harpsichord, oboe, violin, viola, cello. A minuet, I suppose, thought Rory. I believe it takes months to learn how to dance it.

A gentleman in rich attire and periwig left the group beside the marble fireplace and beckoned. The ruler, Rory guessed, and stepped into the monochrome world. The King of Faerie bowed. Rory returned the gesture. He thought the room and its occupants would blind him if they were in colour.

'Welcome to my palace, Mr Redman. It seems you are to be congratulated. The walls of this town, such as remain, echo with your praise.'

The King's tone was sardonic. He took a pinch of snuff and offered the silver box to Rory.

'No thank you, sir. Tobacco and I don't agree.'

'Ha-hah! The man who solved Lekhissa's Riddle doesn't have an amicable relationship with tobacco! Has he an amicable relationship with wine?'

He snapped his fingers and two servants approached. One poured a Lower Vona claret into a glass and presented it to Rory. The other poured a Szipad Riesling and offered it. Surely, thought Rory, servants shouldn't leer when they present wine? The Riesling shone like moonlight. The claret was the only scrap of colour in the ballroom, the palace, the ruined town; the colour of blood, of sunset, of Valentine's Day roses against a monochrome engraving or a Doré print. The King waved away the Riesling. Rory sniffed and tasted the claret, then drank it.

He found himself airborne again, flying who knew whither.

Chapter 66

'Democracy' was a pejorative word until well into the nineteenth century. Not until after the Second World War did it denote an ideal to which all western political parties had to pay lip service. Today, in countries that pretend to this ideal, democracy has become contaminated and fragile. 'Government of the people by the people' is a fine slogan, but in practice the franchise is limited everywhere and always. In modern Britain everyone can vote – provided they are over eighteen and not in prison or certified insane and provided they can prove they are British subjects. Those restrictions exclude a significant portion of the population. Liberal democracies espouse the ideal of majority rule, but most governments are elected by a numerical minority of voters. In the showpiece of modern democracy, Switzerland, women did not enjoy full voting rights until 1991. And women never had rights in the cradle of democracy, Athens. Nor did other slaves.
— *Klarissa Krefin Strlzhava, 'Democracy'. Final Honours Dissertation, 2011*

He was riding along the route he'd taken a day earlier – or three weeks earlier – with Klarissa, Arraitch and Mangler. How he'd reached it again was a mystery. He passed the burnt-out village, where the dead were being buried and rebuilding had begun. Hobunay snorted and tossed his head. Rory patted his neck and urged him into a trot.

He was still hyperaware of his surroundings: crops flourishing, cows grazing, trees whispering, flowers blooming, birds calling; sensations he'd experienced in the Faerie Realm. For the first time he could remember he didn't need dark glasses. The beauty of the land wasn't hurting his eyes. Did he no longer need to seek shade?

The faint sound of Vaughan Williams's *Norfolk Rhapsody* came to his ears and he traced the music to a cowpat. Then he followed the horse-path into woodland, which thickened into forest. Lost in ruminations about the dynamics of Faerie, the beauty of nature ('I must learn more about flora and fauna'), the devastation of the village and the resilience of peasants, the repetitive teaching of Morris-dancing and the inner reality of traditional lore, he failed to notice where he was going. *Déjà vu* had limits. In the blink of an eye he was surrounded by twelve people clad in green, all bearing bows and quivers. Among them he recognised Arraitch.

'*Ciskza!*' whispered Arraitch. His finger slid across his mouth, simulating a zip. '*Halt!*'

Rory stopped, dismounted and walked forwards, holding Hobunay's reins. One of the green-clad dozen pointed northwards and whispered through tears: the Ulyanova had been captured by the oppressors' lackeys. The others seemed close to weeping, too, but their arrows were nocked. And their eyes were suspicious: on what mission, their faces demanded, had Rory been riding alone through the forest? Whence the horse that now walked beside him?

'Krev Strlzhav's people?' whispered Rory.

Arraitch beckoned him forward and he followed. Not a twig snapped. A few fathoms ahead, a track cut east-west through the trees. A score of uniformed riders surrounded a lone figure on a bay mare; Rory recognised both the ekwyor in charge and her denim-clad captive. Klarissa's hands were roped together behind her back. The ekwyor smoked a cigar. To judge from her face and voice she was savouring developments unamusing for Klarissa. Rory nodded and tiptoed back to Hobunay, Arraitch in his wake.

The green-clad group was outnumbered; they had bows and arrows against firearms; they were on foot while the Blue Primrose ekwyroj were mounted; few of them had battle experience, while the ekwyroj were trained and disciplined. Nevertheless, Rory sensed an impending rescue attempt. The phrase 'heroic failure' sprang to his mind, along with 'cock-up'.

'Ekwyor Tupsroot knows me,' he told Arraitch. 'I'll approach her on foot so I won't seem a threat, then I'll talk to her to create a diversion. Then we'll rescue the Ulyanova.'

Arraitch spat and muttered something untranslatable.

'Give me a knife,' continued Rory. He pointed at the knife in Arraitch's belt.

Arraitch hesitated, frowned, and whispered words needing no translation. He gestured to a huge man with a ferocious beard. '*Eldzhay, yif.*'

Reluctantly, Eldzhay drew his knife and presented it to Rory. He too whispered words of menace. He looked weary, as though from travelling many leagues.

Rory patted Hobunay, dropped the reins, murmured to the horse and tiptoed towards the east-west path. A dozen arrows were pointed at his back and twelve pairs of eyes bored into him. Empathising with St Edmund he crashed forward through the undergrowth. Ekwyor Tupsroot spun her horse towards him.

'Ekwyor!' he called. 'Ekwyor! Thank goodness! I have information!'

The ekwyor saw a breathless figure break from the trees and lean on the captive female's horse, gasping. She dropped her cigar stub.

'We have search for you, Pan Redman. You are in much trouble.'

Rory eyed the glowing end of the Havana, glad it had rained the previous night. He propped his elbows on Klarissa's mare and his hands made subtle movements. Eldzhay's knife was sharp but the rope was thick. Klarissa gave no sign of recognition. She sat upright and unmoving on her saddle.

'I know, Ekwyor. You and Colonel Barrington placed me under arrest in St Avicenna's. I was abducted yesterday by three scoundrels dressed in Blue Primrose uniforms. I assumed they were genuine until we'd travelled half a league. Then they threatened to torture me unless I gave them the security plan from the bag I'd carried for Krev Schammerbass.'

Rory seemed to stop for breath but his fingers kept sawing. One strand of rope severed, then another. The ekwyor sat still, trying to make sense of Rory's gabbled English. Nineteen blank faces surrounded her; none of her companions had followed the rapid speech.

'You say, they ask security plan from England?'

'Yes, Ekwyor.'

'You have plan?'

'Had it. I was forced to hand it over. Sorry.'

'Tell, Redman. This is big trouble on you. This woman is one of three who take you from St Avicenna?'

Rory glanced up at Klarissa and frowned.

'Pana Laskesia? No. Why is *she* under arrest?'

'What is Laskesia? This woman is SPAR leader, Klarissa Alterleta. You know it, Redman. She seize you from St Avicenna?'

'Hang on, Ekwyor. This lady is Trellarta Laskesia. I followed her from London thinking she *was* Klarissa Alterleta, or Klarissa Krefin Strlzhava, or whatever the SPAR woman called herself. She looks a bit like her. I'm surprised she's under arrest but I sup-pose that's none of my business. I did find out where the Klarissa woman was supposed to be hiding in Strelsau, though, so I went there.'

The ekwyor shook her head to disentangle spiders of truth from the cobwebs of fiction.

'Continue.'

'Sorry. Out of breath,' said Rory.

Two more strands of rope gave way. Rory's wrists ached. Everyone was watching the ekwyor. His fingers worked unobserved.

'I have say, continue! Where is place you seek Alterleta?'

The words were machine-gun fire. Rory gulped.

'Er … it was a house in Vorgottenstrit, in district 23K. When I got there it was deserted. It had been vandalised. Klarissa What's-Her-Name wasn't there. I searched the house and found a sheaf of paper with the royal crest on it. I knew it was the security plan. I thought, I have to take this to Ekwyor Tupsroot and Colonel Barrington, so I put it in my pocket and ran back to the city centre. But before I could get to Blue Primrose HQ, some idiot threw a miasma grenade and I ended up in St Avicenna's. The plan was still in my jacket pocket. When I recovered I took it out of the pocket and hid it in a niche behind one of the statues. SPAR must have learned I had it. I don't know how.'

His forearms were burning but three quarters of the rope had yielded to Eldzhay's knife.

'You give to them?' The ekwyor looked furious. 'You lie! Why they seize and threat to torture if you have give to them?'

'No, you misunderstand. I held out as long as I could. I didn't go back to the cathedral hospital and give the plan to the abductors until yesterday evening. Then one of them rode away with it. I didn't hear his name. Or any of their names. I'm sorry, Ekwyor. I'd have brought you the plan if I could, but I couldn't handle three armed abductors unaided.'

His hands needed just another moment.

'Tell name!'

'Come on, Ekwyor, I've told you, I never heard their names!'

'Tell name or we shoot you in knee!'

The rope gave way. Klarissa swung her arms, leapt from the stirrups, stood for a split second on the mare's saddle, grabbed a branch and sprang into the trees. Rory whistled. Hobunay charged through the undergrowth into the midst of the Blue Primrose riders, scattering them. The white horse reared, leapt across the track and headed northwards, the direction Klarissa had taken. The bay mare followed.

The twenty ekwyroj regrouped and drew their guns, but by the time they'd fired two or three aimless shots, Klarissa had vanished, her course marked by a line of quivering branches.

'Shoot me, would you?' shouted Rory, sprinting after Hobunay. 'You want names? Tough luck!'

From behind the trees, bowstrings twanged and arrows flew. From the track, guns replied.

Chapter 67

Aristotle defined democracy as a condition in which the freemen and the poor carry the power of the state. He seems to have considered the meaning of the phrase 'power of the state' self-evident, but analysis reduces it to dust. Socrates said democracy comes into being after the poor have slaughtered some of their opponents, banished others, and given an equal share of freedom and authority to the rest. In other words, the poor select their rulers. Is that democracy? Socrates was referring to 'assembly' democracy, yet there is a sense in which the self-styled 'representative' democracies of today are the Socratic version – albeit with little slaughtering and banishing.
[...]
In Ruritanian elections you vote for a count, but in the High Bakery it is the count who votes. The same principle obtains in other states. We might dub the system 'demockracy'.
— Klarissa Krefin Strlzhava, 'Democracy'. Final
   Honours Dissertation, 2011

Nadhan extolled Kjym's prize horse: every year, before the journey to Strelsau for National Cake Day, she groomed Hobunay and dressed his mane and tail with her own hands. Every castle minion was now searching for him; villagers, too, when they could be distracted from Morris-dancing.

'We must recover him quick,' said Nadhan.

'I can't understand why nothing was seen or heard,' said Ariadne. 'Your stables are secure. Could any of your staff have been bribed?'

Nadhan shook his head.

'To find work and hovel in this krefmark is dream for peasant. None would put livelihood or liberty at risk.'

Ariadne kissed Kartor's forehead, smiled, and wondered what punishment a krev's court would impose on a horse thief. What opportunities might await a qualified lawyer? Nadhan said that irrespective of defence, whoever had stolen Hobunay would not be free to vote in the election. 'He must be in dungeon. And court maybe say surgery.'

Their dialogue turned to crime and punishment in general, and then to whether the forthcoming election could change voters' lives. Nadhan said there would be no meaningful change, but the voters enjoyed their illusion of power over government. The fantasy of democracy was justified because it ensured stability, continuity and peace.

'To play devil's advocate,' said Ariadne, 'why *should* voters have power? They're uninformed about political and economic issues. And does democracy truly offer stability or continuity? Those in government only want to be re-elected, not to solve the people's problems. So if the people's problems loom large enough, peace will end.'

Nadhan put his finger to his lips.

'Care, Ariadne; say not these things. It is SPAR argument.' He frowned. 'Something more than theft of Hobunay trouble you. Something more than politics. What, I ask?'

'It's nothing, Nadhan.'

Ariadne forced a smile. An irrational connection had formed in her mind. If Kjym's peasants had taken up Morris-dancing, Rory was responsible; how, she had no idea, but she knew it was he. Hobunay had vanished at the same time. Was Rory responsible for that, too? The notion was absurd. By his own admission, Rory knew nothing of horses, such as how to ride them, so why would he want Kjym's beloved white charger? And even if he did, how could he have accomplished the theft from afar? On the other hand, he had a track record for stealing

247

anything that wasn't screwed down. And if he wanted something that *was* screwed down, he'd steal the screws as well.

She strove to sever the ridiculous mental connection but it was like a loose tooth. Kartor awoke and complained, so she bounced him on her knee and sang to him until he laughed.

Chapter 68

At an election, the voters choose among candidates; thereafter the elected representative makes his or her own decisions and voters' opinions no longer matter. In Britain, an individual MP's opinions weigh like feathers against the cabinet's, and the cabinet's bend to the prime minister's. Thus, representative democracy makes one individual into a potential dictator, several stages removed from the voter. The individual MP, and the de facto dictator, can break every pre-election promise and even change party without consulting the electorate. The voter's sole power is to vote for someone else next time. Thus, the practical effect of replacing overt tyranny with democracy is to shift the mechanism of power from oppression to manipulation. In the USA today, no candidate can be elected to Congress without huge funding, so corporate interests manipulate the manipulators. In Britain and the rest of Europe the manipulation may be subtler but it is no less powerful, and no less omnipresent.

— Klarissa Krefin Strlzhava, 'Democracy'. Final
Honours Dissertation, 2011

'Wrong!' yelled Rory, charging after Klarissa. 'Your friends are the *other* way! For God's sake! Bloody women, no sense of direction!'

Behind him arrows whined, guns barked, people yelled, horses milled and whinnied, bodies fell. Glancing over his shoulder he saw Ekwyor Tupsroot drop from her saddle. Bullets struck trees to his right and left. Three huge hounds chased him, baying. Klarissa was swinging from tree to tree above his head.

'What the hell are you?' he shouted. 'Squirrel or gibbon?'

'Catch!' she called.

Two wooden shoes fell on his head. He bent to recover them and a bullet whined past him.

'Gibbon.'

He accelerated away from the hounds. Klarissa started to croon and chant. After a few seconds the horses changed direction and the hounds followed. Klarissa's voice controlled them from above. Rory blundered through the undergrowth below.

'This is suboptimal,' he thought. 'I've run into a forest, no idea where I am, horse gone another way, half the nation's security force after me because I've freed a dangerous terrorist, her friends are chasing me to get her back, there are three hungry hounds … and if I get away from Blue Primrose, Arraitch's gang *and* the hounds … Still, look on the bright side. Lekhissa didn't eat me, even with chestnut stuffing, and I've spiked some of SPAR's guns by teaching Morris-dancing. Maybe. *And* I haven't been shot yet.'

Klarissa stopped crooning. In the distance, the gunfire ceased. As far as Rory could tell the two events were unrelated. The movements of leaves above him grew slower.

'Again, catch.'

Klarissa's voice had become feeble. With no further warning she dropped from the tree. By instinct or reflex he held out his aching arms. For the second time in less than twenty-four hours she fell against masculine muscles, knocking Rory to the ground and winding him. Several seconds passed before the pair righted themselves. Then Rory blew a gasket.

'You stupid bloody fool! What the hell were you playing at, riding alone through the middle of …? Look at you! How did you get separated? If I hadn't met Arraitch and the–'

'Arraitch? Where?'

'Where you left him! He and his friends were about to attack Tupsroot's crew with bows and arrows against guns, just to rescue one feckless dim-witted female! There's less difference between bravery and rank fucking idiocy than there is between genius and madness!'

'Are they safe? Is Arraitch safe?'

'How the bloody hell should I know? You ran away from them and I followed. There's been a battle royal back there. Well, skirmish semi-royal. I've no idea who's alive and who's dead except you and me. As far as I can …' At last he noticed her injuries. 'Oh, God, what did the bastards do to you? Need to get you somewhere for treatment.'

'Not … oppressors. Fell down wall. Must …'

Fell down wall? What wall? Did it matter? What was he to do? Could he take her to Castle Bauntzi? Could he find his way, even with Hobunay's alleged homing instinct?

'Where the hell are we,' he muttered, 'except miles from bloody anywhere?'

The blood drained from Klarissa's face and her eyes rolled upwards.

'Horses,' she whispered, and fainted. Rory caught her again.

'Bugger. Here I am, lost in a forest in deepening twilight, and a beautiful woman faints into my arms. What am I supposed to do next? What did she mean, "horses"?'

He looked up. Hobunay and Klarissa's bay mare were staring at him from four fathoms away. They snorted, amused. The three hounds lay beside them, tongues lolling.

'Oh,' said Rory. 'I see. Except I don't. How the hell did she manage that?'

He heaved Klarissa on to her saddle, held her in place, took hold of the bay mare's reins and mounted the white charger.

'Okay, Hobunay: take us home.'

Chapter 69

Some people are alive only because it would be illegal to kill them.
— *Old Ruritanian Proverb*

'You must rest, Comrade Mangler.' The leaders spoke with one voice, casting doubt on their fitness to govern. 'You're exhausted.'

The leaders were copying the security plan, their pace furious. Time was emulating water in a leaky bucket. Mangler was now a Hero of the Revolution.

'Thanks, Comrades. But I must brief you about the timing of events on National Cake Day.'

'The briefing will be clearer after you've rested. Your ride was long and hard, in the dark, alone, with oppressors all around. Rest, Comrade. But first, if it won't exhaust you further, tell us what you did with the spy Redman after you'd taken the plan from him.'

Mangler grinned.

'Redman fled from my knife. Our late Comrade Stanislas's miasma grenade had laid him low, but he could run! He entered a maze beside St Avicenna's and I pursued him until I saw the maze was a trap laid by the gargoyle Lekhissa. He didn't reappear. Lekhissa has eaten him.'

Satisfaction purred around the room. No more suitable fate could be imagined. Two voices asked whether Eldzhay had found the Ulyanova and Arraitch. Mangler said Arraitch and the Ulyanova had been safe when he'd left them – rousing peasants to action, gathering comrades, preparing to return to Strelsau – but he hadn't seen Eldzhay.

Another leader began to address the meeting. He'd read a book about oratory.

'Go out to the countryside, Comrades, and hear the winds whispering insurrection among deserted hovels. A noiseless bugle-call resonates through village and town, summoning peasant and trader, striking harmonics from the earth beneath battered boots and bare blistered feet. The centuries-old visage of oppression trembles before it! They are rising, the people are rising, and we shall lead them to victory! Long live the Revolution!'

Mangler yawned, went to the window and let his thoughts drift into the black night. The city slept. At least, the law-abiding bits of it slept; the rest was wide awake as usual after sunset. But Mangler's orator comrade had a point: you could sense the unrest and excitement simmering beneath the dark sky that curved over Strelsau.

Mangler wondered what post the Revolutionary government would grant him. After his achievements with the metacake and the document he'd be able to choose whatever he pleased! He'd enjoy himself as Head of Security. Secretary of State for Bakery Busting could be fun, too.

Finance Minister was still more appealing, though he'd need deeper pockets.

Chapter 70

Never judge a krev by his or her castle.
— Old Ruritanian Proverb

Hobunay stumbled from the forest on to a track that wound among rich fields and meadows, raised his head and whinnied recognition and relief. The sun climbed above the trees and drove his shadow before him.

The vista was closed by the northern mountains; snow clinging to the topmost peaks glowed magenta against a periwinkle sky. Never thought of early sunlight *painting* skies and mountaintops before, mused Rory, delighting in his newfound photo-tolerance. Could he discern the headwaters of the Vona among the pinnacles? Weary and sore though he was he revelled in the diamond clarity of the young day, the miracle of the world renewed. Dew glittered on crops and the air was vibrant and vital. He wished it would rouse Klarissa. Throughout the journey she'd remained motionless, strapped to the saddle, murmuring indecipherable words. The long hours on horseback had surely worsened her injuries. It might be crazy to bring the Ulyanova to a krev's castle for help, but Krev Bauntzia was Ariadne's friend so he dared to hope.

Traversing a gentle rise he saw Castle Bauntzi at last; small, radiant with many colours, set on a mound embraced by a crystal stream. Even in the early light Rory found it dazzling, the antithesis of the ruined monochrome town in the Faerie Realm. He walked Hobunay forwards, leading Klarissa's mare. A curved wrought-iron drawbridge decorated with roses led them over a glittering moat ornamented with water-lilies and carp and fringed with marigolds. On the studded oak door, surrounded by images of Donald Duck and his friends, was a big smiling gnome that shrieked with joy when Rory dismounted and punched it. Rory quieted the horses and lifted Klarissa from her saddle. She remained either unconscious or asleep.

Kjym Krev Bauntzia watched their arrival from her chamber. When the gnome shrieked she ran downstairs and flung open the door, waving her minions aside. Rory saw a slim young woman of moderate height. Her ankle-length dress matched her yellow hair, and the child on her back had inherited her angelic eyes. Three Ruritanian Spitzes yapped and wagged around the horses. The baby wept with displeasure but his mother hushed him, ordered the dogs to their hazelwood baskets, folded her arms and addressed Rory. Her tone was not welcoming.

'*Ki sai du, kai was oznaczakh sai–?*'

'Your pardon, ma'am, I can't speak Ruritanian. Are you Kjym Krev Bauntzia? If so, I'm honoured.'

'I am. You are Rory Redman?'

'Yes, ma'am. Since you recognised me, I suppose Ariadne is here and she's mentioned me?'

'She is here. You have much to answer. First: why were you riding my stolen horse, and why have you exhausted him, and what woman do you bring here, and why?'

Rory supposed the krev might be as pretty as her castle, albeit less kitsch, if she didn't emulate a small blonde thundercloud. He told her it was a long story, asked whether the horses could be stabled and rubbed down and fed, and begged help for the injured woman in his arms. Kjym ran her eyes over Klarissa, froze in recognition, stroked Hobunay and whispered to him. At her command, minions scurried to lead the horses to the stables and a medipriest tiptoed from the castle entrance and took charge of the patient.

'Now you will explain.' Kjym didn't smile. 'Enter my hall.'

Rory wiped his shoes on the grass and followed her. The hall was lime green and the furniture scarlet. The floors were well sprung; it was hard even for an exhausted traveller not to leap and dance on them. From the top of an orange staircase decorated with plastic flowers, a mauve corridor led to private chambers. Sunglasses notwithstanding, Castle Bauntzi would have hurt Rory's eyes a day or two earlier, or three weeks earlier. Now it didn't. However, most of the rest of him had been hurting for days. Some parts ached for the first time in their lives.

'If you'll allow me, Krev Bauntzia, I'd like to wash and shave before I answer your questions. Unfortunately, my suitcase was lost during my adventures so I've no razor and no change of clothes. I've been in St Avicenna's and … it *is* a long story.'

Kjym directed him to a private chamber and detailed a minion to take him hot water, razor and towels. 'Nadhan, lend clothes to our guest,' she called. 'He is your size.' Then she lifted Kartor from his harness, hugged him, wiped his nose and kissed his brow fifteen times. She stopped kissing the child long enough to command Rory to present himself in the drawing room after his ablutions. He would then tell his long story. Then she went to tell Nadhan and Ariadne that Hobunay was safely back in his stable and they would soon be apprised of the horse's recent history.

Leaving her husband and her friend to speculate in two languages, she went upstairs to a chamber decorated in relatively subdued purple. It was her duty to visit the woman she'd placed under the medipriest's care.

In any case she wanted to talk to her.

Chapter 71

If you wish to hit a target, shoot. Call whatever you hit 'the target'.
— Old Ruritanian Proverb

Flanked by the moustachioed captain and a hung-over sergeant from his eighty-strong squad, Colonel Barrington stuck coloured flags into the street map of Strelsau adorning the conference room wall. Two Blue Primrose ekwyroj stood nearby; one was fifty years old and had lived all her life in Strelsau. Outside the room, the daily bustle of Blue Primrose HQ hummed and jangled.

'This deployment,' said the colonel, 'should suppress trouble in 23K and 17B. Now, 7R?'

'Police send team with armour,' said the veteran.

'Intelligence says 7R shouldn't give much trouble, sir,' said the captain. 'Ekwyor's right: police can handle it.'

'Hmm. What about the north-west quarter and 11S?'

'We check copy of original plan,' said the other ekwyor. 'It say nothing of them.'

'Yes, SPAR could have added that info. Question is: bluff or double-bluff?'

Thad Masim had given them the photocopy of the original security plan, which differed in several particulars from the version Colonel Barrington had brought from the Hilton. Persuaded of the copy's authenticity by Thad's status, the colonel had requested a further one hundred and seventy troops from London. His request was now entangled in Whitehall bureaucracy.

'We have mobile phones, sir,' said the captain. 'A scout in each of those districts can alert us if there's trouble.'

'Scouts need experience and cool heads. And precise orders. Ekwyor, you'll need most of your forces in St Galen's Square. My people will deal with other parts of Strelsau. It'll be easier if my reinforcements arrive in time. I'll stay here and coordinate the operation.'

The room stood to attention. Everyone studied the flags on the wall map. The ekwyroj regretted that continuing unrest throughout the country had depleted Blue Primrose numbers in Strelsau.

There was a scratching at the door and a junior ekwyrin entered.

'What?' demanded the veteran.

The ekwyrin scuttled forward and whispered to her. Her wrinkles deepened. She murmured to the colonel. The colonel addressed the room, his voice and expression controlled.

'We've just received news of an operational setback and a tragic loss. Grizelina Ekwyor Tupsroot and six of her detachment have died in a SPAR ambush led by Rory Redman, who escaped custody in St Avicenna's two days ago. Under Ruritanian law, I believe Redman will face the death penalty. I shall not plead for mitigation. Ekwyor Tupsroot had arrested the so-called Ulyanova but she escaped during the ambush. Presumably she's with Redman.'

The air quivered.

'How many terrorists were involved, sir?' The captain's voice sounded close to its elastic limit.

'According to this report, twelve to fifteen. Three dead, the rest escaped. Some possibly wounded.'

'Why British man help SPAR? Britain supposed to be friend.'

'Redman's a criminal. Criminals are no one's friends.' The colonel squared his already-square shoulders and tugged his beard. He needed whisky. 'Once again, the terrorists have killed without compunction. They threaten the Queen's peace and the nation's security. After this outrage they can expect no mercy.' He cleared his throat. 'Also, they too may have a copy of the original security plan. Seems Redman gave it to them. One more crime to his name.'

Grizelina Tupsroot merited a state funeral, he decided. He'd speak to the new krevjalem after the election.

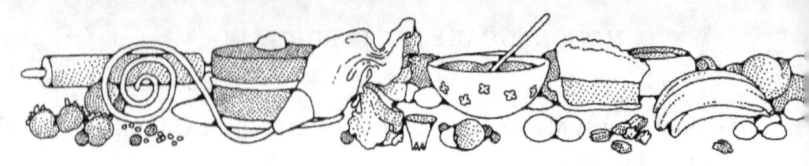

Chapter 72

*Like most personable young men who cannot be trusted
with pocket-sized objects, women or lockfast places, Mr
Redman was always the soul of courtesy, a perfect guest for
any host blind to the losses incident upon hospitality.*
— *Cerberus D. Gardog: 'A College Porter's
Recollections of Unconventional Undergraduates'*

A wash, shave and change of clothes made Rory's aches and
pains more bearable. Among the aromas from the castle kitchens
he could smell coffee; the prospect of food and drink spiced his
mood. He took off his shoes and Morris-danced along the mauve
corridor, hoping it might defuse the aggression simmering in
Krev Bauntzia. He skipped down the orange staircase and blinked
at the vibrant colours.

A minion conducted him to the drawing room, another riot
of hues. Three other people were present: Ariadne, Kjym and a
young man with a relaxed smile. Ariadne's figure, he thought,
must be the envy of ninety-one percent of her friends, and her
navy blue jersey and leggings and court shoes didn't detract from
it. But the incipient interest she'd shown in him during Professor
Reciprocus's lecture in Hrincacz seemed to have faded; she
greeted him with the briefest of smiles. Was this because the
carriage had deserted her outside the physics department? Kjym
was sipping a drink. She looked frosty.

'Pan Redman.' The young man with the relaxed smile
extinguished his cigarette, rose from his scarlet chair and
extended a hand embellished with a garnet ring. 'Nadhan Krefin

Bauntzi. I am happy to encounter you, and to see my clothes upon you.'

Rory thanked Nadhan, shook his hand and acknowledged the ladies.

'I am happy you look better, Pan Redman,' said Kjym. 'Please sit. Ariadne says you drink coffee. Coffee will brought to you. You will then speak.'

She too was drinking coffee, from a mug decorated with bright cartoon figures. She lit a cigarette and offered one to Ariadne, who declined it. Coffee appeared before Rory in another indescribable mug. He sipped it and began his story: his abduction from the cathedral surgery by SPAR agents in Blue Primrose disguise, their threats, the massacre of the village, his return to St Avicenna's, the cow sacrifice, his escape from Mangler, the logical maze, his encounter with Lekhissa.

'Her riddle made my brain hurt, but after I'd solved it she more-or-less answered the question I'd embedded in the solution.'

Kjym set down her cup and silenced him, her face an icon of incredulity.

'You – solved – *Lekhissa's – riddle*?'

'She'd have eaten me if I hadn't. It was challenging, but she gave me half an hour to work on it so it was manageable. Anyway, she was pleased with my question so she persuaded her sisters to grant me wishes. I had to find my way here, so my first wish was for a horse and the skill to ride it. Sporota granted it by bringing Hobunay to me. He's beautiful, Krev Bauntzia. I was honoured to ride him.'

'You – solved – *Lekhissa's – riddle*?' Kjym's disbelief wasn't disposed to yield without a fight. 'And this is how you explain the theft of my horse?'

'Taking Hobunay wasn't my idea, Krev Bauntzia. Somehow, Sporota knew I wanted to go where Ariadne was.'

Nadhan intervened.

'No one find solution for Lekhissa riddle. You enter Faerie Realm and meet gargoyle, you solve riddle, you live? It is miracle.'

'He's not bad at logic puzzles.' Ariadne raised her eyebrows and gave a half-smirk.

'Tell rest of story, Pan Redman,' said Nadhan. 'What is third wish?'

Rory explained how SPAR were planning to stir the peasants of every krefmark into a rampage of arson and looting and slaughter.

'It would be civil war. I had to try to prevent it. So I spent three weeks in Faerie time, less than a day in ours, riding from village to village teaching the peasants Morris-dancing. You know about Morris-dancing? It's an English tradition. Othloc and Lekhissa made the clothes and secured the bells, and somehow they acquired the instruments.'

'The dancing of our villages!' said Nadhan. 'So this is how!'

At last, Ariadne smiled.

'I knew it was you. And I guessed you'd somehow taken Hobunay. So now you *believe* in the Faerie Realm, do you?'

Rory nodded. He recounted his re-emergence into the mundane world, his meeting with Arraitch and his companions, the rescue of Klarissa and the escape into the forest. Kjym frowned.

'Blue Primrose arrested her and you *rescued* her? It is a bad crime, Pan Redman. Blue Primrose do not arrest without reason.'

'I'd no choice. Twelve arrows were pointed at my back. Also, I'd witnessed her kindness at the ruined village. And whatever you say, Krev Bauntzia, I've seen evidence of wrongdoing by Blue Primrose. And they were planning to torture Pana Alterleta. She was already injured. I put her on her horse and let Hobunay bring us here so her hurts could be treated.'

Silence hung cold and grey in the gaudy room. Then Kjym spoke again.

'You did what you thought right. And if this Morris-dancing prevents rioting among the peasants you have done good for Ruritania. We might be safe here, but raging mobs in other krefmarkoj could attack the castles with pitchforks and scythes

262

and flaming torches and ceramic utensils. But the woman you rescued and brought here… it puts me in … Ariadne, what is English for *dilemma*?'

'Same word,' said Ariadne.

'Yes. A dilemma. I know who and what she is, Pan Redman. *What* she is I must hand over to Blue Primrose. *Who* she is I cannot; I owe her my krefmark.' Kjym drank the rest of her coffee. 'Until I decide, she will receive care of cathedral hospital standard.' A sudden smile lit her face. 'Ariadne, you were right about Pan Redman. But indeed he brings trouble.'

Ariadne said, 'Invariably.'

Rory said, 'Please call me Rory. And it seems you too have a story to tell, Krev Bauntzia. Why do you owe your krefmark to Pana Alterleta?'

'You may call me Kjym.'

A minion scratched at the door, entered, bowed, and spoke to the krev. She nodded.

'Rory, Pana Alterleta is awake and wishes to speak to you,' she said. 'This minion will lead you to her room. The medipriest will remain in attendance.'

'I'll be more comfortable about visiting Pana Alterleta if Ariadne will come with me,' said Rory. 'Will you, Ariadne? Please?'

Chapter 73

You hear it said that the krevoj are all alike: arrogant, self-seeking, greedy, idle, lustful, avaricious, vengeful and envious. They're so out of touch with the common people of Ruritania they seem to inhabit a different planet. I've met too few krevoj to know whether this is true, but I can vouch for one exception. Kjym Krev Bauntzia is considerate, hard-working, faithful to her husband, generous, understanding, peace-loving and moderate in her ways. I won't speculate whether this is because she's one of the few female krevoj. However, she's not a pushover.

— Ariadne Sowerby, 'First Impressions of Ruritania'

'So you finally found Klarissa.' Ariadne's tone was casual. 'By coincidence, it seems.'

She stalked along the mauve corridor beside Rory, who sensed or imagined an air of *nole me tangere.*

'Something like that,' he said.

'When you were carrying her up to the castle I noticed what a mess her hair and eyebrows were, and her nails were frightful. I didn't think much of her dress sense, either. But everyone, you not least, finds her attractive.'

'Certainly,' said Rory. 'Beautiful as a Bengal tiger.'

'And that's why you followed her to Ruritania.'

'Hardly, Ariadne. She'd mugged me, kicked me unconscious, robbed me and landed me in trouble with MI7, so I had questions for her. I have most of the answers now.'

'I'm pleased to hear it. I must confess I'll be interested to meet her.'

Klarissa was lying on an antique four-poster in a room redolent with herbs and freshness. A modest white sheet covered her to the neck. An empty plate and cup stood on the bedside table next to her handbag. The medipriest hovered beside the window. Outside it was clear and a crescent moon vied with the sun for mastery of the sky. It was losing the contest.

'She's well enough to eat and drink, I see.'

Ariadne spoke in Ruritanian. The medipriest nodded.

'She was exhausted and hungry and stressed, but the injuries are superficial and peasants are quick to recover. Is this Pan Redman? She wishes to talk to him. It must not be for long.'

Rory approached the bed, wondering who else had eyes of such vivid green.

'Why?' said Klarissa.

'Why what?'

'Why did you risk your life to rescue me? You hate me. With reason.'

'I don't hate you. I don't like you, but I like Grizelina Tupsroot less.'

'Nevertheless, thank you. Tell me what happened. I cannot remember.'

Rory summarised their escape but couldn't report the fate of Arraitch and his companions. Klarissa's eyes filled with emerald emotion. Ariadne stepped forward.

'Why is the Socialist People's Army of Ruritania led by a woman as young as you?'

Klarissa gave a painful laugh.

'Young? I celebrated my one hundred and sixty-fifth birthday this year, pana prejosza.'

Ariadne's eyebrows rose.

'You've worn well.'

'Thank you.' Klarissa closed her eyes. The medipriest stepped forward but she gestured him away. 'I must tell the story. Sit down.'

Ariadne hesitated, then sat beside Rory on a dark oak chair

with a padded seat. Fleur-de-lys and fairy-cake designs embellished both woodwork and upholstery.

'Four years after the Peasants' Revolt of 1848,' said Klarissa, 'Efeef Krev Strlzhav raped a peasant girl called Bresina Alterleta. I was born on the first of May 1853, two weeks after her fourteenth birthday.'

'Much as I'd guessed, except for the date,' murmured Rory. 'Did the Strlzhavs lose control of the capital after the Peasants' Revolt?'

Klarissa blinked.

'You know Strlzhav history?'

'I guessed from the name. But wasn't the Peasants' Revolt a bloodless revolution?'

'Anaemic. Soon the Teesporn King was back on his throne and everything was as before, except many peasants were hanged, and Dzhumpinpork Palace was rebuilt, and a Swiss Consortium was blamed for the insurrection. But you are correct, Pan Redman. Strlzhav lost his land rights in the capital and was bitter.'

'And raping a thirteen-year-old girl was his revenge?' said Arladne.

Under the sheet, Klarissa's shoulders shrugged.

'Ruritania has changed little. She remains as she was, and as Britain was two hundred years ago. Aristocratic men exploit lower-class women, though a peasant is more liable to assault by her own kind – in barn or haystack, on her way home, even *in* her home if the assailant is drunk. Tradition requires women to resist advances even within marriage, so the man is obliged and expected to use force. Received wisdom says "A woman's nay is a double yea".'

'The confusion between "dakh" and "khad" can't have helped,' said Rory.

'It has helped many men plead innocence,' said Klarissa. 'Rape is impossible to prove unless there is great injury or witnesses can testify. It is part of the culture. Men use it to settle scores, avenge insults, recover unpaid loans in kind. Former lovers use it against women who marry other men. Some of us learn to deter men by kicking them in the rising passion, but many do not because self-defence is deemed unseemly for a woman. You see some reasons why the Revolution is necessary, Pan Redman? There was nothing to protect my mother against Strlzhav. She could expect no sympathy.'

'I see it all too clearly,' said Ariadne. She blew out her cheeks. 'Didn't the krev give your mother any support or recognise you as his daughter?'

'Of course not. Everyone in the village knew Bresina had borne the krev's bastard so she was whipped and pilloried as a whore. Then in the summer of 1858, when I was five years old, Krev Efeef died.'

'Ah. Inheritance dispute,' said Rory. 'Inconvenient nieces and nephews vanish, armed conflict becomes *de rigueur* ... If people knew you were the late krev's daughter you could have been seen as a threat.'

Klarissa's mouth set hard.

'My mother died. I would not have lived had I not been carried to the Faerie Realm overnight.'

'How did it happen?'

'I have no idea. I was only five years old. I missed my mother but I was cared for. I was taught to fight, use weapons, tell stories, ride, subdue animals, climb ... When I was older I discovered how to appear to my fellow-mortals like either a cultured lady or a common peasant. I mastered languages. Fourteen years ago I was returned to the village where I was born and to the house of Egrienne and Bresina Alterlet. Egrienne was chosen because he had enjoyed contact with the Faerie Realm since childhood. Perhaps it is coincidence his wife shares my mother's name. Perhaps it is also coincidence the present Krev Strlzhav shares my father's name. There are those who study coincidence ... But during the previous one hundred and forty-three years I had aged just eight, so to mortal eyes I was thirteen when I reappeared – as my mother had been when Strlzhav used her. I learned to work in the fields and in the house and I studied in the village church surgery; the yasimak was educated. Five years later I went to university in England to read politics and economics.'

'And you learned to speak perfect English.' Rory rose from his chair. 'Those who study coincidence ... Did you make friends with Krev Schammerbass in England or in Ruritania, Pana Alterleta? And the woman at the London Hilton who called herself Sura Marnikova?'

Klarissa drew a deep breath.

'Krevoj are not friends of our people, Pan Redman. With one exception. Have you at last found commitment?' Her green eyes scanned Ariadne and then fixed on his face. 'Now I will sleep. We may talk again later.'

Rory and Ariadne tiptoed from the chamber, to the relief of the medipriest.

'You see: no competition,' said Rory. He grinned. 'Never been attracted to older women.'

'Oh dear, how sad for me. *I* grew up, *ergo* you're younger than I am.' Ariadne paused. 'Remind me, what's her family name – Alterlet?'

'If she's told us the truth her foster-parents are called Alterlet, but it seems "Krefin Strlzhava" is correct.'

'Alterlet. Yes. Taken by the Faerie Realm and subsequently returned. For "alter" read "change". For the suffix "-let", read "-ling". What did she say about coincidence?'

Rory blinked.

'You know, there are times when I find your intelligence almost as attractive as your ...'

'Yes?'

Rory hesitated, grinned, shook his head and said, 'Never mind.'

'Intelligence is the capacity to make quick decisions on the basis of incomplete information,' said Ariadne, 'not to notice the obvious.'

Rory almost said something about men's capacity to concentrate on two things at once, but he opted for silence.

Chapter 74

*Some claim that a modern democracy can have a non-
capitalist economy. In principle this should be possible
because democracy and capitalism have different aims:
democracy constrains economic processes to protect basic
rights, though it does not limit wealth, while capitalism has
no interest in basic rights and generates a large, wage-
dependent class with negligible political influence. However,
global capitalism has created undemocratic, unelected
multinational bodies that can with impunity override the
environmental and labour laws of any sovereign legislature,
in Europe or elsewhere. In practice, therefore, every modern
democracy has become – cannot help but become – subject
to such bodies, making it just one more slave of capitalism.*
— *Klarissa Krefin Strlzhava, 'Democracy'. Final
  Honours Dissertation, 2011*

Conversation during dinner in the Castle Bauntzi banqueting
hall was less constrained than Rory had feared. The meal ended
with cakes made by the krev herself.

'Kjym, these are delicious!' said Rory. 'Such baking should
make you krevjalem!'

Ariadne mouthed 'Arse-licker', but Kjym was gratified.

'I love my bakery, Rory. My Faerie Cakes are made to a true
Faerie recipe. Please, take more! Our injured guest upstairs will
of course not eat them. As for being krevjalem, thank you, but I
am not physically designed to urinate on trees. I care for my
own family and krefmark.'

269

'So you'll be at the rear of the procession on National Cake Day?'

Kjym nodded. 'Like all krevoj who have no desire for power.'

'You'll be in good company,' said Rory. 'The President of the National Academy of Science seems to keep a low profile.'

'Krev Schammerbass is seldom in the country, let alone the High Bakery, so … Yet he has … help me with English again, Ariadne – what is *drujetsz*?'

'Er … Charisma.' Ariadne grinned at Rory. 'A few Ruritanian words have Gaelic roots rather than Polish and German and so on.'

Rory knew no Gaelic and didn't comment. But Kjym was right: whatever might be said of Krev Schammerbass, he had charisma.

'Do Krevoj Strlzhav and Hvimpy have charisma, too, Kjym?' he asked.

Kjym laughed.

'You wish me to be indiscreet, Rory. I will answer, but the answer will not be repeated outside these walls. Krevoj Strlzhav and Hvimpy are utterly devoid of *drujetsz* and do as much for Ruritania as a verruca for one's foot. Krevjalem Strlzhav is a sorry little sadist with a moustache. Krev Hvimpy is a shudder looking for a spine to run up. But it is useless to oppose them because in all democracies the elected representatives coalesce into two groups, government and opposition, and each must have a figurehead.'

The door opened and Klarissa entered, handbag over her shoulder. As if to confirm Ariadne's aspersions she was wearing an unsuitable pale blue dress, tight at the bust and too short, so it exposed several of her injuries. Her left ear was swollen. The purple bruise on her cheek had acquired yellow edges. Laughter and conversation stopped and everyone stared. Ariadne wondered whether Klarissa was trying to look like a rainbow or to match Kjym's décor.

'Ah,' said Kjym. 'Welcome, Pana Alterleta. If you wish for more food it will be brought upstairs to you.'

Rory leapt to his feet and punched the table. It hurt less than the wall in Vorgottenstrit.

'*Get back to bed! You're not fit to wander around! What was the medipriest thinking to let you out?*'

His voice echoed around the multi-hued masonry and dislodged dust from the roof timbers, to the annoyance of a family of roosting bats and a cascade of invertebrates. The Frog Prince would have feasted on the fallout.

'I wish to talk more to you before I leave,' said Klarissa. 'May we use another room, Krev Bauntzia? Also, thank you for your care, but no more food for now.'

Nadhan answered. Rory guessed the words meant, 'You will not leave; you will remain in Castle Bauntzi until after National Cake Day and then we shall decide what to do with you'. Klarissa responded with a smile. Ariadne shook her head like a wet terrier. The balletic undulations of her hair distracted Rory.

'Are you willing to talk further to our guest, Rory?' said Kjym.

'Twenty minutes,' said Rory, 'provided she'll then return to her room.' In a murmur, he added, 'I want to talk to you, too, Ariadne, in private.'

'Oh, do you.'

'Yes. Not long ago you chaired the Slug Defence League AGM in the London Hilton. Our friend here attended. She was in disguise and used the name Gottlieba Weissfeld but you imagined her to be a German businesswoman and you took a dislike to her. I wondered why. On the other hand you *welcomed* another guest, who called herself Sura Marnikova and claimed to be Slovenian. You didn't challenge her non-Slovenian name or her travelling arrangements. Going via Vienna and Budapest isn't a *direct* route from London to Ljubljana, is it? So yes, Ariadne, I do want to talk to you. After Pana Alterleta has told me what she wants.'

He led Klarissa from the banqueting hall to a small adjoining chamber. Kjym told Nadhan to go and check the horses and the new batch of vermicelli machines. Alone with Ariadne, she said, 'Rory won't try anything on with her.'

'He's a man. Men always try it on given half a chance. If you leave a man alone in a room with a tea-cosy he'll try it on.' Ariadne pondered. 'When he said you'd be a good krevjalem, Kjym,' she continued, 'why did you dismiss the idea? And what *is* the story about you owing your krefmark to Klarissa Alterleta?'

Chapter 75

Democratic elections do not guarantee social progress, nor are all elected leaders who foster progress celebrated. In 1945, Britain elected a prime minister whose government revitalised a war-wearied and impoverished country, built a million new homes and a thousand new schools with twenty-five thousand new teachers, created the world's first National Health Service, passed laws that ensured fair wages, improved working conditions and ended much industrial exploitation, founded the first national parks, and conferred on Britain the blessings of child benefit, sickness pay, invalidity benefit, maternity pay and social security. Thirty-four years later she elected a prime minister whose government halved Britain's manufacturing capacity and created record unemployment, closed numerous hospitals and hundreds of schools, decimated the social housing stock, deregulated the financial sector, abolished free milk for primary school children, befriended and supported brutal dictators and murderous regimes all around the world, and oversaw the biggest transfer of wealth from the poor to the rich in British history. For the latter of those prime ministers, who at the time of writing is approaching death, an expensive state funeral has been planned. Her memory will be lauded. The former of the two died many years ago. He was privately buried, his passing almost unremarked.

— Klarissa Krefin Strlzhava, 'Democracy'. Final Honours Project Dissertation, 2011

Klarissa's eyes, thought Rory, evoked the silent explosion of spring: the eruption of new life in field and hedgerow, the burgeoning of the tree canopy – 'green fire', 'fairy fire'. Her traumas should have laid her low but her spirit had triumphed. He understood why Arraitch and the others revered her, why she had the power to lead. He folded his arms.

'What do you want to say?'

'Not to say; to question. Alone. You could not answer without constraint if Pana Sowerby were with you.'

'Forget it. You're not going to interrogate me again. Last time, you called me a "British spy", which was taurocoprology, threatened me with torture, ordered Mangler to kill me once I'd given him the security plan … and that was on top of the assault in my own garden.'

Klarissa shook her head.

'Barrington and Tupsroota recruited you. Nevertheless, your attitude to authority … Perhaps you did not become a spy. But you love your country, yes? Your *democracy*? Have you grown to love my country, too?' Another smile illuminated her bruised face. 'I didn't order Comrade Mangler to kill you. He was supposed to hand you over to Blue Primrose when he returned to Strelsau. He made a … How would you say, "executive decision"?'

I sort of understand, thought Rory: Mangler didn't want to be burdened with a liability who couldn't ride his own horse. He's off my Christmas card list, though.

'With executives like Mangler you won't need executioners. As for your questions: I love my country when I talk to foreigners but I slag her rotten when I'm at home. Our democracy might be a joke because it's run by a self-serving political class but it beats the hell out of any other form of government. And yes, I *have* grown to love Ruritania, so I'd like to see your idiotic feudal system overturned and your public health and life expectancy improved. And your customs and immigration officers replaced with humans. But I'm not on *your* side. Ruritania needs evolution, not revolution.'

'You mean she needs *capitalist democracy*? So we replace a

hereditary élite with a money-based élite? What sort of democracy, Pan Redman, assembly or representative?'

Rory shrugged. As far as he knew, assembly democracy wasn't feasible in any polity bigger than a city state.

'Call me "Rory", for Asclepius's sake. Okay. Back in the 1640s, Rhode Island established a constitution: the people collectively made the laws in "orderly assembly" and the appointed ministers "faithfully executed" them. But a hundred and thirty years later, one signatory of America's Declaration of Independence dubbed the Rhode Island experiment "a recipe for anarchy". I can't remember who it was but everyone agreed.'

'Alexander Hamilton, 1777,' said Klarissa. 'He defined representative democracy as one "where the right of election is well secured and regulated, and the exercise of the legislative executive and judicial authorities is vested in select persons". It's what the West has today, ripe for manipulation by global capitalists. Americans were scared of the *canaille* during the early days after Independence. Considering what happened in France a few years later, and what will shortly happen in Ruritania, they had a point.'

Rory's eyes scanned the multicoloured walls and decorated ceiling of the little chamber. He wanted to talk to Ariadne, not to listen to a lecture by a Communist zealot. Nevertheless he felt constrained to respond.

'Hamilton was echoing Aquinas: democracy is a tyranny in which the common people oppress the rich by force of numbers. You want to impose the tyranny of the mob on Ruritania.'

'That "tyranny of the mob" will succeed where your democracy fails because the time has come when the rich *must* be oppressed. Have you forgotten the euro crisis of 2007 to 2009? The EU accrued powers that allowed it to override the voters' wishes in every so-called sovereign nation. Global capitalism was in crisis but the perpetrators weren't punished; they were bailed out and granted renewed power. The EU, ECB and IMF together imposed austerity measures and neo-liberal policies of privatisation, deregulation and reduced public services on governments and populations.'

It's obvious she plans to leave after she's harangued me, thought Rory, with or without Kjym's consent. Is she trying to recruit me to the SPAR cause, or does she just want me to help her escape from Castle Bauntzi? Either way, she's starting to annoy me.

'Look at Greece,' Klarissa continued. 'The birthplace of democracy. George Papandreou sought the views of his *demos* but his referendum infuriated Merkel and Sarkozy, who had exacerbated the crisis. They ousted Papandreou and replaced him with a former ECB vice-president, Lucas Papademos, who was *unelected*. Papademos installed in government a far-right group that had been banned when the military lost power in 1974. And in Italy, Europe's money men pressurised the president into replacing Berlusconi with a former Goldman Sachs executive called Mario Monti. Italian voters were not consulted. Berlusconi was absurd but he had been *elected*. So much for democracy. We must outgrow those delusions of "people power" and impose *real* people power. If you have grown to love my country you will understand this. You will support Ruritania's Revolution.'

Oh, so you *do* want me to join SPAR, thought Rory. No chance. You know a hell of a lot more about politics than I do, but I'm better at logic. I can refute your arguments.

'If your Revolution succeeds your country will be politically isolated,' he said.

'No we won't. Ruritania moves into contact with other nations. Our word will spread. People everywhere are disenchanted with *democratic* governments. Our country will become a shining symbol of freedom. Others will emulate us.'

Rory launched into an angry diatribe about pipe-dreams, of the naïveté (remarkable in a one hundred and sixty-five-year-old woman) of believing in a world where people stop being greedy and are nice to each other and a chicken can cross the road without having its motives questioned.

'I understand about oppression and exploitation and inequality and all the rest, I understand about unmerited privilege and economic mismanagement and unfair wealth distribution and

276

alienation of labour from profit and blah blah blah blah, but what will your Revolution achieve? In any revolution, the fool on horseback brandishing the whip swaps places with the fool on foot who's being whipped.'

Had he just quoted Yeats? He paused, took a deep breath and closed his eyes. If he yielded to his annoyance, even rage, he realised, he'd be less persuasive. Kjym, he thought, would have responded more succinctly and effectively to Klarissa's lecture without raising her voice.

Klarissa waited, knowing he'd say more. After a few seconds he continued, his tone more measured:

'There'll still be oppression and exploitation, just a different gang of exploiters and oppressors. The economic resources will still be mismanaged and wealth will still be unequally distributed, though it'll mostly be in different hands. A new group will enjoy privilege, a new group will profit from labour, a new group will be alienated. And so what? In a thousand years, who'll know the difference? And in the meantime the fools on horseback and the fools on foot will change places again and again, round and round in a pointless dance – which is why revolution is called "revolution".'

He turned back towards the banqueting hall and Klarissa called after him: 'You are still a fool, Rory Redman, on horseback or on foot. What does your country want of us? Why does your MIOCIA support our oppressors?'

'Our what?'

'MIOCIA. Your Ministry for Interfering in Other Countries' Internal Affairs. The ministry responsible for MI7. What do you British want of Ruritania? It involves exploiting the Faerie Realm, but how?'

It cost me a near-death experience with a hungry gargoyle to find the answer to that, *pana prejosza*, thought Rory, so I'm damned if I'll share the information with *you*.

'Your guess is as good as mine,' he said, and walked out of the room.

Chapter 76

Woman's place is in the home. Man's place is in the wrong.
— *Old Ruritanian Proverb*

Ariadne had gone outside. Rory found her standing beside the ornamental maze, staring past the vermicelli machine worksheds towards the mountains. She glanced at him and then looked away again. How, he wondered, can I get this right? He knew she considered him an immature womanising kleptomaniac with no intention of securing legitimate or useful employment, which was a fair assessment, but was she also jealous of Klarissa? He half hoped she was. It would confirm her interest.

Personal concerns aside, there were important matters to discuss. Ariadne was clever and cool-headed, she planned to live and practise law in Strelsau, and she counted Kjym, Nadhan, Thad and Tomen as friends. He strolled to the maze and stood beside her.

'There are two or three things I didn't mention when I recounted my adventures,' he said.

'You amaze me.'

'I amaze lots of people. I amaze myself. I amazed myself by not stealing anything from Thad and Tomen while we were in Strelsau, and I haven't nicked even the smallest jewel from Castle Bauntzi. In fact, I don't think I've stolen *anything* since I lifted these sunglasses from the airport shop. But failure to pinch stuff isn't among the things I didn't mention.'

'Come now, Rory, if you've truly resisted pinching stuff it's a major achievement for you. Don't men always boast about their achievements?'

'You know the wrong sort of men. But it suggests you were right about me.' He allowed a five-second pause to stretch Ariadne's curiosity, then added: 'When we met in Vienna airport you told me, "You haven't changed, but if you go to Ruritania you will". And I have.'

Ariadne was quiet for half a minute and then said, 'When we went to Klarissa's room she asked, "Have you at last found commitment?" Did she mean commitment to the Glorious Revolution or to her?'

The mountains were picture postcard material, but staring at them was making Ariadne's eyes water. Restraining an urge to seize her and either shake her or hug her, or both, Rory kept his voice gentle.

'If she was being as perceptive as I supposed, she meant *you*. You're right, I do want an intelligent, educated, articulate and strong-minded girlfriend, but I don't want a dangerously fanatical one. Or one who's a hundred and thirty years older than me.'

Ariadne's throat made an odd noise and her next words were muffled.

'Rory the Rational believed that guff about her age?'

'I told you I'd changed. You've read Dai's *Primer*? He tells us the Faerie Realm changes people who venture into it. I've ventured into it. And there's no doubt about the time dilation. So yes, I believed her. So did you.'

She turned and buried her face in his shoulder. His arms went around her of their own volition. Other parts of him also responded of their own volition. She gulped twice before she spoke again. Her words were still muffled.

'Have you *any* idea how worried I've been about you, you stupid bugger?'

Rory watched his left hand stroke her hair. It had seldom relished such a texture. It went on stroking.

'Thad told me how long you'd sat beside me in St Avicenna's while I was unconscious. I won't forget it. But you shouldn't have been concerned. You know I'm as adept at getting out of scrapes as getting into them.' He sensed she couldn't reply, so he stumbled on: 'I'm sorry I worried you, though, and I'm sorry I had to bring Klarissa here, partly because it's put Kjym in an invidious position but mostly because I was worried about how *you'd* react. Under the circumstances I'd no moral choice, but if there'd been a portal handy I'd have sent her back to the Faerie Realm to sort herself out.' Ariadne still showed no inclination to reply, so he continued: 'You were right again, of course: when I talked to her just now she tried to convert me to the SPAR cause. Needless to say, she failed.'

Ariadne eased herself out of his embrace.

'I didn't like "Gottlieba" at the Hilton because she walked into the meeting as though she owned the place, and you'd been staring at her as though you … I wanted to kick her face in. I suppose her aristocratic genes and long life explain her arrogance, but … And Sura was so unassuming and we felt so … The name and the odd route to Slovenia didn't register with me.' She wiped her sleeve across her face and made eye contact. 'Rory, what's going to happen? I'm scared. Kjym's scared too but she won't admit it.'

'What's going to happen right now is that you and I are going to sit down and go on talking. I'm going to tell you the two or three things I didn't tell Kjym and Nadhan. Then I'll tell you what might happen to Ruritania. What will happen between you and me in private is more important but we'll save it for later.'

She didn't reply; he guessed her voice was still not in working order.

They sat side by side on the grass and Rory put his right arm around her. She leaned against him and rested her head on his shoulder. Her hair caressing his cheek, her delicious aroma, the sound of her breathing, conspired to close his eyes with anticipatory bliss. He forced his mind on to a less personal track and explained about the security plan: one copy of the original delivered to SPAR via Mangler, one given to Thad, who'd no doubt share it with the authorities; and the spoof version, concocted by Klarissa, which he'd put into Colonel Barrington's hands.

Ariadne sat upright and frowned.

'Whose side are you on, Rory? You give the real document to SPAR, you rescue their charming leader – under duress, but willingly – and you give the spoof document to the colonel who's cooperating with the Ruritanian government. But then you give the real document to Thad and therefore *to* the government, and you concoct this Morris-dancing plan to stop the peasants wreaking havoc. Running with the hare and hunting with the hounds?' She stared at him. 'What was this wall she fell down?'

The sun was sinking behind the hills beyond Strelsau. The scene was a perfect watercolour.

'I neither know nor care. To answer the important question … Coincidence, isn't it? The Ruritanian for "dilemma" is "dilemma".'

Anyone could sympathise with SPAR, Rory argued, because the feudal system condemned most of the population to poverty and early graves and social mobility was non-existent. 'Look at Thad and Tomen. They wouldn't have their wealth and position if they weren't from aristocratic families. They're good people, but how many good people lack comparable opportunities?'

He railed against the brutality of Blue Primrose and the massacre unleashed by Krev Strlzhav. 'The krevjalem – the prime minister – ordered innocent people to be murdered. I don't believe Kjym would have done that, but feudalism *invites* atrocities.' On the other hand, he said, SPAR wanted to throw the baby out with the bathwater, destroy the country's traditions, terminate her interaction with the Faerie Realm, and achieve those aims through bloodshed. 'They plan to kill everyone in power and they'll use National Cake Day to do it. I sympathise with their ends but I'd never condone their means.'

Ariadne hadn't known about SPAR's intentions for Faerie Realm access, but she evinced no surprise.

'Do you know exactly what SPAR are planning?'

'I can surmise.' Rory took a deep breath. 'Suppose you wanted to wipe out the entire royal family, most of the High Bakery and the senior mediclergy in one fell swoop. How would you do it, bearing in mind the massive security in Strelsau on the fourth of July, or the twenty-first of June, depending on calendar?'

'I don't see how it *can* be done. Anyone carrying weapons anywhere near St Galen's Square will be arrested unless they're Blue Primrose or British Army.'

Rory nodded.

'Exactly. So you'd need to trick the official party into bringing the weapon or weapons to the ceremony with them. Anyway, thanks to Lekhissa, I know why our government's keen to help Ruritania's. If SPAR's revolution succeeds it will scupper British military ambitions.'

He paused again. He knew Ariadne was waiting for him to explain, but this wasn't the right time; it would take too long. Instead, he continued:

'If Kjym were krevjalem … Ariadne, she has more political clout than she admits. She's made a fortune exporting vermicelli machines, and someone, probably her, has made it illegal to import any. Remember Thad saying she could broker a deal between SPAR and the government? But when I tried to suggest it to her–'

'Rory, if she'd expressed interest in being krevjalem you'd have told Klarissa. At least, she thought you would. But she's in a real dilemma. Apparently the previous Krev Bauntzi was Kjym's uncle. When he died there was the usual inheritance dispute. Klarissa saved Kjym's life and a few competitors *disappeared*, so Kjym's indebted to her. On the other hand, Klarissa's a serious threat to the government and Kjym's a member of the High Bakery. She has her duty.' Ariadne stood and dusted grass from her clothes. 'Sorry, Rory, got to go indoors. Need time alone. To think.' She bent and kissed the top of his head. 'I await with bated breath your explanation about SPAR versus British military ambitions. Later, perhaps?'

'Yes, later. Though other matters might take priority.'

Ariadne stumbled, smiled, blew another kiss to him, and went indoors. Rory sat beside her absence and mused. Matters were more complicated than he'd supposed. Klarissa, the dedicated revolutionary, had ensured the friendship of at least one influential aristocrat. She had a taste for designer clothes and expensive hotels. And she said she was the daughter of the present krevjalem's great-great-great-grandfather and was therefore a claimant to the Strlzhav krefmark.

Twilight was thickening. There was a distant rumble of thunder; clouds had massed over the mountains. Wind rose from the north.

'Didn't think the weather was forecast to deteriorate,' said Rory.

No one was there to reply.

He stared upwards. Stars began to appear but cloud had obscured half the sky.

'What will she do to Ruritania,' he asked, 'if she becomes President of the Socialist Republic or whatever they decide to call it?'

As if in answer, something thumped on to the grass beside him. It was his suitcase.

Chapter 77

I wanted a handbag you can put all of your things in, and you can open it, you can close it, you can hide all your tricks in it, but it's never lumpy.
— *L'Wren Scott, quoted by Egrienne Alterlet*

Ariadne knocked at the door of the purple chamber and heard Klarissa call '*Tulae spravaja*'. She complied. The medipriest was asleep on one of the fleur-de-lys and fairy-cake chairs. Klarissa turned from the window to greet her visitor. Her eyebrows rose and her voice was cool.

'Pana Sowerby. I did not expect you. You have something to say?'

'I believe I owe you an apology for supposing you were after Rory.'

Klarissa looked puzzled, then laughed.

'You say "were after" to mean "desired"? Indeed, your supposition was wrong.' She shook her head. 'He is attractive but more than a century too young, and I will not encumber myself with a personal relationship.' She looked out of the window again. 'Also, he has reason not to like me. You disliked me too when we met in London.'

'That was then. This is now.' Ariadne conjured a smile. 'Call me Ariadne, please.'

Klarissa walked from the window and picked up her handbag.

'Be careful not to trust certain people. I do not mean Pan Redman. He is … Oh, he is more than *after* you.'

'Is that what you meant by "commitment"?'

'If he is now committed to a productive life he will wish you to be part of it. After the Revolution, Ruritania will be a free country. All who are not counter-revolutionary will be welcome here.'

Klarissa conjured from her handbag a Victorian-style navy blue riding habit, matching hat, leather boots, makeup and perfume. Ariadne's envy was blended with astonishment.

'I'd give my eye teeth for a bottomless handbag! All my bags cost a fortune and I can never fit everything into them. May I ask where you got it?'

'Egrienne made it. He understands Faerie Realm physics. The bag encapsulates a spatiotemporal anomaly so it contains whatever I wish. I take a suitcase when I travel, otherwise people think it strange, but the suitcase is always empty.'

'Egrienne? Oh yes, your foster-father.'

'So called, though he is a hundred and twenty years younger than me. If you become a citizen of the People's Republic of Ruritania, Ariadne, perhaps he will make one for you. Now, please excuse me. I wish to change.'

Ariadne went downstairs, half relieved, half confused. Klarissa was obviously dressing for travel. Kjym and Nadhan had ordained she must remain at Castle Bauntzi until after National Cake Day, and she couldn't leave the building without their consent, so how did she plan to escape? In any case, was she fit to ride?

As she reached the multicoloured hall a commotion erupted outside: shouting voices, including Rory's; and then a noise like a circular saw on steroids, remarkable in a country innocent of both steroids and circular saws. She ran through the hall and dragged the portal open.

'What in the name of the wee man from Milton Keynes is *that*?' she demanded, seizing a heavy copper warming pan from the wall beside the door.

Chapter 78

There are said to be three categories of shape-shifters: those with the power to change species, gender, size or appearance as they choose (e.g. Lekhissa); those on whom change of species, gender, size or appearance is imposed by a magical spell (e.g. the Frog Prince); and those who are transformed by Divine intervention either for protection (e.g. Syrinx) or for punishment (e.g. Actaeon). However, when you meet a shape-shifter, it is seldom possible to identify the category to which he, she, or more usually it, belongs.
— The Unideker Guide to Ruritania

Rory walked to the side of the castle and scrutinised the gathering. He recognised Arraitch and the giant Eldzhay but not the other two dozen green-clad men and women emerging from the forest. They seemed neither hostile nor friendly. He nodded a greeting.

'Thanks for returning my suitcase. And,' (he held out the knife, haft-first, to Eldzhay) 'thanks for this. It proved useful.'

Eldzhay waved his massive arms, pointed to another knife in his belt and said 'You comrade. Keep.' Then he pointed at the castle. 'Lady here? Safe?'

'The Ulyanova's being cared for. Her injuries have been treated by a medipriest. Yes, she's safe, fed and housed in comfort. But the krev doesn't intend to release her.'

There was a mumbled conversation among the Ruritanians. Rory feared they hadn't understood, but his search for alternative wording was interrupted by a buzzing and whining from the forest.

'What's that? Sounds like a circular saw on steroids ... It's – Oh, what the –?'

The noise came from its transparent wings, which were beating so rapidly that the four dark blotches ornamenting them were invisible. Its legs and antennae bore stiff bristles. Its enormous compound eyes were multifaceted. Its abdomen was segmented, its mouth parts flexible and formidable. It measured a fathom from mandible to anus. As Rory watched, it seized the nearest green-clad figure. The mandible sliced through the screaming victim's skin, then the mouthparts rolled into a tube and the creature began to suck.

Arraitch fired an arrow that should have been fatal; it went right through the mega-insect's thorax. Undisturbed, the creature went on sucking. Panic began to spread.

'*Panculikeut!*' shrieked a voice.

The invertebrate left the exsanguinated bowman and buzzed into the air again, its eyes seeking further nourishment. Arraitch and five of his companions fired more arrows; every one hit the target but without effect. Then the hairy antennae pointed forwards and the creature charged towards Arraitch and Rory.

'Oh no you don't!'

Ariadne sprang from the shadow of the castle and clobbered the attacker over the head with the warming pan. There was a coppery clang and the insect hit the ground, bounced, and rose again.

'What the hell *is* it?' shouted Rory.

'*Panculikeut!*' said Arraitch.

'What?'

Ariadne brandished the warming pan and watched the predator perform lugubrious saccades against the darkening sky.

'Never heard the word, but from the morphology I guess it means "weremidge". You know, like a werewolf but – *Get out of here, you biologically implausible–*'

So that's why arrows have no effect, thought Rory. Ordinary weapons can't harm werethingies. However ...

'Arraitch! Quick! Push this into the tip of an arrow and shoot it again!'

Rory tugged Colonel Barrington's remaining cufflink from his pocket and held it up against the deepening twilight. It shone into half a dozen facets of a compound eye and the insect retreated with a petulant buzz. Arraitch nodded, took the cufflink, pressed it into an arrowhead and fired. The predator emitted a thin cry and fell. The circular saw sound ceased.

For half a minute, no one moved or spoke. Then everyone crept forward to surround the fallen body. It was no longer a giant insect but a naked man. Not an impressive one.

'Well, well,' said Rory. 'Huipi Krefin Hvimpy. I remember wondering what had bitten him when we met in Strelsau.' He put an arm round Ariadne's shoulders. She was shaking. 'Well done, lady with the warming pan. Not your first demonstration of smart thinking but one for which I'm particularly grateful. We must tell Kjym and Nadhan because they'll have to break the news to Krev Hvimpy's family. Tragic, of course, but Hvimpy will get a sympathy vote if people hear about his son's sudden death.'

'If there's an election,' whispered Ariadne. She looked around the green-clad assembly. Eldzhay was cutting off his dead comrade's head with his new knife. 'Ugh! Why –?'

'Prevention's better than cure,' said Rory. 'Nobody wants another weremidge, especially if it was formerly a friend.'

Arraitch stepped forward and spoke. He sounded angry. Ungracious, thought Rory, considering I just devised a way of killing an unkillable killer that threatened all his friends.

'Rory,' said Ariadne, 'he asked whether you've been in the Faerie Realm and failed to seal the exit. Did you?'

Rory shrugged.

'I've no idea how I was ejected from the Faerie Realm. One moment I was in a ruined town beside Lake Brojginzha drinking claret with the King of Faerie, the next I was in the mundane world, riding north near the burnt-out village. So I don't know where the exit was. And what do you mean by sealing it?'

Exasperation shook Ariadne's head.

'You place two slugs side by side on the path behind you, both looking in the direction from which you've come. You've visited Faerie so you ought to know.'

She spoke to Arraitch. Arraitch uttered what Rory guessed was an unclean expletive, then started to issue orders to his companions. Suddenly he stopped, turned thirty degrees to the left and inclined his head. The other Ruritanians did likewise.

Rory and Ariadne looked. A bay horse approached. On it, clad in navy blue riding habit, matching hat and leather boots, sat Klarissa. She smiled at the British couple.

'It is time to bid you adieu. I hope we will meet again in the People's Republic of Ruritania.'

She nodded and rode from Castle Bauntzi towards the last lingering light of day. Arraitch and his companions followed, a small silent army.

'How did she get out of the castle?' said Ariadne.

Rory pointed to the window of the purple chamber, then to the rugged stone wall below it.

'She hurt herself falling down a wall two days ago so she needed to climb down another one. Like going back up a ladder after you've fallen off, only the other way round.'

'Kjym won't be happy.' Ariadne sighed. 'Let's hope somebody finds your Faerie Realm exit and seals it before anything else gets out. I can't. If I'm to witness National Cake Day I must leave for Strelsau tomorrow. Kjym and Nadhan will go in the morning, too. What are your plans?'

'To travel with you. Up to a point.'

Rory lifted his suitcase, Ariadne gripped her warming pan, and they went back indoors hand in hand. Above them, the crescent moon had won its contest for mastery of the sky. The couple ignored it.

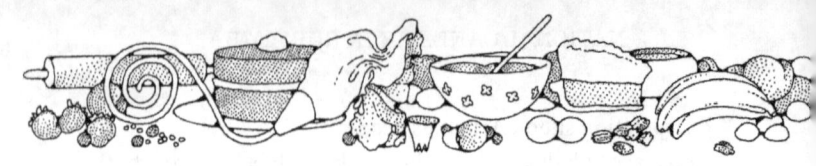

Chapter 79

When you travel around Ruritania, try to follow the advice given to European travellers during the early 19th century. You should rise early so you have ample time to arrange everything needful for the journey. Direct a servant to waken you at a suitable hour. Dress plainly and avoid unnecessary embellishment so other travellers will respect you. Ensure that your most reliable servants supervise the transport of your heavy baggage, and carry nothing with you on horse or trap except a travelling satchel containing only a comb and mirror, a book and a light snack. Keep your money hidden, especially if you are travelling through forests. If you dine at an inn, adapt your taste to the fare provided, though this can challenge even the most robust palate.

— *The Unideker Guide to Ruritania.*

It was raining. Dry weather was prescribed for the weeks before and after National Cake Day, so what was amiss? No matter: it would surely be fine in Strelsau. Kjym and Nadhan had risen early to prepare for their journey. Ariadne hadn't found time to pack and Rory was yet to renew acquaintance with the contents of his suitcase. When Ariadne entered the breakfast room, Kjym greeted her by not sniggering.

'Is Rory still asleep? He must be tired. Sound travels well in Castle Bauntzi, Ariadne.'

Ariadne gave a non-committal answer and focussed on not blushing. She repeated none of Rory's confidences: his explanation of Britain's opposition to SPAR, his conjecture about SPAR's plans for National Cake Day. In return, Kjym said nothing about Klarissa's nocturnal departure. Perhaps, thought Ariadne, she'd connived at it to evade an impossible decision.

'I suppose you will come to Strelsau and Rory will travel with you?' said Kjym after cakes and coffee. 'I shall ride Hobunay. If Rory wishes he may take Hobunay's brother, Yahimees. Stay here as long as you please, both of you; but in three days it will be National Cake Day.'

She and Nadhan and Kartor departed a few minutes later, followed by two carriages full of luggage and minions and an abundance of freshly-made fairy cakes. It was midday before Rory and Ariadne were ready to follow. Rory had dressed in his own clothes, anorak and white shirt and jeans, but he'd borrowed Nathan's riding boots and rode Yahimees. Ariadne wore a Barbour jacket and jodhpurs and rode her hired gelding, Boris. Such luggage as they'd chosen to carry was strapped to a third horse, which they took turns to lead.

They had travelled scarcely three leagues through the unrelenting rain before Ariadne witnessed Ruritanian Morris-dancing for the first time. The village side lacked polish, though considering the weather its vigour was commendable. The new dance fashion was spreading – forty villages had now formed sides – but more than three weeks would have been needed to lick them into shape. Ariadne watched Rory's face and giggled.

'Klarissa won't be pleased when she learns about this outbreak of Morris-dancing. The peasants ought to be primed for revolution by now, attacking their krevoj's castles.'

'Klarissa and friends aren't the only ones who'll be displeased with me,' said Rory. 'I freed a SPAR leader from "legitimate custody" so the authorities will have taken umbrage. So in order to enter Strelsau without being arrested again, or shot, I've devised a cunning plan.'

'I'll bet you have. Rory, wasn't it a *coincidence* that you were guided through the maze at Hrincacz by logic puzzles? Suppose you hadn't been a logician.'

'I'd have received different guidance. If you'd been in the maze you'd have had legal tangles to resolve, not logic puzzles. Let's stop for lunch at the next inn.'

'We only had breakfast an hour and a half ago.'

'True. And your point is?'

They stopped at the next inn and rested their horses. Meals at Tomen's house, the cathedral hospital and Castle Bauntzi had met reasonable standards of hygiene if not nutrition. Meals at village and wayside inns were less constrained and were served under a pall of tobacco smoke. Rory said smoking in a restaurant was on a par with peeing in a swimming pool, from the high diving board. A small portion of his lunch, fleeing the nicotine fumes, scurried across his plate and took refuge under a depressed piece of foliage masquerading as salad.

'Lively lunch, Ariadne.'

'So what's this cunning plan?'

'It involves you. You must place me under citizen's arrest before we cross the city boundary and then take me directly to Blue Primrose HQ and hand me over.'

'What?'

'Think about it: you'll get a medal for delivering a dangerous criminal to the authorities.'

'Not funny, Rory. Are you going to eat that?'

'Not unless I can catch it. Ariadne, in order to save lives I must talk to Barrington before July the fourth, or June the twenty-first, or whatever. If you arrest me I can get to him without being shot *en route*. I haven't a pussy in the Inferno's chance if I try to make it on my own. The streets will be full of Blue Primrose ekwyroj and police, all hyped and trigger-happy as a posse of pissed cowboys, and someone will recognise me.'

'What do you mean, "save lives"? How am I supposed to arrest you and take you to …? I don't like this one little bit.'

Rory handed Eldzhay's knife to her.

'Brandish this in a bloodthirsty manner and I'll consider myself arrested. I'll explain as we ride. I've told you what I believe to be the core of the plot, but I need to explain a few things about Krev Schammerbass, too. And, I think, about the so-called Sura Marnikova. After you've taken me to Blue Primrose HQ, go to stay with Thad and Tomen again. I'll join you there as soon as I can. Meanwhile, share everything I tell you with Thad. Ariadne, darling, please do as I ask. Lives *will* depend on it.'

Ariadne handled the knife as though it was about to slither round her arm and bite her.

'I'm beginning to regret ever having met you, Rory Redman.'

Rory sighed. She wasn't the first woman to say those words. She was just the first he wanted not to mean them.

As they went to collect their horses, Ariadne stopped and knelt on the wet earth.

'Oh, darling, look! A pair of netted slugs, mating!' She stood again, smiling. 'Netted slugs are a delight, aren't they? And watching them evokes such a vivid memory of last night.'

There, thought Rory, romance isn't dead. He smiled and kissed her.

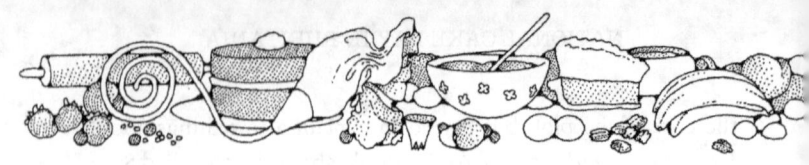

Chapter 80

The best tourist accommodation in Strelsau is in Districts 4D-5H, within walking distance of the Opera House and the National Theatre. There are several hotels where the rooms range from the expensive to the extortionate, but there is also the nine-storey Musement Block, which faces the Opera House. At most times of the year, several apartments in the Musement Block are available for short-term rental. Each floor is named after one of the Muses and is credited with inspiring residents with appropriate modes of creativity.
    — The Unideker Guide to Ruritania

Kjym and her family took an apartment on the Calliope Level of the Musement Block, so she'd have no stairs to negotiate with Kartor. Nadhan ensured she and Kartor were settled, then took the lift to the eighth floor to visit the editor-in-chief of the *Journal of Terpsichorean Meteorology*. On the way he discussed the rebellious weather with the conveyance. He hoped to acquire confidential information in advance of his visit; he knew the editor-in-chief often confided in lifts, as many journal editors do.

The lift in the Musement Block was a good listener, unlike its kindred in the local hotels, but could only say that the weatherdancers' recent forecasts had been 'optimistic'. As Nadhan ascended it announced the character of each floor in the tones of a lift discharging its duty: 'Second floor, Clio for those interested in history, where you may hear clarion and guitar … Third floor, Euterpe for dialectic – listen to the delightful flute and other … Fourth floor, Thalia for geometry, architecture and agriculture – the sounds of merriment are from comedy writers … Fifth floor, Melpomene for rhetoric, beware of low-flying bats and ignore the weeping and gnashing of teeth from tragedians … Sixth floor, Erato for all your wedding plans and love poems, not to be confused with errata, though she often is … Seventh floor, Polymnia for grammar, mimicry and divine hymns – my favourite floor, sir, I love the sound of the lyre; and here we are, the Eighth floor, or Eighth Dancer as the vulgar call it, Terpsichore. I'll stop here, per your request.'

Nadhan was no wiser about the weather. He alighted, punched the little gnome on the editor-in-chief's door, entered and shook hands with the occupant. The editor-in-chief was staring at the sky through his plate glass window. He was a worried man.

'I apologise for our loquacious lift, Krefin Bauntzi. *What* are we to make of this weather? I'm told a new dance is being practised in the villages. Could it be related? Cause and effect? I've sent five senior weatherdancers to watch the village performances and report back to me. Initial impressions are that the new dance *could* have brought this unseasonal rain but its provenance is unknown.'

A minion scurried into the room with coffee and cake.

'Perhaps I can elucidate,' said Nadhan. 'Among our recent guests at Castle Bauntzi is an Englishman who entered the Faerie Realm and used time-dilation to teach our villagers this new dance. It is called Morris-dancing. He told us various forms of it are traditional in communities throughout England. Its origins are debated, but it was brought to England during the fourteenth century.'

The editor-in-chief frowned. He nibbled a cake. Then illumination dawned.

'The fourteenth century? Precisely when the climate changed in Britain, heralding a cooler and wetter era culminating two centuries later in the Little Ice Age! This cannot be coincidence. Morris-dancing *must* have caused the rain we're now experiencing, but more importantly, we have a plausible explanation for British weather! Krefin Bauntzi, I beg you'll bring your English visitor here. My colleagues and I must discuss Morris-dancing and its meteorological impact with him. I shall invite him to co-author what could prove the most significant paper ever published in my journal.'

Nadhan returned to the lift and joined a party of astronomers and astrologers from the ninth floor, Ourania. They were chatting about a comet and an eclipse and arguing about local restaurants. They ignored the lift's floor by floor observations as they descended.

Back in his apartment on the Calliope level, Nadhan learned that his noble wife had also been making inquiries.

'Klarissa's gone to the Lenmir,' she said. 'She's made herself look plump, and the blonde wig and blue contact lenses rendered her barely recognisable. I've often thought the Lenmir management could be pro-SPAR. I wonder if I should alert Blue Primrose ...'

Two days to National Cake Day. A quick decision was needed.

'No, let them do their own work,' decided Kjym. 'It's what they're paid for.'

Chapter 81

Four aspects of the Rule of Law are universally agreed.
First: individuals, private entities, and government and its
agents are all accountable under the law. Second: the laws
are clear, publicized, stable and applied evenly, and protect
such fundamental rights as the security of person and
property. Third: the process by which laws are enacted,
administered and enforced is fair and accessible. Fourth:
justice is delivered in reasonable time by a sufficient
number of competent, ethical, neutral, independent
representatives who have adequate resources and reflect the
values of the communities they serve. In Ruritania, these
principles are not applied consistently, so the courts require
a corrective: the monarch has the power to override their
decisions. This power is seldom exercised.
— Principles of Jurisprudence in Ruritania

Colonel Barrington's desk was at once hectic and disciplined. The
flag-ornamented map of Strelsau formed a backcloth to his
satisfaction. His beard bristled. Two ekwyrinoj beat a polite tattoo
on his door and ushered in the captive and his captor. He nodded.

'Lock him up. Bread and water from now 'til the trial. And
tell the lady who captured the scoundrel she's earned Ruritania's
thanks, and mine.'

Rory looked at the map and shook his head.

'The lady's English, Colonel,' said Ariadne, 'and before you
lock Mr Redman away I must advise you that he *asked* me to
arrest him and bring him to you. He has important–'

'*Asked* you, ma'am? Do you know the …? Good grief, you're Ms Sowerby! So you *do* know him. In which case you won't believe anything he says.' The colonel frowned. 'You, get Redman downstairs. And stay alert. The blighter can run.'

'Please, Colonel, let him report,' said Ariadne. 'What's he alleged to have done?'

The colonel signalled the ekwyrinoj to execute his order. He counted off the charges as Rory was dragged from the office.

'One: knowingly interfered in a security operation. Two: handed a top secret security plan to terrorists. Three: skipped custody while under arrest. Four: ambushed a Blue Primrose detachment and enabled the terrorist leader to escape from lawful custody. Five: was party during the ambush to the deaths of several ekwyroj including the most respected senior ekwyor, Grizelina Tupsroot. On the latter two charges he's liable to the death penalty.'

Rory's voice echoed from the stairwell: 'What? Ekwyor Tupsroot? Killed? My God! No!'

His shock was manifestly unfeigned but his antagonist was unmoved.

'He led the ambush so he's responsible.' The colonel nodded to Ariadne. 'No doubt interrogation will reveal details, but we already have more than enough to convict him.'

Rory's voice was heard no longer. Ariadne watched the colonel trying not to stare at her chest, which the Barbour jacket failed to conceal. She was determined not to break down and cry.

'Regarding the deaths of the ekwyroj,' she said, 'the court will have to prove intent on Mr Redman's part. That would be difficult, Colonel. Regarding the other charges, his defence will establish that he never attempted to interfere in a security operation, he was forced to hand over the security plan under extreme duress, and he was abducted from St Avicenna's and therefore can't be held to have skipped custody.'

The colonel looked as though he'd drunk sour whisky.

'Of course. Bloody lawyer, aren't you?'

'Not yet licensed to practise in Ruritania, so Mr Redman can't instruct me in his defence. However, I can advise.'

The colonel's disgust stuck in his gorge.

'Even if he could persuade a jury with those feeble lines of defence, which I doubt, there's no argument about him leading the ambush.'

'A more interesting charge, but the defence will show him *not* to have led the ambush.'

Only someone of the colonel's rank, nationality and vintage could have spat 'Pah!' without sounding risible.

'Mr Redman was trying to tell Ekwyor Tupsroot the names of SPAR leaders when the ambush struck and he was forced to run,' said Ariadne. 'This isn't just *his* version of events; I've also heard the SPAR leader's account, which corroborates it. Unfortunately I was in no position to detain her.'

'Was that before or after Alterleta broke into the krevjalem's private chamber, threatened him and injured him?'

For a moment, Ariadne was nonplussed.

'I wasn't aware of that incident, Colonel. But I know two reasons why she might have attacked the krevjalem and neither has much to do with SPAR. Did she *kill* Krev Strlzhav?'

'The krevjalem's recovering.'

'But if she broke into his chamber and injured him I suppose she *could* have killed him.'

'So what? She didn't.'

'So you contend that the leader of an organisation dedicated to overthrowing the Ruritanian government had the head of said government at her mercy but didn't kill him? What will a court make of that?'

Whether Colonel Barrington was more impressed by Ariadne's argument or her bust wasn't clear, but he leaned back in his chair and raised his eyes to her face.

'Do you seriously believe Redman has worthwhile information about SPAR's plans?'

'Yes. He wouldn't share all the information with me because

he said it would put me at risk. He wanted to tell *you*. But he told me enough to convince me he should be heard. He can give you the names of several SPAR leaders. And he's deduced the core of their National Cake Day plot. If he's right, it has little to do with the flags on your map. And there are only two days to go.'

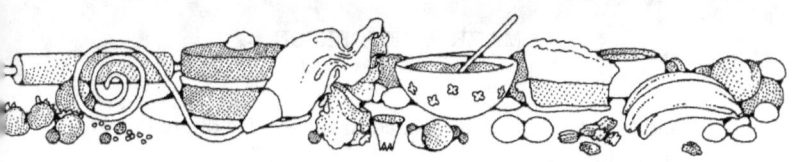

Chapter 82

The monarch has the inalienable right to hear appeals from non-native persons convicted under the law or claiming unlawful arrest or detention.
  — Principles of Jurisprudence in Ruritania

The sun was setting when Ariadne punched the gnome at Klatzierstrit 27. She was enraged at the colonel and frantic about Rory. Thad listened to her story.

'Thad, please understand, it's not just my concern for Rory. He says he's deduced SPAR's plan for National Cake Day. People *must* listen in case he's right.'

Thad inclined his head.

'Your representations failed to move Colonel Barrington?'

'He'd made up his mind about Rory and wouldn't listen.'

'Military men are intransigent. Now, Ariadne, please try to disengage your feelings and tell me whether you *believe* Rory's deduction.'

Ariadne paused. How had Thad discerned her feelings?

'*He* believes it and he's smart. He wouldn't tell me all the details but he's told me the core of the plot. And on the way to Blue Primrose HQ we did see that red-haired so-called Slovenian woman going into the National Bank … There's only one way to prove whether Rory's right and it needs permission from the highest authority.'

Thad's lips sketched a smile.

'Which you believe I can secure.'

Ariadne nodded. 'I wouldn't ask if the situation weren't desperate.'

Thad lit a cigarette and smoked in silence. He offered one to Ariadne. She took it.

'I will do what I can,' he said.

It was dark when he reached Dzhumpinpork Palace.

Chapter 83

The advantage of solitary confinement is that complaints about prison conditions – inadequate lighting and ventilation, extremes of temperature, insect and rodent infestation, and insufficient or non-existent hygiene supplies and sanitary provisions – cannot be independently corroborated.
  — *Principles of Jurisprudence in Ruritania*

It wasn't Rory's first experience of a cell but it was the worst: as smelly and Spartan as any in England but also cramped and airless. The bare floor was more comfortable than the mattress. The pitch darkness and the prospect of a death sentence didn't conduce to relaxation. Tired though he was, his sleep was fitful and his dreams lurid.

He was already half awake when the door fumbled open. He blinked and shaded his eyes. In the doorway stood Colonel Barrington, dishevelled and irate.

'Get dressed and upstairs, Redman, on the double!'

'Why?'

'Never mind bloody why! I gave you an order! And where are my damned cufflinks?'

'Shove your order up your arse.'

The colonel strode into the cell. Go on, thought Rory, give it your best shot. He stood and bunched his fists.

'Her Majesty Queen Anastassia commands your presence at the Palace.' The colonel's voice quivered. 'Do you understand? *The Queen has summoned you!* Get dressed and upstairs!'

Rory shook his head and blinked.

'The Queen? Why?'

'Maybe that lawyer bitch got the old biddy to listen to the same cock-and-bull–'

Rory's right fist smashed into his mouth and the left struck the side of his jaw.

'Take that back, Barrington, now!'

The colonel half fell, grasped the wall, righted himself, shook his head and wiped blood from his beard. His face betrayed shock, rage and disbelief.

'You'll pay for that, Redman.'

'One more insult to Ariadne, you bastard, and *you'll* pay. I'll hit you a bloody sight harder next time.'

'Dare to threaten me and you'll pay double.'

'I'm shaking in my shoes.' Rory fought for self-control. 'Now fuck off. I'll be upstairs when I'm ready.'

Awaiting him beside the Great Azure Door were the colonel, dabbing his lips, and three other men. Two were senior ekwyroj in full uniform. The third was Thad Masim, wearing his best suit. No one smiled. Thad addressed him formally.

'Her Majesty Queen Anastassia is graciously pleased to command Rory Redman to an audience. Pan Redman will travel under armed guard. At the Palace he will observe full protocol. Colonel Barrington will travel in my coach and will be present at the audience.'

'I couldn't wish a less desirable travelling companion on you, Thad,' said Rory.

A day and a half until National Cake Day, he thought. What chance do I have of averting disaster?

Chapter 84

Love has been defined as 'giving someone the power to destroy you and trusting them not to'. In truth, it is Nature's way of tricking us into reproducing. Trust is essential, destruction incidental.

— Dai O'Genies, A Primer of Ruritanian Philosophy

'Thad went to see the Queen,' said Ariadne, 'but he can't make Her Majesty grant Rory an audience, or compel the bank to reveal confidential information.'

'He has a lot of influence, Ariadne,' said Tomen.

'Unless he can persuade the Queen, Rory's in trouble and so is Ruritania. May I make coffee, Tomen?'

Ariadne rose from the chaise longue, dodging the tusk. Tomen followed her into the kitchen.

'You are in love with Rory.'

Ariadne plugged in the kettle, scanned a shelf and examined a cupboard.

'Here.' Tomen handed her the coffee jar.

Ariadne spooned coffee into cups. Tomen's house, crockery included, seemed dingy and wan after the lurid colours of Castle Bauntzi.

'I shouldn't be.' Ariadne frowned. 'Rory goes through women like a Glaswegian through deep-fried pizzas.'

'Perhaps he is growing up.'

'Impossible. He's a man.'

'Good point.'

Ariadne's face crumpled. She blinked.

'I'm so worried, Tomen. I could have killed that bloody colonel.'

Tomen put her arms around her.

'I will not say, "Try not to worry," because I am not stupid. But you say Rory has spent his life getting into scrapes – and out of them again.'

'So far.'

Ariadne sobbed on Tomen's shoulder.

Chapter 85

Notwithstanding the principles of jurisprudence in Ruritania, the monarch and the krevoj are largely immune from the rule of law. Hereditary privilege decrees that a krev accused of a crime can only be charged and tried on the specific order of the monarch.

— The Unideker Guide to Ruritania

Queen Anastassia was smoking a cigarette. She was small and stout with coiffured white hair and clever eyes. Each of the guards standing behind her held a silver battle-axe, one of which sported a cobweb. Her Majesty addressed the arrivals in her audience chamber in English.

'Colonel Barrington, you are permitted to speak in your own language. Also you, Pan Redman. Speak slow with no hard words. Professor Masim, you will translate when need.'

Thad bowed.

'Colonel Barrington,' continued the Queen, 'you say Pan Redman commit crime. Tell.'

The colonel said, 'If it please Your Majesty,' and enumerated the charges. Thad translated.

'Professor Masim, you say these charges are answered. Tell.'

Thad summarised Ariadne's defence. Then the Queen's eyes turned to Rory.

'Your Majesty, I didn't interfere in a security operation; I was illegally detained and taken to London by Colonel Barrington and Ekwyor Tupsroot. I escaped and flew to Ruritania to find the woman who'd attacked me. And, Ma'am, I was curious to visit your country.'

Thad translated and Rory related his visit to Vorgottenstrit, the miasma grenade, his abduction from St Avicenna's, and the threats compelling him to relinquish the security plan.

'The man who took it is called Mangler. He'll have arrived in Strelsau within the past two or three days.'

Thad's translation was accompanied by a glare from the colonel, who confessed ignorance of Mangler.

'Where in Strelsau have this document and this Mangler arrived?' said the Queen.

'I don't know, Ma'am,' said Rory. 'But the SPAR leaders are probably lying low in a hotel with a sympathetic management.'

Her Majesty snapped an order to her guards. One of them bowed, turned to march out of the room and tripped over his battle-axe, injuring the cobweb. The Queen shook her head, lit another cigarette and commanded Rory to continue.

Rory described the rescue of Klarissa.

'I'd no choice. Twelve arrows were pointed at my back. I thought I could prevent bloodshed, but I was forced to run because as soon as the captive jumped to freedom a fire-fight started. This evening I heard Ekwyor Tuperoot and other ekwyroj had died in the skirmish. I'm grieved by this tragic news.'

The colonel snorted.

'The group responsible for the ambush numbered twelve men and women,' added Rory. 'Their leader is called Arraitch; a brilliant archer.'

Colonel Barrington hadn't heard Arraitch's name, either. The Queen issued orders to the ekwyroj. Soon, Blue Primrose were combing the dark streets of Strelsau.

'If he's telling the truth,' said the Queen to Thad, 'he's more a victim of ill fortune than a miscreant. Do you believe him?'

'I do, Ma'am,' said Thad. 'I consider him honest and well-intentioned.'

'Nevertheless, freeing a dangerous terrorist from custody is a serious offence. Only if he can prove his claims about the planned insurrection will a Pardon be considered.'

Thad translated the Queen's message. Rory gulped.

'Ma'am, Colonel Barrington's men and Your Majesty's ekwyroj are well prepared to suppress insurrection in the capital. But there will be relatively few of them in St Galen's Square for the National Cake Day ceremony.'

'Do you imagine we won't have the Square covered?' barked the colonel. 'Terrorists won't get past the cordon unless they use tanks and fighter jets, and they don't have any!'

'Speak in your turn!' Her Majesty stubbed out her cigarette. 'Translate, please.'

Rory resumed: 'I don't doubt the colonel's preparations, Ma'am. But if I were a terrorist leader I wouldn't try to attack St Galen's Square during the ceremony. To put the royal family and the leading krevoj and mediclergy out of action in one fell swoop, I'd booby-trap the metacake. The Surgeon Archbishop's sacred scalpel would wreak havoc. I don't know what they'll use, but after what I experienced with the miasma grenade–'

'Taurocoprology!' roared the colonel. 'Ma'am, the scoundrel's trying to buy a Pardon with fantasy! It's impossible–'

'Silence!' shouted the Queen.

'But Your Majesty, this is ridiculous! The metacake has been behind locked doors since it reached Jubetitstrit, guarded twenty-four hours a day! No one could have tampered with it!'

Thad translated, and added: 'Krevjalem Strlzhav oversaw the baking of the metacake in person, Your Majesty. His most trusted people guarded it along the route to Strelsau. And of course the colonel's right about security in Jubetitstrit.'

'So on this matter, you don't believe Pan Redman?'

Thad hesitated.

'Not unless he can explain how the metacake could have been booby-trapped.'

'Then order him to explain.'

Simple case of baking and entering, thought Rory. Aloud, he replied: 'Guards can be bribed and keys can be stolen. There isn't time to locate and question everyone who's been on guard duty in Jubetitstrit, but what about asking whether any of the overseers mislaid their keys after the metacake arrived, even for an hour?'

The Queen gave the order.

'And inform the krevjalem,' she added. 'He will personally inspect the metacake for evidence of tampering, and he will report immediately to me.'

She turned to Rory again.

'We will see. Now you return to cell until it is known.'

But tomorrow is National Cake Day, thought Rory. By the time it's known it'll be too late.

'SPAR isn't the only threat, Ma'am,' he said. 'There's also–'

The Queen emptied the audience chamber with a gesture. As Rory was taken from the Palace she re-lit her cigarette, summoned secretaries and gave more orders:

The Surgeon Archbishop was to be indisposed on the morrow and the drunken Surgeon Bishop of Szipad would be brought to Strelsau to take his place in St Galen's Square.

She too planned to be unwell and unable to fulfil her traditional National Cake Day role. Crown Prince Elharic was to be recalled from his pond in the enchanted forest to officiate on her behalf

Chapter 86

Anyone with eyes to see and a mind to reflect will perceive that all current governments must be abolished so that liberty, equality and fraternity will become living realities, not empty words. All forms of government yet tried, including modern-day democracies, have proved to be just so many devices for oppression.
— *Klarissa Krefin Strlzhava, 'Democracy'. Final Honours Dissertation, 2011*

Klarissa and her comrades studied a map of Strelsau more detailed than Colonel Barrington's. The epidemic of Morris-dancing among Ruritania's villagers was irksome but everyone was focussed on plans for the capital. The tines and edges of the scheme were honed, ready to wield. Everyone knew his or her role. All were eager.

Three activists brimming with news were admitted to the Lenmir Hotel, questioned by a junior SPAR member and at length allowed access to a leader and thence granted admission to the Ulyanova. They trembled.

'Well?'

'Ulyanova, Redman has been arrested!'

'We saw it with our own eyes!'

'We know it was Redman, his name was on many lips!'

'An unknown woman forced him to the Great Azure Door at knife-point!'

'When?'

'Several hours ago, Ulyanova – we tried to report earlier–'

'But we weren't allowed–'

'At first.'

'Did Redman subsequently leave Blue Primrose HQ?' said Klarissa.

'No, Ulyanova, he hadn't left when we came here–'

'He was still–'

'They'll have interrogated–'

Klarissa dismissed the activists and addressed the assembly.

'What information could Redman divulge?'

'He knows nothing of our plans,' said Mangler. 'Of course he knows our identities, but surely Blue Primrose have that information already.'

'Mangler, Arraitch, Eldzhay – Redman knows your names and faces, so find somewhere to hide until noon.'

Klarissa's fingers drummed the edge of the desk. Then she returned to the map. Redman's arrest was troubling. He was clever, unpredictable, a latent fly in the revolutionary ointment. He should have been eliminated. Had he not escaped from Mangler – and afterwards saved her life – he *would* have been eliminated, albeit belatedly.

Yet he had potential. He could be an asset. She'd tried at Castle Bauntzi to convert him to the Revolutionary cause.

Perhaps she still could.

Chapter 87

SPAR, the Communist Party in Ruritania (if an underground organisation can be called a 'party'), differs in important ways from the Party that unleashed the 1917 Revolution in Russia. In modern Ruritania, as in early 20th century Russia, some 85% of the population are peasants, but there the similarity ends. By the eve of the October Revolution the Russian feudal system was disintegrating, there was a rising urban proletariat that proved instrumental in ensuring Bolshevik ascendency, and the peasantry had differentiated into haves and have-nots. In modern Ruritania the feudal system remains intact, there is no significant urban proletariat, and the peasantry remains mostly undifferentiated. SPAR depends more on support from the peasants than from the urban poor.

— Ariadne Sowerby, 'First Impressions of Ruritania'

Crown Prince Elharic stamped his foot and waved his fist and shouted. The Queen ordered him from the audience chamber. He slammed the pearl-inlaid door behind him. His tongue shot out and caught a bee. It stung him.

'Your future King, Professor Masim.' Her Majesty lit a cigarette. 'I'd like to say, "Over my dead body," but why state the obvious? And don't search for a diplomatic reply, there isn't one.'

'No, Ma'am,' said Thad. 'I regret that Prince Elharic was so dismissive of Pana Sowerby's submission.'

'I can now give proper attention to it. Repeat it.'

Thad bowed.

313

'First, Krev Schammerbass's scheme for the bag of papers in Manchester was so convoluted it seemed designed to fail. Alterleta must have known where to find the security plan, and the krev was one of only a handful of people who could have told her. They visited the same hotel in Manchester at the same time.'

The Queen pointed her cigarette at Thad.

'I cannot imagine anyone less like a Communist than Krev Schammerbass. He is rich. He has international prestige as a scientist. He has everything to lose and nothing to gain from a revolution.'

'Nevertheless, Ma'am, Pan Redman discovered him living with armed guards in an isolated house behind electronic locks and bullet-proof windows. Why, in a friendly country such as Britain? His house in Switzerland is also isolated ...' Thad collected his thoughts. 'Your Majesty, no dictator in history has gained or held power without support from his nation's armed forces. In Ruritania, that means the Order of the Blue Primrose. Would any of Your Majesty's ekwyroj follow a leader who was not a krev?'

The Queen nodded.

'They would not. But Alterleta pretends to be a krev's daughter, I understand she carries off the act to perfection.'

'Blue Primrose wouldn't recognise her as a krev, Ma'am.'

The Queen snorted and stubbed out her cigarette.

'You prove nothing. I will not believe Krev Schammerbass is associated with SPAR.'

'No, Ma'am. But what is the source of SPAR's money? SPAR feeds and houses numerous orphans. They help the poor and the sick. Those are expensive activities. Klarissa Alterleta spent a fortune in England – five-star hotels, designer clothes–'

'Krev Schammerbass is rich but not as rich as that. And what would motivate him to finance SPAR if he isn't associated with them?'

'Ma'am, his contacts include the military of powerful nations. They can provide big money.' Thad stared at the Queen. 'According to Pana Sowerby, Pan Redman believes Krev

Schammerbass is using SPAR as a parasitic wasp uses a caterpillar. He intends their revolution to succeed, then he'll recruit Blue Primrose support and step into the power vacuum. Once he rules the country he can return value for the money that foreign military sources have given him, and his income will continue. SPAR will be eliminated. But he believes Alterleta discovered his intentions, so he has been in fear for his life.'

The Queen frowned.

'More than half the research the Academy of Science finances concerns the Faerie Realm. Why would the American or Russian or Chinese military be interested in the Faerie Realm?'

'Pan Redman suspects Britain's military of such interest,' said Thad. 'He has visited the Faerie Realm and believes someone who understands its physics, as Krev Schammerbass does, could manipulate its powers to military advantage.'

A millstone of silence hung. Then the Queen shook her head.

'Nonsense. Redman sprang Klarissa Alterleta from lawful detention. He's woven a fantasy in the hope of escaping the consequences. What he claims is impossible.'

Someone extinguished the lights. National Cake Day had dawned, and despite an unseasonal gathering of rain clouds the rising sun caressed the Palace. Birds sang, though they were inaudible to those in the audience chamber.

'Impossible indeed, Ma'am; but as Pan Redman discovered, the impossible is commonplace in the Faerie Realm,' said Thad.

The Queen snorted again.

'A well-worn observation. Do not repeat well-worn observations here, Professor Masim. You are in the Royal Palace, where the commonplace is impossible.'

Chapter 88

To 'rain on someone's parade' is an English idiom meaning to disappoint or discourage a person or organisation by ruining their aspirations. But no rain on the parade entering St Galen's Square could discourage or disappoint Ruritanians on National Cake Day; not that it ever rains on National Cake Day.
— The Unideker Guide to Ruritania

The crowds gathering around St Galen's Square frowned at the sky and muttered. Along with the prospect of unforecasted rain there was the nebulous threat of insurrection, and disturbing rumours had radiated from the Palace: the Queen was unwell after dealing with affairs of state overnight, so Prince Elharic had been recalled to take her place at one o'clock. Could National Cake Day be celebrated without the reigning monarch presiding? It was also rumoured that the Surgeon Bishop of Szipad would usurp the Surgeon Archbishop's role. Sensible people regarded these stories as nonsense, but they spread quickly because less sensible people confided them far and wide.

Blue Primrose was assiduous. Every office, every rooftop, every doorway, every underground pipe, every parked carriage within half a league of St Galen's Square was searched by ekwyrinoj with trained sniffer Spitzes, which attacked the parked carriages. Every square smallbit of the Gardens was inspected. The bright balloons and bunting were scrutinised. The seats upon which the shabby old cripples sat were examined with magnifying glasses, making the cripples look even shabbier. Wooden legs were sawn in half to check for hidden weapons. The very flowers were viewed with mistrust. The statue of St Galen was assessed for evidence of tampering.

In district 7R in the north of the city, jittery police officers struggled with Kevlar vests, visors, riot shields and big black sticks with knobbly ends.

The investigations ordered by the Queen had yielded nothing. No hotel housing SPAR's leaders had been identified, neither Mangler nor Arraitch had been located, and Blue Primrose were now too busy to search further. Krev Strlzhav had inspected the metacake; he reported minor distortion of the metadecorations, typical of the effects of travel and temperature fluctuations.

'Damn Redman and his bloody lies and fantasies,' spluttered Colonel Barrington. 'Wasting the krevjalem's time, today of all days!'

Three Jubetitstrit bakery overseers admitted they'd mislaid their keys once or twice during the previous fortnight, but the keys had been recovered within an hour. One reported that his key-ring had been returned by a labourer who'd only worked in the bakery for one shift.

'Stupid fellow, but a first-rate quality control man. Name? Cineas or Pélleas or something. Never seen him since.'

The sun climbed above the Gothic rooftops of Strelsau and then hid behind thickening clouds. The editor-in-chief of the *Journal of Terpsichorean Meteorology* looked at the sky, pursed his lips, checked his records, and descended from his high place carrying a pink umbrella and a pair of antique galoshes.

'The weatherdancers have erred,' he said.

'It happens,' said the lift, 'but the people must be warned – if there's time.'

Rory had managed to speak to Thad for three minutes before the guards took him back to his cell below Blue Primrose HQ.

Colonel Barrington heard the key turn in the lock and was satisfied.

'At least the old biddy had the sense not to believe the scoundrel,' he said, and turned to important matters.

Chapter 89

War is Asclepius's way of teaching us geography.
— *Old Ruritanian Proverb*

At the edge of the south-east quarter, a scout shook his phone and fulminated.

'Bleedin' signal's had a dose of bromide. Can you hear me, mate?'

'Strength two, Scout. Pretend I'm foreign: talk slow and loud. Over.'

'Over what?'

'Bloody hell. Report, you wanker!'

'Fifteen or sixteen folk banging buckets and shouting. No weapons visible except the buckets. Couple of 'em waving placards. Couple of folk, I mean, not buckets.'

'What do the placards say, Scout? Over.'

'Can't hear them say ... Oh, right. Two words, written in foreign: *Z-i-t-a-g-u* and *E-p-a-n-a-s-t-i-j-a-n*. Er ... Over, okay?'

'Right, Scout. Similar report from south-east quarter: dozen rag-bags trying to march, one with a drum, two or three placards– same message, except one says "Zitagu Ulyanovan".'

'What's it mean?'

'Guys here say it's "Long live the Revolution", so the other's "Long live the Ulyanova". The Ulyanova's the chick they say leads SPAR. We're supposed to look out for her. Over.'

The Scout's reply was politically incorrect. It elicited a chortle.

'Yeah, but me first. Watch the bucket-bangers, Scout, and report if numbers increase. Over.'

'How long for? Most residents have gone into town. If this is a revolution it's bloody boring. Are they trying to overthrow the government by sending it to sleep? Over.'

'You never know. Stay on post pending further orders. Over and out.'

The scout glared at his phone and rehearsed his repertoire of naughty words. Then it began to rain and he rehearsed them more loudly.

*

As noon approached, Mangler emerged from hiding and marshalled his forces. He inspected their weapons and reviewed the battle plan.

'The police outnumber us two to one, but since one of us is worth three of them we have numerical superiority. You, stop trying to count, you'll drop your cream cakes. You, put that dictionary away.' He checked his watch. 'The police have formed a single line with locked riot shields. So: three ranks, forward march, ammunition cart to follow. Keep in step; don't fire until I give the order. Any questions? Good. Sillias, hit the drum, one hundred and twenty beats per minute. Yes you can, I've explained it fifteen times.'

The revolutionaries marched round the corner and the police saw them. The riot shields trembled, emitting a dissonant grating, but the line stood more or less firm. The marchers strode forwards, almost keeping time with the drum, until they were fifteen fathoms from the shivering shields. Then Mangler ordered, 'Halt!' and they halted.

'First rank: Fire!'

A volley of cream cakes flew at the police line and splattered on the Perspex visors.

'Second rank forward! Fire!'

Cakes rich in jam and treacle smote the beleaguered officers. The visors became opaque.

'Third rank forward! Fire!'

Ceramic utensils smashed against helmets and shields. The line broke and the police lashed out blindly. Their big black sticks with knobbly ends struck walls, air, stray dogs and other officers. A few grappled hand to hand with the revolutionaries but were handicapped by poor visibility. Within five minutes they were overwhelmed. The victorious SPAR forces cheered lustily and sang a song with unclean words and imaginative rhymes.

'Back in marching order!' roared Mangler. 'To St Galen's Square! Ammunition cart, don't fall behind!'

'Yes, Voyalem,' said the cart.

The stray dogs licked up the remains of the cake ammunition. Rain began to fall, too late to wash the Perspex visors clean.

*

Rory inspected his cell door: old-fashioned mortise lock, economical on tumblers but big and heavy. Strong bolts on the outside. The hinges looked more promising. He fished in his pockets and located nail clippers and nail file, which more perceptive jailors would have confiscated.

He checked his watch and set to work.

Chapter 90

*Lack of electricity hurts when you're an electricity addict, as
we all are in the west. You have no refrigerator or freezer, you
have to use other energy sources to cook, lighting depends on
lamps and candles so the nights are dark, no computers work
except laptops with good batteries, phones are useless. If you're
an electricity addict in a Ruritanian city, all will be well for
you – if and only if the hamsters remain on their treadmills.
The countryside, though, will give you withdrawal symptoms
until you adjust to life without electric power.*

— *Ariadne Sowerby, 'First Impressions of Ruritania'*

Colonel Barrington received news of Mangler's victory.
Denouncing the police as blithering idiots unworthy of their big
black sticks with knobbly ends, he grabbed the phone.

'Captain! Take forty men up the road to 7R. Gang of terrorists
got through the police line and they're heading for the Square.
They're armed. Stop them.'

'Yessir. On our way. Arrest them all?'

'If they surrender. Otherwise shoot to kill.'

'Sir. What about the other two districts?'

'Twenty men in each under the command of a lieutenant.
When you've dealt with the north-western gang, report and we'll
redeploy.'

'Don't have two lieutenants, sir.'

'Grant on-the-spot temporary commissions to two NCOs.'

As the colonel barked the order there came an emergency call
from the generating station, followed by yells of panic.

321

'God's buttocks, who let the hamsters out?' bellowed the colonel. 'Ekwyor, we need every vet in the city; tranquilliser darts, cranes, animal carts. Immediate action! And get a force to the power station pronto and shoot the blighters responsible. We don't need distractions but we do need electricity!'

On cue, the lights went out.

The ceremony was due to begin in fifteen minutes. The power station crisis would deplete the Blue Primrose forces around St Galen's Square.

The scout in the south-east reported increasing numbers of protesters, now forming a dangerous mob. He requested support from a dozen armed ekwyroj and begged permission to leg it. The colonel's beard bristled.

At least there was no trouble in the city centre so far, though the bunting had started to droop as the rain grew heavier.

*

Three fathoms beneath the colonel's polished boots with their freshly-ironed laces, four of the screws securing the cell door's lower hinge had yielded to Rory's nail file and clippers. The fifth was proving tough.

Rory glanced again at his watch and redoubled his efforts.

Chapter 91

Ever since Orpheus enchanted with the lyre and David calmed the dark soul of Saul, indeed for tens of thousands of years before that, music has been valued for its capacity to charm, captivate, mesmerise, stimulate, seduce, energise or sedate. The wise and wayward Odysseus stopped his sailors' ears with wax when a certain singing would otherwise have lured them to doom. The Ruritanians have made constructive use of this idea: the singing, not the wax.
— Ariadne Sowerby, 'First Impressions of Ruritania'

'Remember what Colonel Barrington said,' shouted the captain. 'These villains kill without mercy, threatening the Queen's peace and the nation's security. So we'll show *them* no mercy! We'll give them one chance to lay down their weapons and surrender. If they don't take it, then on my command, shoot! Understood? Right. Positions!'

The forty squaddies exhibited well-trained dubiety and discipline.

'Wonder what weapons the enemy's carrying.'

'Ceramic utensils and cakes. Be a joke if they don't come this way.'

'Won't be a joke if they reach the Square and His Nibs finds out they've dodged us.'

'Yes it will. Captain'll get his balls fried.'

'They'll take this route. Alternatives are too narrow and smelly.'

'Any intelligence about numbers?'

'Nah. Enough to break through the police line, though.'

'At least two of them, then.'

Sounds approached: drum, marching clogs. The squaddies trained their rifles on the road to the north.

Then came another sound and they all closed their eyes, lowered their weapons and sighed. Drum and footwear fell silent.

Sillias's arms were tired.

'Mangler, don't like this. Something's wrong. We're walking into a thingummy. You know, an am-whatsit.'

'We're marching, not walking. Need to be in the Square to protect the Ulyanova as soon as the job's … Oh, listen, aren't they lovely? Comrades must have … accomplished … task …'

His beatific smile was reflected in every face. No one moved. From across the city came the singing of emergency vehicles, blue-clad voices uttering wordless melodies, an unearthly polyphony that tingled spine and viscera and rendered every listener powerless.

Slowly, slowly, the glorious music faded as the emergency vehicles galloped from incident scene to church surgery. The world moved on again.

'Forward march!' ordered Mangler.

'Throw down your weapons and step forward with your arms raised!' bellowed the captain.

'Bugger,' said Mangler.

'Told you,' said Sillias. 'Now what?'

'March on. There aren't many of them.'

As he spoke, reinforcements rushed to their aid: seven youths armed with rubber bands and rolled-up comics. Their onset distracted the squaddies.

'Last chance!' shouted the captain. 'Throw down your weapons and raise your arms or we fire!'

A rolled-up comic landed in the middle of the road. A young corporal rushed out under covering fire to seize it. Soon, half a dozen squaddies were cackling over it.

'Grab the stickiest cakes from the armaments cart,' said Mangler. 'Those of you with the best aims, throw them at the rifles and gum up the muzzles. The rest of you, ceramic utensils. We'll drive these puppets of the oppressors back into their holes!'

His troops cheered. They didn't know the power of state-of-the-art firearms. Nor did Mangler.

There was a rattle of gunfire. Bullets screamed in one direction, ceramic utensils flew in the other. Five cake-throwers fell.

Chapter 92

Never try to pat a blazing dog, outmuscle a ghrunli defender, or lock up a lock-picker.
— *Old Ruritanian Proverb.*

From every district of Strelsau, from hotels and rented rooms, from outlying villages, streams of citizens rich and poor flowed towards the city centre. Despite the rain, the sea of humanity around St Galen's Square widened and deepened as the morning advanced. Excited waves of anticipation washed over the Gardens, and the hum of expectation from the damp ranks of hoi polloi swelled to a rumble. No arrow had been fired, no Communist slogans chanted, and not a single hostile placard waved.

Noon passed, though no one noticed because the sun was veiled under asphalt cloud. Then one o'clock approached, and under the drenching rain the rumble of expectation became a roar. Wet voices sang patriotic verses, each in a different key; soggy flags flopped. At ten minutes to the hour the roar grew to a cheer with a descant of booing.

From the High Bakery emerged the procession of thirty-one krevoj and their partners, resplendent in ceremonial bakers' robes, hats and aprons. At their head marched Krevjalem Strlzhav, pushing the metacake on a gilded trolley protected by a jewelled umbrella. The Royal Band of sackbuts, shawms, crumhorns, serpents and dustbin lids played a jolly march that drowned the mingled cheers and cat-calls from the dripping crowd around the Gardens. Among the wet Ruritanian flags, sporadic hammer-and-sickle banners had appeared.

From Dzhumpinpork Palace issued a bronze carriage drawn by four white horses decorated with red, white and blue plumes. In the carriage sat Crown Prince Elharic, his face sulky. Beside him sat a portly blonde, eating cake, and a lutonist who looked resigned. The Royal Band struck up the National Anthem. Listeners who were not tone deaf supposed that the National Anthem had been not so much struck up as struck down by a harmonic miasma. There were more cheers and louder cat-calls.

From the Surgeon Archbishop's palace staggered the Surgeon Bishop of Szipad, squelching with the cautious dignity of chronic intoxication towards the statue of St Galen. His clerical hat wilted under the rain. In his fist, the sacred scalpel shuddered.

Whispers ran around the Square. Were the rumours true after all? No Queen, no Surgeon Archbishop? No sunshine? What was afoot?

But the ceremony was choreographed to perfection. The bronze carriage halted and minions in royal livery sprang forward to open the doors and lower the steps. Crown Prince Elharic descended with the stateliness of hereditary privilege, scanning the rain for insects. Behind him, the blonde wobbled from the carriage in a shower of cake crumbs. The lutonist remained where he was, arms folded. As the Prince advanced towards the statue, Krevoj Strlzhav and Hvimpy moved forward and stood one on each side of him. The other krevoj stepped back, leaving a clear circle around the focus of the ceremony: the metacake enthroned on its crystal cake-stand on the gilded trolley.

The jewelled umbrella was moved aside with reverence. The crowd gasped and applauded: there before their eyes, in all its calorific majesty, gleamed the metacake.

The Surgeon Bishop of Szipad stumbled forward, brandishing the sacred scalpel. The band stopped playing. The crowd held its breath.

Unnoticed by anyone in the Square except Krev Bauntzia, one krev and his red-haired companion donned rubber masks.

*

From her position in the crowd near the cathedral hospital, Klarissa watched and frowned.

'Where is the Queen? Where is the Surgeon Archbishop? Why have the Frog Prince and the fool from Szipad taken their places? Why has the weather turned foul? Where are Mangler and his people? And who are those with the rubber masks? Surely they …'

Over St Galen's Square the downpour was unrelenting. Balloons and bunting drooped and dripped.

*

The final screw was half-undone. Rory tugged. The hinge sprang free and the door tilted. He squeezed himself into the gap, squashing his rib-cage. A minute's wriggling and cursing saw him outside the cell with watering eyes, contusions and skinned knuckles. According to his watch it was three minutes to one.

The corridor was lined with lockers. Rory applied his nail clippers to the nearest door, then the next, then the next. The fourth opened. The locker was empty. He went to the fifth. The sixth. At last! It wasn't his size but it would have to suffice.

*

All eyes behind the Great Azure Door were fixed on St Galen's Square. The colonel and the ekwyroj congratulated each other: despite the unrest, the fighting and the freed hamsters, the terrorists hadn't reached their target. The captain had dispersed the gang in 7R, shooting many, arresting a few, and seizing a consignment of ceramic utensils and cream cakes. Incipient trouble elsewhere had been suppressed. The stirrings of unrest had come to nothing. The Gardens were safe. All was well.

Then an ekwyrin with an ill-fitting uniform leapt out through the Great Azure Door. His swift march segued into a run. He

328

headed straight for the centre of the ceremony. Klarissa recognised him and began to push forwards.

'Arraitch!' she called. 'Arraitch! Emergency!'

Colonel Barrington spotted the intruder at the same time. He reached for his binoculars.

'What does that damned idiot think he's doing?'

A moment later, recognition came.

'God's knickers, it's Redman! What bloody fool let him out and gave him a uniform? You, you, you, after him! Stop him!'

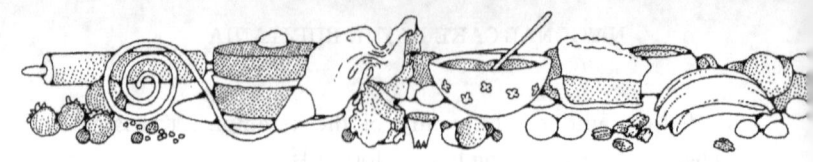

Chapter 93

Anger, unrest and panic are contagious, but some people are immune.
    — *Old Ruritanian Proverb.*

Rory scanned the scene before him. There was the metacake at the foot of St Galen's statue. Ranged around it in attitudes of wet veneration were Crown Prince Elharic, Krevjalem Strlzhav, Krev Hvimpy and the Surgeon Bishop of Szipad. Some fathoms apart from them, the rest of the aristocracy awaited the climax of the ritual. Their ceremonial robes sagged under the downpour. Stoical ekwyroj bearing ceremonial swords and battle-axes flanked the assembly. Then bugles were blown by four people wearing outfits for which they'd have been arrested in many countries, not least because they were now translucent with rain-water. The great crowd cheered and booed. Wet flags flopped in a parody of exuberance.

Rory's legs went into marathon mode. It's a good crowd despite the weather, he thought, but the space would accommodate thirty percent more of them if they weren't all so fat. Now all I have to do is get to the middle of the Gardens before–

It was too late.

The bugles blew again. The Surgeon Bishop mouthed a short prayer and raised the sacred scalpel. His arm wobbled, but he thrust the blade into the yielding flesh of the metacake with all the alacrity and a caricature of the precision proper to his calling.

And the metacake exploded.

The Surgeon Bishop only had time to mutter, 'Never known a patient do that,' before the pressurised miasma overwhelmed him.

At first, eighty-three percent of the crowd thought the explosion was part of the entertainment, but their merriment swiftly yielded to dismay. Thousands of tongues murmured about SPAR: a Communist Revolution was all very well, but not if it spoiled everyone's enjoyment, and blowing up the metacake was a hanging offence.

As the green fumes of the miasma bomb rose and the Crown Prince, the fat blonde, the two election rivals and the Surgeon Bishop collapsed into the puddles beneath the statue, the other krevoj and their partners scurried for cover. Some fell, ensnared by tendrils of green fumes, but those who'd been at the rear of the assembly escaped; the rain was drenching the miasma and limiting the bomb's range. Two of the escapees abandoned their protective rubber masks and ran towards the Palace, cursing the downpour and the Morris-dancing that had caused it.

In Blue Primrose HQ, orders were shouted from five different directions. It took Colonel Barrington two minutes to regain control. By then, Rory was half-way across the Gardens and racing towards Dzhumpinpork Palace, pursuing the pair who'd dropped their protective masks. The fourteen ekwyroj who'd been sent to stop him trailed several fathoms behind. They were losing ground.

'He knew!' shouted the colonel. 'He told us, but he made it sound so far-fetched no one could believe him!'

Redman and Alterleta were in it together, he decided: co-conspirators. Most people's certainties are undermined by stress but the colonel's became more deeply entrenched.

'Captain! Get your men into St Galen's Square on the double! Riot control! Ekwyor, we need every available medipriest and every emergency vehicle not already occupied. Get the Faerie Flight link to Hrincacz activated. You, what's the situation with the generating station? We need the hamsters back on the treadmills and this power outage ending *now*. You, take a dozen ekwyroj into the Gardens to protect the krevoj who're still on their feet – get them into the High Bakery for safety pending further orders. And stay away from the miasma. You, contact the television centre. Announce a one thousand raldol reward for the capture of Alterleta or Redman, dead or alive! You, bring me a carriage, a fast one. I must get to the Palace.'

From the northern side of the Square, Klarissa saw Krev Schammerbass loping towards the Palace, the red-headed woman beside him, not limping. Rory Redman was pursuing them and fourteen ekwyroj were pursuing him. One of them raised her gun and a bullet parted Rory's hair. Still running, the ekwyor took fresh aim.

Confusion and dismay surged through the hoi polloi. The mob sought a leader, any leader.

'Get me to the television centre,' shouted Klarissa. 'As soon as power is restored I will tell Ruritania she is free under the Revolutionary government, her people no longer slaves of an effete aristocracy!' She pointed towards Rory. 'Arraitch, stop the interference.'

Arraitch bent his bow and shot the ekwyor with the gun.

'Not her! *Redman*!'

Rory vaulted a wooden seat. He was twenty fathoms behind Krev Schammerbass and 'Sura Marnikova' and closing.

'Lady, you must go to the Palace, not the television centre,' said Arraitch. 'You are our President!'

'Stop Redman, Arraitch, or the Revolution will falter!'

Arraitch raised his bow, then lowered it again. He risked hitting the wrong target: Redman had grasped Klarissa's friend Krev Bauntzia. Both appeared to be talking.

'Kjym, you're going to be needed at–'

'Rory, Schammerbass–'

'I know, I'll stop him – take command of Blue Primrose.'

Kjym stepped in front of the pursuing ekwyroj and shouted orders. Krev Schammerbass reached the Palace and loped through the door, 'Sura' in his wake. Seconds later, Rory followed.

Arraitch's arrow missed Rory; either his legendary accuracy had failed him, or he'd chosen to aim to the left, or Klarissa had nudged him as he released the bowstring.

Chapter 94

When presented to the monarch, men should bow and women should curtsy. The bow should be made by bending from the neck or shoulders (not the waist) while briefly lowering the eyes. Bow or curtsy again on departure. Do not speak first; if the monarch addresses you, you must reply. Never turn your back on the monarch. When you are permitted to leave the audience chamber, walk backwards.
— *The Unideker Guide to Ruritania*

Music permeated the ground floor of Dzhumpinpork Palace; a string quartet was performing a work by Avarn Ghard based on Ruritanian peasant songs and dances. Rory didn't stop to listen. The ekwyroj on guard duty didn't listen either; they stood impassive and impressive while Krev Schammerbass strode past them, pistol in hand. Rory's entry, in contrast, stirred them into action. Aristocrats could enter the Palace freely but scruffy ekwyrinoj in ill-fitting uniforms couldn't, especially if they were so ignorant of protocol as to run. Ceremonial battle-axes were lowered to form a barrier. Rory jumped over them. Within seconds he'd been seized and wrestled to the ground. The ensuing verbal exchange proved that the guards didn't understand colloquial English.

Krev Schammerbass stopped at the far end of the ornate hall, turned and smiled. 'Sura' clung to his arm. She was out of breath. He wasn't.

'Ah, the running man.' Krev Schammerbass shook his head. 'So much trouble you cause to us, Rory. It matters not; you are apprehended. I add icing to cake of Revolution; we decide later your fate.'

The string quartet went on playing.

'It won't work.' Rory spoke through a mouthful of thick red carpet. 'You think assassinating the Queen will give you power? You think you can *sell* access to the Faerie Realm for military manoeuvres by foreign governments and international terrorists?'

The krev's smile faded.

'You know this how? Who tell you?'

He glared at 'Sura', who shook her head.

'Call it a lucky guess,' said Rory. 'What's your answer? You really believe you can?'

'Of course.' Krev Schammerbass shrugged. 'All country must use resource for economic prosperity and stability. Ruritanian economy will depend no longer on cake, so what put we in its place? You like we make profit from recreational drug, or people traffic, or art theft? Military agreement is more moral choice, is it not? Access to Faerie Realm is national resource.'

'And how do Klarissa and Arraitch and Mangler rate your *moral choice*? No, don't bother to answer. When they abolish feudalism, access to the Faerie Realm will be blocked and that will scupper your scheme.'

Another shrug, another smile.

'Mangler is no longer concern. The others will acquiesce or die. We have support from Swiss. In 1848, Swiss Consortium was rumour; now it is fact. If one lady constitute "Consortium".'

Consortium? Consort, more like, thought Rory.

The krev beamed at his companion, but then his expression changed. Fourteen ekwyroj burst through the gilded double door, Kjym Krev Bauntzia in their van. Schammerbass pointed his gun at her, thought better of it, turned on his heel and loped out of the hall. Kjym stepped forward and barked commands at the Palace guards. Confused, they released their hold on the prisoner. Rory scrambled to his feet.

'Thanks, Kjym. I don't need to tell–'

'You said you would stop Schammerbass. Do it!'

She snapped orders in Ruritanian. Blue Primrose obeyed her; she was an aristocrat. Rory raced in the wake of Krev Schammerbass and a dozen of the ekwyroj followed. The other two seized 'Sura' and evinced an appetite for interrogation.

A carriage skidded to a halt outside. Colonel Barrington alighted, umbrella in hand, galloped up the Palace steps and staged a one-man entry. He paid cursory respect to the junior krev and attempted to take control, but he'd underestimated the junior krev.

The string quartet segued into a lively scherzo with a high content of dissonance. The performance was immaculate. Avarn Ghard would have applauded.

*

The Queen had graciously commanded Thad to bring Ariadne and Tomen to her audience chamber. She heard Ariadne's testimony and was impressed; never before had she met a Brit fluent in Ruritanian, or one who wore an immaculate business suit. As she listened she grew more favourably disposed towards Rory and less venomous towards Klarissa. She also smoked several of Ariadne's cigarettes, clear evidence of royal approval.

'Pan Redman saw furthest regarding the metacake, though his accusation against Krev Schammerbass was far-fetched. However, Alterleta committed serious crimes. She must be brought to trial.' She accepted another cigarette and an ekwyor knelt to flick a gold-plated lighter. 'Someone tell that string quartet to shut up before I order all four of them to be disembowelled as a preliminary warning.'

Another ekwyor bowed and went to do Her Majesty's bidding, brandishing his silver battle-axe. At the pearl-inlaid door he almost collided with Krev Schammerbass; he stepped aside, tugged his forelock and went on his way. Krev Schammerbass strode forward and infused his excessive bow,

335

from the waist, with still more excessive irony. The Queen raised her eyebrows.

'It is most gratifying to see Your Majesty recovered from your overnight indisposition,' purred the krev.

'No doubt your uninvited intrusion and your impertinence in speaking before I addressed you betoken more than a desire to applaud my health,' said the Queen.

'Your Majesty is most perceptive.'

'Not especially. I failed to heed advice about you, and the gun in your hand is a dead give-away.'

'Not subtle, I grant you,' the krev continued. 'However, in view of today's tragic events, Ruritania requires new leadership. The loss of Krevoj Strlzhav and Hvimpy along with so many other notable members of Ruritanian society, to say nothing of His Eminence the Bishop of Szipad and His Royal Highness Crown Prince Elharic–'

'*Most* tragic,' said Her Majesty. 'There will be half a day of national mourning.'

'That will more than suffice. This is regrettable, Ma'am; but as I observed, a new administration is required. After my business here is complete I shall visit the Surgeon Archbishop, since he too has been indisposed.' He glanced around the room and sneered at Ariadne. 'Another British visitor, I believe. I have begun to find the British superfluous, their military personnel aside. My government will expel them.'

Krev Schammerbass pointed his gun at the Queen. Ariadne skipped sideways and stood in the line of fire.

'Oh no you jolly well don't. I'll give you *superfluous*, you cad!'

The krev sighed.

'I have more than one bullet, dear lady. Pray feel free to remain in the line of fire if you prefer death to expul–'

Rory erupted into the room and rugby-tackled him. Both men fell to the carpet, struggling. The gun fired twice. A crystal chandelier disintegrated and a cherub's head in the rococo ceiling acquired a look of terminal surprise. The delicately-carved slug upon which the cherub had been seated became non-viable. Thad and Tomen took cover, sneezing under the cascade of plaster dust. Ariadne's legs gave way and she subsided, shaking. The Queen sat and smoked.

A dozen ekwyroj tumbled into the chamber and paused. The junior ekwyrin they'd been ordered to follow was wrestling on the floor with a krev, and there were three other people in the room besides Her Majesty. Whom were they supposed to detain?

The Queen told them. She was not amused. The ekwyroj obeyed. Rory picked up the gun.

By the time Colonel Barrington entered the room the show was over. He stared at Krev Schammerbass, who was struggling to maintain his dignity while the ekwyroj manhandled him, and then glared at Rory.

'Give that gun to me, Redman. And where is Krev Schammerbass's Rolex watch?'

'How should I know, Barrington? And what do you mean by speaking in Her Majesty's audience chamber before Her Majesty commands you? No, I'll keep the gun. It's safer in my hands than yours.'

Ariadne tried not to giggle. The Queen smiled and held out her hand for another cigarette.

Chapter 95

It is said that a mystery story must involve a near-perfect criminal scheme, red herrings that mislead the authorities, a protagonist with superior perception and brilliant mind, and a startling and unexpected dénouement. However, from the protagonist's standpoint, the dénouement is neither unexpected nor startling. He has arrived at it by reasoning, which is a mundane process.

— Dai O'Genies, 'A Primer of Ruritanian Philosophy'

'They're blaming Morris-dancing for the weather,' said Ariadne.

The Palace entrance sheltered them from the worst of the rain.

'Bollocks. But gratifying.' Rory's mouth twisted. 'If it hadn't rained, a lot more of Ruritania's aristocracy would have died from the miasma bomb. On the other hand, if bloody Barrington had had the sense to listen to me, lives would have been saved.'

'But the Queen is minded to add Honorary Ruritanian Citizenship to her Royal Pardon.'

'I should bloody well think so,' said Rory. 'Saving the monarch's life and thwarting a Revolution and a hostile political takeover ought to merit more substantial recognition, like a few thousand raldoloj. I'm nearly out of cash.'

'Can't you find an expensive watch to pawn?'

'You accusing me of something, woman? I'll phone Paul and get money transferred to your account here and then get cash … By Asclepius, if this weather *is* my fault–'

'There'll be a load of succession disputes shortly. How many died, Rory?'

'Didn't have time to count. But irrespective of numbers, my love, a good lawyer will profit. Especially if she's a personal friend of the new krevjalem.'

Thad emerged from the audience chamber. The Queen, he said, had denied Colonel Barrington's request to send Rory back to prison. Rory was a free man and a Ruritanian citizen.

'So I gathered,' said Rory. He relinquished the pistol to his friend. 'Thanks, Thad. I'm in your debt again. What'll happen to Schammerbass and the pseudo-Slovenian Swiss woman?'

'Her Majesty will decide,' said Thad, 'after they've been questioned. If you can explain the background, Rory, it will help.'

'It would help me, that's for sure,' said Ariadne. 'I'm still not clear about what happened in there. Except Her Majesty smoked most of my fags.'

Thad gave Ariadne a cigarette. Across St Galen's Square and through the neighbouring streets, frightened and excited citizens jostled under the relentless downpour. Few were willing to go home. Rory watched and shook his head.

'Someone needs to take control before the election. Time she started distributing her cartload of fairy cakes … Yeah, well, Thad, it started when Britain's armed forces were reduced to near-impotence by government cuts. MIOCIA saw prospects in Ruritania's connection with the Faerie Realm.'

'My what?' said Ariadne.

Thad explained. Ariadne shook her head. She'd never heard of the Ministry for Interfering in Other Countries' Internal Affairs, though like all British subjects she was familiar with its consequences.

'MIOCIA contacted Schammerbass because of his expertise in Faerie physics,' said Rory, 'and they involved MI7 in their strategy.'

'What *was* the strategy?' said Thad.

'I believe the plan was to exploit the dimensional expansions and contractions of the Faerie Realm in order to transport a military unit from Ruritania to anywhere in the world in zero time. The element of surprise could be decisive in a conflict. The ministry would need to pay an expert to manipulate the time and space distortions – an expert like Schammerbass – but other costs would be minimal. Schammerbass realised there'd be huge profits, so as RAS President he secured massive funding from the British military for "research" and used it to finance SPAR. He wanted the Communists to succeed well enough to create a power vacuum, then he'd step in and take control. And he nearly succeeded. Britain was helping the Ruritanian government against SPAR because they knew a Communist takeover that abolished feudalism might block access to the Faerie Realm and kill the scheme. Schammerbass pretended to be MI7's ally but he was playing both ends against the middle. He'd have sold military access to the Faerie Realm to all comers. But knowing he was up against smart people on both sides made him fear reprisals, so he was always on guard.'

Thad nodded.

'As I thought … The Swiss woman is called Sonja la Limace, not Sura Marnikova. Can you tell us anything about her, Rory?'

'I don't know how Schammerbass recruited her, but I'm certain they were together in Budapest and probably Lucerne. She was his eyes and ears around Klarissa, at least in London and Vienna. She knew who "Gottlieba Weissfeld" really was. Klarissa – "Gottlieba" – probably thought "Sura" was MI7. Schammerbass needed her to confirm that Klarissa had returned to Ruritania with the security plan she stole from me, thus putting SPAR ahead of the game and improving the Revolution's chances – as far as he was willing to allow. No doubt he had a Plan B. I wonder whether Sura-Sonja was naïve enough to believe she'd become rich and powerful if Schammerbass's plot succeeded. I'm pretty sure Schammerbass used her account in the Bank of Ruritania to funnel money into SPAR, so the financing couldn't be traced to him. Klarissa and maybe other SPAR leaders must have had authority to withdraw cash from that account … But I suppose Parliamentary or Royal consent will be needed to investigate the bank records.'

Ariadne said she needed time to get her head round it all, but had anyone wondered where Klarissa was now and what she was doing? Thad looked thoughtful. Rory said it was obvious.

Colonel Barrington marched past them, umbrella raised, and jabbed his beard at Rory.

'Your wild guesses proved better than they'd any right to, Redman. And the Queen's gone soft on you.' He stepped closer and lowered his voice. 'But I haven't. As soon as you step on to British soil again you'll be arrested, facing charges for more crimes than you can count. And you owe me a pair of silver cufflinks.' He accorded Thad a brusque nod and ignored Ariadne. 'I have a terrorist leader to catch. Bloody woman's vanished again. *You there, bring my carriage, at the double!*'

Rory yawned.

'Of course she hasn't vanished.'

The colonel turned his back on Rory and strode to the carriage. The wheel rims were under water. Thad frowned.

'Rory, you know where Klarissa Alterleta is?'

'If you'd usurped the government and wanted to establish your grip on power, Thad, you'd need to inform the people. The *electorate*. So where would you want to be as soon as the hamsters were back on their treadmills?'

Thad's eyebrows acknowledged the revelation. Ariadne pointed an admonitory finger.

'Rory, don't you dare!'

'Not much choice, love. The colonel's carriage won't get through the mob on the streets for hours. Situation calls for someone who can *run*. Give me a candle stub.'

Chapter 96

Television has become a powerful force in the country during the past twenty years. It has brought drama, music, documentaries, interviews, news updates and weather forecasts to the people of all three cities. It has provided a rich source of rumours that the people can spread willy-nilly. It has transformed Ruritanian society and will remain a major influence for the foreseeable future.

— The Director of Ruritanian Television, 'An Impartial Assessment of the Impact of Television on Ruritania'

Immediately after the power supply was restored, a female ekwyor with curly hair stood before the cameras recording the promise of a one thousand raldol reward for information leading to the capture of Klarissa Alterleta or Rory Redman. The offer would be broadcast as soon as the equipment had been checked. Now the ekwyor with curly hair was studying the Presence entering the television centre and pricing its outfit: red Lancaster lace turtleneck dress and black court shoes by Marc Jacobs, top-quality makeup, Christian Dior perfume. The very handbag exuded authority.

The ekwyor with curly hair recognised the Presence as a krev who'd survived the terrorist outrage and would now assure the people they were safe. One of the bowmen accompanying the Presence unfurled a relatively dry Ruritanian flag. Superimposed on the flag was a hammer and sickle, but to the ekwyor with curly hair, eighteen hundred raldoloj of clothing and accessories was a more powerful statement than a Communist symbol. She bowed and cleared a passage through the foyer. Klarissa strode forwards and snapped a question at a middle-management suit.

'How soon can I broadcast to the city?'

'Normal service should be resumed at any moment, Your Excellency.'

'Take me to the best-prepared studio. My message must reach the people without delay. Let the cameras roll!'

*

Rory overtook the colonel's carriage, the candle-wax in his ears blocking the expletives. Another emergency vehicle appeared in the Square but he was deaf to its charm and continued to run. By the time the ethereal singing had faded into the distance, leaving all other occupants of the Square tied to masts of enchantment, he was a hundred fathoms ahead of the colonel.

As I recall, thought Rory, the television centre's next to the Academy of Science building. She'll have reached it by now. Let's pray to Asclepius for recalcitrant hamsters.

He took out his mobile phone and called Paul Edict's number. As he dialled, he jumped over a symbolic mess of fallen bunting and discarded flags, demonstrating that men are capable of multitasking. He took a wrong turning, lamented his inability to ask directions (he couldn't speak Ruritanian and in any case he wouldn't have heard the answer because of the wax in his ears), then recognised the permanent scaffolding around the Academy of Science portico.

'Paul – it's Rory. You and Christine okay?' He took the wax out of his left ear. 'Yes, sorry – running. Been around the country, back in Strelsau, got a little local difficulty … Yes, interesting ceremony, but it got washed out … Look, I need money. To access my account online, my password …'

Three minutes later he squelched into the television centre and was accosted by the ekwyor with curly hair.

'Ekwyrin, why is your uniform the wrong size? Why aren't you controlling the crowd in the Square?'

Rory shook his head.

'Even if I could hear you I wouldn't understand. I don't suppose you can speak English?'

He glanced around the foyer. Klarissa, her attire conspicuous, was issuing orders to a cheap sharp suit. As Rory scraped the wax from his other ear and elbowed forward, the suit bowed and opened a studio door.

'*Klarissa!*' yelled Rory. '*Klarissa! Stop! It's over!*'

She turned. Through the milling crowd her brilliant green eyes met his. Her face paled but her aura was undimmed. Her mouth sketched a smile.

'Ekwyor!' she called. 'That man is an imposter. His uniform is stolen. Arrest him!'

'Whatever you intend to say to the people, Klarissa, it's past its sell-by date! The Queen's alive and well and in control. Schammerbass has been arrested. The authorities are coming. Give yourself up and plead for clemency. Krev Bauntzia will be krevjalem, so–'

'Pan Rodman?' said a damp man with galoshes and a pink umbrella. 'Forgive; English not majestic. You tell how dance make rain?'

'What?'

'You teach dance for peasant? Peasant dance, rain fall – please, tell how! I am chief editor of *Journal of Terpsichorean Meteorology.*'

'Do a Google search for "Morris-dancing" – it'll tell you all you need to know.'

The ekwyor with the curly hair seized Rory. The editor-in-chief protested and Rory spoke slowly and loudly but to no effect. He sighed.

'Sorry, ma'am, but needs must when the gargoyle drives.'

He punched the ekwyor with the curly hair in the stomach and kicked her shin, making her gasp and hop. Klarissa's laugh verged on the hysterical.

'Your plans have ganged agley, Klarissa,' he shouted. 'For your own sake, surrender!'

Colonel Barrington barged into the foyer brandishing his umbrella, twelve ekwyroj in his wake. Klarissa fled towards the rear of the building. Rory followed.

'The lady who just ran–' gasped the ekwyor with curly hair, hopping with puzzlement.

'Is Klarissa Alterleta,' said the colonel, ignoring Rory. 'You six, round the back, cut her off! The rest, with me!'

Klarissa ran up a flight of stairs. Rory saw her turn the corner and pounded after her. Colonel Barrington and his team arrived ten seconds later, ignored the stairs and raced towards the rear exit. Klarissa forced open a window and climbed out on to a narrow ledge. Her designer outfit had disappeared. She now wore a blue one-piece swimming costume and her feet were bare. The handbag swung from her shoulder.

She'll head for the hotel where she stayed, thought Rory, recover her horse and gallop out of town. Where are the most expensive hotels?

He ran back to the ground floor, out of the television centre and into the noisome lane beside the Academy of Science building. Klarissa was climbing down the wall at the far end, out of sight of the colonel and his entourage. She saw Rory charging towards her, turned and sprinted westwards behind the Academy building. Rory redoubled his pace.

'*Klarissa! Stop! I'll do all I can for you! The Queen owes me a favour or two!*'

The reply was a faint laugh. He knew he'd outrun Klarissa over a marathon but she might match his speed over a shorter distance. However, she wasn't running towards the hotels. She was heading through the rain, through the crowds, back to St Galen's Square, towards Blue Primrose HQ, towards certain capture.

Or so Rory thought. But as he watched, Klarissa skirted the Great Azure Door and, her eyes on the Palace, disappeared into the Labyrinth. He hesitated, looked sideways, and plunged after her.

Chapter 97

After a month's silence he rang me again. It was midsummer's day. He was running. I could hear crowds of people around him, as you'd expect in Strelsau on National Cake Day. He said it was raining and he was facing a 'little local difficulty' and needed money, and he gave me all his banking details so I could transfer a few thousand from his account in Manchester to Ariadne's account in Strelsau. Apparently Ariadne had agreed to draw cash for him. I'd no problem believing he was short of money, and in difficulties, and running, but I've no idea how he persuaded Ariadne to do a financial deal. And I didn't believe it was raining, not on National Cake Day. He said nothing about SPAR or plots to overthrow the government, so I supposed all that revolution stuff had turned out to be so much hot air.

    — Paul Edict, 'Rory Redman as I Knew Him'

The slug-trails, the *nerjaportikhnoj*, ran like electric cables through an underground tunnel. Rory couldn't see Klarissa. She must have taken one of the three paths from the node ahead, but which? Each path was guarded by one of the three gargoyle sisters in miniature form.

'Which way did she go?' said Rory.

'She went down the left-hand path,' said Othloc.

'She went down the central path,' said Lekhissa.

'At least two of us are lying,' said Sporota.

'Thanks,' said Rory.

He turned right, dodging mini-Sporota's shears. The path curved through an avenue of chestnut trees. Klarissa was halfway up the trees on the left, swinging from branch to branch more quickly than she could run.

Rory began to sprint but Klarissa vanished around the curve. There was another node, this one with a signpost. The sign pointing to the right read, 'Exactly one of these two signs is true'. The sign pointing to the left read, 'Klarissa didn't go this way'. He took the path to the left.

He was in a convoluted tunnel that rose and fell and twisted. Overall, he seemed to be going downhill. Klarissa's lead over him had grown, but even Klarissa couldn't climb the smooth walls in this part of the Labyrinth. If the tunnel had continued another half league he'd have caught her, but it opened into sunlit fields beside a reed-fringed lake. Klarissa rushed forward, dived, and swam away underwater. Rory stopped and blinked.

'Good afternoon, Mr Redman.' The fisherman in the rowing boat reeled in his line. 'Would you care for a ride, or do you wish to swim in Ms Alterleta's wake through the miasmagenic waters of Lake Brojginzha?'

The weather had changed. It was warm and sunny. Nothing about the lake seemed miasmagenic.

'I'd like to catch her and thump some sense into her, Professor Weisheitsliebhaber.'

'Can you find any to thump, Mr Redman? You never had a surfeit of sense to share.'

'Take me to where I *can* catch her.'

'You're persistent. Climb aboard.'

Morris-dancers were performing in the village on the hill overlooking the lake. The ghrunli field was deserted but the inn was busy. The fisherman-professor rowed towards the forest.

'Have you considered that you could be chasing an illusion, Mr Redman?'

'Klarissa's real, Professor. Though whether she's the illegitimate daughter of a krev is another matter.'

347

'You miss my point. What is your image of her? What do you want with her? Or in view of your personal history, is the answer obvious?'

The professor shipped the oars and pointed his fishing rod towards the forest. The boat rocked on the sunlit water. Rory sat up. In a small clearing sat Klarissa. She was crooning, as she'd crooned to charm the horses and hounds when he'd rescued her from Ekwyor Tupsroot and her detachment. She wore a long green mediaeval gown; her feet remained bare. The handbag lay beside her. As Rory watched, a white unicorn emerged from the trees and laid its head in her lap.

'Plausible, I suppose,' said Rory. His mouth was dry.

The professor chuckled, picked up his oars and rowed on. Soon the air above the lake grew misty. The further they rowed, the thicker grew the mist, until the little boat was surrounded by grey opacity. The rhythmic splashing of the oars sounded oily. The odour grew noisome.

'I'll wait here,' said the professor, 'pending your decision.'

The boat's keel grated on shingle. Rory stepped ashore. Once again he stood in the ruined town, the monochrome Doré print, broken walls rising from rubble, the half-standing mill, the church with smashed windows and roof. The mansion, the palace, stood no more than ten fathoms from the edge of the lake, its open ballroom replete with ornate furnishings, mirrors, candelabra, servants dispensing wine and dainties, the small ensemble playing a minuet. And the King in rich attire and elegant periwig watched from beside the marble fireplace, advanced to meet his visitor, and bowed.

'Welcome back, Mr Redman. It seems you're to be congratulated again. Not everyone will thank you; not everyone will know what you have done, but some will praise you. All in the Faerie Realm will do so.' The King of Faerie offered snuff. 'Ah, I forgot: you eschew tobacco, as does our noble lady.'

He nodded towards the dancers. Among them was Klarissa, magnificent in eighteenth century silken gown, the verdure of her eyes muted to sepia. She smiled welcome. Rory wished he knew how to dance the minuet.

Two servants approached, bowed and poured wine for Rory: one glass of claret, one of Riesling; sunrise and moonlight. This time, the King didn't wave away the moonlight. He watched Rory, his eyes amused.

Somewhere behind Rory, unseen, the professor waited to row him back to – where? Strelsau? Hrincacz? Castle Bauntzi? Manchester? Surely to Ariadne! Rory glanced at the claret, reached for it, and withdrew his hand.

Years would pass and Ariadne would age. So would he.

Before him, Klarissa repeated her inviting smile. He could stay in the Faerie Realm for centuries, ageing little if at all, companion of the beautiful woman whose life he'd saved at least once, perhaps twice. And her beauty would endure. And Barrington's threat of arrest would be vacuous. His left hand reached for the Riesling. Then it retreated again.

The Faerie Realm was unpredictable, full of dangers. And in fifty years, a hundred years, Klarissa might return to the mundane world and renew her revolutionary quest.

In any case, surely he loved Ariadne? He reached for the claret.

There were dangers in the mundane world, too. Nothing was predictable. No matter which party he chose, it could prove to be the wrong party.

'The either-or moment,' he murmured. 'The Ruritanian for "dilemma" is "dilemma". Oh, why can you never find an existentialist when you need one?'

The End

Afterword

The Logic Puzzles

The puzzles in the maze at St Avicenna's (chapter 57):

1. At the openings of the three paths lay stones, each bearing an inscription. *This way is good*, said the first. *This way is not good*, said the second. *The first way is not good*, said the third. Over the junction of the paths hung a banner with the legend 'At most one of the three stones tells the truth'.

Rory assumes the banner is truthful (otherwise the puzzle is insoluble). Since, therefore, a maximum of one stone tells the truth, either the first or the third must be true and the other false, because they contradict each other. No matter which is true, *one* of them is, so the second stone's inscription must be false. Therefore, the second path is the right one to choose.

2. Within a few fathoms the path bifurcated, and at each of the openings was a stone bearing an inscription. *This is not the right way*, said the first. *Exactly one of these two inscriptions is true*, said the second.

Suppose the second inscription is false. In this case, the first statement must also be false. Suppose the second inscription is true. This would also make the first statement false. Therefore, no matter whether the second inscription is true or false, the first one must be false, so the first path *is* the right way.

3. Once again, stones with inscriptions lay at the three entrances. *This is the way*, said the first. *This is the way*, said the second. *At least two of these inscriptions are false*, said the third.

This time, Rory's reasoning is explicit in the text. Assuming the third inscription to be false means only one inscription can be false, i.e. the third one, so the other two are true … but they can't be because they contradict each other. So the third inscription is true, which means the other two are both false. Therefore neither the first nor the second path is the way, so the third path is the right choice.

I won't explain the puzzles Rory meets in the labyrinth in the final chapter because they're of much the same kind.

*

The solution to Lekhissa's riddle: A statement of the form 'A if and only if B' is true if both A and B are true *and true if both A and B are false*. It's false if A is false and B true, and it's false if A is true and B false.

In Rory's solution, 'A' is the question: *Will you tell me why Britain has chosen to become involved in the Ruritanian government's attempts to eliminate SPAR?* It counts as true if Lekhissa *will* tell him why Britain has chosen to become involved and false if she *won't*.

'B' is the statement *Lekhissa answers 'dakh' to the question 'does two plus two equal four?'*

Now there are four possibilities: 'dakh' might mean 'yes' or 'no', and Lekhissa might lie or might tell the truth. Rory's solution forced Lekhissa to answer 'dakh' if A was true and 'khad' if it was false, *no matter which of the four possibilities obtained*, i.e. no matter what 'dakh' and 'khad' actually meant, and no matter whether Lekhissa was lying or telling the truth.

In what follows, let's assume that A is true, i.e. Lekhissa *will* tell Rory the reason for Britain's involvement (as, in fact, proved to be the case, though she gave him the answer obliquely). Had

A been false, i.e. if Lekhissa had *not* been willing to explain the reason to Rory, the same four possibilities would have obtained, but the answer in each case would have been 'khad', not 'dakh'.

First: suppose 'dakh' meant 'yes' and Lekhissa told the truth. Then B must be true: she *would* answer 'dakh' to the question 'does two plus two equal four', since two plus two *does* equal four. Since we are assuming A to be true, then both A and B are true, so Lekhissa must answer 'dakh' (= yes).

Second: suppose 'dakh' meant 'yes' and Lekhissa lied. This case is a little more mind-bending. As a liar, Lekhissa would deny that two plus two equals four, so she would not answer 'dakh' to the question; she would answer 'khad'. The 'B' statement now becomes false, while A remains true. Therefore the whole 'A if and only if B' contrivance is false. But being a liar, Lekhissa would deny that it is false, so she would say 'dakh' (= yes) instead of the correct 'khad'.

Third: suppose 'dakh' meant 'no' and Lekhissa told the truth. In this case, Lekhissa would not answer 'dakh' to the question 'does two plus two equal four'; she would answer 'khad'. So as in the previous case, 'B' is now false, and therefore the whole 'A if and only if B' is false. Lekhissa, being truthful, would *say* it is false by answering 'dakh' (= no).

Fourth: suppose 'dakh' meant 'no' and Lekhissa lied. In this case she *would* answer 'dakh' to the question 'does two plus two equal four?' so the 'B' statement is true. This makes the entire 'A if and only if B' true, so Lekhissa the liar would say it was false – by answering 'dakh'.

Therefore, Rory can discover whether Lekhissa will explain Britain's involvement by making her answer 'dakh' if she will and – as the reader can establish by amending the foregoing four cases appropriately – 'khad' if she won't.

As I admitted in the Foreword, I'm indebted to the late Raymond Smullyan for the maze riddles and for the idea of Lekhissa's riddle, which appears in a different guise in his *What is the Name of this Book?* Smullyan's splendid book also provides a delightfully accessible introduction to a pillar of mathematical logic, Gödel's incompleteness theorem, of which my 'Gödelpus unsatisfiability theorem' is an obvious parody.

About the Author

After he retired from a career in medicine and university teaching, Mark Henderson moved to the Peak District of Derbyshire, England, where he started to write fiction and to collect and tell local folktales. Mark has many publications to his name, long and short covering many genres, including a collection of 62 traditional Peak District stories and a collection of performance pieces, Cruel and Unusual PunNishments.

Mark is secretary of his local creative writing group. He regularly performs at storytelling gigs and is in demand for his talks about his work and life experiences.

Find out more about Mark on his
website: www.markphenderson.com

If you have enjoyed this book, please consider leaving a review for Mark to let him know what you thought of his work.

You can find out more about Mark on his author page on the Fantastic Books Store. While you're there, why not browse our other delightful tales and wonderfully woven prose?

www.fantasticbooksstore.com